11 Dec 19

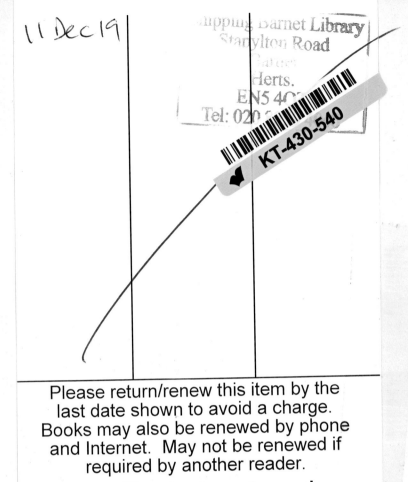

KT-430-540

Please return/renew this item by the
last date shown to avoid a charge.
Books may also be renewed by phone
and Internet. May not be renewed if
required by another reader.

www.libraries.barnet.gov.uk

BARNET
LONDON BOROUGH

Seven Letters

SINÉAD MORIARTY

PENGUIN
IRELAND

PENGUIN IRELAND

UK | USA | Canada | Ireland | Australia
India | New Zealand | South Africa

Penguin Ireland is part of the Penguin Random House group of companies
whose addresses can be found at global.penguinrandomhouse.com.

First published 2019
001

Copyright © Sinéad Moriarty, 2019

The moral right of the author has been asserted

Set in 13.5/16 pt Garamond MT Std
Typeset by Jouve (UK), Milton Keynes
Printed and bound in Great Britain by Clays Ltd, Elcograf S.p.A.

A CIP catalogue record for this book is available from the British Library

ISBN: 978–1–844–88407–0

www.greenpenguin.co.uk

For sisters

There are things that we don't want to happen
but have to accept, things we don't want to know
but have to learn, and people we can't
live without but have to let go.

Nancy Stephan, *The Truth about Butterflies*

I

Sarah smiled to herself as two more bottles of wine were ordered. Some of the school mothers were getting very loose-tongued and it was extremely entertaining.

'Wait until you hear this.' Molly's mum leaned forward and the others huddled and strained to hear her. She milked the attention, pausing for dramatic effect as she took a sip of her wine. Then, in a very loud attempt at a whisper, she said, 'Did you know that Ethan Kennedy's mother –'

'Who's Ethan Kennedy?' Frank's mum interrupted.

Molly's mum frowned. She was not used to being cut across. Sarah suppressed a grin. Frank's mum was new to the class and clearly still hadn't figured out that Molly's mum was queen bee. She'd want to cotton on quickly, Sarah thought, because Molly's mum had a tongue like a sword.

'He's in the other second class. Small, weedy, with glasses,' Molly's mum said impatiently. 'Anyway, his mum came home early from work last week to find her husband being *serviced* by the Brazilian au pair.'

Gasps, and some giggles, around the table.

'What do you mean exactly?' Frank's mum was not playing the game.

Sarah sat back in her chair, enjoying the show.

'What do you think I mean? He was getting a blow-job up against that marble-topped island she's always boasting about.'

'Oh, my God!' Frank's mum was shocked into silence.

'That's awful,' a sympathetic voice said.

'Mind you,' Sally's mum said, narrowing her eyes, 'I wouldn't mind if someone else serviced my husband. It'd save me the trouble.'

All of the women cracked up laughing, and Sarah couldn't help laughing too, although she definitely didn't want this to descend into drunken confessions about their sex lives. She was way too sober to deal with that.

'In fact,' Sally's mum went on, 'maybe we should put it in the contract. *Au pair must be adept at looking after kids and servicing husband*.'

'Oh, come on, ladies, sex can still be mind-blowing,' Sadie's mum slurred. She was sitting opposite Sarah and had been drinking the wine as if it was water.

'Wow, your husband must be a total stud.' Bobby's mum failed to hide the envy in her voice.

Sarah had seen Sadie's dad at the school gate once and he certainly didn't look like a stud, more like a dorky accountant.

Sadie's mum snorted dismissively. 'God, not *him*. I'm talking about my personal trainer. He's Australian. I tell you, ladies, the sex is off the charts,' she declared.

The other women's eyes widened, and they oohed.

'What's his name and does he do house calls?' a mother at the end of the table shouted, making them all laugh.

Sarah laughed along with them but, truth be told, she was uncomfortable with this level of private information being shared. If she ever saw Sadie's dad again, she'd feel awful knowing about his wife's extra-marital carry-on. This was exactly what she'd been dreading about tonight. Being pregnant and not drinking, she'd known it would be a bit of an effort. On nights like these you needed a glass of wine to relax you. After all, none of these women were her friends. They were a bunch of mothers thrown together by one solitary common denominator: their children were in the same class.

Sarah was always careful to be friendly, but not too friendly. She didn't want to get sucked into any of the little cliques and listen to gossip about other children or parents. She'd been stung badly as a teenager. She knew what it was like to be part of a group and think they were your true friends, only to be dumped when one of their ex-boyfriends fancied you. It wasn't Sarah's fault Brian Morrissey had taken a shine to her, but Georgia had taken it very badly. Suddenly, Sarah had found herself on the receiving end of bitchy comments, lies about being a flirt, a slut and a bad friend. Georgia and the others had dumped her unceremoniously. Sarah had spent the last year of school enduring the days, waiting to get the hell out of there. She'd been wary of groups of women ever since. Once bitten, twice shy.

She'd seen school mums becoming best friends, only to fall out a few months later when they realized they didn't have much in common. Sarah had no interest in that type of drama. She'd had enough of it as a teenager. She had friends, but she'd never allowed herself to get really close to any women since her schooldays. She didn't need that tight female bond because she had Mia. Having a sister she was so close to meant that she always had someone to talk to or confide in. She had grown up with a ready-made best friend, so she wasn't as needy as some of the other women she met who had no sisters or didn't get on with the ones they had. Women needed a best friend, and Sarah knew she was lucky that hers happened to be her sister. It was Mia she had gone to when Georgia and her gang were horrible to her. It was Mia who had told her to hold her head high and 'ignore those bitches'.

Molly's mum suddenly turned her laser focus on Sarah. 'You must have insider school gossip. Your sister's a teacher and the deputy head. Come on, Sarah, spill the beans. Are any of the teachers shagging each other? That Mr Grogan's fit. I'd shag him myself,' she said, laughing too loudly.

Sarah smiled patiently. 'As you know, Mia is the most discreet and professional person you could ever meet. I know nothing.'

'I don't believe you. Come on, we won't tell anyone, will we, girls?' She poked Sarah in the chest.

Sarah swallowed the urge to bend the finger backwards and kept smiling. 'I've got nothing to tell you. Honestly.'

'You're no fun.'

'Give her a break. She's driving and we're all drunk,' Tim's mum said, waving her glass in Sarah's direction.

'Eshcuse me, I am not drunk,' Sadie's mum slurred.

'Paralytic more like,' Mary muttered.

'Embarrassing,' Rebecca's mum agreed. 'She's so tacky.'

Sarah would take Sadie's mum's drunkenness over these two witches judging everyone and everything. She got up to go to the toilet. It was time to leave before people got more confessional and judgemental. She didn't want to know about their private lives and she had no intention of discussing hers. Nor did she want to see someone who'd drunk too much being judged by pious, disapproving women.

She wove her way through the overheated restaurant towards the sanctuary of the Ladies. It was empty and the window in the corner was open, which gave her some much-needed air. She splashed some water on her red cheeks, then went into a cubicle and locked the door. Even though she was only eleven weeks pregnant, her bladder was already causing havoc. She was just buttoning her trousers when she heard the door open and voices.

'Oh, my God, she's so drunk, it's mortifying. She's going to wake up tomorrow and die. Does she actually think we're impressed by her shagging some Australian half her age?'

'He's bound to give her an STD.'

Sarah winced, feeling sorry for Sadie's mum. That was why she never gave away any private information: it only gave people a reason to gossip about you.

'How's Rebecca getting on?'

'To be honest, I'm not a bit happy about the class.'

Sarah recognized their voices. Mya's and Rebecca's mums. They were Tiger Mothers, *über*-ambitious for their kids. They had the girls so over-scheduled, they constantly looked exhausted.

'Why?'

'Because that girl Izzy is holding the class back.'

Sarah froze.

'Do you think?'

'Totally. She's the youngest and the stupidest. She should be put into the class below. Rebecca said she's always getting stuck on maths and holding up the lesson. It's ridiculous.'

'Now that you mention it, Mya did say that Izzy is reading the *Secret Seven* books. Can you believe it? Mya read those two years ago. She's clearly not very bright.'

Every hair on Sarah's body was standing on end. Her breathing quickened and she felt nauseous.

'She's sucking up Miss Dixon's time because she's so slow to catch on. Rebecca said she's quite babyish, too. She's clearly immature. I wanted to speak to the headmistress, but then I realized that the deputy head is Izzy's aunt, which means we have no hope of getting her moved down.'

'Well, unless we get a few of the other mums to ask. If five or six of us complain, it might work. They'd have to listen to us then. We can't have our kids being slowed down by a girl with a low IQ. I don't care who she's related to.'

'You're right. How about I set up a WhatsApp group and invite some of the other mums to join and see how they feel? I'll have a word with –'

Sarah flung open the cubicle door, which banged against the wall. The two women spun around and stared at her, open-mouthed.

'You should always make sure there is no one in the cubicle before you set about slating an innocent child,' Sarah snapped at them. She was so angry, and their daft shocked faces made her even angrier. 'How dare you speak about Izzy like that? She's keeping up just fine, thank you very much. She's a very happy, well-balanced child, which is more than I can say for your over-worked, miserable kids. Then again, no wonder they look so unhappy. They're being raised by malicious, spiteful bitches.'

Sarah pushed past them and walked back to the others, legs shaking. Trying to look composed, she told them she was heading off, left money on the table and made a swift, if slightly wobbly exit.

When she got to her car, she fell sideways into the seat. Her whole body was trembling. She tucked her legs in and closed the door. She'd never spoken to anyone like that in her life. She felt elated and proud of herself, sticking up for Izzy, but she was also worried about the repercussions. No doubt those two witches were panning her to the other mums. She could see them now, loving the drama, telling the others that Sarah had verbally abused them and playing down what they'd said about Izzy. Lovely, innocent Izzy. Sarah felt tears prick her eyes. She'd never let anyone hurt Izzy. She'd never, ever let Izzy be bullied or made to feel left out. Never.

She needed to talk to someone, to process what had just happened. She picked up her phone.

'Hi.' Her sister answered on the first ring.

'You're not going to believe what just happened.'

'Aren't you on a class mums night out?'

'Yes. Things got a bit messy. I need to discuss it with you. Can I call in?'

'Of course. I'm intrigued.'

Sarah drove to Mia's house, threw the car up on the pavement outside, rushed up to the front door and rang the bell.

After a minute, Riley opened the door. She was wearing tartan pyjama bottoms and a black hoodie. Black eyeliner was smudged around her eyes. 'Hi, Sarah.'

'Hi, love.' Sarah kissed her teenage niece's cheek. 'Not out tonight?'

Riley rolled her eyes. 'As if. The Wicked Witch of the West has grounded me for two weeks because I got home an hour late last night.'

Sarah smiled. 'Well, curfews are there for a reason.'

'Come on! I'm nearly sixteen. Having to be home at eleven is ridiculous. She's a tyrant.'

Sarah laughed and put her arm around her niece's shoulders. 'No, she isn't, she's just protective of you. I would be, too. I love you too much to have anything bad happen to you, which is exactly what your mother's thinking.'

Riley rested her head against Sarah's shoulder. 'Will you talk to her? I really want to go to a party next Friday.'

Sarah kissed the top of her head. 'I'll put in a good word for you, but you have to be back at whatever time she says, OK?'

Riley hugged her tightly. 'I will, I promise. If you get her to agree, I'll love you even more than I already do.'

Mia opened the kitchen door. 'I thought I heard voices. Come in, I'm dying to hear what happened.'

'Sounds interesting, what's the gossip?' Johnny asked, from the kitchen table, where he was nursing a beer.

Sarah smiled at her brother-in-law. 'Stupid school mums' dinner that went a bit awry.'

'A cat fight?' Johnny's eyes twinkled.

'Not quite, but not far off. I behaved quite badly.'

7

'You?' Johnny looked surprised. 'I don't believe that for a minute. You didn't even snap when a barman poured an entire pint of Guinness over a brand new dress, remember?'

'Must be the pregnancy hormones. I lost it tonight,' Sarah said, taking off her coat and hanging it on the back of one of the kitchen chairs. 'Brace yourselves.' She sat down and filled them in on her lively evening.

'*What?*' Mia threw back her head and laughed. 'God, I wish I'd been there. Good for you! You couldn't let those two cows get away with it. I'd say they nearly died. Everyone thinks you're this calm, laidback person, but I know inside you're a lioness who'll defend her cub to the death. My God, I'd say they were in complete shock.'

Sarah giggled. 'They did look pretty taken aback.'

'Go, Sarah!' Johnny grinned. 'They deserved a tongue-lashing. Anyone who would say that about Izzy is a certified idiot.'

'Yeah,' Riley said. 'How dare those bitches knock Izzy? She's the best.'

'Language,' Mia said.

'But they are bitches,' Riley protested.

'To be fair, they sound like it.' Johnny backed up his daughter.

'They are,' Sarah agreed. 'But, still, I'm not sure I was much better in the end. I may have slightly overreacted, but then again, I won't let Izzy be picked on, no way. I've been there and it's awful.'

'Exactly,' Mia said. 'You were absolutely right to put them in their place. That's just a horrible way to behave.'

'Actually, I wanted to talk to you about Izzy and school,' Sarah said.

Johnny stood up. 'Right, Riley, let's leave them to it. Come on, I recorded the new episode of *The Young Offenders*.'

'Cool.'

'Seriously, Johnny? It's utter rubbish,' Mia complained.

'It's good fun,' he said, walking out of the room with his daughter in tow.

Sarah waited for the door to close, then asked her sister, 'Mia, I need you to be honest with me. Is Izzy falling behind? Is she holding up the class?'

Mia shook her head firmly. 'Absolutely not. As you know, I was a bit worried about her because she's the youngest, but Izzy is well able to keep up, Sarah. She's got more common sense than half of the kids in her class.'

'Yes, but is she able to keep up academically?' Sarah persisted. 'The teacher said I need to encourage her to read more and help her learn her tables, but she never said there was a problem. Is there?'

'She didn't say there was because there isn't. Look, you know I'd tell you if there was, for Izzy's sake as much as yours. I speak to Vanessa Dixon all the time and Izzy is doing fine. Don't let those women get into your head.'

Sarah exhaled, relief flooding her. Izzy was OK. She knew Mia would be honest. Mia was always honest, plus she had Izzy's best interests at heart because she adored her.

'I'm worried they might complain to the headmistress about Izzy, like they said, or after tonight they'll probably complain about me.'

Mia snorted. 'They wouldn't dare, and if by some tiny chance they do, she'll dismiss them. We see this type of parent every year, the ones who think their kids are geniuses and need to be challenged more. They want the teacher to give them more difficult maths problems and higher-level reading material. The head knows as well as I do that they're delusional. Sure, their kids might be slightly ahead of the game at seven and eight, but in a year or two the others will

9

all catch up. Honestly, Sarah, don't worry. Keep calm – think of the baby.'

Sarah placed her hand protectively on her stomach. 'Thanks, Mia, you're a star.'

'The only thing you need to worry about is looking after yourself and that little miracle inside you.'

Sarah smiled. The little thing inside her did feel like a miracle. It had been a long, bumpy road, but so worth it. 'I don't know what I'd do without you, Mia.'

'Thank God you were sober tonight. Imagine if you'd been drunk when you heard them.' Mia giggled. 'You'd probably have punched their lights out.'

Sarah laughed. 'Well, that's the last mums' night out I'll be going to, I can tell you. I don't need that drama in my life.'

'At least it'll be something different to write in your diary.'

'It'll certainly make a change from my fairly boring entries recently.' Sarah stifled a yawn. 'Now that the adrenalin has died down, I feel exhausted.'

Mia nodded. 'Go home and get some rest. For the moment, it's probably best to stick to nights in with herbal tea and Netflix.'

Sarah groaned as she pulled on her coat. 'I'll have to go to the school gate in a wig and dark glasses.'

'Hold your head high,' Mia said, as she walked her sister to the front door. 'You aren't the one in the wrong.'

Sarah kissed her. 'Night, Mia, and thanks.'

'Sleep well.'

As Sarah drove home, she thought about Izzy, vowing to keep a close eye on her schoolwork and encourage her. She'd had her reservations about starting her in school when she was only four, and she often found herself wishing she'd stuck to her guns. But Adam had been so certain that an early start was right for Izzy. Her birthday was in June, which meant she started in junior infants when she was only four years and two months. Some of the other kids had turned five that summer, which gave them a big advantage, Sarah reckoned. Adam had argued and argued, insisting that Izzy was clever enough, 'the next Sheryl Sandberg' apparently, and that leaving school at almost nineteen was ridiculous. Sarah had argued, too, but he was so sure that she'd ended up giving in and enrolling Izzy. It was her fault, really, if it affected Izzy in the long run, and she hated herself for that.

She tried to push away the dark thoughts and focus on what Mia had said. She was right: she shouldn't let those nasty women get into her head. She took a few deep breaths, reminding herself that Izzy was happy to go to school and ran out smiling each day. There was no evidence of her being under pressure. Thank God for Mia, who had always been her go-to person. Five years older, Mia had always seemed to know what to do and say. While Mia had been really close to their mum, it was to Mia that Sarah had always gone for advice or help. She was her rock. A rock that drove her nuts at times, but her rock, nonetheless.

2

Mia opened the door to her daughter's bedroom and stepped over the piles of clothes, the discarded shoes, the guitar lying on its side, the scattered schoolbooks and the damp towel. Riley was buried under her duvet, like a hibernating animal. Only a few strands of her long black hair were visible.

Mia tried to suppress her irritation at the state of the bedroom and not start the day with yet another argument. She gently shook the mound on the bed. 'It's seven thirty, Riley. Come on, up you get.'

Riley didn't budge. Mia could hear her deep inhalations. How was it that teenagers never wanted to go to bed and then never wanted to get up? Mia shook her a little harder. Nothing. She put both hands on the duvet and rocked the body underneath.

The top of the duvet snapped back. 'For God's sake, you don't have to be so rough.'

'I tried to . . . Never mind. Just get up now or we'll be late for school.'

Riley pulled the duvet back over her head and groaned.

Mia tried not to, but she couldn't help herself. 'And will you please clean up this mess?'

'It's a pigsty in here,' Riley mimicked her mother's voice.

'Well, it is, Riley, seriously.'

'It's the middle of the night. Stop nagging.'

Mia left the room before she snapped at her daughter. All they did was argue these days – morning, noon and night. It was exhausting. Her friends said their teenagers had come out of the really moody stage at about sixteen. Only three months to go . . .

When Mia reached the kitchen, Johnny was sitting at the table sipping coffee, bent over his iPad, reading the news. 'Is she up?' he asked.

'Nope, but she's awake, so that's something.'

Mia poured herself a coffee from the pot on the table. 'Remember the days when you'd wake her and her face lit up with joy to see you?'

'Yep,' Johnny said.

'I wish I'd cherished them more.' She sighed.

Johnny waved his hand. 'Ah, it's only hormones. She'll grow out of it. Give her some space.'

Mia gripped her cup. That was Johnny's favourite line, 'Give her some space'; the other was 'Leave her be.' But if you left a teenager 'be', and didn't set boundaries and guidelines, they'd go wild. The rude way Riley spoke to Mia was bad enough. There was no way she was going to give her space to get drunk or take drugs.

Johnny had grown up with five brothers, and his parents had basically let them do whatever they wanted. They'd all turned out OK. Well, except for Stephen, who was 'fond of the drink', a.k.a. a raging alcoholic. Johnny reckoned it was a good way to grow up, free and unrestricted.

Mia's parents had been very strict, especially her mum, who always knew where she and Sarah were, who they were with and what they were up to. True, sometimes it had been a bit much, but now Mia respected her mother's concern.

But Mia didn't want to be the 'bad cop' all the time with Riley. She was always the one chastising and disciplining. Sometimes she wished Johnny would step in and take the reins a bit more. She was the disciplinarian all day in school. As deputy head she had to deal with all the kids who got into trouble. She wanted to come home and take her foot off the pedal. But, no.

Johnny got to be Fun Dad, the parent who joked around and made Riley laugh. But it was Mia who had to keep on her back to study, have better manners, eat vegetables and on and on. She'd love to come home, kick off her shoes and ignore it if Riley was flaked out in front of the TV instead of doing her homework. Or not care if Riley never ate any vegetables or fruit. She'd love to ignore Riley's rudeness when she was in one of her many teenage moods, but she couldn't. Johnny kept saying, 'She'll grow out of it,' but in the meantime Mia wasn't going to let her become a monosyllabic, bad-mannered person.

She missed the old days when she'd been a lot more carefree, unburdened by responsibility and being the only breadwinner. She missed drinking too much wine and having spontaneous sex on the couch with Johnny. She missed laughing. Mia couldn't remember the last time she'd belly-laughed. She was always worried about money. She had a permanent knot in her stomach. When did life get so tough? Where did all the fun go?

She looked at Johnny. She'd like to talk to him about it, to ask him to step up more with discipline and getting Riley to study, but she couldn't nag her husband now. She needed to build up his confidence. He'd lost his job five months ago and she knew it upset him deeply that he wasn't providing for them.

'So, any meetings lined up?' she asked, trying to keep her voice casual.

Johnny swiped his finger across the iPad. 'No, but I've one or two people to contact.'

Mia said nothing. Since the *Daily Business Post* had shut down, there seemed to be no movement in the industry. Newspapers seemed to be the past. What was the future for her forty-one-year-old journalist husband?

It was almost impossible to survive on her income alone. She'd accepted the role of deputy head, on top of her teaching job, last year because she'd wanted to earn more to pay for maths tutoring for Riley this year. But now . . . Well, now there was no extra money for anything. She felt so hemmed in by her work, so trapped in the daily grind, but hers was the only pay packet in the house so she had zero choice in the matter. Every month that passed without Johnny finding a job she felt as if a noose was tightening around her neck, threatening to overwhelm her.

She crossed the fingers of her left hand under the table, like so many of her young pupils did. It was childish, but in a small way calming.

Riley shuffled in, skirt rolled up to mid-thigh, hair tied up in a messy bun. Mia could see her daughter had put make-up on to hide the smattering of spots that had appeared on her cheeks a few weeks ago. They weren't half as bad as some of her poor friends had, but she was very conscious of them.

'There she is, the light of my life.' Johnny grinned at her.

Riley rolled her eyes, but her lips twitched.

Johnny reached over and laid a hand on her arm. 'Ah, hang on now, I think I saw a smile, did I? No, couldn't be, not this early.'

'Go away, Dad.' Riley pushed off his hand gently, but she was half smiling.

'What'll you have? Eggs? Bacon? French toast?'

Since losing his job, Johnny had taken to cooking with gusto. Mia reckoned it helped him fill the long hours and she was delighted to hand over the job to him. It was the one positive thing to come out of the rotten episode.

'Black coffee,' Riley said.

'You have to eat something. You can't sit through school on an empty stomach, love,' Mia said. She'd heard from the head of the senior school that some of the girls in Riley's year were teetering on the edge of eating disorders. Last year's obsession had been self-harm. What next?

'I'm not hungry. The coffee will keep me going. Stop fussing all the time.'

Johnny waved a spatula at his daughter. 'Here, I'll throw an egg on and you might be tempted.'

Five minutes later, Riley was tucking into a poached egg and brown bread. Johnny was so much better with her. Mia knew she needed to try a lighter approach, but banter with Riley didn't come naturally to her. It sounded fake.

She glanced at her watch. 'OK, we have to go. I promised Sarah I'd pick Izzy up on the way. She has an appointment with her obstetrician for her twelve-week scan.'

Riley got up and went upstairs to get her schoolbag.

'Do you think she'll find out the sex?' Johnny asked.

'They can't always be sure this early in the pregnancy, but I think she's going to ask if they can tell on the scan or not.'

'I know one man who'd be very happy to have a son.' Johnny put the saucepan in the sink.

'Yes, Adam would definitely love a mirror image of himself.' Mia grinned.

'Ah, sure, what man wouldn't?'

Mia bit her lip.

'I didn't mean me, Mia. You know I'm happy with Riley. She's our miracle and I know how lucky we are to have her. But do you mind Sarah having another?'

Mia walked over and kissed her husband. 'No, and don't go bringing that up. Riley is enough. I have no regrets and don't think I ever do.'

Johnny held her close. 'Thanks.'

*

Izzy sang 'Let It Go' for the zillionth time as Sarah plaited her hair. Her headache was throbbing but, still, the sound of her little girl singing made her smile.

'Will you tie the plaits back with this bow, Mummy?' Izzy asked.

'Of course.' Sarah did so and smiled as her seven-year-old swirled around, trying to get a good view of the back of her head in the mirror on her wardrobe door.

The room was a princess parlour. Sarah knew she'd gone a bit overboard, but she was a girly girl and so was Izzy. The carpet was pink, the curtains were pink, the bedspread was white with pink hearts on it. The lamp beside her bed was pink and her desk chair was also pink. Sarah had chosen different shades, so it wasn't a complete pink onslaught.

'I love my hair.' Izzy threw her arms around her mother's waist. 'Am I squishing the baby?' she asked.

'No, sweetheart, not at all. No matter how big my tummy gets, I want you to give me your amazing hugs.' Sarah stood up and began to tidy up the hair bobbins and clips, putting them back into the glass box on Izzy's desk. Keeping her voice breezy, she asked, 'Izzy, are you finding school OK? Is maths getting too hard for you?'

'Not hard, just boring. I only got three wrong in the test yesterday. I got seven right.'

'So you're not struggling to follow any of the work?'

Izzy admired her plaits in the mirror. 'No. Why?' She suddenly looked anxious. 'Did Miss Dixon say something?'

'No, sweetie, she didn't. I just wanted to check everything was all right.' Sarah kissed her daughter's button nose. 'But if you ever find anything difficult just tell me.'

'OK, Mummy.'

Sarah folded Izzy's unicorn pyjamas and placed them under her pillow. 'Are Rebecca and Mya being nice to you?'

It had been a week since the 'incident' and nothing had been said at school, but Sarah wanted to make sure Izzy wasn't having any trouble with the witches' daughters.

'Why do you keep asking about them?' Izzy rolled her eyes. 'I told you already I don't play with them. They just read books at breaktime, which is *sooooo* boring.'

'That's fine. I just want to make sure everyone is being nice to everyone else. And if anyone is ever mean to you –'

'Tell me straight away,' Izzy imitated Sarah's voice. 'I know, Mummy, you've told me lots of times. But no one is being mean to me. Everyone is nice to everyone. Well, except Max and Ben who fight all the time, but we just ignore them. Boys can be so silly.'

Sarah laughed. 'Good. I promise I won't ask again for at least a day.'

They headed downstairs. Adam was standing in the hall, dressed in a suit, his car keys in his hand.

Izzy twirled. Adam looked to his wife for guidance.

'Hair,' she mouthed.

'Wow, Izzy, your hair looks amazing!' he exclaimed.

'Thanks. Mummy helped me.'

'Right, gotta go.' Adam headed towards the door.

'Daddy!' Izzy shouted. 'You never kissed me goodbye and you didn't kiss me goodnight either.'

Adam turned back. 'Sorry, Sweet-pea. I had to work late last night.'

'You're always working late,' Izzy complained.

Adam picked up his disgruntled daughter and swung her high in the air, covering her face with kisses.

'Stop, Daddy!' she squealed. 'Too much kissing.'

He put her down. 'You can never have too many kisses, can you, Sarah?'

Sarah shook her head. 'Nope.'

Adam kissed her and winked at Izzy. 'I'll see you ladies later.'

'Bye. Good luck with the meeting today. Don't be late for the scan,' Sarah reminded him.

Adam smiled. 'I should make it in time. I've a good feeling we'll get this contract, and if we do, I'm booking us a fancy holiday this summer.'

'Make it early June so I'm not hugely pregnant in my bikini.'

'You're gorgeous pregnant,' he said, kissing her again.

'Enough kissing. Go to work, Daddy.' Izzy pushed him out of the door.

Sarah packed Izzy's lunchbox while her daughter sat at the counter, chatting to her.

'Not carrots again, Mummy,' Izzy complained.

'They're healthy and good for you and will make your eyes shine.'

'My eyes *are* shiny. You just can't see them through my stinky glasses.'

Sarah looked into her daughter's blue eyes and smiled. 'They're beautiful, and they shine through the glasses, which are cute and cool.'

Izzy wrinkled her nose. 'I hate them.'

Sarah leaned forward to look at her daughter. 'I know you do, sweetie, but you'll get used to them and you do admit they help you see better – and you *are* a gorgeous girl with them.'

'I'm not wearing them on my Communion Day. I don't care if I can't see perfectly.'

'That's a deal. You can take them off for that special day.'

Izzy's frown faded. 'I love my dress so much, Mummy.'

'Me too. You look like an angel in it.'

Izzy clapped her hands together. 'Only a few weeks to go!'

The bell rang as Sarah packed a water bottle into her

daughter's lunchbox. Izzy clambered down from the stool and ran to open the door. Mia was standing on the step.

'Morning, sunshine. Ready to go?' Mia asked her niece.

'Yes. Is Riley in the car?'

'Yes, she is and she's grumpy, as usual.' Mia came into the kitchen followed by Izzy, who grabbed her schoolbag and lunchbox, gave her mother a quick kiss and ran to the car.

'She's obsessed with Riley,' Sarah said.

'God love her, she'll get no joy from her this morning. Riley's in a foul mood.'

'Quick coffee?' Sarah asked.

'No time.'

'You look nice. I love that colour on you,' Sarah said.

Mia was clearly surprised. Sarah knew her sister wasn't feeling good about herself, these days.

'Thanks.'

'Green has always been your colour. It matches your eyes.' Sarah grinned at her sister.

'Pity about the big saggy bags underneath.' Mia sighed.

'Stop that! You're gorgeous. Thanks for taking Izzy.'

'I can take her every day. After all, we're going to the same place.'

'I know, but I like taking her to school. Well, I used to, but now I have to avoid certain mothers.'

'Have you seen them?'

'Yes, but only from a distance. We all ignored each other.'

'Did any of the other mums mention it?' Mia asked.

'Harry's mum told me she'd heard there was an altercation in the Ladies.'

'What did you say?' Mia asked.

'I said I'd heard some mums being mean about Izzy so I defended her. I didn't name names.'

'Nicely handled. I asked the headmistress to let me know

if anyone approached her about Izzy or anything to do with Izzy. I checked again with her yesterday and there's been nothing so far.'

'Phew.' Sarah smiled. 'Tell me, how's Johnny getting on? Any sign of something turning up for him?'

Mia shrugged. 'There don't seem to be any jobs for journalists. I think he may have to retrain as something else.'

'Like what?'

Mia rubbed her eyes. 'I don't know. I need to look into options.'

Sarah thought it was up to Johnny to search into options, but she said nothing. Her older sister had always liked to control everything. She couldn't help herself – it was in her DNA. Their mother had been the same.

'Well, hopefully he'll get sorted soon.'

'Thanks. Let's not talk about Johnny. How are you feeling? You look pale. You might need iron. You're probably anaemic. Ask the doctor today for a prescription.'

'I'm fine. I just slept badly. Don't fuss.' Sarah didn't want another lecture on looking after herself. Mia had always been bossy, but since their mum had died three years ago she'd gone into overdrive. It was as if she felt her role now was leader of the family. She was even bossing their poor dad, Charlie, about. Sarah thought Charlie's romance with Olivia was an attempt to get away from Mia telling him what to do. Mind you, Sarah wasn't sure Olivia was the best choice, but Charlie seemed content.

'Well, good luck with the scan later. Will you find out the sex, do you think?'

Sarah was still undecided. 'I think so. It depends if they can see anything on the scan or not. Adam's mad keen to know. He has a big meeting today and I'm worried it'll run on. If he misses the scan, I'll kill him.'

Adam will always put work first, Mia thought. She picked up her bag and headed out of the door. 'Call me if you want me to bring Izzy home. You might need a lie-down – you really do look tired.'

Sarah didn't bother responding. She walked to the front door and waved them off. She could see Izzy chatting to Riley, while her teenage cousin stared at her phone. She hoped Izzy would love the new baby as much as she loved Riley.

3

Sarah sat in the waiting room at the clinic, flicking through a fashion magazine. She kept one eye on the big clock ticking in the corner of the surgery. Photos of celebrities on the beach with big red circles around their stretchmarks couldn't distract her from the anger rising in her chest. Where the hell was Adam? Her scan was scheduled for half past two. Knowing Adam's disastrous time-keeping, she'd lied and told him it was at two o'clock. It was now twenty past and there was no sign of him. She dropped the magazine onto the coffee-table and picked up her phone. She dialled his mobile. Straight to voicemail. She left a third grumpy message.

Damn him. He knew how important this was to her. And it should be just as important to him, for God's sake. She'd told him to be there, no matter what. This was a really big deal. This was their longed-for, wished-for, prayed-for baby. She did not want to do this alone.

A text flashed up. *So sorry. Negotiations still ongoing. Good luck. Ax*

Sarah wanted to throw the phone against the wall. She felt emotion well up. She wanted support today. She'd been feeling really tired and headachy lately and she didn't want to do this without her husband. She stared at the phone, silently cursing Adam for being so bloody unavailable all the time. Then she began scrolling through her contacts, stopping at 'Dad'.

Charlie lived ten minutes away. If he was at home, maybe he could come and support her if her husband couldn't.

Charlie answered on the second ring. Sarah explained the situation, struggling to hold back tears.

'I'll be there in ten minutes,' he said.

'Thanks, Dad, you're an angel.'

Sarah sat back and tried to calm her breathing. Getting worked up before the big scan was not a good idea. She was only twelve weeks pregnant, but she already had a tiny little bump. She'd thought it might be twins because she'd had no bump until about sixteen weeks with Izzy, but the original scan had shown just one baby. Mind you, it could be down to the daily scones she was scoffing. She'd have to be careful not to put on too much weight this time.

She didn't care what sex the baby was. A girl would be wonderful because Izzy would have a sister, like Sarah had Mia, but a boy would be amazing too, a little Adam.

The sonographer, Frankie O'Sullivan, called her name. Sarah looked towards the reception door. Charlie hadn't arrived yet.

'My father's on his way. Can you show him in when he arrives?' she asked the receptionist.

'Of course, no problem.'

Sarah followed Frankie into the small, dark room. She hopped onto the bed, undid her belt and the zip of her jeans, pulling them down to just below her hips. Frankie squeezed cold gel on her stomach and began to run the probe over her pregnancy bump.

Sarah held her breath. She hadn't had any bleeding or spotting, but you never knew until you heard the heartbeat and saw the screen if all was truly well. The probe moved around and then . . . the beautiful thump of her baby's heartbeat filled the room. Sarah smiled. The most wonderful sound in the world.

'Everything looks good,' Frankie assured her.

The door opened and Charlie rushed in. 'Sorry. Traffic. Am I too late?'

'No, Dad, just in time. Look, there's the baby.'

Charlie sat down beside his daughter and stared at the screen. 'Well, now, isn't that something?' He was transfixed.

They stared at the screen and Charlie took Sarah's hand in his. 'I'm so glad for you, love.'

'Thanks, Dad.' Sarah tried not to cry. Turning to the sonographer she asked, 'If possible, I'd like to know the sex.'

'Are you sure, love? Would you not like a surprise?' Charlie asked.

Sarah shook her head. 'No. Either way I'll be thrilled. With Izzy I was happy for it to be a surprise, but I've decided this time I want to know.'

Sarah turned back to face Frankie.

'Well, Sarah, I can't say with one hundred per cent certainty, but I can say that I'm very confident that it's . . . a boy.'

'Oh, a boy,' Sarah whispered, as tears of joy ran down her cheeks.

'A grandson.' Charlie beamed. 'The first boy in our family for decades.'

'It's perfect,' Sarah said. 'We'll have the perfect family.'

'You deserve it, pet.' Charlie squeezed her hand.

Sarah sat in the café next door to the hospital, staring at the printout of the ultrasound. The café was small and warm, full of students from the nearby college of art. Charlie came back to the table with a tray. He plonked down two cappuccinos and a large slice of sponge cake dripping with cream and jam. 'To celebrate my grandson.' He winked and handed Sarah a fork.

She groaned. '*Daaaad!* I'm supposed to be trying not to eat too much in this pregnancy. You know cake is my downfall.'

'Ah, will you stop! No man likes a skinny woman.'

The cake was calling: 'Eat me.' Sod it. Sarah dug in her fork and put a chunk into her mouth. God, it tasted so good.

'Do you think that person behind the counter is one of those transvestite or transgender types?' Charlie asked.

Sarah looked over. 'No. She's a girl with really short hair and a lot of tattoos.'

'In my day you'd know who was a girl and who was a boy. Nowadays you can't be too sure. And you'd be afraid to say anything in case you'd get it wrong or insult someone. I don't know, I think it was easier in the old days.'

'Easier for some, oppressive for others,' Sarah remarked.

'It's hard for us oldies. We don't know what to be saying to anyone any more. You'd be afraid even to tell a girl she looks nice. The world has gone mad.'

'No, Dad, it's just that people who were once marginalized can now openly be who they are. And women don't have to put up with being sleazed over. It's a good thing, believe me. I had a really creepy boss in the call centre who was always making lewd comments. I hated it. It made me feel so uncomfortable.'

Charlie ate a large chunk of cake. 'Fair enough, point taken. Anyway, my little grandson will be a boy and that's that.'

Sarah laughed. 'He'll be whatever he wants to be.'

'He'll be marvellous. I can't wait to take him to football matches and kick a ball about with him. I've been outnumbered by women for too long – me and this little fella will be great pals.'

Sarah smiled at her father. He'd be a fantastic granddad to her son, just like he'd been a wonderful father and grandfather to her and Mia, Riley and Izzy. She was extra glad it was a boy for Charlie to hang out with.

Sarah's phone buzzed on the table between them and the screen lit up. It was Adam. *Well? All OK?* She ignored it.

'Are you not going to tell him?' Charlie said, nodding at her phone.

'No. He can wait. I'm really furious with him. I begged him to be there, but he got stuck in some negotiation. It's always work with him.'

Charlie put down his fork. A group of loud students left the café, bringing a lot of the noise with them. It was a relief. Sarah's headache was back and throbbing.

'I know you're angry but, to be fair, if he was stuck in negotiations for a new contract, he couldn't really walk out. He's a very driven man and you have to admire that.'

Sarah pushed a strand of hair out of her face and tucked it behind her ear. 'I do, Dad, but sometimes I think he's too driven. In the last year he's been so busy in work he's rarely home for dinner or even to tuck Izzy in. I miss him. Izzy does too.'

Charlie sighed. 'It's hard for him to turn down contracts – you have to make hay while the sun shines. Look at Johnny. Will he ever get another job in journalism? Poor old Mia is worn out with the worry and stress. She's very short-tempered, these days. Jeepers, she ripped my head off the other day just for telling her she looked tired.'

Sarah winced. No woman wanted to be told she looked tired, especially a woman who was tired and under pressure. 'I guess you're right, Dad, but there has to be a better work–life balance for Adam. Izzy is growing up so fast and I don't want him to miss it. We don't need a bigger house or fancier cars. I just want him to be there more.'

'Talk to him, love. The key to a good marriage is communication. Even if you're roaring at each other, at least you're communicating. It's when you stop talking that things go wrong.'

Sarah polished off the last bite of cake. What the hell? She was eating for two. She glanced at her watch. It was half-past three. She'd put Izzy into after-school care until four.

'I'd better go, Dad. I need to collect Izzy.'

Charlie stood up and they walked out to the car park. He hugged her. 'I'm thrilled for you, love. A little boy. I can't wait to meet him. I'm so proud of you.'

Sarah kissed his cheek. If Adam could be half the father Charlie had been to her, this little boy would be very lucky indeed.

4

Mia hadn't sat down all morning. She glanced at her watch. A quarter to three: no wonder her stomach was rumbling. Between Communion practice, a meeting with the head-mistress, the endless form-filling, then dealing with three children who seemed to have a vomiting bug and needed to be picked up early, she hadn't had a second. Work was piled up on her desk, but there was no way she could get to it. Her chest tightened at the thought of all that still had to be done today.

She took a deep breath to calm her racing thoughts. Harry's parents were waiting for her in her office, and it was going to be a difficult meeting. Poor Harry was falling behind in his senior infants' class and the tests she'd asked the learning support teacher to conduct showed that he was within the autism range. The family had two other kids in the school who were bright academically, so this would be new territory for them. She took another deep breath, then straightened her shoulders and opened the door. 'Joan, Peter, lovely to see you,' she said, extending her hand. 'Thanks so much for coming in.'

Over the next hour, Mia listened as Harry's parents went through all the stages of shock, disbelief, questioning, anger, upset and, finally, acceptance. She felt for them, but it was essential that they get to grips with the diagnosis and focus on helping Harry to cope with school and fulfil his potential. He needed them to be strong now.

'I'm here if you have any other questions,' Mia said, standing up and smiling at them. 'The staff are here for you and

Miss Coakley is one hundred per cent behind Harry, there to support him every day.'

When she closed the door behind them, Mia heaved a sigh of relief. Another tick on her unending list. The next thing she wanted to sort out was the broken curtain rail in the sitting room at home. It was driving her crazy looking at it every evening. She texted Charlie, as he'd promised more than a week ago to do a run to the hardware shop, get the necessaries and come over to fix it. Johnny was hopeless at DIY. Her phone pinged almost immediately: *Just with Sarah. Can't today. Sry.* Mia cursed under her breath. The curtain would never be fixed at this rate. She'd just have to try to do it herself. No doubt the two of them were having coffee or out on a walk. God, what Mia wouldn't give for some time out, just five non-pressured minutes in her day. A leisurely cup of coffee with nowhere to be and nothing to do would be utter bliss.

Mia spent an hour trying to tackle the work on her desk, but eventually realized it was impossible to get through it all. She'd have to stay late again tomorrow. For now, she had to be at the post office before it closed, pick up her dry cleaning, and Johnny had texted her to buy some pork chops for a new recipe he was trying. Now that they only had one car, Mia ended up doing all the bloody picking up and shopping. She fired some work into her bag, grabbed her car keys and set off at a brisk trot to the car park. Hers was the only car there. The last to leave, as usual, she thought crossly.

She hit roadworks on the way to the post office and got there just as they were pulling down the hatch. Then she had to dash to make it to the dry cleaners before they shut up shop as well. She decided to drive to the supermarket, as their meat counter was the cheapest. It never ceased to amaze her that she had become the woman who carefully cut out coupons and knew the discounts offered in every shop in a five-mile radius. When Johnny was working and Riley's demands didn't stretch beyond Barbies, she'd been able to buy as she pleased. She wouldn't have had a clue how much pork chops were, she'd just have paid whatever was asked. *And* she would have gone to the organic butcher near Sarah's house and paid way over the odds without a second's thought.

Her life was almost unrecognizable to her now. She tried to tell herself that family was all that mattered, but it was hard to keep your chin up when everything fell on your shoulders. Mia felt old and tired. Tired right down to her bones. She was sick of having to carry everyone on her back. She earned the money, budgeted, nagged Riley to study, tried to keep track of her movements, and did the majority of the shopping. She did most of the worrying as well. It was great that Johnny was into cooking now, but texts with ingredient orders weren't so great. He could have got the bus to the supermarket.

The worst thing was, it was impossible to go from Mrs Coping With It All to Mrs Might Just Want Sex Occasionally. Johnny had tried it on last night, but she was so tired and felt so deeply unsexy that she'd swatted him away. How was she meant to do the household accounts, argue with Riley, tidy up, then be all hot and seductive at the drop of a hat? She just couldn't do it. The imbalance between her and Johnny had crept into their bedroom, and while it upset her deeply, she couldn't see a way out of it. All she wanted to do after ten o'clock at night was collapse into bed and sleep.

As she walked towards the checkout with the pork chops in hand, she saw Rebecca's mother coming towards her. Great, thought Mia. Now I have to be nice to this cow who was mean about Izzy. It was such a pain to have to put her work face on outside school, but everyone expected her to be deputy head at all times.

'Mia, how are you?'

'Hello, Grainne. Just grabbing a few dinner things on the way home.'

'Same here,' Grainne said, rolling her eyes. 'The work never stops, does it? We working mothers are heroes. Mind you, you teachers have it easy with the short days and the long holidays.'

'Not really. I think everyone is busy, Grainne,' Mia said evenly.

'I'm not so sure,' Grainne said. 'Those stay-at-home mums have no clue about the pressures of the corporate world. They just don't understand the demands of being in a high-powered, high-pressured job. It's all coffee mornings and yoga with them.'

Mia felt the irritation prickle across her like a skin rash. Could this woman be more judgemental? She had no idea of the lives of the other mothers with children at the school. Those who didn't hold down day jobs did Trojan work, throwing themselves into school fundraising events, committees and every other task going, regardless of difficulties at home, like money worries or elderly parents who needed minding. From her years of experience in dealing with families, Mia was all too aware that no one got away lightly.

'I think you'll find they do a lot more than that,' she said, trying to keep the irritation out of her voice. 'Everyone has their own stress and pressure. It's easy to judge from the outside but looks can be deceiving.'

'Oh, sorry. I forgot your sister doesn't work. Oops, hit a nerve, did I? Anyway,' Grainne said, 'speaking of Sarah, how is Izzy getting on? She's in my Rebecca's class, you know.'

Mia smiled tightly. 'She's getting on extremely well. She's a bright little girl. Sorry, Grainne, but I'll have to dash. My husband is waiting for the ingredients to arrive.'

'Sure I'm rushing myself,' Grainne said. 'Never get a minute to sit down. It's non-stop conference calls and meetings. Mind you, the hefty bonuses always help ease the pain.' She winked. 'This is last year's bonus.' She shoved a hand in Mia's direction to show her a huge diamond ring. 'Present to myself.' She tittered.

'Very nice.' Mia walked away with clenched fists. What a piece of work, judging everyone else, then crassly shoving her success in Mia's face. It had the desired effect, though. Mia did feel a bit envious. Working so hard would be easier if you were getting paid tons of money, but a teacher's salary was never going to buy a diamond of any size. Still, all her success couldn't save Grainne from being a total idiot. Mia needed to focus on the good things in her life and somehow find a better work–life balance before she broke.

The house was in darkness when she pulled into the driveway. She hated it when Riley and Johnny sat in the kitchen and forgot to put on the porch light. It looked so unwelcoming, as if they'd forgotten about her. Wearily, she gathered her stuff from the back seat, kicked the door closed with her foot and locked it. She couldn't wait to take off her shoes and be served a hot meal, preferably with wine, if there was a bottle knocking around. Sarah had given her one last week, so if Johnny hadn't got his mitts on it, she was going to treat herself to a glass to unwind after what had been a pretty lousy day, all told.

She let herself into the house. Inside it was cold and dark. There were no sounds of life, and certainly no smells of dinner cooking. She went down to the kitchen, switched on the light and dumped all her stuff on the table. She looked around. There were dirty dishes on top of the dishwasher, a habit of Riley's that drove her insane. Johnny had obviously been cooking something earlier, and there were pots on the hob and spoons on the counter. The washing-machine was flashing 'End', with a full load inside, waiting to be taken out. There were newspapers strewn across the table. It looked messy and unloved. Where was everyone?

Mia took out her phone to check her messages. Sure enough, there was a text from Johnny: *Riley had a tough day, so I've taken her to cinema. Be home by 10.30. Reheat soup if hungry.*

If hungry? Mia wanted to scream at the top of her lungs and fling the shagging pots on the floor. She had worked like a maniac all day, done all the extras on the way home, collected the damn chops and he was suggesting she *might* be hungry. Was he for real? And, as usual, he was off playing best dad in the bloody world. Fun Dad. Dad who never gives Riley grief. Never nags. Mia felt completely alone. Who was going to take her out for a treat after her crappy day? Who was going to make her feel better? Cheer her up? As usual, no one. She was on her own. Suck it up, Mia. This is your life.

Mia sank into a kitchen chair and put her head in her hands. The silence of the house was heavy around her, and her limbs felt as if they were made of concrete. She should get up and put on the heating. She should tidy and empty the machine. She should reheat the soup. She knew those were the sensible, grown-up things to do, but she felt broken with exhaustion and disappointment. Instead, she cried. Mia was not one for crying, and she knew her mother would be utterly horrified at the sight of her giving in like that, but it was just too much. She had nothing left to give. *I'm sorry, Mum*, she thought, *but my life has gone down the toilet and I don't know what to do*. Sitting alone at the messy table, Mia cried until her throat was sore. She felt absolutely wretched.

When the front door opened at ten thirty, the kitchen was clean and tidy, all the pots put away, everything in its place.

Mia had eaten the soup, and she had found the wine bottle, half full, then realized she just couldn't stomach it. The clothes were out of the dryer, folded and in the hot press. There was another load on in the washing-machine. She'd tidied the house, and was now sitting on the sofa, a smile glued to her lips, her face washed and showing no sign of the tears that had overtaken her earlier.

Johnny and Riley came into the room. 'You would have enjoyed that film,' Johnny said cheerfully, falling onto the sofa beside her.

'I'm sure I would, but I was kind of busy doing everything in the house after a really tough day at work. So . . .'

'There's no need to be like that, Mum.'

Mia looked at her in surprise. 'What? Grumpy? Fed-up? I dunno, Riley, how would you feel if you'd come home after your "tough" day at school to a cold, empty house and had to spend two hours cleaning and washing?'

'You should have left it, Mia. I would have done it,' Johnny said.

'When?'

He shrugged. 'Now, or tomorrow morning.'

'He was just cheering me up,' Riley said. 'Don't nag him.'

Mia looked at her daughter, then stood up. 'Someday, you might think about cheering me up. I'm a person with feelings, too. Goodnight, everyone.' She left the room. She literally couldn't take another second of this day. She craved the oblivion of sleep.

5

Izzy lay back in bed and put her hands over her head. Sarah gently took her daughter's glasses off and placed them on the bedside locker. She sat down beside her on the bed. 'Are you tired, sweetie?'

Izzy stifled a yawn. 'No.'

Sarah kissed her soft cheek. 'I think you are. Swimming on Wednesdays always tires you out.'

Izzy reached up and played with Sarah's hair. 'I wish mine was lovely blonde like yours, Mummy. It looks like a princess's hair in fairy-tales.'

Bleach and hair tongs, Sarah thought. 'Thank you, Izzy, but your hair is blonde and beautiful too.'

'But it's not shiny gold like yours, Mummy.'

'It is shiny, just like your blue eyes. You are the prettiest girl in the world.'

Izzy sighed. 'You always say that.'

'Because it's true.'

Izzy twirled Sarah's hair around her fingers. 'Mummy, is the baby going to take you away from me?'

Sarah frowned. 'No. Why would you think that?'

'Because Caroline's mummy had twin babies and she said her mummy is always busy-busy, and she never reads Caroline stories or tucks her into bed or anything.'

Sarah chose her words carefully. Taking Izzy's hand in hers, she said, 'I will have to look after the baby, feeding and changing nappies and stuff, but I'll still be able to read you stories and tuck you in.'

'Do you promise?'

'Yes. I'll love you the same, look after you the same, hug you and kiss you the same.' Sarah covered her daughter's adorable face with kisses.

Izzy giggled, but was only temporarily distracted. She was clearly fretting over the baby more than Sarah had realized. 'So you won't love the baby more than me?'

'Of course not, sweetie.'

'But how do you know? You said when I was born your heart was full to the top with love. There's no room for you to love the baby unless you love me a bit less.'

'Oh, Izzy,' Sarah said, resting her forehead against her daughter's. 'My heart is big enough to love lots of people. You, Daddy, Mia, Riley, Granddad and Johnny, and Rob and Ellen in Canada and lots of other people. The heart is a muscle, so the more you love, the bigger and stronger it gets.'

'For real?'

'Yes. I will always love you, Sweet-pea.'

'So when the baby comes, you'll love it the same as me?'

'Well,' Sarah whispered in her daughter's ear, 'I'll let you in on a secret. I'll love the baby so much, but I'm not sure I can love anyone more than I love you.'

Izzy beamed. 'Me too, Mummy. I love you the best.'

They hugged, and Sarah inhaled the scent of her daughter. She felt as if her heart might just overflow.

Adam came into the bedroom and handed Sarah a mug of tea. She was sitting up in bed, wearing her most comfy brushed-cotton dove-grey pyjamas. Mia always joked that Sarah's 'worst' pyjamas were better than her own best ones. Mia usually slept in an old pair of leggings and one of John-ny's big T-shirts. Sarah had lots of silky pyjamas that Mia said were far too good to wear. But Sarah liked making an effort to look nice, even in bed. But not tonight: tonight she was cross and tired.

'You're not forgiven,' she said to her husband.

He sighed. 'For the millionth time, I'm sorry.' He had loosened his tie and the top button of his shirt was open. His brown eyes had dark shadows under them. But Sarah was not going to feel sorry for him, not now. She didn't care how tired he was: she was tired too.

'It was really important to me, Adam. I wanted you there with me for the scan.'

'I wanted to be there, but the meeting ran over and I couldn't just get up and leave. This is a huge contract for us. It's going to make us a lot of money.'

Sarah put the mug down carefully on a magazine on her bedside locker. 'I don't care about having more money. I care about you being around for this baby, Adam. You work all the time. Izzy's growing up and you're missing it. I feel like a single parent, you're so busy all the time.'

Adam rubbed his jaw. 'Look, the recession almost destroyed my business. No one wanted new bathrooms when they couldn't pay their mortgages. I have to grab these big opportunities when they come along. I can't let up now things are good again. I won't let my family down like my dad did. I'm doing this for us, for security, for our future, for our kids.'

Sarah took his hand. 'I know your dad went off the rails and lost everything after your mum died, but you're not him. We're not them. You're a strong man who's always been so responsible, and I love that about you. I'm not going anywhere so I'll be here for the kids, always. But you don't need to prove anything to anyone any more. You're successful, you're together, you provide well for us financially and I really appreciate that. But Izzy and this new baby need you to be their dad as well as their provider. Izzy craves more time with you. When you're home, you're on your phone all the time. Please, Adam, promise me you'll try to get a better life–work balance. Being at that scan on my own was grim. Dad had to step in and hold my hand.'

Adam kissed her. 'I'm sorry. I'll try, I promise. I guess I'll never feel safe. When you've grown up with a deadbeat dad and had to rob your classmates' sandwiches as your only food for the day, you always worry about the future.'

'Your childhood was horribly tough, but look at what you have now. We have a great life. Don't miss it by working all the time.'

Adam kissed her again. 'How did I get so lucky with you?'

'Charm, good looks and great sex.' Sarah laughed and sank back into her pillow, yawning.

'Are you OK?'

'Yeah. I just feel wiped out. I'm going to get some iron tomorrow – I think I need a boost. Mia very kindly offered to take Izzy to school in the morning.'

'She loves helping you out. It makes her feel like she has control.'

'Stop it.'

'It's true. She's so domineering. She treats everyone like they're her students. Poor Johnny's completely bitch-slapped.'

'No, he's not. He's really happy with her.'

Adam raised an eyebrow. 'Is he?'

'Yes, he is.' Sarah wished Adam and Mia got on better. They'd always had an edgy relationship. Adam had found Mia 'too much' from the day they'd first met, when she'd peppered him with questions.

'It was like an interrogation,' he'd complained to Sarah afterwards.

'She's just protective of me. There's five years between us, so she's always looked out for me.'

Over the years Adam and Mia had learned to tolerate each other and sometimes, usually when wine was involved, they even got on quite well, but they were never going to be close. Mia was too forthright for Adam and he, in turn, spent his life winding her up.

Sarah had tried to bring them closer by highlighting each one's best qualities to the other, but they were just too similar. Both wanted to have their own way, both were stubborn as mules and both had very strong personalities. While they argued heatedly about pretty much every topic under the sun, Sarah and Johnny would sit back, wink at each other and sip their wine, or go outside and have sneaky cigarettes. They were the total opposite – Sarah had fallen for Johnny's humour and warmth from day one, and that had never changed. She always said he was the best brother-in-law she could have hoped for. Whenever she said that, Mia went quiet. She would never be able to say that about Adam.

'Now that I've got this new contract, I want to take you and Izzy on a blow-out holiday. I was thinking we could go and visit Rob and Ellen in Toronto. I've always wanted to see Canada. I'd like to spend some time with my brother and for Izzy to get to know him and Ellen better. She hasn't seen them since they came back for Christmas two years ago.'

Sarah's head throbbed. The thought of going two hours down the road to Cork on holidays seemed like too much of an effort at the moment. All the way to Canada?

'I'm not sure I should fly that far when I'm pregnant. I think I'd be nervous. I'm afraid to risk anything when it's taken us so long to get this far. Can we go after the baby's born?'

Adam nodded. 'Of course. I wasn't thinking. No risks, no way, not this time.' He bent down and kissed her stomach. 'This baby is a keeper, I just know it.'

Sarah smiled and rubbed her stomach. 'I didn't carry any of the other four pregnancies past seven weeks, so it's looking good. The scan went so well. The baby is growing normally and looking healthy. Thank God.'

Adam lay down on the bed beside her and held her hand. 'Thank God is right. I so want a sibling for Izzy . . . Rob's my best mate.'

'I don't know what I'd do without Mia.'

'It's been a long road, but it'll be worth all the disappointments to have a sister or brother for Izzy.'

Sarah rolled onto her side to face her husband. 'Actually, Adam, it looks like it's going to be a baby brother.'

Adam stared at her. 'What? Seriously? You found out the sex?'

Sarah nodded, smiling at his delight.

'Oh!' he said, kissing her. 'I'm going to have a son? Really?'

Sarah's eyes filled with tears. It was wonderful to see Adam so happy. The miscarriages and the constant hoping had been draining, but even though he had almost given up hope, she never had.

'Yes, they're fairly confident it's a boy. Your son.'

'Woohoo!' Adam said, punching the air. He threw his arms around her. 'Sarah, this is just brilliant. I'll teach him how to play football and we can go to rugby matches together and watch the *Star Wars* movies and – Oh, God, it's going to be amazing.'

'So you're a bit pleased, then?' Sarah said, laughing.

'A girl and a boy! It's exactly what I've always wanted. And you are the most amazing woman. I know it's been hard on you, much more so than on me, but you've been so strong. And now we'll have a son. It's just fantastic news.' He held her close.

Maybe a boy would bring Adam home more, Sarah thought,

as she cuddled into his embrace. He'd want to play sports with his son and do boy stuff. It might work out for all of them. It could make Adam really step up and spend more time being a father. She couldn't wait for their future.

6

Olivia reached over and fixed Charlie's tie. Mia caught Sarah's attention and they rolled their eyes. It was the fourth or fifth time she'd done it. His tie was perfectly straight – she just couldn't help herself: she was constantly touching him or fixing his clothes. It reminded Mia of a dog peeing to mark its territory. She didn't like Olivia. Neither did Sarah, but she wasn't irritated by her like Mia was.

Olivia had dropped into their lives and plonked herself down. Mia didn't want her father to mourn her mother's death for ever, and she was glad Charlie had found a companion, but Olivia was suffocating. She wanted to be with him day and night. All she talked about was the golf club, going on holidays and how successful her sons were, which really bugged Mia. It was bad enough having to put up with Olivia pawing her father without having to hear about Robert, her barrister son, 'senior counsel, you know', and Tim, with the PhD. It made Mia, the teacher, and Sarah, the ex-call centre manager, seem pretty lame. Not to mention Johnny, the unemployed journalist. At least Adam, the successful businessman, was something for Charlie to shout about, even if he 'just owns a bunch of bathroom stores', as Johnny grumpily pointed out.

Mia missed her mum. They'd been so close. Penny was the one person in the world who really *got* her. They were very similar, and Mia missed being able to call her and talk to her about things, good and bad. Her mum would always listen and give the best advice. She'd understood why Mia was het up about something because she'd got het up about the same things. They were two peas in a pod, and she'd made Mia feel cherished.

Sarah and Charlie were different. They were more relaxed and didn't let things bother them. On the one hand, Mia envied them and wished she could be more like them, but on the other, it annoyed her that they didn't get more wound up about things. How could you go through life like that? Mind you, Mia felt so strongly about so many things that sometimes that in itself was exhausting.

Charlie poured everyone more wine. Sarah waved her hand over her glass. 'Not for me, Dad.'

'I must say, it's very nice having a driver again. I could get used to this, Sarah,' Adam said, accepting a refill with relish.

Sarah punched him playfully. 'Don't get too comfortable. As soon as this baby's born, I'll be swigging white wine by the neck.'

'I find one or two glasses perfectly sufficient,' Olivia said. 'I never like to see a woman drunk. It's so unseemly.'

Mia picked up her glass and drank the contents in two large gulps.

'Easy there, Tiger,' Johnny muttered. 'You don't need to get paralytic to prove a point.'

Ignoring him, Mia reached over and poured herself another glass.

'So, how are things, Johnny?' Adam asked. 'Any sign of a job yet?'

Johnny looked at his plate. 'Not yet, but hopefully something will come up.'

'I love your enthusiasm, especially when newspapers seem to be a dying format. These days, anyone can write a story and post it online. You don't need to be a journalist. Pity you didn't see online publishing coming when you chose your career. People will always need bathrooms, but newspapers, not so much.'

Mia gulped more wine to stop herself speaking. She could feel anger bubbling up inside. Had Adam so easily forgotten that during the recession, when he'd had to close down two of his bathroom shops, Johnny had sent his way any colleague who was even thinking about buying a new tap? Had he forgotten how difficult it was when things were going badly? Just because his business was booming again, did he have to be such a smug git?

Sarah leaned across and squeezed Johnny's arm. 'People will always want to read what Johnny has to say. He's brilliant. Always was, always will be.'

Mia felt tears well up. Good old Sarah, always with a kind word, always sensitive to others. Mia polished off her wine and poured more. Beside her, Johnny knocked his back too. At this rate, they'd both be face down on the table by the time the main course arrived.

Since Johnny had been laid off they'd cut back on all unnecessary expenses, and wine was one of the first things to go. They bought cheap beer and drank a couple of those to take the edge off after a long week. Posh cheeses had been replaced with lumps of Cheddar and artisan bread with sliced pan. They'd sold Johnny's car and were sharing Mia's. When their friends suggested meeting up for dinner in town, they made excuses not to go. Tonight was Charlie's treat, so Mia was able to relax and not worry about the bill. She was determined to keep meeting their mortgage repayments, no matter how much they had to tighten their belts.

Their food arrived, and Olivia made a fuss over the amount of salt Charlie put on his fish. 'Darling, it's so bad for you. You promised to cut back. Here, taste some of mine.'

Olivia proceeded to fork-feed Charlie half of her meal and make 'yummy' sounds each time he took a bite.

Sarah caught Mia's eye and made a vomit face. Mia, loosened by wine, laughed.

Olivia and Charlie looked over.

'It's lovely to see you smile, Mia,' Olivia said. 'It transforms your face. You always seem so preoccupied and stressed. Those frown lines are very hard to reverse without Botox.' Olivia whispered the word. 'I trained myself not to frown, you know. You can do it too – it's not that difficult. All you have to do is say *Frown and your face falls down* over and over and eventually you'll just stop and look relaxed and happy all the time, like me.'

Mia stared at her fork and imagined sticking it into Olivia's salon-coiffed head.

'Breathe,' Johnny whispered, 'and lower the weapon.'

Olivia nudged Charlie, who tapped his wine glass with his fork.

'I . . . that is we . . . ah . . . well, we have a little bit of news.' Charlie struggled to find the right words.

'More of an announcement,' Olivia said grandly.

'Yes, well, I suppose that's right. The thing is that we've . . . well . . . we've decided to get hitched.'

'What?' Mia and Sarah exclaimed.

Charlie's face reddened. Olivia took his hand firmly in hers. 'Isn't it wonderful? I know you want to congratulate your father, girls. I'm sure you're pleased to see him happy again.'

'You've known each other for ten minutes,' Mia spluttered.

'Five months actually, Mia,' Olivia said sharply. She straightened her back and puffed out her considerable chest.

Maybe that was it, Mia thought, through her wine haze. Olivia's boobs. Maybe that's what Charlie liked so much

46

about her. Olivia was all boobs and touching. Their mum, Penny, had been flat-chested, witty and, truth be told, sharp-tongued at times, but very loving, too. She hadn't endlessly groped their father, like Olivia did, but Penny had loved him, supported him and made him laugh.

Mia could feel an epic frown down the middle of her forehead right now. This was ridiculous.

'It does seem quite impulsive,' Sarah said. 'What's the hurry?'

'Are you up the duff, Olivia?' Adam said. 'Shotgun wedding, is it?'

Olivia glared at him. 'Don't be silly. We both feel that, as we're not getting any younger, we want to commit to each other now, don't we, Charlie?' She held Charlie's hand to her cheek.

'Oh, yes, that's right.' Charlie was a bit sheepish.

Mia was furious with her father. Why did he have to announce this in the middle of a restaurant in front of Johnny and Adam? Why couldn't he have taken her and Sarah out for a coffee and told them privately, so they could discuss it? Allow them the time to process this news. It was a big deal. It meant that Olivia would be in their lives for good and their mother would fade into the background.

Mia glared at her father, who avoided her eyes and looked at Sarah, the 'nicer' daughter. 'I know it's a bit of a whirlwind romance, as they say, but we get on well and have fun together, and I want to make an honest woman of Olivia.'

'So this was your idea?' Mia folded her arms across her chest and eyeballed her father.

'Of course it was.' Olivia pretended to be insulted. 'I hardly twisted his arm. Charlie proposed very romantically, over breakfast in bed.'

'After sex, I presume.' Adam laughed at his own joke. 'The feel-good hormones carried you away, did they?'

'Adam!' Sarah thumped his arm.

Olivia giggled. 'I'll tell you this and no more. Charlie is a very fit man.'

Charlie blushed, but looked flattered at the same time.

'Jesus, I need a stronger drink,' Johnny muttered.

'Stop! Enough! We don't need the sordid details.' Mia got up from the table and headed to the Ladies. Her feet were like lead and her head was spinning. She felt a hand on her arm.

'OMG, we need to talk.' Sarah hurried her into the powder room. Mia plonked herself down on the chair in the corner.

'What is he doing?' Mia said. 'She's a pain in the arse.'

'I agree.'

'Talking about sex with our dad!'

'Well, Adam did wind her up.'

'Did you see Dad's face?'

'He looked proud of himself about the sex. Oh, God.' Sarah squeezed her eyes shut.

'Do you think it's the boobs?'

'I guess so. But I thought you were either a boob man or a leg man. Mum had no boobs and good legs, so I presumed Dad was a leg man,' Sarah said.

'Well, he seems to like boobs now. He's always staring at Olivia's.'

'They're hard to miss in those plunging tops.'

'Don't.' Mia covered her eyes.

'To be fair, although she's a pain he has been happier since he met her,' Sarah said.

'Fine, so date her and shag her, but don't marry her!' Mia slapped her hand on her thigh.

'She's an operator. She knows exactly what to do and she's played him like a violin.' Sarah pulled at her face in the mirror.

'He likes being looked after – all men do. She fusses over him and he loves it.'

'Do they?' Mia chewed her lip. Did men like being fussed over? She never fussed over Johnny and he seemed fine. Did he really want her spoon-feeding him and making 'yummy' noises while flashing her boobs?

Sarah turned away from the mirror to face her sister. 'Absolutely. Adam loves me to fuss over his sore back or tell him how wonderful he is for working so hard or to cook his favourite dinner.'

Mia sat back in the chair. She couldn't remember what Johnny's favourite dinner was. Was it steak and chips? Or roast lamb? Maybe roast chicken. She actually didn't know. But she'd never fussed over him. She loved him and supported him and encouraged him and looked after him if he was sick, but she definitely wasn't a fusser. Maybe she should fuss more. Then again, given how tired she was most days, she could barely speak when she got home, let alone fuss.

'What are we going to do? Will we try to get him to have a long engagement?' Sarah asked. 'I'm worried he may regret it. I think he needs to get to know her better.'

'A *very* long engagement.'

'I don't want to upset him, though,' Sarah said. 'He does like her a lot.'

'Well, he'd bloody well want to if he's just agreed to spend the rest of his life with her,' Mia said, the alcohol making her sound angrier than she'd intended.

'Will you say it to him?' Sarah asked.

'No way. He'll take it better from you. He prefers you.'

'No, he doesn't. Don't be silly.'

'Yes, he does, and we both know it, but it's OK because I know Mum preferred me.'

'You cow,' Sarah said, laughing.

Mia grinned. 'I love you the most.'

Sarah leant down and kissed her sister's cheek. 'Ditto.'

'Thank God we have each other,' Mia said. 'The only sane ones left.'

Sarah pulled her to her feet. 'I'll talk to Dad tomorrow, quietly and alone. For now, we have to pretend we're happy.'

'Do we really?'

'Yes, Mia. Now behave.'

'I'll be good.'

'Smile and say nothing.'

'How's this?' Mia turned to her sister, a fake smile plastered across her face.

'That's really scary. OK, forget the smile. Just keep quiet.'

'But Olivia said my smile transforms my face.' Mia bared her teeth again.

The two sisters arrived back at the table, laughing.

Olivia beamed at them. 'Didn't I tell you, Charlie? They're delighted with the news.'

'Thrilled.' Mia threw her arms in the air.

'Over the moon.' Sarah giggled.

'My lovely girls,' Charlie said fondly. 'Best sisters in the world.'

7

Riley poured vodka into the plastic cup and topped it off with a splash of Coke. Taking a deep breath, she knocked it back. It burned her throat and made her want to throw up, but she needed it.

She glanced up from under her fringe and watched him flirting. How could he do this to her? He'd said she was special. He'd said she was the only person he wanted to be with. He'd said . . . he'd said so many things. They were together. They were a couple. Riley and Zach, Zach and Riley. She'd loved it. She'd loved being part of a pair. It had been the best five months of her life.

Until last week, when she'd made that joke about the stupid high jump. It was no big deal, but he'd looked all hurt and then he'd stopped answering her calls and then he'd sent that text: *I think we need to take a break*. A text! A break? Because of a stupid comment?

Zach was the one good thing in her life. He made her feel ten feet tall. He made her feel beautiful, which no one had ever done before. She knew she wasn't, but when Zach said it, she kind of believed him. Stupid of her, because he obviously hadn't meant it. He'd been avoiding her, and now he was humiliating her in front of everyone. Riley needed to numb the pain quickly.

It was crazy that he was acting like he was into Zoë. She was so not his type. He'd always slagged off 'those girls' with their fake tan, bleached hair and dresses barely covering their arses. Zach always said they looked like cheap Barbie dolls.

He said he liked Riley because she was different. Well, it didn't look that way now. Riley crunched the plastic cup between her fingers as Zach twirled Zoë's long hair around his finger and laughed at some stupid remark she'd just made.

'Hey.' Shocko sidled up beside her at the kitchen counter. 'What's up?'

'I'll tell you what's up,' Riley hissed. 'Zach is a dickhead, that's what.'

Shocko followed Riley's eyes and saw Zach kiss Zoë. He turned back to Riley. 'He was always a dickhead.'

'Yeah, but he was my dickhead. Mine, not hers. Look at her, she's pathetic. Peroxide toothpick.' Riley roughly wiped a tear away.

Shocko put his arm around his best friend. 'Dude, he's not worth it. Don't let him get to you. You're in a different stratosphere from Zoë. If he can't see that, he's a fool.'

Riley grabbed another cup and filled it with vodka. 'He told me I rocked his world.'

Shocko poured water into a cup and handed it to Riley. 'I think you should drink this.'

Riley pushed his hand away. 'I need to get really drunk and block this out.'

'I'm not sure that's a good idea. Besides, you're pretty smashed already.'

'Not smashed enough.'

Riley blinked. God, the lights were so bright. She went to sit up but fell back onto the pillow. Her head ached. She looked around. Where the hell . . .

'You're awake,' Shocko's voice said.

Riley turned to see her friend sitting in a chair beside her. 'Jesus, Shocko, where am I?'

'A and E.'

'*What?*'

'Yep. Let's just say the vodka had a negative influence on your balance. You fell and cut your head.'

'OMG, did anyone see?'

'Pretty much everyone at the party, yeah.'

'Don't sugar-coat it.'

'I thought we swore to always be honest with each other,' he said.

Riley bit her thumbnail. 'Did Zach see?' she asked, looking down at her hands.

'Kinda hard for him to miss it. You were throwing a drink over him when you tripped.'

Riley covered her face with her hands. 'Oh, God, did I?'

'Yep. Most of it went over Zoë, though.'

Riley smiled. That was something. 'How did I hit my head?'

'You were throwing the drink and, like, shouting a lot and then you sort of just lost your balance and fell over and whacked it on the coffee-table. It was pretty dramatic – people thought you were like dead and stuff. Because there was a lot of blood.'

'Did Zach think that?'

'Yeah, he looked pretty freaked out, but when he bent down to check on you, you told him he was a scumbag, so he knew you were alive.'

Why did she have such a big mouth and why did she get so drunk and why was she such an idiot? Now everyone in school would be talking about what a loser she was. Not only had Zach publicly humiliated her with Zoë, she'd humiliated herself by making a scene.

Riley's head throbbed. 'How did I end up here?'

'Someone, who thought you were like dead or dying, called an ambulance. I came with you.'

'You didn't call my parents, did you?'

Shocko's cheeks reddened. 'I had to, Riley. Because you're a minor, they said I had to get an adult to pick you up.'

Riley began to sob. Not only was she now going to be a pariah in school, but her parents would go mental. Her mother would lock her up and never let her out again.

Shocko stood up and shuffled his feet. 'I'm sorry, dude, I had to.'

Riley cried even more.

Shocko wrung his hands. 'Jeez, Riley, don't cry. Come on, it won't be that bad.'

'My mum is going to freak.' Riley wiped her tears with the back of her sleeve.

'Yeah, she probably will but . . . well, I'll talk to her. I'll say . . . I dunno . . . Oh, I've got it. I'll say your drink was spiked.'

Riley sniffed. 'Yes. That's perfect. You're a genius.'

Shocko shrugged. 'Well, I wouldn't go that far, seeing as I failed almost every subject in my Christmas exams, but . . .'

Riley took his hand. 'You're a genius to me.'

Shocko's face turned pink.

The curtain around the bed was yanked backwards.

'Riley! Are you OK?' Mia asked, rushing over and examining the bandages.

'I'm fine, Mum. It's just a bump.' Riley was desperate to play this down.

'You gave us a fright, sweetheart.' Johnny reached down and hugged her.

'They glued it.'

'What?' Mia glanced at Shocko.

'Her head, they glued it. No stitches, just glue.'

'Sounds sore, you poor thing. How are you feeling?' Johnny held her hand.

'Honestly, it's fine. It's no big deal.'

'Thank God you're all right. How did it happen?' Mia asked.

'Well, I tripped and hit my head off a coffee-table.'

'Were you drinking?' Mia's eyes were like lasers.

Riley flinched. 'I had one beer.'

'One beer?' Johnny asked. 'You smell like you had twenty.'

'No, just one,' Riley said. It was true: she had only had one beer. She'd had about six vodkas as well, but at least it was partly true.

'You fell over after one beer.' Johnny's eyebrows rose.

Riley glared at Shocko.

'What?' He looked confused, then his brain caught up. 'Oh, yeah, sorry, I think her drink was spiked,' he blurted out.

'Spiked?' Mia was horrified. 'With what? By whom?'

'Oh, eh, well, I'm not sure, like. I didn't see obviously, but one minute Riley was fine and then she wasn't.'

'This all happened in Violet's house, at the party?' Mia asked.

'Yes,' Riley said.

'Where were her parents? Were they not supervising? There wasn't supposed to be any alcohol at all.'

'Her parents went out for a bit.' To London for the week-end, Riley thought, but you don't need to know that. 'And some of the kids brought drink.'

'What was your drink spiked with?' Mia asked. 'Should we ask for a drug test? I think we need a drug test.'

'No!' Riley sat up in the bed. She'd smoked a joint with Shocko in his garage before going to the party. That would show up and then her mother really would put her in prison.

'Riley, I'm afraid we have to. If your drink was spiked with a drug, we need to know which one. It could affect you in the future, flashbacks, psychotic episodes . . . Who knows what damage it's done and will do?'

55

'It's very serious,' Johnny agreed. 'In fact, we may even have to get the police involved.'

'Yes,' Mia agreed. 'I'll have to call Violet's parents first thing in the morning and get statements from all the kids who were there. Someone must have seen who spiked your drink. It's illegal.' Mia patted Riley's arm. 'I'm going to call the doctor in and get tests done. We need to know exactly what's in your system.' Mia turned to leave.

'Stop!' Riley shouted. 'Don't get the doctor. It wasn't spiked.'

Mia folded her arms across her chest. 'I didn't think so. How about you tell us the truth now?'

Riley's jaw clenched. She didn't know how, but Mia could always tell when she was lying.

'I drank some vodka as well as the beer and then I tripped and that's it.' Riley put her hands up. 'I know I'm grounded for ever so you don't have to go off on one.'

Mia leaned over the bed. 'I'm not going to "go off on one", but I am incredibly disappointed in you for disobeying me and your dad, for getting drunk and injuring yourself. You made some really bad decisions tonight, Riley, and, yes, there will be consequences, serious ones.'

Riley looked to her dad for help. Johnny shook his head. 'We asked you not to drink, you lied, and now you've hurt yourself into the bargain. Not cool, Riley.'

Riley began to cry. Her mother was always annoyed with her and on her case about something, but her dad was her ally. She'd really blown it this time. Still, who cared if her parents locked her up for ever? She never wanted to leave her room again anyway. Zach had hurt and shamed her publicly, and she'd made a complete fool of herself. She was a total loser.

'Hey, now.' Johnny sat beside her on the bed and put his arm around her. 'It'll be all right. Let's get you home.'

*

Mia was signing the release form when she felt a tug on her arm. It was Shocko.

'Can I talk to you for a sec?'

Mia just wanted to get Riley out of the hospital and home to bed. She was exhausted, upset and really angry with her daughter. She was only fifteen – how could she get so drunk that she'd fallen over? What if she'd hit the side of her head and died? What if she'd swallowed her own vomit and choked to death? What if she'd ended up alone with a boy and done something she regretted? What if, what if . . . Life was so complicated and there was danger everywhere for teens, these days.

Riley was so bloody difficult. Why couldn't she just study, go out and drink Coke and stop being so angry and hostile? Where was the little dark-haired angel who used to throw her chubby arms around Mia's neck and kiss her face and say, 'I dove you, Mummy,' over and over? Mia closed her eyes. She missed that Riley so much it hurt.

'Mia?'

She opened her eyes. 'Sorry, Shocko, what is it?'

Shocko fidgeted with his skull-head ring. 'So, like, I know you're pissed with Riley and all.'

'Annoyed.'

'Sorry, yeah, annoyed. But, like, she had a really good excuse to get drunk.'

Mia blinked, what in the name of God was he talking about? She was fond of Shocko, who was a sweet boy and had been a good friend to Riley. They'd become pals three years ago when he'd moved in next door, and Mia had had her doubts. Shocko was the kind of boy who liked to sit inside all day and play video games or draw comic books. She'd have preferred Riley to choose a sporty, outdoorsy best friend, but Shocko was a nice kid. He had a big heart and

57

Mia had seen how he could boost Riley's confidence and make her laugh. He had Riley's back, and Mia was grateful to him for that.

'Shocko, please explain to me what could be a good reason for my fifteen-year-old daughter to get staggering drunk?'

'So, like, she was seeing this guy, right? I can't tell you his name cos she'd kill me so let's just call him "Kevin".'

Mia had no idea Riley had been seeing anyone but she was too embarrassed to admit she had no clue about her daughter's life so she just nodded.

'Well, she really likes him. I dunno why, to be honest, he's not so great, but anyway . . . So, tonight "Kevin" was all over Zoë, right?'

'Is that Zoë Karsdale, the hurdler?'

'Yeah. She's good at jumping over hurdles but, whatever, she's a total douchebag.'

'Douchebag?'

'You know, all, like, dyed hair and big white teeth and sporty and bouncy and fake.'

Since when had having white teeth and being sporty become a bad thing? Mia let it go. She wanted to find out more. 'So what happened?'

'"Kevin" was all touchy-feely with Zoë in front of Riley, which shows a total lack of respect and also it was, like, really humiliating for Riley cos everyone knows she was with him until last week. But then "Kevin" was all cold with her, like she'd done something wrong, which Riley says she didn't.'

'Poor Riley.'

'I know, right? Riley is crushed but pretending she's not – you know how she is. So she starts hitting the vodka big-time. I'm like, "Dude, drink some H₂O," but she's having none of it because she's watching her boy all over another girl. And then she goes all Hulk Hogan and starts shouting at him and calling him a . . . well, bad names, and then she throws her drink over him, but she trips and falls and then it's all major drama because there's blood and . . . Well, that's how she ended up here.'

Mia knew it was childish but she was proud of Riley for throwing a drink over 'Kevin'. How dare he treat her like that and humiliate her in public, the little shit? Still, though, getting plastered and making a spectacle of yourself was not the right way to go about it. But she understood why Riley had done it. At least there was a valid reason for her actions. She'd love to get her hands on 'Kevin'. How dare he hurt her daughter, how bloody dare he?

'So I know you're all furious with her drinking and stuff, but don't go too Hulk Hogan on her because she's had a really rough night.'

Mia smiled. 'I promise not to go Hulk Hogan on her. Thank you for telling me. You're a good friend, and she's lucky to have you. Thanks for bringing her to hospital and for calling us. I really appreciate it, and I know Riley does too.'

Shocko shrugged. 'It's no big deal. She'd do the same for me. But you absolutely cannot tell her I told you about the ex-boyfriend because she'd kill me. Seriously, I'm dead meat if she finds out I spilled the beans.'

Mia placed her hand on Shocko's shoulder. 'I promise I won't break your trust. But by the sound of it, she's well rid of this boy.'

'I think so.'

'She deserves a lot better.'

'Damn straight.'

'Right. Let's get you kids home.'

Mia and Shocko walked back to Riley's cubicle.

'Let's go,' Mia said. 'We'll pick up some McDonald's for you two on the way home. You must be starving.'

Johnny looked surprised, and Riley's mouth hung open in an expression of pure shock.

'Is this a wind-up? I presumed I was going to be locked away in a dungeon for ever,' Riley said.

'Oh, you'll be locked away all right, but I'm not going to starve you.' Mia grinned and pushed Riley's hair back. 'I love you too much for that.'

Riley pushed her hair forward again, but she almost smiled.

8

Sarah was mopping the kitchen tiles when the doorbell rang. She glanced at her watch. Two o'clock. Maybe it was another delivery. Adam had been sending her bouquets for the last four days since she'd told him about the baby. She was running out of vases, but it was nice that he was making an effort. Plus he'd been home for dinner two out of the four nights, which was an improvement.

She put down her mop and went along the hall to open the door. It was Riley. She was in her school uniform, her rucksack slung over her shoulder.

'Hi, is everything OK?'

Riley never called in during the day. Sarah was worried.

Riley shook her head and began to cry.

'Is it Mia? Johnny?'

'No,' Riley sobbed. 'It's me.'

'Oh, you poor thing, come in.' Sarah guided her into the kitchen and sat her up at the counter. 'Would a hot chocolate and a brownie help?'

Riley nodded.

Sarah busied herself microwaving the milk and mixing in the chocolate powder, while Riley's sobs subsided, then handed her the steaming mug and put a plate with a homemade brownie beside her. Riley took a sip and a bite and sighed. 'I wish I lived here. It's always so peaceful and calm and, I dunno, nice.'

Sarah wiped the counter and put the cloth in the box under the sink. She moved around and sat opposite her niece. 'It's not always calm, I can assure you. Now talk to me.'

Riley filled her in on the party, falling over, the concussion and the hospital fiasco. 'I'm the big joke in school. Everyone is talking about what a fool I made of myself. Mum's gone mental and grounded me pretty much for life.'

Yikes, Sarah thought. This was not good. Riley should not have been drinking, certainly not getting paralytic and falling over. But she couldn't help feeling sorry for her: she'd been dumped and humiliated. 'Oh, Riley, that sounds like a total nightmare. You know, I was bullied a bit in school so I do understand a little of what you're going through.'

'Mum told me, but I just can't imagine anyone bullying you. You're so cool and nice.'

Sarah laughed. 'Flatterer! It was in my last year of school, so it wasn't too bad. I had just a few months to put up with it. But I remember how long and lonely the days were. The best thing to do is ignore people and their comments. It'll pass – it'll be yesterday's news soon. Someone else will do something and the attention will move to them. You just need to brave it out. If you act like you don't care, people will stop talking about it.'

'I'm trying, but it's hard. I see Zach every day in school and stupid bloody Zoë.'

'I can imagine that's really difficult. But on the drinking thing, please tell me that you've learned your lesson and won't drink again.'

Riley dabbed some brownie crumbs on her finger and licked them off. 'I'll never drink again. I've never felt so sick in my life.'

Sarah smiled. 'At least that's one positive to come out of the mess. Look, Riley, I know you like him, but maybe Zach isn't for you. Maybe this needed to happen so you could see that he's not such a great guy.'

'No, he is great,' Riley said. 'Honestly, he's so nice and – and he made me feel really special and said all these amazing things about me and . . . Well, it was kind of magic.'

Sarah rubbed her temple. Her headache was back again. 'I'm glad he made you feel good about yourself because a boyfriend should always make you feel that way. Besides, you *are* amazing. But there are lots of other nice boys out there.'

Riley chewed her thumbnail. 'Not like Zach. I know he and Zoë are wrong – I just know it. I'm not like one of those delusional girls who thinks someone way out of their league will fancy them. I've been with Zach and we work well together.'

'Maybe he'll get sick of Zoë soon and break up with her.'

'Yeah, but even if he does, we'll never get together. I might as well join a convent because I've basically been locked up until I'm eighteen. Mum is being such a cow. She keeps saying, "I never should have let Sarah talk me into letting you go to that party."'

Oh, great. Now Sarah was in trouble, too. Still, she wasn't surprised that Mia had flipped out. She wouldn't be too happy if Izzy ended up in hospital drunk out of her mind at fifteen. 'Look, Riley, you need to be on your best behaviour for a few weeks. Let your mum cool down. It's understandable that she's cross with you.'

'Isn't losing Zach and making a complete fool of myself punishment enough?' Riley's eyes filled with tears. 'I don't need Mum going on about it all the time.'

Sarah reached over and patted her hand. 'As parents we worry. It's our job to keep you safe from harm. Mia's probably just really concerned about you and about what happened. You have to understand it from her point of view. She got a call in the middle of the night to say you were unconscious in hospital. No mother wants to get a call like that.'

Riley shrugged her shoulders. 'I guess so.'

'You gave her a fright. Give her some time. It only happened five days ago.'

'If she mentions it to you, will you please try to put my
side across? I was devastated. I didn't mean to get drunk – I
was just so miserable.'

'I'll try, but you have to be patient, Riley. It'll probably
take Mia a while to get over this.'

'I feel like such a loser.' Riley wiped a tear away.

Sarah stood up and put her arms around her. 'You're not a
loser. You're wonderful, smart and gorgeous, and any boy
would be lucky to go out with you. Don't settle for second
best. You deserve a great guy who puts you on a pedestal.
Being a teenager can be really hard, but being a parent can
be hard too. Mia loves you so much, she just wants the best
for you.'

'She's got a weird way of showing it. She's on my back all
the time, telling me I need to study harder, get better results,
stop going out, eat healthier, clean my room – she never
stops.'

Sarah knew how much strain Mia was under. She wanted
Riley to go easy on her mother. 'She doesn't mean to be on
your back, but she needs you to help her out, Riley. Please
try. Mia has a lot on her plate with your dad out of work,
and when we mums are worried, we can all be a bit short-
tempered. I really think that if you try to react less, and not
push back against her all the time, things would be easier.
Will you try? Please?'

Riley finished the brownie. 'OK, but when you're talking
to her, will you please ask her to lay off me? I'm stressed
about Dad, too, and I've just had my heart smashed into
pieces.'

Sarah smiled inwardly. Riley was so like Mia. Her sister
had been the exact same at that age: she'd felt things so acutely.

Her emotions and reactions were always strong, no matter what the situation. Riley was her doppelgänger. But her poor niece needed reassurance. 'Of course I'll talk to Mia, love. And don't let any boy ever crush your spirit. You're really wonderful, Riley.'

Riley got up from her stool and hugged her aunt. 'Thanks. You're the best. I'd better go. I snuck out of school early to come and see you. Don't worry,' she said quickly, as Sarah opened her mouth to say something. 'I only missed hockey, which I hate. But don't tell Mum – it'll just give her something else to freak out about.'

As Sarah waved her off she prayed that Izzy's teenage years would be less dramatic.

Mia sat at the table in her sister's lovely, sunny kitchen. Sarah always had fresh flowers in a vase on the table while the counters were always clean and uncluttered. Mia's kitchen was full of newspapers, bills and Riley's books. Jackets were slung over chairs, shoes were kicked off in the corner . . . It was always messy. Sarah's house was spotless. It was such a relaxing space to be in.

Sarah came over and handed Mia a glass of wine. She sat opposite her, a cup of herbal tea in her hand.

'It feels a bit strange drinking alone,' Mia said. 'I feel like someone with a problem.'

Sarah laughed. 'It's Friday, you've had a long week, and you deserve it. Believe me, if I wasn't pregnant, I'd be joining you.'

Mia raised her glass. 'Well, cheers.' She savoured the wine as it slipped down her throat and felt herself begin to unwind.

'So, how's Riley?'

Mia put her glass down. 'Riley is being Riley but worse. She's her usual teenage self, plus heartbreak plus public humiliation plus rage at being grounded. I'm kind of avoiding her, to be honest. Johnny's tried talking to her, but she's like a bear.'

'Ah, the poor thing. She's had a rotten time. Can you imagine the hurt and embarrassment she must be feeling? There's nothing worse than seeing your ex with someone else.'

'I feel really sorry for her, but she won't talk to me about it so I can't help. I've tried broaching the subject from all angles, but she just freaks out and runs to her room. At least she's got Shocko.'

Sarah smiled. 'He seems like a nice kid. I always think he's a bit in love with Riley.'

'Yeah, maybe, but they're just pals. He's such a good friend. She talks to him, so at least she has an outlet for her angst. She's also been playing that song "I Hate U, I Love U" on repeat for a week. I'm going nuts.'

Sarah laughed. 'God, do you remember the days of playing soppy break-up songs to get over guys? Mine was Justin Timberlake's "Cry Me A River".'

Mia giggled. 'You must have played that a million times. Remember Mum coming in and begging you to find "a different bloody break-up song"?'

The two sisters laughed at the memory.

'I suppose it's a rite of passage. Hopefully she'll start playing some slightly more cheerful music soon,' Mia said, taking another sip of the delicious wine.

'She will. But go easy on her. She's crushed.'

Mia bristled. She didn't need to be told what to do about Riley. Her daughter had to grasp the consequences of her actions. Otherwise, she'd just do it again. Sarah didn't understand because she didn't have a teenager. 'I can hardly ignore the drinking and ending up in hospital.'

Sarah held up her hands. 'No, of course not. But don't ground her for too long. It'll just make her more unhappy.

Remember when Mum grounded you for a month because you came home drunk? You went mad.'

Yes, Mia did remember, but she'd been seventeen and tipsy, not out-of-her-mind drunk, like Riley. And what if it happened again and Riley was taken advantage of by some boy? Anything can happen when you're that drunk. Mia was scared for her daughter.

She didn't want to talk about Riley any more. She had thought of nothing else all week and had barely slept. 'I'll think about reducing her grounding. Have you seen Dad?'

'Yes, we went for a walk and had a chat about Olivia yesterday.'

'And?'

Sarah shrugged. 'He's happy. He really likes her and the companionship. He said Olivia makes his life better, happier and fuller. He said he hates being on his own. He wants to marry her and live with her.'

Mia sipped her wine. 'I didn't realize how lonely he was. But she's so irritating. I wish he could have found someone less over-the-top. She's always pawing him and talking over him and she's just so . . . so . . .'

'Annoying?'

'Yes, very bloody annoying.'

'Look, I know she can be a bit overpowering and terri-torial around Dad, but the important thing is that he's happy. And, you know, he really is. His face lit up when he talked about being married again.'

'Well, I guess I'll just have to suck it up, even though she drives me nuts. God, I miss Mum. She'd hate Olivia. I'd say she's shouting from the grave, "Get that cow out of my house."'

They laughed.

'She'll probably haunt them,' Sarah said.

'I still talk to her sometimes,' Mia admitted.

'Do you?'

She nodded. 'When Johnny lost his job, I asked her to help me with the stress, and I ask her advice on what to do with Riley.'

'Does she answer?' Sarah asked tentatively.

Mia grinned. 'I'm not nuts – of course she doesn't. But . . . I often remember her advice, things she said to me growing up, and I try to use her wisdom. She was always good at giving advice. I miss that.'

'It bothered me that she never really liked Adam.'

'She did like him,' Mia lied. Her mother had never warmed to him. She could see he was good to Sarah and that he adored her, but she felt his ambition would be a problem in their marriage. His desperation to prove himself as a businessman in order to put his awful childhood behind him had worried Penny. 'I admire his drive,' she'd admitted to Mia once, 'but it seems to consume him. He might never stop trying to prove himself and never be able to enjoy what he has. I'm worried Sarah will end up raising her kids alone while he's working all the time.'

She'd been right. Adam did work day and night, and Sarah was alone all the time. She said she didn't mind and she understood him, but Mia knew it bothered her.

'She always used to say, "Make him come home for dinner," or "Make him take holidays,"' Sarah said, 'but Adam is rarely home for dinner, and when we go on holidays, he's on his phone a lot of the time. We had a big fight the day of the scan when he didn't show up, and I told him that he has to be around for this baby. I think he will be because it's a boy and he wants to teach him football and all that stuff. I hope so anyway.'

Mia patted her sister's hand. 'It'll all work out. Adam's a family man at heart. He adores you and Izzy.'

They were silent for a bit. Then Mia said, 'Is it normal that I'm jealous of my father's sex life? Dad and Olivia seem to be having great sex. Johnny and I are in a total slump.'

Sarah covered her eyes. 'Stop! I really don't want to picture it. All I can see is wriggly bits and saggy bits and . . . arggh . . .'

Mia laughed. 'And her boobs swaying. I mean, they're like watermelons.'

'Imagine Dad's face stuck between them!'

They both cracked up laughing.

Izzy came in from the TV room wearing a white T-shirt with purple bobbles across the chest and purple leggings to match. 'What are you laughing about?' she asked.

Mia wiped her eyes. 'Just something your mum said.'

'Tell me,' Izzy said, climbing onto her mother's knee.

'I was just being silly, Sweet-pea.'

Mia decided to distract her niece. 'Are you getting excited about your Communion?'

'Yes! I can't wait. Mummy's getting me a bouncy castle and a chocolate fountain, and we're making special party bags for everyone and there'll be millions of pink balloons and pink cupcakes with sparkles on them!' Izzy squealed.

'Seriously?' Mia looked at Sarah.

'Yes, the party is going to be completely over the top and fabulous.' Sarah kissed Izzy.

Mia smiled. Sarah's parties for Izzy were always over the top and fabulous. Mia wondered if she should have had bigger and better parties for Riley. Izzy's childhood memories were going to be of magical times and a calm, loving, endlessly patient mother. She was a very lucky little girl. 'It sounds amazing, Izzy. I can't wait to come, and you know how proud I am to be your godmother.'

'I'm proud too.' Izzy beamed at her aunt. Then she said,

'Was Clara in big trouble today? I saw you giving out to her in the corridor after break.'

Mia shook her head. 'She did something a bit silly.'

Clara was an over-indulged, spoiled eight-year-old who had ordered the teacher to pick up her jumper from the sports pitch because she was too tired. When the teacher had reprimanded her for being so rude, Clara had said she'd get her fired.

Mia had spoken to her about her behaviour and told her to go and apologize. Clara had refused. Mia had called her mother, who seemed to think it was hilarious.

'Oops,' she'd said. 'We have a lot of help at home, you see, so she's just used to people doing things for her. She didn't mean to be rude.'

'Whether she did or not, Clara must apologize, and she must understand that in school the only person picking up her belongings is herself.'

'I'll talk to her tonight. Maybe we could send in a gift to the teacher. What do they like? Red or white wine? A voucher for Harvey Nichols?'

'No wine or voucher is necessary, just a simple verbal apology.'

Mia had tried not to let her frustration show. Wine? Vouchers? Seriously? The woman needed a reality check, as did her daughter. The Celtic Tiger was well and truly back if this was going on in people's homes. Staff running around picking up after an eight-year-old? Ridiculous.

Mind you, it would be nice to have no money worries.

'All right, I'll have a word with Clara, but I really think this teacher is overreacting. It's just a silly misunderstand-ing,' Clara's mum trilled.

Misunderstanding? A teacher being mistaken for a slave? Mia thought.

'Good. I'll bring Clara to Mrs Hagan tomorrow to say she's

sorry.' Mia hung up before Clara's mother could try to backtrack.

'Mummy, can we do baking tonight?' Izzy asked Sarah.

'Sure. What will we make?'

'Cupcakes.'

Sarah laughed. 'We always make cupcakes.'

'I know, but they're so yummy and we can put melted chocolate on top and eat them all.'

'OK, sweetie, whatever you want.'

Izzy reached up and hugged her.

Mia smiled at them. Sarah was so good with Izzy. She was never impatient or short-tempered with her. Mia felt ashamed as she remembered Riley asking her to bake after a long day at school and her own response: 'Not today, love, maybe at the weekend.'

She'd rarely baked with Riley. She was always too busy or tired, or something else had taken precedence. Mia felt bad about that. Still, Sarah didn't work: she had more time and no financial worries. Maybe if Mia had given up work when Riley was young, she and her daughter would be closer. But they had been close. Mia closed her eyes and remembered the feeling of Riley's soft cheek against hers as they cuddled in her bed when she read bedtime stories. Mia longed to put her arms around her spiky teenager and tell her she loved her. She'd do it when she got home, she decided. No time like the present.

Johnny was sprawled on the couch, reading the paper. Two coffee cups and a half-eaten packet of Chocolate Digestives were strewn on the coffee-table. Johnny jumped up when he saw Mia.

'Before you ask, I haven't been lounging about all day. I had a meeting with a head hunter earlier.'

Mia had to admit that she hated coming home to find

Johnny lying about. She knew he was looking for a job, she understood it was hard, but it upset her if she found him on the couch reading or watching TV. She felt he needed to be constantly looking, meeting people, networking and trawling the internet for jobs and options. She was terrified he'd be out of work for years and they'd lose the house, or that he'd get depressed and never work again. His self-esteem would be in the gutter and he'd end up on anti-depressants feeling like half a man.

She knew she was a catastrophist, her mother had often told her to stop worrying so much, but Mia couldn't help it. She always imagined the worst-case scenarios. She was really worried about Johnny and had a constant ache in the pit of her stomach. She wanted him to be happy, she wanted him to be fulfilled and, if she was being honest, she wanted him to be earning money so that all the pressure wasn't on her shoulders. Bills seemed to mount daily, and the stress was keeping her up at night as she tried to tally incomings with outgoings in her head.

'Great,' she said enthusiastically. She wanted to show support. Mia pointed to the ceiling. 'I see Riley's still listening to the same song.'

'That's the sixth time since she came home from school. She's in a foul mood. I'm making her chocolate pancakes to try to cheer her up.'

'You're so good.' Mia went over and put her arms around her husband.

'Well, thanks. You're not too bad yourself.'

Mia pulled back from the embrace. She took off her jacket and hung it over the back of the couch where the fabric had split. She sat back, untucking her shirt and kicking off her shoes. 'I was watching Sarah with Izzy. They're so close. I miss that with Riley.'

Johnny nodded. 'Me too. But our little girl is still in there, underneath the teenage angst and anger.'

'It's hard to see it sometimes.'

'We have to be patient with her. It's just a phase.'

'You've always been better at patience than me.'

'True.'

'You didn't have to agree quite so readily,' Mia said.

'Much as I love you and much as I admire all of your good qualities, patience has never been among them.'

Mia grinned. 'I'm trying to work on it. In fact, I'm going up to Riley now to tell her I love her and give her a hug.'

Johnny's eyes widened. 'Are you sure? She's in a grump.'

'Yes.'

'Good luck.'

Mia climbed up the stairs and opened Riley's door. The usual mess greeted her and music blared from the speaker in the corner. Riley was lying face down on the bed, bawling into her pillow. Above her hung the poster of Caitlin Moran with a bubble coming out of her mouth: *'Do you have a vagina? And do you want to be in charge of it? If you said "Yes" to both, then congratulations – you're a feminist!'* Riley had bought it with her birthday money from Charlie last year and proudly hung it up. Mia would have preferred a more eloquent quote about feminism, but she was pleased that Riley was embracing the empowerment of women.

Her heart went out to her sobbing daughter, her baby girl. She went over and put her arms around her. Riley jerked up, hitting her mother accidentally in the face with her elbow.

'Ouch!' Mia cried.

'What the hell, Mum? Don't sneak up on me like that! You gave me a fright.' Riley quickly wiped her eyes with her sleeve.

Mia rubbed her cheek. 'Oh, sweetheart, I know you're upset about your ex-boyfriend. Break-ups are so difficult.'

'I don't give a crap about him,' Riley snapped.

Mia tried putting her arms around her daughter again. Riley wriggled to get free.

Mia held on firmly. 'I love you, Riley, and I know you're upset. I want you to know I'm here for you. I've loved you since the first moment I set eyes upon you, almost sixteen years ago.'

Riley pulled out of her mother's embrace. 'Oh, my God, stop.'

'You are a beautiful, brilliant girl. Don't ever forget that.'

'If I'm so great, how come he doesn't want to know me?' Riley sobbed, then pushed past Mia and locked herself into the bathroom.

Mia sat on the floor outside the door, listening to her daughter's sobs. Her heart ached for her.

9

Sarah clutched the basin and bent over. She tried to breathe deeply in and out. God, this headache was worse than any of the others. She tried to relax her body, but the pain was making her feel nauseous. She retched but didn't vomit. She could feel perspiration running down her back and beading on her forehead.

'Mummy?'

Sarah held a cold facecloth to her forehead and turned to her daughter. 'Yes, sweetie?'

Izzy was standing in her navy school skirt and white blouse. 'I can't find my school jumper.'

Sarah rinsed the facecloth under the cold water tap and rubbed it on the back of her neck. 'I'll help you. Just give me a second.'

'Is your head sore again, Mummy?' Izzy pointed to the facecloth.

'A bit, yes, but I'll be fine in a minute.'

Izzy pottered downstairs to talk to her father while Sarah tried to fight the urge to crawl back into bed. She didn't want to call Mia, but she really didn't think she could drive. This headache was so bad that her eyesight was blurring. She'd have to ask her sister to take Izzy to school. But the last thing she wanted was Mia fussing over her. She just wanted to go to bed and sleep it off.

Adam was chatting to Izzy when Sarah came into the kitchen. He turned to look at her. 'Izzy said you've got another headache. You're very pale. I think you should go back and see Ingrid Johnston.'

Sarah waved her hand. 'I'm fine. It's a bit better already,' she lied. 'I think the bedroom was too stuffy last night.'

'Are you sure?' Adam asked.

'Yes.' She forced herself to smile, even though it hurt to move her facial muscles.

'Well, if you feel worse later, please go and see her. I'm paying her a bloody fortune to look after you and the baby, so don't be shy about booking in.'

Sarah nodded. Ouch, that hurt too.

Adam kissed Izzy, then bent to kiss his wife. 'Seriously, you don't look great, call her. You need to mind yourself and my son. I've gotta fly. I've a meeting at nine. I'll be late again tonight so don't cook me dinner.'

'Adam!'

He put his hand up. 'I know. I'll try to be home for dinner tomorrow, but it's a crazy week.'

'It's always crazy,' Sarah said.

'Will you not tuck me in again tonight, Daddy?' Izzy grumbled.

'Sorry, Sweet-pea, but I have to work so I can earn money to pay for our house and all the things in it.'

'I wish you didn't have to work so hard. Riley sees Johnny all the time.'

'Yes, well, that's a whole other story,' Adam muttered.

'Let's not go there,' Sarah said. 'I guess I'll see you when I see you.'

Adam kissed her. 'Don't be annoyed with me. I'll make it up to you. I'll book Franco's for dinner on Saturday night.' He glanced at his watch. 'Damn it, I'm late. See you, guys.'

When the front door closed, Sarah sank onto a high stool at the kitchen counter. This headache was flooring her. She'd have to go to the doctor and get something for it. She could barely stand up. 'Izzy, can you help me make your lunch today?' she said.

'What shall I do?'

'Get me two slices of bread and some ham and cheese from the fridge . . .' Sarah instructed her seven-year-old on what to do because she was afraid if she stood up, she'd faint. She decided that, once Izzy had left for school, she'd call Ingrid to make an appointment. This headache was in a different league from any of the others.

While Izzy got her lunch ready, Sarah texted Mia to ask her to pick up Izzy.

No prob. U OK?

Mia always texted her straight back. It drove her nuts when Sarah didn't do the same. But Sarah hated her phone beeping and pinging. Half the time she didn't even know where it was. Now she typed a lie: *All good. Just ate something that didn't agree with me.*

Izzy wrapped her sandwich in a large piece of tinfoil, then put her apple and crackers into her lunchbox. 'I made my own lunch!' she said, delighted.

'Well done you.'

'When the baby comes, I can help you loads,' she said.

'That would be amazing, Izzy.' Sarah reached out to hug her. 'You're such a star.'

'I don't mind so much about the baby, now I know it's a boy. When I thought it was going to be a girl, I was worried you'd love her more than me. But you can't do girly stuff with a boy, so I know you and me can still do our own thing. Daddy and the baby can do stuff together, can't they?'

'You never needed to worry even if it was a girl. You know how much I love you, don't you?'

Izzy nodded. 'To the moon and back.'

Sarah kissed her head. 'Yes, and don't ever forget that.'

They heard Mia beeping her horn outside. Sarah walked Izzy to the door. Mia jumped out of the car and came towards them. 'Are you sure you're OK?' she asked her sister.

'Yes,' Sarah said, in as strong a voice as she could muster. 'Thanks for bringing Izzy. Go on, I don't want to make you late.' She tried to hustle them into the car, so she could go and lie down.

'Call me if you need anything.' Mia turned to get back into her car.

'I will. Thanks, you're a life-saver.'

Mia smiled at her. 'That's what sisters are for.'

Sarah forced herself to stand at the door and wave them off.

'Oh, no!' Izzy shouted. 'I forgot my maths workbook. I left it in my bedroom. Miss Dixon is going to be cross with me.'

Mia cursed silently. If she turned back now, she'd be a few minutes late for school. She hated being late – it looked really bad, especially for the deputy head. Still, Izzy was upset and she didn't want her to worry.

'OK, pet. We'll whizz back and get it.'

'Thank you so much, Mia.'

'Great! Now I'm not going to be able to finish my home-work before school,' Riley huffed.

'You should have finished it last night,' Mia reminded her.

'I was working on my art project until eleven and I left my history book in school. Give me a break.'

'I do nothing but give you breaks,' Mia muttered.

'Yeah, right. It's like living in prison.'

'Well, next time you decide to lie, get drunk and end up in hospital, think again.'

'Are you ever going to stop going on about that?'

'We can forget my maths book. I don't want Riley to get in trouble,' Izzy said.

'It's fine, don't sweat it,' Riley said. 'My life's a pile of shit anyway.'

Mia clenched her jaw. 'Watch your language,' she hissed.

'It's OK,' Izzy piped up. 'Daddy says that word too.'

Mia hurtled into the driveway. 'You stay there,' she said to Izzy. 'It'll be quicker if I just grab it.'

She rang the doorbell. Nothing. Mia rang again. Come on, Sarah, hurry up, she thought, glancing at her watch anxiously.

No sound of footsteps. Mia peered in through the bubble glass on the side of the door. She could see something. She cupped her hands and peered through. It was Sarah. She seemed to be on the floor. Was she cleaning it? Mia knocked loudly.

She squinted through the glass again. Dread gripped her. Something was wrong. Sarah wasn't moving. Mia's heart began to pound. She banged on the glass and shouted through the letterbox. Her sister didn't move.

Damn! She'd have to break the glass. Mia shrugged off her blazer, wrapped it around her hand and punched the glass. It didn't shatter.

She ran back to the car, her fist throbbing.

'Is Mummy not answering?' Izzy asked. 'Maybe she went to bed. She said she had a bad headache.'

'Everything is fine, sweetie.'

Mia grabbed Riley's arm and yanked her out of the car.

'What the hell?' Riley snapped.

Mia shut the door and pulled her aside. 'Sarah's collapsed on the floor inside. I have to break the glass. I don't want Izzy to be freaked out so I need you to distract her.'

Riley's eyes widened. 'Is Sarah OK?'

'I don't know.' Mia's voice shook. 'I have to get that bloody door open.'

79

She opened the boot of her car and found the jack for changing the tyre. She ran back to the front door, and while Riley turned up the music in the car and got Izzy to sing along to some pop song, Mia smashed the side glass of her sister's front door. She reached around and pulled the catch back to open the door, cutting her arm on a piece of glass.

'Sarah!' she shouted, as she ran towards her sister.

Sarah was lying in the hall. Mia shook her and slapped her cheeks. 'Wake up, Sarah! Please wake up!' There was no reaction.

'Oh, Jesus, please. Sarah, please wake up. Oh, God!' she cried.

Mia checked her sister for a pulse. Yes. She was alive. She grabbed Sarah's phone, which was lying on the floor beside her, and dialled 999.

'Please help. Help me. My sister has collapsed in her house. She's not responding but she has a pulse. She's fourteen weeks pregnant! Please help . . .'

Week One

10

Adam burst through the doors of A and E. 'Where is she?' he said, his eyes wild.

Mia jumped up and rushed over to him. She put her hand on his arm. 'It's OK, Adam. They've taken her for tests to find out what's wrong.'

'How is she? Can I see her?'

'I think she's OK. She had a pulse, although she was non-responsive, but the paramedics got to the house fast, then raced her straight here. They asked us to be patient. They said they'd update us as soon as possible. They just need to do some tests so they know how to treat her.'

Adam took a deep breath and rubbed his jaw. 'That sounds all right, doesn't it? I mean, she was fine this morning. She looked a bit pale, but nothing serious. I told her to go and see Ingrid Johnston, get checked out. Maybe it's blood pressure. Or the baby taking too much of her supplies or, I don't know, something like that or . . . What is it, Mia?'

He was squeezing Mia's arm tightly. She'd never seen him so upset. 'I don't know, Adam. It could be any of those things. The doctors will find out. She did seem fine before we left, so maybe it was some kind of fainting episode. At least she's in the right place now. They'll help her.'

Izzy and Riley came through the door into the waiting room. Riley was carrying a tray of coffees and Izzy had a chocolate bar in one hand. Izzy ran to her father and wrapped herself around him. 'Mummy fell down, Daddy. She hit her head hard so she needs to rest in hospital. Isn't that right, Mia?'

'Yes, pet, it is.'

'What's going on, Mum?' Riley whispered. 'Is she going to be OK?'

'I honestly don't know.' Mia wiped a tear from her cheek. 'Just say a prayer, Riley.'

'I don't believe in God.'

'Are you seriously going to start on about your atheism now?'

'I'm just saying, I can't pray if I don't believe.'

'Send positive vibes or do whatever you kids do then.'

'Positive vibes? Please! I'm not a hippie.'

Johnny and Charlie arrived before Mia could shout at her daughter for being insensitive.

'Where is she? Where's my Sarah?' Charlie went straight to Mia.

Mia put an arm around him. 'Dad, she's in good hands. They're checking her out to see what the problem is. It could be something simple like high or low blood pressure. It happens in pregnancy.'

'Good, that's probably it. She might need blood thinners or something. Right?'

'Yes, Dad, hopefully it's something like that.'

Johnny pulled Mia aside. 'What's really going on?'

Mia bit her lip. 'I don't know, but it doesn't look good. She was completely non-responsive when I found her, and she was still unconscious when she got here. I'm really scared, Johnny.'

Johnny put his arms around his wife and pulled her close. 'She'll be OK,' he whispered into her ear.

'Don't be nice to me. I need to keep it together for Izzy and Dad. If you're lovely, I'll go to pieces.'

'Would it help if I shouted abuse at you?' he said, kissing her cheek.

'No, I have Riley for that.' Mia gave him a watery smile.

84

'She'll pull through, Mia. Sarah's a toughie.'

But that was just it: she wasn't. Sarah wasn't tough like Mia. Sarah had always been the one who got bugs and viruses when they were young. She was the sickly sister who got a cold if she didn't wear a jumper to school. Mia could go out in a T-shirt in the snow and be fine.

Sarah had always had a boyfriend. From the age of fourteen she'd gone from one relationship to another. She'd always had a boy there to look after her. Boys, and later men, loved Sarah. They wanted to look after her. She had that way about her. Mia scared men off because she was too assertive, but Sarah attracted them like moths to a flame.

'It'd be better if it was you in there, Mia. You're a big strong lassie. Sarah's a delicate thing.' Charlie confirmed what Mia was thinking. She tried not to let the comment sting.

'He didn't mean it like that,' Johnny muttered.

'What the hell is taking so long?' Adam paced up and down.

'Don't worry, Daddy,' Izzy said. 'Riley told me that Mummy just needs a big sleep for her sore head.'

'Well said, love.' Mia squeezed her daughter's hand.

'Mia could carry triplets and not skip a beat, she's strong as a horse. But Sarah was always a delicate flower,' Charlie mumbled.

'Sarah's not that delicate. She's strong too. Come on now, let's be positive,' Johnny said.

The door to the waiting room opened, and a man and a woman came in, both wearing scrubs.

'You're Sarah's family?' the man said.

'I'm her husband,' Adam said, walking over to him. 'This is her father and sister.'

'And I'm her daughter, Izzy,' Izzy said, sounding put out.

'Well, I'm Dr Mayhew,' the man said, 'and I'm very pleased to meet the most important person in the room, Miss Izzy.'

85

Izzy looked delighted. 'Are you making my mummy better?' she asked.

'We're doing our very best,' Dr Mayhew said. 'Are you happy to have a talk here?' he said to Adam.

Adam nodded. 'We're all desperate, waiting to hear. What's the news?'

'Mr Brown, I'm an intensive-care physician. My colleague here,' he said, gesturing to the woman beside him, 'is Professor Irwin, head of the Department of Neurology. We're both on the team caring for your wife.'

'A neurosurgeon?' Charlie said. 'Doesn't sound good.'

The woman looked around them. 'Was Sarah suffering from any head pain recently?'

'Yes,' Adam said. 'She had mentioned headaches. I thought she might need iron because of the baby.'

'Mr Brown, we think your wife has suffered a brain injury, and we're working to ascertain the type and the level of damage.'

'Jesus Christ,' Adam said, his shoulders sagging.

'Riley,' Mia said quickly, 'I'd say Izzy would love a hot chocolate, wouldn't you, sweetheart?'

Izzy was looking worriedly from face to face, obviously trying to work out what was going on. Riley nodded at her mother. 'I'd murder a hot chocolate myself,' she said. She bent down to Izzy's eye level. 'The doctors are using hard words I can't understand, so how about we go to the café? When we come back, Mum can explain it to us so we can understand. What do you think?'

'Em . . . OK,' Izzy said uncertainly. 'Did Mummy's headache make her sick?'

Mia didn't trust herself to speak. She was going to break down at any moment. Neurosurgeon, brain injury . . . She could barely keep herself standing. This was like a surreal nightmare. Thank God for Riley, even if she didn't believe in him.

Professor Irwin smiled warmly at Izzy. 'Did Mummy have headaches, Izzy?'

Izzy nodded. 'She kept saying she was OK, but I think her head was hurting a lot. And it was really sore today because she couldn't even make my lunch. I did it myself.'

'Good for you,' Professor Irwin said.

Mia looked at Adam, whose eyes were red, as if he were holding back tears. The poor man, she thought. He'll be feeling guilty now that he wasn't there to help.

'We're going to do everything we can to help your mummy,' Professor Irwin said. 'And I think you deserve a hot chocolate after all that helping you did today.'

'OK,' Izzy said, seeming reassured. 'We'll be back soon.'

The door closed behind the two girls and all the adults dropped the fake smiles.

'Why don't we sit down?' Dr Mayhew said. 'This is a terrible shock for you all.'

They sat into the chairs, and Mia took Johnny's hand. She needed to feel something solid and real because the world was spinning and she was trying hard to stay upright.

'The headaches were a warning sign,' Professor Irwin said. 'We think there may be bleeding in an area of Sarah's brain, which has triggered the injury.'

'W-will she be OK?' Adam stuttered.

'It's difficult to say at this point,' Professor Irwin said. 'We have to run a number of tests to verify our suspicions, and it would be unwise to jump to conclusions at this early stage. For now Sarah is intubated and on a life-support machine. This is necessary, although I know it will be hard for you. She's not conscious, but we would encourage you to talk to her.'

'Is that it? Just . . . tests?' Adam said, and his voice sounded faint. Mia's heart went out to him.

'For now, yes, I'm afraid that's the situation. I'm terribly sorry that we can't give you certainties, but we have to ask you to bear with us over the next forty-eight to seventy-two hours. This is a complicated case, as you can appreciate.'

'It's further complicated,' Dr Mayhew added, 'because, of course, Sarah is pregnant. We're monitoring the foetus closely and so far the heartbeat remains strong. Our obstetric and neonatal paediatric teams will be keeping a close eye on the baby's progress.'

'Thank you,' Mia said, but she wasn't sure why. This was crazy. Sarah had waved them off from the front door just a while ago. This couldn't be happening.

'Please save them,' Adam whispered.

Dr Mayhew's eyes were full of sympathy. 'We'll do our utmost, Mr Brown. I know this is uncharted territory for you all. I'm sure you'll have questions and concerns. We have assigned your wife to a very experienced trauma coordinator nurse, Angela Fanagan, and she will be available to you at all times to answer questions and liaise between the various teams and yourselves. She's an excellent senior nurse and will take good care of you, and of Sarah.'

'What do you think of Sarah's chances?' Charlie asked.

The two doctors exchanged a brief glance.

'It's too early to say,' Professor Irwin said. 'As I said, it would be unwise to speculate. But her condition is very serious.'

'Oh, God,' Mia said, biting her lip hard.

'Can I see her?' Adam asked again.

'Very soon,' Dr Mayhew said. 'We're just making sure she's comfortable, but I'd say in about twenty minutes Angela will bring you in. I wouldn't recommend that everyone enters the room, however. We need to be mindful of infections and so forth. So perhaps, for tonight, just her husband should visit.'

Mia felt a visceral urge to be near Sarah, to see her, to hold her hand, but she fought against it. Adam had to come first, she knew that, but it didn't make it any easier. She looked at her father and knew he was fighting the same emotions.

'If you've no more questions for now,' Professor Irwin said, 'we'll leave you for the time being. I'll ask Nurse Fanagan to come in and introduce herself.'

They left the room and everyone sat in silence. Then the door pushed open and they all sat up, but it was Riley and Izzy coming back in.

'Daddy,' Izzy said, running to him and climbing onto his lap. 'What did they say?'

Riley was looking from one to the other, obviously trying to read the mood.

'They said,' Adam said, putting his arms around Izzy, 'that Mummy is very tired and needs to sleep for now, so that she has the strength to get better. Does that make sense, Sweet-pea?'

Izzy nodded. 'I think she'll feel much better after a good sleep. She always says that to me, so it must be true.'

'Exactly,' Adam said. 'So I think we'll ask Aunty Mia if you could maybe sleep over at her house tonight.' He looked at Mia and Johnny.

'Absolutely,' Johnny said immediately. 'I need someone to help me flip pancakes, and Sarah always says you're a star in the kitchen.'

Izzy giggled. 'I am, and I *love* flipping pancakes. Although I love eating them even more.'

'Then you're my kind of assistant chef,' Johnny said. 'We'll make a big stack of them and gobble them all up.'

'Yum!' Izzy said, her eyes shining.

'Thank you,' Adam said, to Johnny.

'Don't worry about Izzy for a second,' Johnny said. 'We've got your back.'

'I'll stay a while, if you don't mind, Adam,' Charlie said. 'I don't want to leave.'

Adam nodded. 'Of course, Charlie.'

Mia tried to think practically. She needed to go into organizational mode now. It would help her get through this.

'How about I go to the house and get some things for Izzy?' she said. 'I can collect some stuff for you as well, Adam, if you're going to stay the night.'

'That would be great, Mia, thanks so much. And I'll call immediately if there's any change or news.'

The door opened again and a tall woman with tightly cropped grey hair strode in. She was dressed in a nurse's green scrubs and smiled warmly at them. 'The Brown family,' she said. 'You must be Adam.' She extended her hand to him. 'I'm Angela Fanagan, and I'll be your liaison between all the medical teams and your good selves.'

'Thank you.' Adam shook her hand. 'We're still shell-shocked.'

'Of course you are,' Angela said. 'This has been a terrible shock for you all. The medical team are working hard to discover exactly what we're dealing with and I'll keep you updated throughout. Now, you'd better introduce me, Adam, so I know who *I'm* dealing with.'

Adam made the introductions.

'I'm here for any of you to ask questions at any time,' Angela said, 'but my key point of contact is Adam, as Sarah's next-of-kin. I'll give updates directly to him, and he can ask to receive them in private or not.'

'We're all in this together,' Adam said, gesturing at the

family. 'Whatever you have to say to me, you can say to anyone here.'

'That's great,' Angela said. 'A family who can support each other is a huge comfort to everyone during a stressful time. And now this,' she said, hunkering down in front of Izzy, 'must be the wonderful Izzy I keep hearing about.'

'That's me!' Izzy said, making them all laugh.

'Well, I'm delighted to make your acquaintance,' Angela said. 'And do you understand what's happening with Mummy?'

Izzy glanced up at Adam, then shook her head. 'I sort of do, but not really,' she said slowly. 'She has to sleep to make her better. But I don't really know why she got sick.'

'Well, Izzy, we aren't one hundred per cent sure yet either. The doctors are doing some tests and those tests will tell us why your mum fell down and why she needs to sleep now. But we're taking good care of her, and she's very comfortable and not in any pain at all. She's just resting for now, OK?'

'Can I come back and see her?'

Angela glanced at Adam. 'Daddy will be able to arrange that with me. We'll let Mummy sleep for now and once the doctors say you can visit, you'll be able to come back. Is that all right?'

'Not really,' Izzy said, 'because I miss her, but I know I have to be brave. Daddy said so.'

Mia had to swallow hard to prevent the threatened tears from falling. Poor Izzy.

'I'm glad I can rely on you,' Angela said. 'And Daddy misses her too, so you can help each other, can't you?'

'Yes,' Izzy said, smiling at Adam. 'And Uncle Johnny is going to let me make pancakes and eat them all.'

Angela grinned. 'That sounds like the perfect thing to do right now. You enjoy that.' She stood up again. 'I'll get back to the ICU now. Adam, I'll bring you in shortly to see your wife. Did the doctor explain only one visitor tonight?'

91

'Yes,' Adam said, 'but Charlie would like to stay here. Is that OK?'

'Of course,' Angela said. 'The coffee shop stays open until ten o'clock. There's a takeaway just outside the main gate and a coffee machine down the hall. Right, I'll check on Sarah and be back as quickly as I can.'

She went out and Adam sank into the nearest chair. Charlie went over and put his hand on Adam's shoulder. 'You doing all right there, son?'

'Just feel like I'm in a nightmare,' Adam said quietly. 'How did this happen?'

'OK, Izzy-bizzy,' Johnny said, clapping his hands. 'Let's get on home, shall we? Those pancakes won't cook themselves. You say goodnight to Daddy and Granddad and we'll see them in the morning.'

'Night, Daddy,' Izzy said, wrapping her arms around his neck. 'Tell Mummy I love her.'

'I will, Sweet-pea,' Adam said, kissing her cheek. 'Although she already knows it – and you know that, don't you?'

Izzy nodded. 'I tell her every day.'

'Me too,' Adam said, his voice raspy with emotion.

Johnny bent down and hugged Adam. 'Hang in there, mate,' he said. 'And ring if you need anything at all.'

Riley squeezed Adam's hand, then Mia went over to him. He stood up and enveloped her in his arms. 'Thanks for getting her here so fast, Mia.'

'We'll come through this,' Mia said. 'I'll pick up some stuff and be back soon.'

They drove home to the sound of Izzy's nervous chatter. Mia stared out of the window, pushing her fears back down her throat and deep into her abdomen where they lay, causing cramps and pain but at least allowing her to breathe and function.

When they got home, Izzy ran up to Riley's room to see which side of the bed she'd sleep on.

'Seriously? Does she have to sleep in my actual bed?'

'Jesus, Riley!' Mia hissed. 'Just work with us on this, just for one night.'

'But I'm not going to get any sleep! She's like a kitten on speed.'

'Could you for one second not think about yourself and consider the feelings of your seven-year-old cousin whose mother is . . . is . . .'

'Is what? You haven't even told me properly. You're all banging on to Izzy about Sarah sleeping. Like, hello, I'm not thick. Is she in a coma or something?'

'Keep your voice down,' Mia said, her every nerve on edge. 'Yes, she's in a sort of coma. She's suffered a brain injury.'

Riley's face drained of colour. 'Shit, really?'

'Yes, it is shit.'

'Will she come out of it soon?' Riley's voice shook.

Mia leaned against the kitchen table as a pain shot through her chest. 'I don't know. No one really knows.'

11

Mia had told Johnny that she'd head over to Adam and Sarah's house to pick up some things for Adam, but on the way there she realized Charlie might appreciate the same gesture. Olivia was in Limerick, visiting her 'brilliant' son with his 'amazing' PhD, so Mia took the turn that brought her towards Charlie's house and went there first.

She let herself in and was struck immediately by how tidy the house was. It was completely different from how it had been after Penny died and before Charlie had met Olivia. A bunch of cheerful purple tulips sat in a vase on the kitchen table. The kitchen didn't smell of fried food, and dirty dishes were not piled high in the sink. Charlie's jumpers, socks and shoes weren't strewn about the place. Everything was fresh and clean and smelt lemony. Clearly, Olivia was a good influence on Charlie in some ways. That, or he was scared of her and tidied up more.

Just as Mia was feeling slightly more charitable towards Olivia, she spotted it: the beautiful photo of Charlie and Penny on their wedding day was gone. Both had their heads thrown back and were roaring laughing. Penny often said she didn't like that photo because her mouth was wide open and all you could see were her teeth, but Mia and Sarah loved it. It captured their parents in a moment of pure joy, young, carefree and in love.

Instead, in the spot where it had been, there was one of Olivia and Charlie taken at some golf outing. Mia wanted to throw it against the wall and hear the glass shatter. How dare she? How dare Olivia try to erase her mother from her own home?

Mia went into the TV room to see if the photos of her and Sarah on their wedding days and photos of their children had also been moved, but they hadn't. Sitting proudly on the mantelpiece above the gas fire were all the family photos, as they had always been. Penny was there, at the weddings and christenings, beaming out from the frames. Mia felt her heart slow down. Olivia hadn't wiped them all out of existence . . . yet.

Mia picked up a photo of her mother holding Riley as a baby. 'Oh, Mum, where are you when I need you? Sarah's bad, Mum. I'm terrified, but I'm trying to be positive.' She kissed her mother's face and sobbed into her hand. 'I need to be strong, Mum, I know I do, for everyone, but I can't bear anything to happen to Sarah. I love her so much. I wish you were here. You'd know what to do.'

Mia remembered telling her sister recently about her habit of talking to Penny.

Was that just the other day? Time seemed to have expanded in the hours since Sarah's collapse. It was a strange feeling.

Mia went upstairs and threw a jumper, some toothpaste, a toothbrush and a deodorant into a bag. She checked Charlie's bedside locker and added his Kindle, some Polo mints, his reading glasses and earphones. She unplugged his phone charger and put that in as well. Then she opened the chest-of-drawers that stood in the bay window to get socks and fresh underwear. As she grabbed a pair of boxer shorts, something fell to the floor.

Mia bent down to pick it up. Oh, my God! It was a small packet of condoms. Gross! Why the hell did they need condoms at their age? Olivia was hardly going to get pregnant. Wait until I tell Sarah, she thought . . . and froze. Would she ever be able to tell Sarah this story? Yes, she thought fiercely. I'll be telling her this story soon and we'll crack up laughing together. She pictured the scene, her sister hanging on her every word, then exploding with mirth at the mention of condoms. She willed it to be true by picturing every detail. Sarah would wake up, she told herself. Her sister would come back to her.

After she left Charlie's house, it took fifteen minutes to get to Sarah's. The alarm wasn't on because they'd left in such a rush earlier, so she turned Adam's key in the lock, opened the door and stepped into the silence.

She stood in the hallway, staring down at the place where she'd found Sarah that morning. It took an effort of will to walk forwards and into the house.

It was so quiet. She kept expecting Sarah to pop out of a room and tell her the kettle was on or the wine was in the fridge. Even the silence sounded different now, deeper and sort of sinister. Mia shivered, then chided herself for being silly. She walked down to the kitchen, the beautifully clean and neat kitchen that Sarah maintained to perfection every single day. She had created a photo-montage on the back wall, with happy memories from their lives. In every one, Sarah was smiling, beaming, radiating joy: holding Izzy as a baby, marrying Adam, giving Riley a piggyback, with Mia and Penny and Charlie at Christmas years ago . . .

Mia had to turn away. It was too painful. She needed to focus on the future, on the positive, stay strong for Sarah and Adam and her dad.

Sarah's handbag was on the kitchen counter. Mia opened it and looked inside. There was a box of paracetamol, and Mia's heart lurched. If only Sarah had told her about the headaches, she'd have made her go to the doctor. Sarah's phone was in there as well now, so she decided to bring the bag with her to Adam.

She went upstairs to their dressing room and opened some drawers – all neatly organized. She chose a pair of bright red silk pyjamas. Sarah would like to look good in hospital. She added her sister's hairbrush, slippers, make-up bag and face cream. She was about to leave when she decided to get a second pair of pyjamas. They'd no idea how long Sarah would be kept in, so it would be good to have a fresh change. She opened the drawer in which her sister kept them and took out a soft grey cotton pair. As she lifted them out, she saw Sarah's diary. The famous diary. Mia smiled through her tears. She'd bought the big, chunky book for Sarah just before her wedding. But it was still going strong, all these years later. Sarah said it was the best gift because, although she only wrote in it occasionally, it created a record of her life and the good times.

Mia picked it up and held it to her nose. The leather cover smelt of Sarah's perfume. She inhaled deeply. Just holding it made her feel closer to her sister.

Mia put Sarah's belongings and some things for Adam and Izzy into a gym bag. But she kept the diary aside. As she was about to leave the room, she saw a beautiful photo of Izzy on Sarah's bedside locker. She put it into the bag. If anything was going to make Sarah fight for her life, it would be Izzy.

Mia went downstairs, put the diary into her own handbag, collected Sarah's, then took the whole lot out to the car. She felt a bit guilty about keeping the diary, but she needed something of Sarah to keep her going. Adam might not even know about it. She couldn't really explain it, but she wanted to keep it close to her, keep it safe for Sarah.

Mia went into the waiting room and found Charlie sitting on his own. Her heart broke at the sight of him, looking so forlorn. She went straight over and sat down beside him, wrapping her arms around him and laying her head on his shoulder. 'Are you OK, Dad?'

He patted her hand. 'I've been better, love, but I'm glad to see you.'

'I hope you don't mind,' she said. 'I ran into your place on the way and grabbed a few things I thought you'd need if you decided to stay over.'

'That was very thoughtful,' he said, smiling at her. 'Thanks for thinking of me. Olivia's coming back tomorrow. She wants to be here.'

'Great,' Mia said, hoping her tone didn't give away her actual thoughts. Olivia would be overwhelming in this tiny room, but if she brought Charlie comfort, that was all that mattered.

The door opened and Adam came in. Mia was taken aback by the change in him in such a short space of time. He looked exhausted and he was stooping, as if he'd aged twenty years since that morning. 'Sit down,' she said. 'You look done in. How is she?'

'I got to sit with her for a bit,' he said. 'It's so hard because she looks just like herself, but there's no movement. She's hooked up to all these tubes and machines . . . I tried talking to her, but I don't know if she could hear me. She didn't react at all. Not even a flicker of her eyelids.'

'Did the doctors say anything more?' Mia asked. She just wanted someone to say, 'It's fine. She'll wake up shortly, panic over.'

'Nothing,' Adam said. 'Just that we have to be patient for all the tests to be done. But apparently that can take days. I'm already half out of my mind. This is just torture, waiting and not knowing.'

'I suppose no news is good news,' Mia said. 'But it's not very reassuring.'

'I just want her back. I need her.'

Mia rubbed his back. 'That's just how I feel.'

'I remember being in this godforsaken place with Penny,' Charlie said sadly. 'I can't believe I'm back with Sarah.' His voice caught and he bent his head.

'Mum will be watching out for her,' Mia said. 'And what about the baby? Have they said anything?'

Adam nodded. 'He's OK. The neonatal team are monitoring him closely. So far, so good.'

'That's great news,' Mia said. 'And Sarah will wake up soon.'

'What if . . .' Adam pressed a fist to his forehead '. . . what if she's brain damaged, though? What if we don't get our Sarah back? I can't stop thinking about it and it's driving me insane.'

She felt as if she'd taken a punch to the stomach. 'Don't go there, Adam,' she said. 'Modern medicine is incredible. There's so much they can do. We have to be hopeful.'

'I know,' Adam said. 'It's just so hard. I've a million things that are freaking me out right now. All sorts of images going through my head. It's just the damn not knowing.'

The door opened and blue light from the corridor stretched across the tiled floor. Angela stepped into the room. 'Just letting you know that my shift is ending in five minutes,' she said. 'Hi again, Mia.'

'Hi,' Mia said. 'Any news?'

Angela shook her head. 'It'll take time, I'm afraid,' she said. 'The tests are complicated and need to be repeated over a few days, so there won't be any news for a while. I know it's frustrating for you. I'd recommend you all go home and get some proper sleep. Sarah is in safe hands.'

'I'm staying,' Adam said. 'But Angela's right, you two should head off and come back tomorrow.'

'I will,' Mia said. 'I want to help with Izzy and I'll drop her to school tomorrow. I'll come back in then.'

'Great, thanks,' Adam said.

'My house is empty,' Charlie said, 'so I'm happy to stay.'

'There's nowhere for you to get proper sleep, Dad,' Mia said. 'I mean, do stay if you feel you need to, but it looks like we'll be here for a few days, and you should keep your strength up. Why don't you stay with us? I can make up the couch for you.'

Charlie sighed deeply. 'Maybe you're right,' he said. 'I could stay tomorrow night, Adam, let you sleep? Now I'll head home to my own bed, but thanks, Mia.'

'We'll play it by ear,' Adam said. 'But if that works out, then, yes, taking turns might be the best idea. I don't want Sarah to be alone at any time.'

Charlie got heavily to his feet. 'Thanks for everything, Angela.'

'No problem,' she said. 'I'll get you a pillow and a blanket, Adam. I'll be back at eight in the morning.'

'Right so,' Charlie said, gripping Adam's shoulder. 'I'll be back in bright and early too. I doubt I'll sleep anyway.'

'Night, Adam,' Mia said. 'Don't forget to call any time.'

'I won't. See you in the morning.'

Mia and her father walked slowly through the quiet corridors, feeling the distance from Sarah with each step.

'This is an absolute nightmare,' Charlie said. 'I feel so useless.'

'We all feel the same,' Mia said. 'I feel stupid as well because I don't have a clue what tests they're doing. I don't even know what to ask.'

'Maybe we'll get good news tomorrow,' Charlie said, taking her hand. 'A new day and all that.'

'Yeah, hopefully,' Mia said.

Charlie's phone buzzed and he pulled it out of his breast pocket. His face softened into a smile. 'Ah, thank God, Olivia raced back. She's waiting for me at home.'

Hearing 'Olivia' and 'home' in the one sentence made Mia want to cry for her mother, but she could see how relieved and happy Charlie was not to be going home to an empty house. 'That's so good of her,' she said.

'She must have broken the land-speed record getting here,' he said, chuckling softly to himself. 'What a woman.'

Mia's heart thawed, just a little, towards Olivia.

12

'Morning, girls,' Mia said brightly. She was determined to put her best foot forward and be positive.

Izzy opened her eyes, registered where she was, and her face broke into a wide smile. 'Hi, Mia,' she said, sitting up.

Mia marvelled at how instantly she was awake. It was hard to believe that in just eight short years she'd be like Riley.

'Jesus, curtains,' her daughter grunted, pulling the duvet roughly over her head.

'I'm not closing them. It's time to get up,' Mia said. 'Your dad has a delicious breakfast on the go, so have a shower, get dressed and come down. I'll help you, Izzy. I washed your uniform last night, so it's all ready for you.'

'But I never did my homework,' Izzy said suddenly. 'I'll be in trouble.'

'Don't worry about it,' Mia said soothingly. 'I'm going to bring you in and explain everything to Miss Dixon.'

'What's that smell?' Izzy said, sniffing the air.

'That's your uncle's French toast,' Mia said. 'Come on, let's get you dressed and your hair brushed and plaited. Then we can eat.'

An hour later, everyone was fed, Riley had graduated to full sentences and Mia was anxious to get the girls to school, then go on to the hospital. Adam had texted to say no change and no updates yet, but Mia was itching to be near Sarah.

'Everybody got everything?' Mia said. 'Then let's go.'

Izzy was quiet on the journey to school, and Mia kept glancing at her in the rear-view mirror. She was obviously preoccupied, and Mia could only imagine how unsettling this was for her. Sarah disappearing so suddenly wouldn't make any sense to her. Mother and daughter had never been apart and did everything together, so Izzy's world had been turned upside-down. Mia prayed that Sarah would pull through quickly and they could all get back to normal.

At the school, Mia brought Izzy to her class and watched her until she was seated and ready. Then she motioned to Miss Dixon to step outside the room. 'Vanessa, Izzy's mum was hospitalized yesterday.'

'I'm so sorry,' the teacher said, looking concerned. 'Will she be all right?'

Mia swallowed. 'They aren't clear yet on the problem. They're running tests. Anyway, Izzy is upset and naturally worried about her mother, so I just wanted to let you know. I'm heading to the hospital now, but if there's any trouble, you can get Riley over from the senior school to sit with Izzy or call me on my mobile.'

'Sure, no problem. I'll keep a close eye on her. Good luck.'

'Thanks.'

Vanessa went back inside and Mia took a deep, steadying breath. She hadn't realized it was going to be so hard to say the words aloud. It made everything sickeningly real.

She went to the headmistress's office, bracing herself for the conversation. Mia enjoyed working with Fiona Kelly, but she wouldn't say she was a friend. At sixty-two, Fiona was a good bit older than the other teachers and kept a slight distance from them, Mia included. But she was extremely professional and compassionate in her own slightly cool way.

'Morning, Mia.' The head frowned. 'Has something happened? You look shaken.'

'It has, actually,' Mia said, shutting the door behind her. She sat down opposite Fiona at the desk. 'My sister collapsed yesterday. She's in the hospital. They aren't sure what's wrong with her, but it could be a brain injury.'

'Oh, Lord, that's terrible,' Fiona said, leaning forward. 'I'm very sorry, Mia. I know you and Sarah are close.'

Mia nodded. 'We are,' she said. 'So it's a difficult time. We're really hoping she'll come round soon.'

'Do you mean she's in a coma?' Fiona asked, cutting straight to the point.

'Well, she's non-responsive.' Mia's voice wobbled. 'So we think it's a coma. It's hard to follow what the doctors are saying, to be honest. I feel completely out of my depth.'

'Your poor family,' Fiona said. 'You'll need time off. Don't worry about it for a moment. I can hold the fort here and obviously I'll keep a close eye on Izzy. Does she know what's going on?'

'Not really, but she's upset, obviously, and worried. I've spoken to her teacher already.'

'Poor little pet. I'll make sure to pop in to see her.'

'I'm worried about my Communion class,' Mia said. 'The rehearsals have been going well, but I don't want to let them down.'

'I can step in there,' Fiona said firmly. 'Hopefully Sarah will respond to treatment and you'll be back here with us in no time.' She gazed at Mia with such kindness that Mia nearly burst into tears.

'Thank you so much,' she said. 'I know this is bad timing, but I really appreciate your understanding. I should be able to drop in and out, try to stay on top of things.'

'Family comes first,' Fiona said. 'It's at times like these we realize the truth of that. I lost my brother,' she said. 'He was only thirty. Leukaemia. I can relate to what you're going through, and I'm here to talk any time. If I can help in any way, please let me know.'

Wow, Mia thought. She had never known that. Fiona was not one to share personal details. How sad. 'Thank you,' she said. 'And I'm very sorry about your brother. I had no idea.'

'We all carry scars.' Fiona smiled sadly. 'Scratch the surface and everyone has a burden they're carrying.'

'Thank you again. I've left Izzy in her class and I hope she'll be OK, but I told Vanessa that if Izzy's upset, she can call Riley to come over and sit with her. I'm going to head to the hospital now and see if there's any news.'

'I'll keep an eye on Izzy, too. I hope you hear something positive. I'll send up a prayer for Sarah.'

Mia saw Adam at the coffee machine and went straight over to him. 'Morning,' she said. 'How is she? Any news?'

Adam stared into the empty cup in his hand. 'Same as yesterday. Baby's heartbeat is still strong, so that's something. Sarah is just lying there. Nothing. And the only word they say to me is "tests". I tell you, Mia, I feel like punching someone at this stage.'

Mia took the cup from him and put it down. She doubted coffee was going to do him any good when he was already so jittery and tense. 'I'll check in with Angela,' she said. 'If there's no change, why don't you go home, have a shower and eat something decent? Izzy's at school, so you'll have time to yourself.'

'What if Sarah wakes up?' he said.

'I'll call you immediately,' Mia said. 'And you'll be here within thirty minutes.'

They walked up the corridor to the nurses' station. Angela came out of Sarah's room and smiled at them. 'Morning. Still no change. But I asked Dr Mayhew if you and Charlie could sit with Sarah, Mia, and the good news is he said yes.'

'Really?' Mia felt like she'd won the Lotto. 'Oh, thanks, Angela. It's been killing me not to be near her.'

'I know,' Angela said. 'And it's good for her to hear your voices as well.'

'Has Charlie arrived?' Mia asked Adam.

'Not yet. He texted to say he'd come around ten.'

'So, will you head home for a bit?' Mia asked. 'I'll sit with her until you get back.'

'That's a good idea,' Angela said, backing her up. 'You need to take care of yourself as well, Adam, for your own sake and Izzy's.'

Adam nodded tiredly. 'Well, if there's no change at all, I'll just run back for a shower and a change of clothes. I'll be as quick as I can.'

'I won't leave her,' Mia said. 'Don't worry.'

Adam collected the gym bag from the waiting room and headed off.

'Are you ready?' Angela asked. 'We have to keep the environment germ-free, so you'll need to wear protective clothing.' She fetched a plastic apron and a hair covering and helped Mia put them on.

'Now your hands.' She watched as Mia washed them carefully with the special foam soap. 'Good. Right, I'll bring you in.'

Angela opened the door to Sarah's room and stepped aside. Mia took a deep breath, but when she saw her sister, a cry escaped her. Sarah, her beautiful little sister, was lying on a bed covered with tubes, drips, wires and lines. Her legs felt weak. Angela quickly took hold of her elbow and steered her to the chair beside the bed.

'Breathe for me now, Mia,' she said quietly. 'I know it's a shock, but it's still Sarah. The machines are helping her to stay alive.'

Mia stared and stared at her sister. Her face was pale. Her

lovely hair lay around her on the pillow – it seemed to have lost its shine. All she could hear was the clicking and swooshing of the ventilator. She struggled to come to terms with the scene before her.

'Can I get you a glass of water?'

'No, I'm fine, thanks,' Mia said. 'I got a shock, but I'm all right now. I'll sit with her.'

'I'll be just outside,' Angela said. 'Press that button there and I'll come running.'

She left the room, and Mia let the tears flow. She reached out and took Sarah's hand in hers. It was warm and soft. It felt like life, completely at odds with how Sarah looked. 'Sarah, it's Mia. I hope you can hear me. You're going to be OK. Stay strong, fight back. Let your inner tiger out. Come back, Sarah. We love you. We need you.'

She sat and listened to the whirring of the ventilator as she held her sister's hand. She sat forward so she was right up at Sarah's ear. She vaguely remembered reading somewhere that hearing was the last thing to go, so maybe on some level, in some way, Sarah could hear her. Maybe not, but she was going to choose to believe that she could.

Mia kissed her sister's forehead. She whispered in her ear, 'I'm here for you, Sarah. I'll help you. Fight, Sarah, fight like you've never fought before, for your baby, for Izzy and Adam, Charlie and all of us.'

Mia wiped tears from her eyes and shook her head, trying to banish any negative thoughts that were trying to creep in. If I believe strongly enough, she'll be OK, she thought.

'Sarah, I'm going to try to shock you awake. Brace yourself for this. I found condoms in Dad's chest-of-drawers.' Mia waited. 'What – nothing? I can't believe you didn't react to that.'

The machines whirred and clicked. Mia wanted to scream,

but she reined in her emotions. She leaned down and pulled Sarah's diary out of her handbag. Sarah always said that writing in her diary had saved her a fortune in therapy. Mia reckoned the idea of someone reading it would freak her out and definitely make her wake up.

'Right. Be warned, I'm resorting to underhand measures now. I found this yesterday and I'm going to read it out loud until you wake up. So you'd want to wake up quickly, because your deepest, darkest secrets are about to be laid bare. I'm not joking.'

Mia flipped open the diary. A bunch of envelopes fell to the floor. She picked them up. They were all addressed to Izzy. Seven of them. On each sealed envelope Sarah had written – *Letters of love from a mother to her daughter – Izzy's first year.* Each letter was another year, *Izzy's second year,* and on up to *Izzy's seventh year.*

Mia felt her throat ache. Izzy, beautiful, sweet, innocent Izzy. Sarah had written love letters to her, and now Izzy would have them for ever. 'Sarah, you really are a brilliant mother,' Mia said. 'It's never occurred to me to write anything to Riley. You're amazing. What a beautiful gift to give your child.'

Mia tucked the letters safely into the back of the diary. Then she looked at the page she'd opened it on: August 2009.

'I'm doing this, Sarah,' she said. She settled herself in the chair and began to read aloud.

'9.30 a.m. I'm lying here staring at my incredible baby girl, Isobel, but Izzy to us. She's sleeping now, and her little rosebud mouth is set in a perfect pout. Her arms are thrown over her head and she looks so peaceful and happy. I never knew such joy existed. Mia told me about it. She kept saying, "Just wait until you hold your baby in your arms," but I didn't understand her. I didn't know that I could feel so much love.

'Adam is besotted too. It's been so lovely to see him so happy. He's been so stressed lately with having to close two of the stores and lay off staff he's had for years. He found it so hard. I'm worried about how stressed he is. Thank God for Izzy. She has lit up his life.

'I keep telling Adam that he mustn't worry about money or earning more. He still has the main bathroom shop and it's keeping us afloat. We're fine. I don't want fancy things. All I want is our little family unit, safe and healthy.

'But Adam's always been so driven. He wants to be successful and keeps saying he feels like a failure. It's because of his rotten father. He's obsessed with proving himself, but I keep telling him that he has no need to prove himself to anyone, and definitely not to me. He is a great guy, a loving husband, and I know he'll be a great dad. I just wish he could put his past behind him.

'I tried to get him to go and see a therapist, but he refused. He thinks he's dealt with it, but he hasn't. His brother Rob went to see a psychiatrist and he told me he found it really helpful. But Adam just said that Rob's gone all Canadian and it's more "normal" for men to see shrinks over there.

'I keep trying to boost him up. I tell him how brilliant he is, providing for me and allowing me to give up work. I want him to stop working 24/7 and spend more time at home. Hopefully he'll be home earlier now to see Izzy and spend time with her.

'5.00 p.m. Mia just called over with Riley on their way home from school. Mia had a face like thunder when she came in. Apparently, Riley got into trouble in school today for telling one of the other girls to "fuck off".

'Mia got pulled aside by the headmistress about it. She was furious. Poor Riley, I felt a bit sorry for her. She's a great kid, just has a very strong personality, which some of the gentler girls in the class find a bit much. Even at only seven you can see she's a fighter – just like her mum. And Mia didn't lick it off a stone either. Mia is like Penny and Riley is like Mia.

'Mia said it's not just that Riley was bold but that it reflects badly on her as a teacher in the school. I get that, but Riley is a chip off the old block. Mia disagrees when I tell her that. She seems to think she was this angel child. But I remember her, and she really wasn't. She argued with Dad all the time and with Mum, but Mum is like Mia, fiery and smart and driven. They get each other.

'I like peace and quiet and harmony. After Mia calls in, I always feel breathless. She can be a bit of a whirlwind. In the thirty minutes she was here she made me a cup of coffee and a sandwich, changed Izzy's nappy, hung out a wash and unloaded the dishwasher.

'I told her not to, but she's not happy when she's not doing something. Mia never sits down and just chills. She can't.'

Yes, I can, Mia thought. I can sit down and watch Netflix. Although . . . she never just watched a programme, she'd also be on her phone checking emails or doing lists in her head or sewing the hem of Riley's school skirt.

'Sarah, you're right about me having to do things all the time, but not about Riley being my mirror image. I was not this troublesome to Mum, no way. I certainly never spoke to her the way Riley speaks to me. She can be so rude. Since I grounded her for getting drunk, she's been even worse. She stomps around the house sulking and making us all miserable. Johnny begged me to let her go out and spare us the moods, but I have to put my foot down or else she'll just go completely wild.

'And sorry if I made you feel breathless, but I was only trying to help. I knew how tired you were after giving birth. I was being practical.' Mia felt a bit stung by that particular comment.

'I could just stare at Izzy for ever. She is so perfect. I feel so blessed. I want to have another baby now. I want to have lots of children, it's so

amazing. I didn't want to say that to Mia obviously. I know she would have liked more kids, she's a great mum, but Johnny had problems – low sperm count. Adam thinks it's because Johnny's not fit and doesn't work out, but it isn't, it's just bad luck.'

Mia's face grew hot. How dare Adam say that? Johnny's low sperm count had nothing to do with not going to the stupid gym. God, Adam was such an insensitive jerk sometimes. Sarah always tried to excuse his remarks as the result of growing up with an alcoholic gambler for a father. Mia did feel bad for Adam – clearly his childhood had been awful and had badly affected him – but sometimes he was really hard to take.

Johnny had been heartbroken when they'd found out they couldn't have any more children. The consultant said that Riley was kind of a miracle child. They'd discussed sperm donors and adoption, but in the end, Mia had said Riley was enough. When she saw the relief on Johnny's face, she knew she'd made the right decision. And Riley was enough for any family. She took up all the space, oxygen and energy of six kids.

If Mia was being totally honest, she had taken a while to come to terms with the fact that she wouldn't have any more children, but she'd kept it to herself so as not to hurt Johnny. And she'd made peace with it a long time ago.

'I think I'd like two girls and two boys. That would be perfect. It might be a pipe dream, though. Adam is so stressed about money and the business I don't want to put any pressure on him. Hopefully the recession will be over soon and things will pick up. I think you have to be optimistic in life. What's the alternative, waiting for the roof to cave in?

'Mia is a worrier. I'm more of a block-out-the-worries-and-focus-on-the-positive person. Mum says I live in La La Land, but I prefer

it that way. I think being bullied made me very self-sufficient. I know I can manage on my own and that I like my own company. It also taught me not to get stressed about things you can't control. I couldn't control Georgia and the other girls being bitches, so I had to learn to work around it. I think that lesson has stood to me. I don't get bogged down in things out of my control.

'Mum and Mia are always worried or stressing about something — if it's not money or work or health, it's the state of the world, refugee crises, famines, recessions . . . They never stop. I want to live in my bubble of joy with Izzy and tune out the bad stuff. I choose happiness and I'm not going to apologize for it.

'Dad always says, why watch a depressing movie when you can watch a comedy? I agree entirely. Mia and Mum can watch their depressing movies and documentaries but I'm going to stick to watching How I Met Your Mother *and laughing.'*

Mia closed the diary and laid it on her lap. She felt guilty for reading it, but it did bring Sarah close to her. It was strange, too, because some of the stuff she knew, and some was Sarah's private thoughts. Obviously, she knew Sarah would have a private take on things, but it was a bit weird to hear it. She felt she knew Sarah better than anyone, but there were things her sister hadn't shared with her.

She stroked the leather cover of the diary and turned it over in her hands, then looked back at her sister, lying so still. 'Come on, wake up, please.' She rubbed the back of Sarah's hand and prayed.

13

Adam walked around his house like a zombie. It didn't feel like home: it was empty and silent and sad. He felt as if he was losing his mind. How could this happen? Why? Was Sarah going to wake up? He stood in front of the fridge, staring at the food, and felt like throwing up. How could he eat when his wife was fighting for her life? Adam inhaled deeply. He had to keep it together. He had to be strong for Izzy and for Sarah. She'd want him to be strong. But Sarah was his world, his love. Sarah had shown him what family looked like. She'd created the warm, loving environment that Adam had craved his whole life. Sarah was home. Without her . . .

He needed to talk to someone who understood him better than anyone. And that person was his brother, Rob. He hadn't told him anything yet, because he'd kept hoping it would end and he'd be able to tell Rob when it was all over and better and fixed. But now, well, now he wasn't so sure about anything. He had to talk to his brother, to hear his reassuring voice.

Adam sat at the kitchen table with his laptop and dialled the Canadian number. The ring tone sounded, then there was a click and his brother's face filled the screen.

'Hey, bro. I was just thinking about you, funnily enough. To what do I owe the pleasure? It's been a while.'

Adam realized he had no idea how to explain this. What the hell did he say? 'Hey, Rob, I kissed my wife goodbye yesterday and now she's in ICU hooked up to a ventilator and I don't know if she'll ever wake up'?

'It's Sarah . . .' was all he managed.

Rob's face fell. 'What's happened? Oh, Jesus, is she OK?'

'She . . . she's in hospital. Oh, Rob, it's awful. It's some kind of brain injury and she's in a coma. They don't know for sure yet exactly but . . .'

'Oh, Christ, Adam, what happened? What do you mean they're not sure?'

Adam began to cry. 'I don't know. I don't understand. I left her yesterday morning and she was fine. She said she had a headache and I told her to go to the doctor and get checked out. Then she collapsed. Mia found her. She hasn't opened her eyes since.'

Rob's face closed in on the screen. 'Are they doing tests? What do the doctors say? What about the baby?'

'They can't tell me if she'll wake up, but our baby is alive. At least I have him.' Adam covered his face and sobbed.

'Oh, Adam,' Rob said, his voice shaking, 'I don't know what to say. Jesus, I wish I was there. I'm in shock. Ellen will be devastated – she adores Sarah. Oh, God, I'm so sorry. I know how much you love her, man. But, look, she's strong, she'll come through this. You hear about people coming out of comas all the time.'

Adam wiped his face roughly with a hand. 'I'm trying to stay hopeful. Sarah's still alive, the baby's still alive. I just have to believe that the tests will explain what's happening and the medical team will figure out a way to save her.'

'Yes, of course. Does she have the best people working on her?' Rob asked. 'It's so serious I think you should definitely consider a second opinion. I could get someone here to look at her test results when they come in.'

'I suppose so, yes,' Adam said. 'I hadn't thought about that, but it's too important not to get a second opinion. They're probably more advanced in Canada.'

'I'll ask around my friends here,' Rob said. 'I'll find the name of a top neurologist. We'll get everyone to have a look and work together to make Sarah better. Hang in there.'

'That's a great help. Thanks, Rob. I'm all over the place – I can't think straight.'

'Of course you are. You've had one hell of a shock. Let me take the pressure off you. Tell me everything you know now and send me all the details as they come in.' Adam watched as Rob searched around for a pen and paper. 'Shoot.'

Adam filled him in with what he knew.

'I have all that. Send me any other details, tests, results, et cetera, and I'll hunt down the best neurologist in Toronto and get you another opinion. I mean, if we have to, we'll fly Sarah over here. I'll do anything to help you.'

'I . . . Jesus, Rob, thank you.'

'Now tell me, how's Izzy?'

Adam shook his head. 'She doesn't understand. I've just told her that Sarah is asleep because she's not feeling well. I couldn't tell her any more. I don't understand it myself. If I can't process it, how could she? Christ, Rob, I feel responsible. Sarah's been really pale and tired the last few days, but I've been so bloody busy with work that I didn't push her to see the doctor. I should have. I should have realized she was sick.'

'Come on, Adam, don't start blaming yourself. This is no one's fault. Brain injuries can be almost impossible to detect. You adore Sarah. You'd lay down your life to save hers. You can't take the blame for any of this.'

'But it's my job to protect my family,' Adam cried.

On the screen, Rob pointed a finger at him. 'Don't do that. This is not your fault. It's a freak accident. Look, we both have this crazy need to be successful, to be the best, to provide for and protect our families because of Dad. But we can't do that. All we can do is show up every day and do our best, and you always do, Adam. You always do.'

Adam could hear the language of his brother's therapy sessions coming out in what Rob was saying. He didn't agree. 'It's not just about showing up, Rob, it's about creating a safe home. All we ever had at home was a drunk, useless fecker either passed out or shouting at us.'

'I know, and it was awful. I'll never forget the feeling of being hungry, cold and abandoned. But we won't undo that hurt by killing ourselves trying to be perfect. We have to accept that we can only do our best. You're a great husband and father, Adam. And Sarah thinks that, too. I know she does.'

He wasn't, though. He was a husband who didn't come home to his wife because he was so busy trying to make more money. He was a father who didn't kiss his daughter good-night because getting a new contract was more important. Adam had sworn, standing beside his father's grave, that he would be a better man. In many ways he had been, but not good enough.

'I can see your face. I know you're trying to blame yourself. Stop it. This is just a horrible twist of Fate.'

Adam rubbed his face. 'She's the love of my life, Rob.'

'I know she is,' Rob said softly. 'You two were made for each other. But she's a strong woman, Adam. She'll fight to get back to you. I'll start working on a second opinion here and we'll do everything humanly possible to help her. You've got to stay hopeful, OK?'

Thanks, Rob,' Adam said. 'I really needed to talk to you. Thanks for being there. I'd better get back to the hospital. I'll be in touch.'

Adam watched his brother's face disappear from the screen. Rob was two years younger than him, but they were as close as twins. When you had no mother and a deadbeat dad, your brother was everything. When Rob had emigrated to Canada ten years ago, Adam had been gutted. He'd missed him so much. They'd gone from talking every day to once a week, and then Adam had got married and had Izzy, and later on Rob had married Ellen, and now they only spoke about once a month. Adam realized with a pang how much he missed his brother. He was his rock.

Adam gathered up his stuff and got ready to go back to Sarah. He felt better after the Skype call – calmer and stronger after hearing Rob's voice and feeling his support and love.

Maybe things would be OK after all.

14

Riley sat in Shocko's desk chair with her feet up on the corner of his bed. Her black school shoes lay on the floor beside her. Shocko lay propped up on his pillows, leaning against the wall he'd painted black, then covered with a huge Che Guevara poster.

'*Duuuuuuude*, that is messed up.' Shocko's eyes were wide. 'A coma is, like, *really* serious.'

'Do people usually wake up from them?' Riley asked, as she flicked through her Instagram page. Her hands were trembling. She hadn't been able to stop shaking since her mum had told her Sarah was in an actual coma. She was trying really hard not to freak out. Sarah had to get better: she was the best aunt ever. Riley loved her so much.

'I dunno. It depends.'

'On what?'

'Well, I'm not totally sure but, like, if you're totally obese I guess that would go against you or if you smoked two hundred a day or were, like, a heroin addict or something.'

'If you're a heroin addict, you're probably going to die anyway,' Riley snapped.

'Not necessarily. Look at whatshisname.'

'Who?'

'You know, the guy in that band.'

'Can you narrow it down a bit?' Shocko never remembered anyone's name. He was like a young person with Alzheimer's, and Riley was not in the mood for a guessing game. She felt like she was going to puke whenever she thought of Sarah being carried into the ambulance on the stretcher – so grey and lifeless. And her mum's face – Riley would never forget it. Mia had looked terrified. She kept opening her mouth to speak, but no words came out. Riley had never seen her like that.

She had stayed calm only because of Izzy. Riley knew she had to make sure Izzy wasn't terrified. The image of Sarah on the stretcher kept coming into her mind all the time. She had looked like . . . Riley closed her eyes and swallowed bile. She'd looked dead.

'That song, you know – something, something ne ne ne ne ne ne,' Shocko sang.

'Nirvana?'

'Yes. Ken? Kobie?'

'Kurt Cobain.'

'Yes, him. He was a heroin addict and he was all right.'

Riley sighed. 'Kurt Cobain committed suicide!'

'Did he? I thought his wife did.'

'He did, and the wife is still going strong.'

'Well, she was into heroin, too, so there you go.'

'There I go? What are you actually talking about? Why are we talking about these people anyway? What has heroin got to do with my aunt's coma?'

Shocko plucked tunelessly at his guitar. 'I dunno. You started it.'

'No, I didn't. You just went off on one of your crazy-arse tangents that go nowhere and have no meaning or purpose.'

'Jeez, no need to rip my head off.'

Riley bit down hard on her nail and tasted blood. It felt good. The sharp pain cleared her head. She thumbed through her phone absentmindedly and then saw it.

'WTF?'

'What?'

Riley turned her phone to face Shocko. He leaned forward. 'Is that Zach and Zoë?'

'Yes, it bloody is.' Riley fought back tears. Could her life get any worse? Zach and Zoë had their arms around each other. She was wearing the Superdry top that Riley had bought Zach for his birthday last month. It had cost her almost all of the money she'd made helping to paint the school during the Christmas holidays. Her mum had got her the job because Riley had said she wanted to earn her own money. She hadn't told Mia what it was for. How dare Zach let that cow wear it? It was Riley's present to him. She wanted to weep.

Shocko plucked a string and sang, 'He's not worth it. You're a cool chick who deserves to be with not a dick. You should be with someone who adores you.'

It was so off-key and awful that Riley laughed. She threw a pillow at Shocko. 'You need to focus more on schoolwork. You have zero musical ability.'

'Way to crush a guy!' Shocko put down his guitar.

'Sorry – you know you're rubbish.'

'Yeah, but I'm trying to get better so a little encouragement from my best mate would be nice.'

Riley stared at the photo of Zach and Zoë. She felt raw fury rise inside her. Her last conversation with Sarah had been about Zach and bloody Zoë. Sarah had got it, how the whole thing made Riley feel. The idea that she couldn't talk to her now made her feel sick. She needed to get outside her head, her memories before she went mad. 'Hey, do you want to do something to make this day less shitty?'

'My day was fine until you showed up and put a downer on everything,' Shocko said.

'I'll make it up to you.'

A plan was forming in Riley's head, one that would distract her and enable her to take her revenge on Zach.

Riley climbed up onto the garage roof and crawled over to her bedroom window, which she always left open a crack in case she needed to sneak in and out. Her mum was like a prison officer, but she hadn't copped on to this little trick yet. Riley had messed around with the lock until she was able to make it look like it was down but was still able to wriggle it up using her penknife. In the room and outside, the window looked closed, but she could still open it. It was her foolproof escape hatch.

She pulled the window down and turned to give Shocko the thumbs-up. He was hiding behind the hedge in the front garden. Riley climbed through the window and stopped to listen. She could hear the annoying 'Let It Go' from *Frozen* and the smell of baking wafted up the stairs. Her dad and Izzy were busy, so she'd be OK.

She rummaged around her room, pulling things out of drawers and wardrobes. She put all of the things she needed into a backpack. She was fine until she got to the card.

He had written her a card. On the front was a picture of Kristen Stewart. Zach had written, '*This hot actress reminds me of you. You rock my world, Riley. Z*'

A lump rose in her throat. Her heart ached for Sarah. Shocko was right: everything was so incredibly messed up.

She went to put the card into the backpack, but she couldn't do it. She hid it under her mattress, pushing it right into the middle. Hopefully her mother wouldn't find it there. The last thing she needed was Mia asking any more questions about Zach.

Riley didn't tell her mother anything about boys. It was too awkward, plus her mum would just interrogate her about anyone she mentioned – was he 'nice', was he a 'good' boy, was he 'sensible' – the kind of stuff that didn't matter at all. She was obsessed with Riley not having sex, too. She kept telling her stories about 'friends' daughters' who had had unprotected sex with their boyfriends and ruined their lives. Riley knew these 'friends' daughters' were made-up. Her mum was so obvious with her lame tales of warning.

Riley hadn't had sex with Zach and he hadn't pushed her. He was nice that way. He said they'd only do it when she felt ready and he'd wait as long as she needed. Riley wasn't going to have sex until she was at least sixteen. She had told him so and he was cool about it. God, she missed him. He was an amazing kisser and, sure, they'd messed around a bit. He was so hot. He had a six-pack from all his athletics training. He was really good at the high jump. At first, Riley had thought that was a bit dorky – only nerdy guys did the high jump, nerds and Sally Peterson, who was, like, ten feet tall and a freak of nature. Sally didn't even have to jump: she just stepped over the bar. But then she'd gone to watch Zach practise and had seen him do the backflip over the bar, and it was kind of sexy when he did it.

Five months was a long time to be with someone. She really liked him. She really, really liked him. If she was being totally honest she kind of loved him and thought he loved her too, so why had he gone off with Zoë?

Riley had been racking her brain for days, but the only thing she could think of was that stupid thing she'd said. She'd only been kidding. How could he not see that? But every time Riley thought about it, she felt nauseous. Why had she said it? Her and her stupid big mouth. She hadn't thought he'd be so sensitive, but the look on his face had told her she'd gone too far.

To hell with him. He'd chosen Zoë and good luck to them. They could do dorky athletics training together. He'd humiliated Riley and broken her heart, so he deserved payback and she needed closure. She picked up her backpack and climbed out of the window, making sure to pull it up behind her.

'What took you so long? I was about to go.'

'Sorry, it took me a while to find everything.'

'What's this all about?'

'Revenge,' Riley said.

'Cool.' Shocko grinned.

They hopped onto their bikes and cycled away, zigzagging through the roads around her estate until they came to Zach's house.

Riley knew Zach's parents worked until at least seven or eight every night. They ran their own bakery, so the hours were long. She looked up at his bedroom window. She could see him at his desk. He was typing on his laptop.

Riley unzipped the backpack and turned the contents out onto the grass in his front garden. She took out the firelighter she'd bought in the Spar shop down the road and lit it. She threw it onto the pile of things and watched as the flames swept over it all. Up went the sweatshirt he'd given her, the baseball cap he'd bought for her on his trip to London, the socks he'd left at her house, the spare school tie he'd let her keep, the Valentine's Day bear he'd bought her. It all went up in flames.

She threw a pebble at his window and watched as he looked over. She saw the surprise, confusion, then shock on his face. He disappeared from the window, and seconds later the front door was yanked open. He ran outside. 'What the hell?' he shouted.

'This is everything I have of yours. Burning, like I hope you do, in Hell.'

123

'Have you lost your mind?'

'You're a bastard.'

'I'm not the one who mocks people for following their dream, Riley.'

'I didn't mock you.'

'Yes, you did. I was gutted when I lost in the final of that competition and all you could do was laugh and say, "Who cares? High jump is for dorks. Just give it up. It's so boring to watch."'

'I didn't mean it like that.'

'Oh, really? What did you mean?' Zach shouted at her.

'I meant . . . I meant it's not exactly the most important thing in the world whether you jump over a bar or not.'

'It is to me,' he hissed, and disappeared inside. He came running back out with a jug full of water and poured it over the fire. The remnants of his gifts to Riley sizzled into a soggy mess.

'At least I didn't go out and humiliate you in public.' Riley poked him in the chest.

'You humiliated yourself,' Zach snapped. 'And what is he doing here?'

'He came to help me.'

'What? Help you start a fire? I'm sure you could have managed that all on your own. You just like to have Shocko around as your adoring lapdog.'

'I'm no lapdog, dude. I came because she's my best mate and you treated her badly. She deserves better.'

'If Riley has something to say, she can say it to me alone.'

Riley turned to Shocko and motioned for him to wait on the road.

'Thanks for making a big mess in my garden. Jesus, Riley, if you wanted to talk to me, you should have just called.'

'Why Zoë?'

'Because she gets it. She gets my passion for the high jump because she feels the same way about the hurdles.'

Riley rolled her eyes. 'She doesn't give a shit about hurdles. She's just pretending so you'll like her.'

'She's actually amazing at the hurdles. She's number four in Ireland. The hurdles are actually a really –'

'Screw the hurdles!' Riley threw her hands into the air. 'I don't want to talk about the bloody hurdles. I'm sorry you feel I mocked you, but you really hurt me at that party, Zach. It was not cool.'

Zach put his hands in his pockets and shrugged. 'Well, you hurt me.'

'Are you going out with her now?'

'Dunno, kind of.'

'Do you like her?' Riley swallowed tears.

'We have a lot in common. It's easy.'

'But you said you liked me because I was different. You said Zoë and those blonde, perma-tanned girls were ridiculous.'

'I do like you cos you're different, but it's just easier with Zoë. I was wrong about her and her friends. They're actually pretty cool.'

'Cool?' Riley snorted. 'Are you having a laugh?'

Zach looked at her. 'Yes, actually, I am having a laugh. We laugh all the time. She's not like you, Riley. She doesn't question everything and take things so seriously and bang on about gun control in America and equality and feminism and religion being a scam and all the stuff you obsess about. She just wants to have fun.'

'Oh, my actual God, can you hear yourself? So that's what you want! To be with someone who is happy all the fucking time, like a puppy! Zoë laughs all the time because she has nothing to say. She has nothing to say because she has a brain the size of a pea. She thought Gandhi was a rapper. A rapper!'

'So what?' Zach stamped out the remaining embers of burned things with his boots.

'Are you kidding me? Do you really want to go out with someone who is that stupid?'

'Maybe I do. It's better than going out with someone who keeps giving me books about *Leaning In* and stuff by Maya Angeline, or whatever her name is. Maybe I want to lean the hell out.'

'It's Maya Angelou and fuck you. You said you liked me knowing so much about women's rights and history.'

'Well, I lied. In the beginning it was OK, but then it all got way too intense and preachy. I'm sixteen. I want to have fun with my girlfriend, not a lecture.'

Riley pushed him back with both hands. 'Enjoy your life with Zoë and her pea brain.'

Zach poked her in the chest. 'I will, thank you.'

'I hate you.'

'Yeah, well, I'm not too crazy about you either.'

'I'm going now.'

'Great. Make sure you read some more of those boring books about women who saved the world and bore some other poor guy about them.'

'I hope your brain shrivels up and you die.'

'At least I'll have had fun before I do.'

Riley walked away before he could see her cry. That hadn't gone well at all. She had intended to stand beside her fire, all righteous and angry, and tell Zach what a bastard he was and then he'd be all sorry and remorseful, admire her fierceness and beg her to get back with him.

But instead he'd seemed happy to be rid of her. The things he'd said, they'd hurt, really hurt. Riley felt as if she'd been stabbed in the heart.

Shocko stood on the other path, holding her bike. 'I guess this day couldn't really get any worse, huh? What with your aunt in a coma and Zach being a dick.'

Riley climbed onto her bike and pedalled furiously to get ahead. She didn't want Shocko to see her fall apart.

15

Johnny twisted one strand of hair around another but dropped the third. 'I give up!' He threw his hands into the air. 'Who invented plaits? Seriously, they're not made for big hands and thick fingers. I'm sorry, love, I've made a total mess of your hair.'

Izzy giggled. 'Daddy's really bad at them too. Mummy's the best. I'll just put on my hairband with the red bow. Mummy likes that one. I can't wait to see her.'

Johnny patted her little shoulder. He didn't think Sarah was going to wake up, not today or maybe ever.

Mia was determined to stay positive, but Johnny had seen the grave faces of the doctors and nurses coming in and out of Sarah's room. None of them looked remotely upbeat. He was praying for good news, but he had a sinking feeling that it wasn't going to come.

He was worried Izzy would be shocked when she saw her mother linked up to all those tubes and drips. She was an innocent little thing. At her age Riley was already cynical and defiant, but Izzy was all wide-eyed innocence and joy.

When they got to the hospital, Adam was waiting in Reception. Izzy ran into his open arms. 'There she is.' He held her close.

'Is Mummy awake?'

Adam looked over her shoulder at Johnny. 'No, Sweet-pea, and she might not wake up today, but that's OK. She needs her rest.'

'I made a picture for her,' Izzy said, ignoring what her

father had told her. 'She's going to like it. Johnny helped me a bit. Look, Daddy, I put the baby in the picture, too, because he's part of our family now, isn't he? Mummy will be pleased about that. Although she told me that I'm her special person and not to worry when the baby comes because she will love me just the same and . . .'

Izzy talked non-stop all the way up in the lift, gripping Adam's hand tightly. Johnny could see the fingers of her other hand crushing the top of the painting. She was putting on a good show, but she was terrified. His heart ached for her.

Adam opened the door to ICU Reception and Izzy stepped inside. Mia and Charlie rushed over and made a fuss of her. Everyone was talking over each other, trying to compensate for the fear they felt. Johnny could see Izzy's grip getting tighter and tighter on her painting.

'Hey, why don't we give Izzy a second to catch her breath?' he suggested.

'Absolutely. You're crowding the poor child,' Olivia said.

'Supporting her, actually,' Mia muttered.

'Izzy, would you like some grapes?' Olivia offered.

Izzy shook her head. 'No, thank you. I just want to see Mummy.'

Angela popped into the room. 'Sarah's ready now,' she said to Adam. Then, to Izzy, she said, 'Hello again, Izzy. Have you come to say hello to Mum?'

'Yes,' Izzy said, beaming. 'I'm coming to wake her up. I have my picture and I'm going to sing. It's my Communion in two weeks and Mummy needs to be better now so we can finish all our plans.'

'Well, that's very exciting.' Angela smiled at her. 'Come and see me before you go. I might just have some chocolate for you.'

'Thank you very much. Mummy likes chocolate too, but she says if she eats too much, she'll be a roly-poly. But I think when you're sick it's good to have treats. When I had a throat infection, Mummy gave me chocolate buttons to melt in my mouth so they didn't hurt when I swallowed.'

Angela smiled, her eyes shiny with tears. 'Your mummy is very clever. Will you follow me and I'll bring you down to see her?'

'Yes, please. Come on, Daddy, let's go.' Izzy pulled Adam's hand.

They all followed Angela except Olivia, who discreetly stayed behind.

'Johnny, I'm scared for Izzy to see her mum like this,' Mia whispered. He squeezed her hand.

'She needs to see her. She won't stop asking until she does,' Charlie said quietly.

'I'm sure you're right, Dad. It's just . . .'

Charlie nodded. 'I know.'

Outside Sarah's room, Izzy paused. She took off her glasses and began to wipe them furiously with her jumper.

Adam crouched down and reminded Izzy that Sarah had a lot of tubes around her and a big one in her mouth to help her breathe.

'I know. You explained it already a trillion times.'

'Izzy,' Angela said, kindly but firmly, 'if you want to wait until later or another day, that's fine. You don't have to see your mummy right now. You can see her anytime.'

Izzy put her glasses back on. 'I need to see her. I'll be able to wake her up. Wait and see.'

Mia covered her mouth with a hand to stifle a sob. Charlie was praying quietly, and Johnny was holding his breath.

She looked so small and vulnerable walking into the room. Adam's eyes were frightened. Johnny reached over and patted him on the back. 'It'll be OK. We're here for you.'

*

Adam and Izzy walked into the room with just the sounds of machines whirring and clunking. Izzy hesitated at the door. 'There are so many things on Mummy,' she whispered.

'It's OK, Sweet-pea.' Adam took her hand and brought her to the side of the bed.

Gingerly, Izzy leaned over and touched her mother's face. She kissed her cheek. 'I'm here, Mummy. I came to wake you up. I miss you. I want you to come back now. Look, I did you a picture. Do you like it, Mummy? Mummy? Open your eyes so you can see.

'I know you're tired Mummy, but if you wake up and come home, I'll help you more. I'll be the best girl in the world. I know the baby is making you tired. I'll tidy up and do anything else you need me to do. I love you, Mummy. I want to snuggle up and watch TV and make cookies and sing songs with you. And we have to finish organizing my Communion party. Remember you said I could choose my cake and we were going to go to the special cake shop to get a fancy one made? But it's only two weeks away, so please wake up. I need you, Mummy.'

Izzy shook Sarah's arm gently. She squeezed her hand. 'Mummy? Can you hear me? I'll sing you a song. It's our song, Mummy.' Izzy's voice shook as she sang 'Let It Go'.

Outside in the corridor, Mia and Charlie wept to hear her sweet voice singing and pleading with her mother to wake up. Johnny put his arms around both of them. He was struggling to hold it together himself. Come on, Sarah, wake up for her, do it for Izzy, he willed his sister-in-law.

'Mummy, come on, sing. Mummy, please. It's me, it's Izzy, Mummy. It's your best girl. Mummy?'

Adam reached out and put his arms around her. Izzy wailed into his shirt. 'Why won't she wake up, Daddy?'

'She's just sick, Izzy, and she might not wake up for a while.'

'But why? Is the baby making her sick?'

'No, but she needs to concentrate on him. She . . . Well, she needs to give him all of her energy.'

Izzy frowned. 'Why? Suzie's mummy has a baby in her tummy and she's awake and walking around.'

'Yes, but Mummy was unlucky. She got sick and now she's trying to keep the baby well.'

Izzy pushed Adam away. 'I hate the baby. I *hate* him,' she shouted. 'Before he came Mummy was happy. But then he came in her tummy and she got bad headaches and was tired and now she's asleep and won't wake up. I want my mummy back!'

Adam picked up his furious, confused, distraught child and held her tight. 'It's OK, Izzy, I'm here. Daddy's here.'

Izzy bawled into his shoulder. He snuggled her to his chest, felt soothed to have her close to him. The kiss of her exhale on his neck was like a salve to his shattered heart. This was his world – Izzy, Sarah, and now the baby. If only Sarah could just open her eyes and this whole nightmare disappear . . .

Izzy's sobs subsided and she pulled back from Adam.

'Are you OK?'

'Yes, I'm fine now, because I know what's happening.'

Adam looked puzzled. 'What do you mean?'

'Mummy is going to rest until my Communion Day so she's all better and able to be at my party. That's why she won't wake up now. She's just not ready. But she would never ever miss my Communion Day. I know that for one hundred per cent sure. That's what's going to happen.'

Izzy stared at her mother, smiling to herself. 'I'd like to go back outside, Daddy,' she said, standing up. 'I'll see Mummy again soon.'

When they stepped outside the room, Mia and Charlie rushed over to Izzy. Angela hovered in the background, keeping an eye on everyone.

'How are you, pet?' Mia asked.

'I'm fine. I know what's happening now.' Izzy filled them in on her Communion Day theory.

Mia looked at Adam. He shrugged helplessly. Charlie coughed. No one knew what to say.

'Well, now.' Angela bustled over. 'I need to hear more about this Communion Day party, I want all the details. Come here with me – I found some chocolate for you. It'll be good for you to have a bit of sugar after all that.'

Angela expertly guided Izzy away while the others stood outside Sarah's room, staring at each other.

Adam rubbed his eyes. 'Christ, that was awful. Was I wrong to bring her in?'

'No,' Mia assured him. 'She needed to see her.'

'And Charlie was right. She wasn't going to let up until she did,' Johnny added.

'It all seems so real now, seeing it through Izzy's eyes. Is Sarah going to wake up? Why can't the doctors tell us what the hell is going on? Why can't they give us a straight answer? All this waiting is driving me insane.' Adam thumped the wall in frustration.

'Let's go out to Reception and sit down for a minute,' Charlie said.

They filed out and sat on the couches facing each other. Olivia fussed over Charlie, trying to force-feed him grapes.

'He doesn't want any,' Mia snapped, as Charlie said no for the third time.

'He needs to keep his strength up,' Olivia retorted. 'This is not going to end well.'

'What do you mean?' Adam glared at her.

Olivia shifted in her seat. 'You need to prepare yourselves for the worst. Severe brain injury is almost impossible to come back from. I think you need to accept the strong possibility that Sarah will not survive this.'

Adam stood up and waved a finger in Olivia's face. 'I think you should leave.'

'Hold on now,' Charlie said.

'No!' Adam shouted. 'I'm hanging on by a thread here and I do not want anyone telling me Sarah's going to die. Leave, please.'

Olivia stood up. 'I'm not trying to upset you, Adam, but you have to face the truth at some point.'

'Since when do you have a degree in neurology?' Mia snapped. 'Who are you to tell us what's going to happen to Sarah? What the hell do you know?'

'Easy now, let's all calm down,' Charlie said.

'Charlie,' Adam's voice shook with rage, 'I would really appreciate it if Olivia left now. I have enough on my plate and she is not helping.'

Olivia picked up her bag and headed for the door. 'I honestly didn't mean to cause offence, but the truth is often a bitter pill to swallow.'

Charlie followed her out.

'Good riddance,' Mia said.

'I don't want her in here again.' Adam paced the room.

Johnny looked at them, the people who loved Sarah most. They were kidding themselves, he thought. The chances of her making it through were getting slimmer by the hour. But he certainly wasn't going to say so. Not today anyway. For now, Mia and Adam needed hope. They weren't ready for the possible awful truth.

16

Izzy kicked Riley in the stomach for the tenth time. She'd been wriggling around all night and muttering in her sleep. Riley had barely slept an hour. She pulled the duvet over Izzy's shoulders and turned to face the window. Daylight was creeping in around the sides of her window blind. She looked at her phone – five a.m.

She checked her messages. None from Zach. She checked his Instagram page: nothing posted. She checked Facebook: nothing. She then looked up Zoë's Instagram page. She'd posted a picture of her beside a stupid hurdle in her training shorts with her hair in a high ponytail, looking all sporty and bouncy and irritating. Her post said, 'Training hard for the finals next week. Zach's been helping me with my fitness!!!!'

Riley's stomach fell. Stupid cow with her stupid exclamation marks and innuendoes and . . . What did it mean? Were they actually together-together? Zach had talked about it like it wasn't fully on, but it didn't look like Zoë had got that memo. And why was he helping her with her fitness? Did the exclamation marks mean horizontal jogging? Were they having actual sex? Or was she just trying to make it look like they were? Did she mean they were just, like, doing sit-ups and laps of the track together?

Riley's head ached. Why are you interested in her, Zach? She's so pointless. She doesn't care about anything except lip gloss and fashion and the stupid hurdles.

How dare he tell Riley she cared too much about stuff? How could you not care? How could you sit around while students in America were being shot in school and girls were used as sex slaves and women were paid less than men for the same work and all of the other wrongs in the world? How could you just say, 'I don't care about gun control but I really care about buying the new Mac lip gloss'? I mean, it wasn't as if Riley didn't care about make-up and stuff. She did. She liked looking good, but in a less obvious way. They weren't from California: they lived in rainy grey Dublin. Why would she dye her hair blonde, lash on fake tan and wear tiny skirts when the average temperature was about eight degrees?

Riley liked her dark hair and black kohl-rimmed eyes. She liked ripped skinny jeans and long-sleeve T-shirts. She liked her leather cuff and her biker boots. It was cold and she didn't freeze her arse off every time she left the house.

Zach said he liked the way she looked, but he'd obviously been lying. She should have known. He was too sunny for her. He was an optimist. He always thought good things were going to happen, that the world was full of decent people and all conflicts would be resolved . . .

But he didn't feel things the way Riley did. Zach felt things at a surface level, while Riley felt things deep down. But she'd liked his optimism: it was nice to be around someone who thought everything would work out. He had reminded her a little of Sarah, because she was always so positive, too. It had even rubbed off on her a bit – she'd felt less anxious about everything when she was with him. She'd thought they had fun. Clearly, she was wrong. She'd pushed him away by being too serious and not 'fun' enough.

How could she be more fun? Life was shit. Her beloved aunt was in a coma and her dad had no job. Riley had heard him on the phone earlier in the week, getting yet another rejection. She'd heard the disappointment in his voice: 'Oh.

I'm sorry to hear that. Well, please keep me in mind if any-thing comes up. I'll take anything you have.' She hated hearing him sound so desperate. He was a good journal-ist. He was a good man. He shouldn't have to beg. It wasn't right. Riley wanted him to be working and happy. She wanted her mum to stop being stressed about money all the time. But right now, most of all, she wanted Sarah to wake up.

She looked at the early daylight around the window blind until her eyes grew drowsy. She didn't believe in God, but right now she needed to pray. What else could she do? 'Please, God or Allah or Buddha or whoever is out there,' she whis-pered, 'please make Sarah come out of her coma and make the baby be OK. Don't take her away. Izzy needs her. It's not right to take a mum away from a seven-year-old. Please don't do this. She's such a great person. We all love her.'

Riley closed her eyes and tried to sleep. She realized she was crying when she felt the damp patch on her pillow.

Izzy jumped up and down on the bed. 'Wakey wakey, Riley,' she shouted.

Riley's eyes were stuck together like concrete. Her head ached. She felt as if she'd been asleep for a minute. It couldn't be seven already.

Izzy pulled one of her eyelids up. 'Are you awake? We don't want to be late for school. Don't be a lazybones.'

Jesus Christ, Riley wanted to weep. She'd barely slept.

Her dad popped his head around the door. 'Ah, great, you're up. And how did you sleep, Izzy, pet?'

'Good. I love sleeping with Riley. Can I stay again tonight?'

'I'm sure you can. Now, off you go and brush your teeth and I'll get the breakfast on. How does sausages and toast sound?'

'Yes!' Izzy did a happy dance, then left to brush her teeth.

Johnny sat on the edge of Riley's bed and pulled the covers back. 'And how did you sleep, my little pet?'

'I didn't. Sleeping with Izzy's impossible. She kicks and twists and turns and wriggles non-stop.'

'Ah, well, the poor little thing is worried sick about her mum.'

'I know.' Riley's eyes filled with tears. 'She thinks she's asleep, Dad. I was talking to her last night and she genuinely believes that Sarah is just having a rest and that she's going to wake up on her Communion Day. She really believes it.'

'Probably for the best. No point upsetting her until we know more.'

'What's going on? Did Mum come home? Can't the doctors tell us anything definite yet?'

Johnny shook his head. 'No. They're being really careful in what they say, which makes me worry. Mia stayed in the hospital last night. She was too afraid to leave. She's working on tracking someone down. Apparently, the mother of that new boy in your class, Pam Neelan, is a neurologist. She was working in some big trauma unit in the US until recently, so Mia's asked her to have a look at Sarah's medical notes. I think she's right, we need as many opinions as we can get.'

'Oh, yeah, he said something about his mum being a doctor. Maybe she'll figure out how to make Sarah better.'

'We're having a meeting with the doctors this morning. Hopefully we'll get some good news then.'

Riley bit her thumbnail. 'Do you think she'll wake up?'

Johnny sighed. 'I don't know, love, but I'm worried. We'll have to wait and see what they say, after all the tests they've been doing. All we can do is hope and try to be optimistic.'

Glass half full, Riley thought. Her dad was a glass-half-full person and her mum was a glass-half-empty person. That was why they worked. That was why she and Zach worked, too – correction, used to work.

'Sarah's the best,' Riley said. 'She's like Mum, but in a calmer, nicer, more relaxed, cooler, more fun way.'

'Ah, now,' Johnny said, swatting her arm gently, 'that's a bit harsh. Mia is a wonderful woman.'

'She's always on my case, Dad. I can't do anything right.'

'She's had a lot on her plate lately, Riley. I want you to be nice to her. Especially now. Sarah is her sister, her only sibling, and she adores her. Remember that. Mia is utterly devastated, and you and I have to support her. She'll be home soon to have a quick shower and then she's heading back to the hospital. Whatever she says or does, you are to bite your tongue and just say, "Yes, Mum," and "Can I do anything for you, Mum?" OK?'

'I promise I will.'

'Good.' Johnny kissed her head. 'Now up you get.'

When Riley shuffled into the kitchen twenty minutes later, Mia was standing at the counter, dressed in jeans and a jumper with wet hair dripping down her back. She looked wrecked.

'Hi, Riley,' she said. She put down her coffee, came over and threw her arms around her daughter.

Riley froze. They weren't huggy people. It felt weird and uncomfortable. She raised her arms and put them round her mother.

Mia pulled back. 'How are you, pet? You've been a bit abandoned in the midst of all this.'

'I'm fine. How are you?'

Mia smiled sadly. 'It's really hard, but I'm hanging in there.'

'So, uhm, how is she?' Riley whispered, so Izzy, who was eating sausages and telling Johnny about her Communion dress, wouldn't hear.

'The same. No change. I don't know what's going to happen. We're meeting the medical team this morning. It's just so . . .' Mia lowered her head and quickly wiped a tear from her cheek.

Oh, Jesus. Riley didn't know what to do. Her mother never cried, like never, ever, ever. She was so strong and tough, Riley often wondered if she felt real emotions. She wanted to put her hand up and lay it on her mother's shoulder or something, but she felt too awkward. She tried to think of something positive to say. Glass half full, she told herself. 'It'll be OK, Mum, I mean, she could end up like that guy Stephen Hawking, and he had a good life. The wheelchair and having to speak with his eyebrows wasn't great, but you know, he did loads and – and – Sorry, that's a shit example, but –'

Mia looked as if she'd been slapped. She rushed out of the room, her hand over her mouth.

'Nice one, Riley,' Johnny hissed.

Riley's eyes filled with tears. What was wrong with her? She should have just kept her big mouth shut. Damn it, she'd upset her mother now and that was the last thing she'd wanted to do. Riley felt sick.

She picked at a slice of toast, then went upstairs to find her mother. She heard her voice and peered around her parents' bedroom door. Mia was brushing Izzy's hair.

'Mummy does two plaits on the side and then she clips them and then she ties them into a ponytail at the back. It looks so pretty.'

'I'm sorry, Izzy, your mum was always better at hair than me. I'll try, though.'

'I don't mind having just a regular ponytail today.'

'Thanks, sweetie.' Mia hugged her from behind. 'You are such a gorgeous girl, do you know that, Izzy? Your mum is so proud of you.'

'She'll wake up soon,' Izzy said. 'And I'm going to tell her all about my sleepovers with Riley.'

Mia concentrated on Izzy's hair. 'You know, Sarah always tells me that the day you were born was the best day of her life.'

Izzy beamed in the mirror. 'She says that to me all the time. I was afraid the new baby would make Mummy love me less, but she said no way.'

'Absolutely no way. You are her little star, always.'

'When Riley was born, was it the best day of your life, Mia?'

Mia held the brush in the air. 'Yes, pet, it was, the very best. I was so happy to meet my little girl at last.'

Riley bit her trembling lip and walked into the room. 'Hey, Mum, I'll do Izzy's hair. You go and finish your coffee. Let me help.'

'Thank you, Riley.' Mia touched her shoulder. Riley put her hand up and squeezed her mother's arm. It wasn't exactly a hug, like in the American TV shows, and she didn't say, 'I love you,' but it was something.

'So I want two plaits at the side and –'

'I'm going to stop you there,' Riley said, sitting down on the bed behind Izzy. 'I don't do good plaits. Today you're getting a messy ponytail and it'll look really cool. Trust me, all your friends will want one.'

'OK, Riley.' Izzy smiled. 'Mummy can do my plaits when she wakes up.' Izzy's jaw jutted out. 'And that's that.'

Riley tied her cousin's hair up in silence and sent up another prayer that Sarah would pull through. The whole family depended on her. They couldn't manage without her. Riley couldn't manage without her. She had to pull through.

17

Mia, Johnny, Charlie and Adam sat at the table facing Dr Mayhew, Professor Irwin, Angela and a woman they hadn't met before. They were in a boardroom on the top floor of the hospital. The walls were painted the same awful magnolia as the rest of the place, but it had a deep red carpet that made it seem a bit more important. In the middle of the room sat a large, oval mahogany table. Sadly, the chairs around it were the same as the ones in the ICU waiting room. Functional, dark blue conference-hall chairs. They cheapened the table and gave the room a clinical feel.

On a trolley at the end of the room there were coffee and tea percolators. Twin towers, surrounded by mugs, a carton of milk and a bowl filled with sachets of sugar – brown and white. A plate of jaded-looking custard creams lay beside the sugar bowl. In the corner of the room was a large water dispenser.

'Can we get you some coffee or tea, or perhaps some water?' Dr Mayhew asked politely.

'If I drink any more caffeine, I'll be climbing the walls,' Adam said. 'I just want to know what's going on.' He looked completely exhausted.

Mia's palms were sweaty, and her heart was pounding. Beside her, her father appeared to be sitting still, but underneath the table his legs were shaking.

Dr Mayhew cleared his throat. 'Professor Irwin will talk us through the results of the neurological examinations that have been carried out over the past three days.'

'Good morning,' Professor Irwin said. She looked down at her notes, avoiding eye contact. That was not good. Mia could feel the woman's dread as she took a deep breath and said, 'I'm afraid it's not good news.'

Nobody spoke. They were all holding their breath. Johnny reached for Mia's hand. Adam clenched his into fists and breathed heavily.

'Sarah has a large cerebellar cystic lesion causing acute hydrocephalus and compression of the brain stem. There is an absence of blood flow in the intracranial vessels to the brain stem or to either cerebral hemisphere.'

Adam thumped the table, making them all jump. 'I don't understand what you're saying. Is she going to wake up? Is my wife going to be OK?'

Professor Irwin looked at Dr Mayhew, then back at Adam. 'I'm very sorry, Mr Brown, but no, your wife is not going to recover from this injury. Sarah had a cyst in her brain that caused her to collapse. The series of tests that we have run repeatedly, both the clinical tests and the scans, indicate that she has sustained a massive and devastating brain injury, one that affects the particular areas of the brain that sustain life, and these areas are no longer working. An angiogram has confirmed that there is no brain stem activity. In other words, there is no brain function. Our conclusion is that her brain injury is so severe, she will not live if we take her off the life-support machine. I am so very sorry, but Sarah is clinically dead. She will not wake up.'

Silence.

Into the awful silence came the sound of weeping. Mia looked over in a daze and saw that Charlie had broken down. Her brain was slowly catching up, as if the doctor's words had been played to her in slow motion.

'No,' Charlie moaned, covering his face with his hands.

'My poor Sarah.' He wept openly, and Mia stared at him stupidly, still trying to process Professor Irwin's words.

Beside her, Johnny took her hand. She turned to him and his eyes were red-rimmed.

She finally managed to speak. 'Are you absolutely sure?' she asked Dr Mayhew.

'I wish I could tell you otherwise, but Sarah will not come back from these injuries. The brain is too damaged. We have repeated the tests and the results are conclusive. I'm really so very sorry.'

Mia felt hope seep out of her. They sounded so sure. The medical jargon was confusing but ultimately they were saying that Sarah was gone, and that she was never coming back. The body in the room down the corridor was being kept alive by machines. But she looked alive, she felt alive . . . It was so hard to believe she was dead. Was she really?

Adam's eyes were flinty. 'I'm not accepting that,' he said fiercely. 'No way. Sarah is still alive. We're not giving up on her.'

The doctors exchanged a look. Angela leaned forward. 'This is incredibly difficult for you, Adam,' she said. 'It is a really cruel blow, but the doctors have been absolutely methodical. That's why we took our time and didn't jump to conclusions. But the fact is that Sarah has no brain-stem activity, which means she is brain dead. It's not possible for her to recover, Adam.'

Adam kept shaking his head, as if blocking out Angela's words. 'I'm getting a second opinion. I've seen reports on the news about medical negligence and – and medical fuck-ups. Well, my wife isn't going to be one of them. We're getting experts to give their opinions. A second one here and my brother is getting a third opinion in Toronto. They're ahead of the game there. They might be able to save her. We'll move her over there if necessary. I will not give up on Sarah, no way.'

'You may, of course, get as many opinions as you wish, but I'm afraid the outcome won't change,' Dr Mayhew said.

'Our expert is coming in this morning to give us a second opinion. I want you to talk to her and tell her everything. I want her to see all the notes and test results. I want her to give me her opinion on this. What's her name again, Mia?'

'Pam Neelan. She's a neurologist. We'd like her to have a look at Sarah and give us her prognosis.'

'She's just back from working in the US, so she probably has a lot more experience working with – with complicated cases,' Adam added, clinging desperately to any lifeline he could find.

'I know Pam Neelan,' Professor Irwin said. 'I'll be happy to have her opinion.'

'And what about my son? He's still alive.'

Dr Mayhew turned and introduced the other lady. 'This is Ms Johnston, the consultant obstetrician working on Sarah's case. She will fill you in on the state of the foetus.'

'Good morning. We believe the state of gestation to be about fourteen weeks. At the moment, the foetus is alive, yes. I am, however, concerned because of Sarah's high temperature. It is currently at 38.5 degrees and rising. Babies are not designed to be incubated in anything but a normal temperature. The higher the foetus's temperature, the quicker it will get through the available oxygen. We also need to control Sarah's blood pressure to ensure good placental function. The problem is that very few drugs are licensed for use in pregnant women and it's not possible to say what effect the drugs we need to use to keep Sarah alive will have on the foetus. As the gestation is only at fourteen weeks, I'm afraid the outlook is extremely poor.'

'Poor, but not impossible,' Adam said. He looked so

wild-eyed, Mia worried he was going to keel over with stress. 'My son can make it. I know he can.'

Ms Johnston remained calm, but Mia could see her jaw twitching. Clearly she didn't know what to say. Suddenly, Johnny leaned down and pulled a bag onto his lap. I've been doing some research and found a study with similar cases, the Heidelberg study. From what I've read, babies have survived in brain-dead mothers.

'Here it says, "*The researchers found that a viable child was delivered in twelve of the nineteen cases they studied. Twelve babies were born and survived the neonatal period. The management of a brain-dead pregnant woman requires a multidisciplinary team, which should follow available standards, guidelines and recommendations.*" '

Adam was staring at Johnny with a half-smile on his lips. 'Now, did you hear that?' he said triumphantly. 'My boy will survive if you all do your jobs. I don't want to hear any more about poor outcome. We all need to stay positive. I am not losing my son.' His voice broke. 'I am not losing everything.'

The room fell silent again.

Ms Johnston explained, 'The foetus is only fourteen weeks. It depends entirely on Sarah for its oxygen and sustenance. Sarah can no longer provide that. Her body has already started to show signs of deterioration, and that will accelerate over the coming days. I'm very sorry, but prolonging Sarah's life won't save the foetus and will be traumatic for all of you.'

Adam stared coldly at her. '*The foetus* is my son, Ben. That's the name me and Sarah had picked. No one is switching off any ventilators.'

'Adam, I know this is awful for you but please listen to what we're trying to tell you,' Angela begged. 'Fourteen weeks' gestation is at least eight weeks before the foetus can reach viability, which means being able to survive outside the womb. And even if it made it to twenty-two weeks and was delivered and had full paediatric ICU care, it's highly unlikely it could survive. And even if it did, the trade-off for extreme pre-term delivery is increased risk of brain bleeds, blindness, lung injuries . . . Adam, you don't want to do that to your son.'

'He can make it,' Adam said stubbornly. 'I know he can.'

Angela bit her lip and looked at her colleagues.

'We'll give you some time and space to process all the information,' Dr Mayhew said gently. 'Let us know when you've decided how you wish to proceed.'

'I don't need time,' Adam retorted. 'You just keep my wife and baby alive.'

Dr Mayhew nodded. 'I'll need you to sign some paperwork. We're here to answer any questions. It's a very traumatic time for you all.' He left the room, followed by his colleagues.

Adam turned to Mia. 'Do you think this woman, Dr Neelan, will find a mistake? Do you think she'll be able to operate on or treat Sarah's brain and make her wake up? Do you, Mia? Do you?' He was like a desperate little boy begging for reassurance.

Mia looked out of the window. Clear blue sky: one of those precious days when you could feel the warmth of the sun wrapping around you, like a blanket. But in here, in this stuffy, overheated room that smelt of fear and grief, all she could feel was the last scraps of hope leaving her mind and body.

The consultants were so sure. Brain dead was dead. Mia had spent hours googling coma and neurology and brain injury. She knew it was a bad idea to ask the internet, but it was impossible not to look for answers. She knew brain dead was final: she'd read it online in black-and-white. *'Brain death is irreversible and is legally and medically recognized as death'*; *'A person who is brain dead may appear alive – there may be a heartbeat, they may look like they're breathing, their skin may still be warm to the touch. But there is no life when brain activity ceases*'; '*A person is con-firmed as being dead when their brain stem function is permanently lost.*'

Despite all of that, Mia had still clung to hope . . . until now. They had done the tests; they had confirmed Sarah's condition. She was gone. Her beautiful sister was gone. Her only sibling, her best friend. Gone. Non-responsive, non-functioning, non-alive.

Gone.

18

The ICU waiting room felt smaller than before. Adam's fizzing energy filled it. The meeting had affected him badly. He was constantly pacing, talking, talking, talking, convincing himself of what he needed to believe. Johnny had headed off to do the school collections. Mia and Charlie sat quietly, watching Adam. There was no point in trying to discuss the situation with him because he was so wound up. Like the doctors, they had to wait until he had processed everything and calmed down.

Mia's phone buzzed and she answered it.

'Hi, Mia. It's Pam Neelan here. I'm with Dr Mayhew now and I'm going to review the case. I'll get back to you when I've gone through it all.'

Mia thanked her profusely and hung up. She filled in Adam and Charlie.

'Fantastic,' Adam said. 'I've a good feeling about this. She's worked in the USA, so she's bound to be right up to the minute. This was a genius move on your part, Mia.'

'Dr Neelan can only review the facts of the case,' Charlie said.

'Exactly,' Adam said, his movements and speech hyper with anxiety. 'The facts. That's all I'm looking for. I'll go and call Rob,' he said. 'I suppose it'll take time for her to get back to us.'

'Definitely,' Mia said quickly. She could do with some time away from Adam, time to think straight. 'You do that, Adam. You could do with a little break. Think over all they said earlier and have a chat with Rob about it.'

Adam said nothing. He headed out of the room. When he was gone, Mia breathed deeply and leaned back in her chair.

The door opened and Mia shot up straight again, but it was just Angela.

'Adam popped out?' she said.

Mia nodded. 'He needed a breath of air.'

'Good,' Angela said. 'That was a very difficult meeting. Are you two OK? Can I get you anything?'

'We're fine, thanks,' Mia said. 'Could we spend some time with Sarah?'

'Give me ten minutes,' Angela said. 'Some of the team are in there with her now. I'll call you when they're gone.'

'Thanks,' Mia said.

Angela left, and Mia looked at her father. 'What do you think, Dad?'

'She's gone,' Charlie said. 'I knew it already, Mia. No amount of opinions are going to bring her back.' He sniffed. 'My little pet, the light of my life. First your mother and now Sarah. It's too much, too cruel.'

'It's not fair. Oh, God, Sarah!' Mia began to cry, reached out to her father and pulled him into a hug. They weren't usually huggers, but she needed him now and he needed her. They were the only two left of their little family unit. 'I'm here for you, Dad. We'll help each other. We'll muddle through – and we have Izzy to look after and mind.'

They clung to each other, crying, until Charlie's phone rang. He pulled back and answered it. Really? He's answering his phone now? Mia thought, feeling hurt.

'Charlie, what's going on?' She heard Olivia's irritating voice booming down the phone.

'Not good,' Charlie said, his voice breaking.

'Oh, Charlie, I'm so sorry. I'm on my way. We'll get through this. I'm here for you.'

'Thanks, that means a lot.' He hung up and looked at Mia. 'Olivia's on her way.'

'Yeah, I heard.' Mia knew it was silly, they were all grieving, but Olivia's offer of support seemed a lot more important to her dad than hers and it stung.

'I don't know what I'd do without her. She's a great woman. She was very fond of Sarah. They got on well from the beginning. Sarah was always very welcoming and warm, Olivia said.'

Unlike me, Mia thought bitterly.

'Right, I'll go down and wait for her outside. Get a bit of air myself. I'll bring her up to see Sarah.' His chin wobbled and Mia felt guilty for being annoyed. The man's heart was broken: did it really matter who he turned to for comfort?

'OK, Dad. I'll be here, and don't worry about Adam. He was just venting when he said he didn't want Olivia here. He didn't mean it.'

'I hate every corner of this bloody hospital. I never want to darken its door again,' Charlie said, as he shuffled off.

Mia saw him out onto the corridor, and as he left, a group of nurses and doctors came out of Sarah's room. Angela walked over to her. 'You can go in and see her now, Mia. It'll be nice and quiet for a while. We've finished washing her.' Angela patted her shoulder. 'It's so tough on you all. She's so young and beautiful. Go on in and talk to her. It'll help you process all you heard at the meeting. I'll try to keep everyone away from the room for a bit.'

Mia thanked her. She entered and sat down. She reached over and held Sarah's hand. It was warm. It was so difficult to believe she was really dead when she looked like she was just sleeping.

'Oh, Sarah, what am I going to do without you? Who am I going to bitch to about Olivia? Who am I going to turn to when I need to give out about Riley and Johnny driving me nuts? Who am I going to boss around? Jesus, Sarah, I can't do this without you.' Mia held her sister's hand to her cheek and sobbed.

When the tears finally subsided, Mia felt about a hundred years old. Her life was falling apart, breaking up and dissolving. She reached into her bag for a pack of tissues, and her hand met the cool leather of Sarah's diary. She took it out and let it fall open at a page. Then she started to read aloud. She needed to hear her sister's words. They'd soothe her, help her . . .

September 2017

'*Why God, why? Just got my period again. It's now been five years and nothing. How can I have got pregnant so easily with Izzy? What's wrong with me? The doctors keep telling me nothing is wrong. Adam's sperm is strong, my eggs are normal. So why isn't it happening?*

'*I want a sibling for Izzy so badly. I want another baby. I love being a mum. It's who I am. It's what I do best. I'm not very good at anything else. Let's face it, I'm never going to get a big important job and earn lots of money. I like being a mum. It fulfils me. I know some people think that's sad and pathetic and all women should be smashing glass ceilings, but I really like being a stay-at-home mum.*

'*I like baking with Izzy and snuggling up and watching Disney movies and going to the park. Mia thinks I should get a job. She says it'll distract me from the baby thing. She says working helped her when she found out that they couldn't have more kids. But I don't want to get a job just to be busy. I want to pick Izzy up from school at 1 p.m. and cherish every moment with her.*

'*Besides, I'm different from Mia, there's nothing "wrong" with Adam or me. We can have more kids. We will have more kids. It's just taking a long time. Mia thinks being alone in the house all morning is bad for me. She thinks I'll get depressed. But I won't. I'd get depressed if I went back to a boring job just to distract myself.*

'Mia likes being a teacher. It gives her great satisfaction. She loves teaching the kids and seeing them thrive. Well, I love seeing my own kid thrive, with me, alone.

'I've never liked big groups and noisy offices and all that chat and bitching about your boss and gossiping about other people. Even when I did work, I always kept out of those conversations. I was nice to everyone but kept my distance. I don't like sitting around giving out about people. I don't see the point of it. If you don't like someone, just avoid them or figure out a way to manage them.

'There was one mum in Izzy's class who kept trying to force me into coming to coffee mornings and boot-camp with some of the other mums. But I didn't want to, so I just kept saying no, in a nice way, and eventually she got the message. I won't be forced into doing anything I don't want to do. I'm no walkover. Mia always says I'm the politest stubborn person she knows. I like that expression – it makes me laugh.'

Mia smiled. She did always say that about Sarah. She was so nice and polite that people often didn't realize how steely she was underneath. If Sarah didn't want to do something, nothing and nobody would make her change her mind.

'It's actually good that I'm free in the mornings because I can take Dad for coffee or a walk while Mum's having her chemo. She hates when he fusses around her. She likes to be left alone to listen to her audio books. She's so like Mia, she hates fuss too.

'Mum can't bear us trying to look after her. She's the one who looks after us. She's the one who minds us when we're sick. She's the one in charge of organizing everything. She really hates being the sick one. But she's been so brave. They said the cancer was aggressive, so they have to fight fire with fire. Poor Mum, she's lost all her hair and she's very weak after the chemo sessions.

'Thank God she only has one more session to go. She's really very worn down from it. I've never seen her so weakened. It freaks me out.

Mum has always been so strong and in control, but now she's like a broken bird. It's just horrible to watch. But her spirit is strong and, as Mia says, if anyone can fight it, it's Mum.

'*Mia's devastated but pretending she isn't. She keeps saying it's all going to be fine because she can't bear the alternative. I'm not so sure. Mum looks terrible and I know it's mostly the chemo but her colour is awful and I'm worried, really worried, that she might not get better. Mia's so close to her she just won't allow the thought of her dying to even enter her mind. I tried broaching the subject yesterday and she cut me dead.*

'"*Sarah, Mum's going to be fine. She's going to get through this and live a long, happy life," she said.*

'*I said nothing. There's no talking to Mia when she's like that. Besides, I know it's only because she can't bear the thought of what could happen.*

'*Poor Dad is devastated about it all. We go for long walks and we chat about everything and nothing. He hasn't ever said it out loud, but I think, like me, he suspects Mum might not get better.*

'*They've been together thirty-seven years. I've only been with Adam eight and I can't imagine life without him. If anything happens to Mum, I'll have to be strong for Dad.*

'*If – no, actually, when I have a baby, if it's a girl, I'll call her Penny after my mum. I really hope she doesn't die. I pray every night for Mum not to die and for me to get pregnant.*'

Mia remembered those dark days well. Her mother, her rock, the strongest person she knew, beaten down by that horrible disease. But even though she was battered and bruised, Mia still saw the spark. Her mother's eyes never lost their light, until the end. Those last two weeks were the worst of Mia's life. Her mother had given up.

'I can't fight any more, love. You have to let me go,' she'd said, one night, in her hospital room.

Mia had selfishly begged her to keep trying. It was Sarah who had pulled her aside and told her to stop. Her sister told Mia she was being selfish, that their mother had suffered enough, and it was time to end the pain.

'If you love her, let her go,' Sarah had told Mia.

So Mia had held her mother's hand, feeling her bones beneath the thin layer of papery skin, puckered with bruises from being jabbed for so many months, and she had said goodbye. 'I love you, and I want you to be at peace. Mum, let yourself go. Thank you for being the best mother a girl could wish for. I feel so lucky to have had you in my life for thirty-five years. You are the most amazing woman. We love you.'

Two days later, her mother had taken her last breath. The pain had knocked Mia sideways. Her anchor was gone, and she'd felt like a boat bobbing around on the sea, lost and alone. Grief was a form of madness – she knew that from bitter experience. And she knew it had Adam in its grip now. She adored Sarah, she wanted her to live, but she knew in her heart that she had lost her.

'You were right, Sarah,' Mia said, rubbing Sarah's hand. 'I couldn't bear the thought of losing Mum. It was so painful to say goodbye . . . and it's too painful now. It's too much. It's just too much.' Mia sobbed, her tears splashing onto the pages of the diary.

Week Two

19

Riley was sitting under the big tree near the athletics track, pretending to read Ingrid Betancourt's account of being kidnapped by the Revolutionary Armed Forces of Colombia while campaigning for the Colombian presidency. She was actually trying to do good, and then she was kept captive for six and a half years before she was finally rescued by Colombian security forces. Stuff like that actually mattered. People like Ingrid Betancourt tried to change the world. How dare Zach tell her she was too intense? How could you just skip through life caring more about jumping over a stupid metal bar than anything else?

Riley fumed inwardly and decided she deserved better. She deserved a boyfriend who knew and cared about the important things in life. Someone who shared her passion for causes that mattered. Who, though? Most of the guys she knew were either sports jocks or maths geeks. The only in-between types were like Shocko and, much as she loved him, she couldn't fancy him if she tried. He was like a brother, he was kind and loyal and, as her mum said, those were two of the most important qualities in a friend.

Riley tried to concentrate on her book, but she was really watching Zoë practise her hurdles. She had to admit she was good – she had great technique and was fast – but she still looked like a complete dork.

Sports Barbie, Riley thought darkly. Her fake-tanned legs were a deep shade of mahogany. And who the hell does athletics with lip gloss on?

The sports coach looked at his stopwatch and whooped.

He went over to high-five Zoë. 'That's your best time this season,' he gushed.

Zoë beamed. Perfect teeth. Those braces she'd worn for two years had paid off. Riley's front teeth had a gap between them. The orthodontist had said he could close it but, in his opinion, it was charming. Mia had agreed, mainly because it was going to save her a lot of money in dental fees.

Mia told Riley she was like some famous supermodel called Lauren Hutton. Riley looked her up, but she was about three hundred years old. So Mia went online and found Elizabeth Jagger and started banging on about her. But Elizabeth Jagger was drop-dead gorgeous, so her gap *did* look cute. Riley was not drop-dead anything. Well, she was drop-dead boring, according to Zach. Anyway, her gap wasn't cute. She hated it. Zach had said he liked it, and for a while, Riley had liked it too, but now she knew everything he'd said was a lie, so she hated her gap again.

Zoë stretched her long, toned limbs. Riley looked down at her own pale, thin arms. Maybe she should take up a sport. But she hated all of them. Her mum had made her play tennis and hockey, and there had been a brief period when she'd dragged Riley to hip-hop dance classes. It had been mortifying. Riley had no rhythm. She just couldn't co-ordinate her arms and legs in time to the music. After three sessions of complete humiliation she went on hunger strike. Of course, her mum wouldn't budge. She said she'd paid for ten sessions and Riley was going to do them, by hook or by crook. But her dad had taken pity on her and stepped in. 'What's the point of making her go?' he'd said. 'All it does is cause a huge argument every week. Let's just write it off as a bad investment.'

Riley did feel bad about the cost of the lessons, but she'd never wanted to go in the first place so it wasn't really her problem.

Riley tried to focus on Ingrid Betancourt's struggles in

captivity. It was all getting a bit repetitive. She knew it wasn't Ingrid's fault, obviously. If you're held captive for six years tied to a tree, there isn't a whole lot of variety to your days. Apart from that, she was distracted by the sound of Zoë's voice, which was being carried to her by the breeze. She was talking to her fellow hurdler and sports Barbie, Kaitlin.

'Yes, it is.' Zoë touched her neck.

'OMG, it's a seriously big love-bite,' Kaitlin said, sounding impressed. 'He's like a vampire.'

'He just can't get enough of me.' Zoë giggled.

Riley clenched the book between her hands. She was hidden by a heavy, leafy branch.

'You guys are just, like, the perfect couple. You look amazeballs together,' Kaitlin said.

'Awww, you are so sweet to say that. He's so amazing and so much fun.'

'I still can't believe he went out with Riley for so long – I mean, seriously?'

'I know. He said he was going through a phase and that she was challenging, which he thought was kind of cool but ended up being a total drag.'

'She's so, like, angry all the time. Seriously, why doesn't she just chillax and enjoy life?'

'I know,' Zoë said, applying more lip gloss to her already glossy lips. 'She's all dark and dreary. Lighten up, dude!'

They chortled. 'Yeah, stop being a Debbie Downer all the time.' Kaitlin cracked up at her own joke.

'That's what we should nickname her, DD, Debbie Downer.' Zoë grinned.

Riley sank down lower behind the foliage. Bitches. How dare Zach say she was a 'phase' and a 'drag'?

Tears landed on Ingrid Betancourt's words. Riley rubbed them away roughly. She'd let Zach in. She'd opened herself up to him and let him touch her, not just physically but emotionally too. Thankfully, she hadn't had sex with him. At least she had that to hold on to. He couldn't say she was a conquest or that she was bad in bed because she hadn't slept with him.

But the hardest part for her was that she'd told him how difficult she found her mother, how she wanted to be close to her but clashed with her all the time. She'd told him it hurt her deep down and she wanted to change their relationship, but they kept locking horns over and over again. He was the only person she'd ever confided that to, and now he'd stamped all over it.

She felt sick when she thought of telling Zach about her hopes and her dreams of becoming a journalist, like her dad. Riley wanted to work for the *Guardian* in London. She wanted to uncover breaking stories, expose fraudsters, crooks, corrupt regimes . . . She had stupidly told Zach all of this. All of these intensely personal things were now in danger of being exposed to and ridiculed by a stupid, insensitive Barbie doll.

'Riley?'

Damn it. Riley pulled her hair down over her face and turned. It was the headmistress of her senior school, Mrs Moloney, and the headmistress of the junior school, Mrs Kelly, who was also her mum's boss. 'We've been looking for you,' Mrs Moloney said.

'We heard about your aunt and we wanted to see how you were doing,' Mrs Kelly said gently.

Riley clambered to her feet.

'It's such a shock for you all. Your mum called me and filled me in. I've told her to take as much time as she needs. It's so difficult, especially for Izzy,' Mrs Kelly said. 'I just wanted to check in with you and let you know that I'll be keeping a close eye on Izzy and you can come and visit her at lunchtime if you like. As you know, we don't normally allow the senior girls to come into the junior playground, but under these circumstances you can certainly come and see your little cousin.'

'Thank you,' Riley muttered. 'I'd like that. Izzy needs to be minded. She was crying in her sleep last night. She's confused. Well, we all are, to be honest.'

She didn't really know what else to say. She hadn't had any further updates on Sarah's condition. She'd texted her dad earlier, but he said he'd had no news from her mum yet.

'We're all praying for your aunt,' Mrs Moloney said.

Riley wasn't too sure how much confidence she had in Mrs Moloney's prayers. She'd prayed for Grace O'Brien's dad last term and he'd died anyway.

'If you ever need or want to talk to someone, my door is open,' Mrs Moloney said.

The only time Riley had ever been in her office was when she was in trouble. She couldn't imagine going in and sitting in that upright chair opposite the principal and pouring her heart out.

Besides, how could she explain the way she felt about Sarah? How could she put into words how the thought of losing her aunt made her unable to breathe? She loved Sarah, like really, really loved her. Sarah was always on Riley's side. When her mum went off on one about something Riley had done or the way Riley had spoken to her, Sarah would wink at Riley and say, 'Come on, Mia, I'm sure Riley didn't mean it like that,' or 'I think you're being a little harsh,' or 'Riley's brilliant and we all love her to bits.'

Sarah was the one person Riley didn't mind getting hugs from. She liked Sarah's hugs: they were warm and genuine. She loved the way Sarah could make her mum laugh. She'd sit in awe as Sarah slagged Mia about something and Mia would just crack up laughing. Mia never got annoyed with her sister for poking fun at her: she loved Sarah too much.

Riley liked the way her mum was when she was with Sarah – relaxed and fun and nicer. Mia was way less narky to her when Sarah was around.

Sarah always tried to look at the positive side of life. When Johnny had lost his job, Riley had overheard her mum telling Sarah. They had gone into the TV room in Sarah's house, leaving Riley and Izzy to eat the brownies Sarah had made. But Riley had snuck out to listen at the door. She knew something bad had happened to her dad and she wanted to know what it was.

Mia was crying and saying, 'What are we going to do? We need his salary . . .'

'You'll be OK, Mia. You're an amazing woman. Johnny is a brilliant journalist and he'll find another job. You have the deputy head job now, so that'll take some of the heat off and you know we'll help you. I'd be delighted to give you money to get you over the hump.'

'Don't be silly. We'll figure it out.'

'I still have the money Mum left me.'

'What? Still?'

'Yes, I never spent it.'

'God, mine's long gone. It went on getting the rotting windows at the front of the house changed and Riley's school trip to Rome. Which she said she hated.' Mia laughed bitterly.

'Come on, Mia, she was only being contrary. She loved it. Remember you coming back from that school trip to Wales and telling Dad it was the worst weekend of your life? It's called being a teenager. Look, I'd be delighted to give you money. Adam's business is flying again and I don't need it. Mum would be thrilled if she knew her money was going to you, Johnny and Riley.'

'I can't take your money.'

'Then let's call it a very long-term loan. Please, Mia, let me do this for you. You've helped me in so many ways. Let me help you. It will make me so happy.'

'No, but thank you. If I get really stuck, I promise I'll come to you for a loan. Knowing I can do that takes the pressure off. Thanks, Sarah.'

Riley could hear the relief in her mother's voice. Good old Sarah, somehow making it seem like Mia would be doing her a favour by taking the money. That day, Riley had fallen even more in love with her aunt.

Sarah always made Riley feel good about herself. Riley knew she wasn't beautiful, but Sarah told her how gorgeous her eyes were and how she had a smile that could stop traffic. She told her to walk tall and not hunch over to hide her height.

'Being tall is wonderful. I always wished I was taller. Being five foot three is rubbish. You have a fantastic figure so show it off. Walk tall and proud. You are a stunner. I wish I had your long legs – skinny jeans look so good on you.'

Riley's mum told her she was gorgeous, but mothers lied to their kids all the time. She'd overheard Sandra Pierce's mother telling her how beautiful she was, and Sandra was by miles the ugliest girl in the year.

Mrs Kelly cleared her throat. 'Of course we'll keep a keen eye on Izzy. I know you're close. She's so fond of you. She was telling me all about your sleepovers. She's such a sweet girl and you seem like a very caring cousin.'

'Good to hear. Keep it up, Riley. Izzy needs all the support she can get right now,' Mrs Moloney said. Glancing at her watch she said, 'Right, time to ring the bell. I'll see you inside, Riley, and remember, my door is open.'

'Thanks,' Riley muttered.

She was afraid to speak. She didn't want to talk about Sarah. It was too much. No, Sarah just had to get better and wake up and be fine. There was no other option. None.

20

Pam Neelan walked into the hospital room where Mia and Adam were sitting, each holding one of Sarah's hands. Charlie was seated in a chair at the foot of the bed; Olivia had gone to visit a friend who was in the hospital, recovering from a hip replacement. Adam jumped up when she entered. She was tall and athletic with an air of authority.

'Mia?' she said. 'Good afternoon, I'm Dr Neelan.'

'Well?' Adam wanted answers.

'Thanks so much for everything. We really appreciate it.' Mia felt it was important to acknowledge her help. After all, neither of them knew her and it was very kind of her to take the time to do this.

'Not at all,' Pam replied. 'Look, I'll get straight to the point. I know you were hoping for good news. I've examined the procedures and measures carried out here and they really did everything they could. I agree with the team's prognosis. I'm so sorry, but Sarah has no brain-stem activity, so there is no hope of recovery. I really wish I had better news.'

Mia gulped back tears. 'Well, thank you for giving us your opinion. I know how busy you are.'

Pam reached out and touched her arm. 'I'm so sorry. It's a terrible and shocking thing to happen.'

Adam grabbed her hand. 'What about the baby? We can save the baby, right? Can't we? I know we can. We've spent hours trawling the internet. There are cases where babies survive. Aren't there, Mia?'

Mia just wanted to lie on the floor and weep for her sister.

She didn't have the energy to hold up Adam and his hopes. She wanted someone to hold her up. She felt as if she was falling down a deep, dark tunnel.

'Mia?' Adam shook her arm.

Mia blinked and forced herself to concentrate. 'Sorry, yes, I did find one case that said, with the advances in medicine and life-support technology, the age of the foetus didn't matter so much. It was a case where a woman had been declared brain dead at sixteen weeks pregnant, but the baby was delivered 110 days later. I know it's not, well, it's not common, but there is hope?'

Pam chose her words carefully. 'It's not my area of expertise. You'll have to discuss this with Ms Johnston. She is an expert in her field.'

'But do you think the baby will make it?' Adam begged.

Pam took a step back. 'You really need to talk to Ms Johnston. I'm so sorry about your wife. I'll leave you in peace.'

'They can't tell you what isn't true,' Charlie said quietly.

'Don't take their side,' Adam said, jabbing a finger in Charlie's direction. 'My son is alive and well.'

Charlie shook his head. 'Ah, Adam, I know how much this hurts, but you'll have to face reality.'

'The reality is that Ben is fighting to survive, and I'm going to do everything in my power to help him.'

'OK, OK,' Charlie said. 'I understand. Let's see what happens.'

'We have to be strong for her,' Adam said, his voice cracking with emotion. 'For her and for Ben.'

The door opened and Angela stepped into the room. 'Sorry to interrupt you, guys, but you have a visitor here. An important one. I've kitted him out in protective gear, so can he come in?'

'Who is it?' Mia said, thinking maybe it was Johnny.

Angela pushed the door wide open and stepped aside. A tall, well-built man walked into the room and his face dropped when he saw the scene before him. 'Oh, my God,' Adam cried. 'Rob!'

Rob opened his arms and Adam walked straight into his embrace. He put his head on his brother's shoulder and wept like a child. Mia felt awkward, witnessing such a private moment of grief, and she motioned to Charlie that they should leave.

Rob held up his hand. 'No, please don't go,' he said. He was crying too, but he held his brother up firmly. 'I'm glad to see you all. Please stay.'

Mia sat back in the chair and focused on Sarah. Rob whispered to Adam over and over, 'It's OK, I'm here,' and slowly Adam's sobs subsided.

'Jesus, I've never been so glad to see anyone in my life,' he said, wiping his eyes with his hand. 'I can't believe you flew over.'

'I couldn't let you go through this alone,' Rob said. 'I know you have Sarah's family,' he said, smiling at Charlie and Mia, 'but it was killing me to talk to you on the phone and not be properly there for you.'

'Thank you,' Adam said, hugging him again. 'Things are so awful, Rob. I'm barely hanging on here.'

'Let's sit down. I want to say hello to Sarah.' Rob swallowed hard as he looked down on Sarah's motionless body. He put his hand on her head and leaned down to kiss her cheek. 'Hey, Sarah,' he said softly. 'I'm sorry I didn't get here sooner. You really need to wake up so we can dish the dirt on this guy.' He looked around at them. 'Has there been any further news?'

'They're saying it's not good,' Adam told him. 'Did you make any headway on finding a neurologist in Toronto?'

Rob nodded. 'Yes, there's a friend of a friend who's at the Scarborough. He said he'd look over all the medical notes and let me know.'

'Great, great,' Adam said, stroking Sarah's arm.

'Adam,' Rob said, 'what did they say to you?'

Adam shrugged. 'I'm not sure if they're on the ball here. I really want another opinion.'

Rob looked at Mia. 'What was the news?'

Mia looked down. 'Em . . . we had a meeting this morning. The team said that Sarah has no brain-stem activity. They said she won't wake up. The life support is keeping her alive. They told us she's . . . uhm . . . that she's gone.'

Rob stared at her. 'Jesus, Adam, I'm so sorry. Can the baby survive?'

Mia looked at Adam. 'We just got a second opinion, and it corroborated the team's conclusion. The baby is still alive, but without the support system of Sarah's body . . .'

'Forget that,' Adam said sharply. 'Ben is alive in there. We're going to focus on that and get him all the help he needs to make it through. They can deliver him early and then we'll care for him.'

Rob looked at his brother, then back at Mia. She could tell that he understood what was happening. 'OK,' Rob said. 'Well, I guess we cling to the positive for now. Right?'

'Exactly. Keep hassling for that opinion,' Adam said. 'We might just get the right answer from your guy.'

'I'll do that,' Rob said.

'I'm so glad you're here,' Adam said. 'Now that you're with me, I feel better. I can't thank you enough.'

'I wouldn't be anywhere else,' Rob said. 'I'm mad about Sarah, you know that. And Ellen really wanted to come, but she couldn't get the time off work.'

'No, that's fine,' Adam said. 'If we do end up moving

Sarah to Canada for treatment, Ellen will be able to help sort it from that end, so it's actually perfect.'

Rob took a deep breath, and Mia could see that he was really struggling to control his emotions. Adam was so hyper and distracted, he was like a different man. The whole thing must be so shocking for Rob – to find Sarah like this, and Adam half crazed with grief. It was all horribly surreal.

The door opened and Angela came in. 'More interruptions,' she said brightly. 'Only me. I just need to do the monitor.'

'Do you want us to leave?' Mia asked.

'I'd really like them to stay,' Adam said quickly.

Angela looked uncertain but she said, 'OK, no problem. It only takes a moment.'

'What's that?' Charlie said.

'It's a Doppler foetal monitor,' Angela said, as she raised Sarah's pyjama top. She placed the device against Sarah's belly and moved it around. There was a sound like radio static, then suddenly the room filled with the pulsing throb of a heartbeat. It was steady and strong. *Du-dum, du-dum, du-dum.*

'See,' Adam said, grinning at them. 'There he is. That's my Ben.'

Mia's heart broke. Oh, Sarah, she thought, your little baby.

'Wow,' Rob said, listening in wonder. 'He's like a little galloping horse.'

Adam laughed. 'Yeah, that's it. He's a fighter, I can tell. Isn't that the most beautiful sound in the world?'

It filled the room, pulsating through each of them. It was the sound of life.

Mia drove home through a fog of tears. She needed to see Riley and Johnny. She needed to be with her little family. She wanted to hug Izzy, too. What were they going to do about Izzy? Adam said he wanted her to think Sarah was still alive and just sleeping. If they were going to save the baby, Izzy needed to think that her mum was sleeping. Getting her head around the reality would be traumatic and unnecessary, he'd said. Mia had felt confused, not sure what her own thoughts were on the matter. She felt Rob was in the same boat. But they had to support Adam because he was in Hell right now.

When she got home, Johnny was cooking dinner for the girls. He was wearing the apron that Riley had bought him for Christmas. It was bright red and said, 'Who needs hair with a body like this?' Johnny had laughed when he'd opened it and put it on straight away. He wore it all the time. It had been a very thoughtful gift. Johnny had struggled with losing his hair. He'd only finally shaved his head in November last year. Mia thought he looked better with it shaved. The receding hairline had been more ageing than the baldness.

It had taken him a few weeks to get used to it, and just as he was beginning to feel better about the hair loss, he'd lost his job.

Riley was upstairs doing her homework and Izzy was watching a movie in the TV room. Mia dropped her bag on the floor and ran to her husband.

Johnny wrapped his arms around her. 'Bad news?'

'She's gone. Pam Neelan confirmed it.' Mia burst into tears.

'What? For sure?' He bent his head against hers and she felt his shoulders shake with sobs. 'Our Sarah. Oh, love, I'm so sorry.' They held each other tightly. He handed her a tissue and wiped his own eyes with the bottom of the apron.

'I can't believe it,' he said, shaking his head. 'I just can't take it in. We didn't get to say goodbye or anything.'

'It's so messed up,' Mia said, sniffing. 'She's dead but she's not. We're keeping her alive for the baby.'

Johnny sighed deeply. 'But she's only fourteen weeks pregnant. I thought it might be viable when I found those few miracle cases online, but hearing what the doctors said, I mean, it makes sense that the poor little thing would likely be severely damaged, doesn't it? He's been through as much as Sarah, and when they said she was going to start disintegrating . . . Man, that's just . . .'

Mia blew her nose. 'I feel so conflicted about it, but Adam wants to try, and I understand that. It's all he has. Sarah would want to try too. I know she would.'

'Fair enough, but he has Izzy to think of now,' Johnny said quietly. 'And I've been doing more research. I have to warn you, love, it says that the dead person's body may deteriorate significantly. It's going to be very hard to watch that. You need to prepare yourselves.'

Mia sighed. 'How can you prepare yourself for anything? I can't believe this is happening. I can't believe my sister is dead because she kind of isn't. She is, but her body isn't. God, it's so hard, Johnny. I feel as if I can't really grieve her because she's not gone, it's not over. It's a nightmare.'

Johnny held her close and rubbed her back. 'What are you going to say to Izzy?'

Mia's face crumpled. 'We have to lie to her and say Sarah's still sleeping. I promised Adam we'd follow his line on this.

He's going to bring her in to see Sarah this evening. He's gone home to shower and get himself together before seeing her. He's a wreck. We can't tell her the truth – it's too awful. How can a seven-year-old process that her mother's corpse is keeping her brother alive? To be honest, we're going to tell everyone that Sarah is still undergoing tests. People will have strong opinions on what's going on and I don't want to hear them. I'm still trying to get my own head around it. Poor Izzy, though, losing her mum so young. It's not fair.' Mia began to cry again.

Johnny dug his fingers into her back. Over her shoulder, he called, 'There she is now. How was the movie, Izzy?'

Mia quickly wiped her face with her sleeve.

'It was good. Mia, is Mummy awake?'

Mia plastered on a big smile. 'Not yet, sweetie, but your dad is going to take you in to see her again tonight.'

'Yes!' Izzy clapped her hands together. 'When will he be here?'

'In about half an hour. I'm hoping he'll join us for dinner, then you two can go and say hello to Sarah.'

'I can't wait to see him,' Izzy said, looking thrilled.

Mia realized that Izzy was bereft of both her parents. Adam was spending every minute at the hospital, so the poor child was probably feeling totally abandoned. Maybe now that Rob was here, Adam could spend more time with Izzy. She needed it.

'You're the best girl ever,' Mia said, smiling at her niece. 'Now come here and give me a big hug.'

Izzy jumped into Mia's arms. She was like a little fairy. Petite like her mum, not tall and big-boned like her aunt.

Izzy looked at Mia's face. 'Your eyes are all red and sad, Mia.'

'I just have a cold and I'm tired because I was at the hospital all night. I'll be fine after some sleep.'

'Right, scamp, are you hungry?' Johnny distracted Izzy. 'Dinner is ready.'

'I'll get Riley,' Mia said.

Riley was hunched over her books in her bedroom. The curtains were closed and the room was dark, except for the lamp on her desk. Clothes and books were strewn all over the floor, but for once Mia didn't care.

She knocked gently on the open door. 'Hey.'

Riley looked up. 'Hi. How's Sarah?'

Mia hesitated. She'd been going to lie, but now she thought Riley deserved the truth and she was mature for her age.

'She's gone, love.'

Riley's jaw dropped. 'What? But I thought ... I ... She can't be, Mum. Sarah can't be dead. She's ... she's ... I just ...' Riley's eyes were wide with shock and grief. 'Mum, please, there must be something they can do?'

Mia bit back tears. 'They can't, love. I'm so sorry. Her brain has stopped functioning. There's too much damage.'

Tears streamed down Riley's face. Mia reached over to her and pulled her into a hug. Riley sobbed into her shoulder. Mia cried silently, holding her daughter, taking a little comfort from their embrace.

Riley pulled back and wiped her face with her sleeve. 'God, Mum, it's just so cruel, to lose Sarah and the little baby too. Poor Adam.'

'The baby is still alive.'

Riley frowned. 'What?'

'Sarah's brain dead, but her body is being kept alive by machines. The baby is still alive. We just have to wait and see if it survives. But the chances are very slim.'

Riley stared at her, open-mouthed. 'Oh, my actual God. That's beyond weird. You're keeping a dead person alive?'

Mia got up and closed the bedroom door. 'Sssh. Keep

your voice down, love. Izzy doesn't know. She thinks Sarah's still asleep. I told you because I don't want to lie to you. It's an impossible situation. I'm devastated. We all are. Poor Adam is beside himself, but we're trying to do what's best for everyone.'

'But . . . how can a dead mother keep a baby alive? A baby needs food and stuff from its mother, doesn't it? I don't understand.'

'It's very hard to understand, I know,' Mia said. 'Sarah's being fed by a tube, and those nutrients are still being passed to the baby by the umbilical cord.'

Riley bit her thumbnail. 'But it just seems . . . like, wrong.'

'Well, there's a very small chance the baby could make it, so we have to try. I think Sarah would want us to.'

Riley crossed her arms. 'Are you sure? It's like some creepy sci-fi film. I think Sarah should just be allowed to be dead and not have her body forced to stay alive.'

Mia didn't want to be questioned about the decisions they were making. She was struggling with it all herself. 'Look, Riley, Sarah was my sister and my best friend and she desperately wanted another baby. She would have done anything to save that baby's life. That's what mothers do. They love their children more than themselves and would do anything to keep them alive.'

Riley was not for turning. 'I think it's wrong, Mum.'

Mia sighed. 'It's complicated, Riley.'

Riley sat down again at her desk. 'It's not complicated, it's wrong.'

Their moment of closeness was over. Mia quietly left the room.

22

The doorbell rang.

'I'll get it,' Izzy yelled, and raced down the hallway.

Mia smiled at Johnny. 'I didn't tell her about the special guest. I thought she'd enjoy the surprise.'

From the hallway they heard the click of the front door opening, then silence, then a high-pitched screech: 'Uncle *Rob*!'

Johnny grinned. 'Yep, I think we can say she enjoyed that.'

Rob came into the room with Izzy clinging to him, like a koala bear. She had her arms wrapped around his neck and wasn't letting him go. He was smiling, obviously delighted with his welcome. 'I'm so happy to see you, Iz,' he said, covering her face in kisses.

'I have to get a hello too,' Adam protested. 'You're hogging my daughter.'

'Silly Daddy,' Izzy said. 'I still love you the best, but I haven't seen Uncle Rob for so long. I missed you,' she said, looking into his eyes.

'My God, Izzy, I won't be able to leave Ireland if this is how I'm treated,' Rob joked.

'Can you stay for a bite to eat?' Johnny asked. 'My exquisite pulled pork is on the menu.'

'Wow, sounds good,' Rob said. 'Can we stay, Adam?'

'Sure, why not?'

Johnny added two settings and called to Riley to bring an extra chair from her room. She came down carrying it and plonked it at the table. 'Hi, Adam,' she said, not meeting his eye.

'You remember Adam's brother, Rob, don't you?' Mia said. 'You met him a few summers ago.'

'Yeah, I remember,' Riley said, giving him a small smile. 'It's good to see you again.'

'This is Riley?' Rob said, eyes wide. 'Wow, you were like Izzy when I last saw you. You're very much a young woman now. What are you, about fourteen? Older?'

'Sixteen soon,' Mia said. 'And still as wonderful.'

They sat down at the table, Izzy chattering. Riley was quiet and morose. Mia was on edge, praying that she didn't tackle Adam about his decision.

'Eat your greens, Riley,' Izzy said. 'You need them to be big and strong. That's what Mummy always says.'

'I'm tall already. You're the one who needs the veg.' Riley could barely look at Izzy. The poor thing had no idea that her life was literally falling apart.

'I'm petite. Mummy says being petite is a good thing. Mummy is petite and beautiful, too. Isn't she, Johnny?'

Johnny looked stricken. 'Yes, pet, she is.'

'I'm bringing my hairbrush in to brush Mummy's hair. She loves when I brush it and I'm going to tell her all about school and my sleepovers here with Riley and I'm going to tell her how much I miss her and how I can't wait for us to be together again at home all cosy.'

Rob covered his mouth with his hand and Adam put down his knife and fork on his barely eaten meal.

'That's lovely, Izzy.' Mia's voice shook.

'You're a great girl,' Johnny said. 'Isn't she, Riley?'

'Totally. Izzy rocks.'

'Is it time to go now, Daddy?' Izzy asked impatiently.

'Sure,' Adam said. 'Let's get off. And would you like to stay here tonight, or at our place with Uncle Rob?'

Izzy looked at Mia and Johnny. 'If it's OK, I'd like to stay at home.'

'Of course,' Johnny said. 'Nothing like your own bed. You can tell Rob all about your Communion and everything.'

'Great,' Izzy said. 'I can tell you the secret, Uncle Rob.'

'Oh, really?' Rob said. 'I love secrets. What is it?'

'On my Communion Day,' Izzy said, bending forward conspiratorially, 'Mummy is going to wake up. She's just resting until the big day. But when she sees me in my dress, she's going to wake up and come home.'

Rob's face froze. He stared at Izzy. With obvious effort, he finally managed to say, 'Wow, Izzy, that's – that's some secret.'

'OK, let's go,' Izzy said, jumping up and heading out to the hallway.

Rob and Adam followed her, looking like they were going to the gallows. Once the front door had closed behind them and Mia had slumped back at the table, Riley turned on her parents. 'It's not right that she goes in there thinking Sarah's coming back when she isn't, ever. You're all lying to her and it's wrong. She should know that her mum is dead.' Riley's eyes filled. 'You all think pretending everything is OK is the right thing to do, but it isn't. It's just lies upon lies.'

Mia leaned forward and pointed a finger at her daughter. 'Listen to me very carefully, Riley. This is not your story to tell. It is up to Adam to decide when he wants to say to Izzy about her mum. It is up to Adam to make decisions about what Izzy should and shouldn't know.'

'I'm not trying to upset Adam,' Riley said, 'but someone has to tell him that lying will only make things worse. Kids hate being lied to.'

'This situation is extremely complicated. It's not for you to decide what Izzy should know. It's for her father to decide. I thought I could trust you with the truth, Riley. Do not, under *any* circumstance, say a word to Izzy. I'm warning you. I've enough to deal with without you upsetting Izzy and Adam.'

Riley felt grief well up inside her. 'I'm sad too, Mum,' she cried. 'I loved Sarah. Maybe someone in this house might remember that.'

Riley fled to her room and slammed the door behind her. Everyone hated her. Her parents, Zach, everyone. She buried her face in her pillow and bawled.

She was a sniffing, red-eyed mess when she heard a knock on the door. 'Please go away. I just need to be on my own for a bit.'

'It's only me.'

The door opened and Riley looked up to see her granddad standing there. She quickly wiped her eyes on her pillowcase, sat up and hugged the pillow to her chest.

'I called in to see Izzy and I heard you were upset.'

'I'm fine. Don't worry about me.'

Charlie was wearing his coat. It seemed too big for him. He looked smaller and thinner, way older and so sad. Riley had to look away from his eyes or she knew she'd start bawling again.

Charlie looked around the dark room. 'It's very gloomy in here. Come on, let's get you out and go for a walk.'

Riley didn't want to go for a walk, she wanted to stay in bed and cry and wallow, but she wasn't going to tell her granddad that. She grabbed a hoodie from the floor and tugged it on. They left the house and turned right towards the local park. It was overcast but not raining. Charlie breathed in deeply. They walked in silence, through the gates of the park and towards the pond.

A breeze gathered, and Riley pulled up her hood to keep her ears warm.

Charlie kept walking. 'How are you doing, pet?'

'I'm all right. Please don't worry about me. I'm so sorry about Sarah, Granddad. I know how much you loved her.' She glanced at Charlie. He'd aged so much in such a short time. He was suddenly like an old man.

'Thank you, Riley. I'm sorry, too. We all loved her to bits. But the person we need to feel most sorry for and protect is Izzy.' Charlie pointed to a bench. 'Let's sit down for a minute. I feel a bit out of breath. It's been a long day.'

'Will I get you some water? Should I run back and get Mum?' Riley was terrified he was going to have a heart attack. What the hell would she do? Please, God, don't let Granddad have a heart attack. Not now, not here. Everyone will blame me.

Charlie sat down heavily on the bench. 'I'm fine, pet, just need to catch my breath.' He stared across the park into the distance. 'What we're all trying to deal with is beyond anyone's imagination. If I saw what is happening to us in a film, I wouldn't believe it. I'm sixty-nine and I can't get my head around any of this, so I can't imagine what it's like for you.'

Riley bit her thumbnail, which was already raw. 'It just seems a bit weird and creepy to keep Sarah's body alive when she's dead. I don't get how the baby could survive in a . . . well, in a dead body.'

Charlie sighed. 'Neither do I, Riley. And, to be honest, the doctors seem to be in shock, too. This is an incredibly rare situation. It's a huge challenge for us to try to understand it and do the right thing by Sarah.'

Riley put her hand into the pocket of her hoodie to protect her stumpy nail. If she bit it any further, it would disappear. 'It's just mad, Granddad, the whole thing. I don't know what to say. I seem to keep saying the wrong thing to Mum. I feel bad because I know she's devastated, but all we seem to do is clash. I want to be there for her, but I don't really know how

I'm supposed to feel or what the right thing to say is because Sarah still seems to be alive. I keep messing up.'

Charlie patted her arm. 'Don't worry about any of that. None of us knows what to say. Your mum loves you more than anything in the world but she's really struggling to deal with this. You do need to try to support her as much as you can. Mia and Sarah were like two peas in a pod. I loved that they were so close. When they were younger, I was worried they mightn't be because they were so different, but as they got older they became inseparable. They could just look at each other and know what the other was thinking. I never had that with my brother – we weren't close at all. They had a very special bond.'

He was right. Sometimes it was as if they could speak without talking. Mia would just look at Sarah and she'd know what Sarah was about to say. Poor Mum, Riley thought, she's lost her best friend *and* her sister. 'I promise I'll try to say the right thing and be a better daughter. How are you doing, Granddad, or is that, like, the dumbest question ever?'

Charlie wrapped his scarf tightly around his neck. 'No, pet, it's not dumb. I think I'm still in shock. I can't believe my beautiful girl is gone. Your children are the most precious thing in the world. To lose one is unthinkable.'

Riley held her breath as Charlie struggled to control his emotions.

'Sarah was the best daughter a man could have wished for. She rang me every day, and when Penny died, she called into me every day to check on me, to make sure I wasn't in bed getting depressed. She was one in a million. Her loss is going to leave a huge hole in my life and in all our lives. No parent should ever have to bury their own child. It's not the law of nature. It's wrong on every level. The only good thing is that Penny isn't here to see this. It would have killed her.'

Riley wanted to say something to make him feel better. But what? 'I guess it's good that Gran died, then. I mean, not good that she died, but you know . . .' Jesus, what was wrong with her? She was a walking liability. She'd better just say nothing from now on.

Charlie patted her knee. 'I know what you meant. At least Penny is up there, with Sarah, able to look after her.'

'But . . . is Sarah actually dead, Granddad?'

'Yes.'

'But not totally dead?'

'No.'

'It's so . . .'

'Unreal?'

'Yes,' Riley said.

'To think that last week my only worry was that Olivia would find the KitKat wrapper in my car.' Charlie laughed bitterly.

'She can't give out to you now,' Riley said. 'You can eat as many KitKats as you want. Would you like me to go to the garage and get you one now?'

Charlie smiled. 'No, thank you, pet. But I might need one over the next few days.'

'Anytime, Granddad.'

'And if you need to talk, just pick up the phone and call me.'

Riley felt a wave of love for him. Here he was worrying about her, when his poor heart was broken. She hugged him. 'I love you, Granddad.'

'I love you, Riley.'

They sat on the bench, holding each other in silence as the light faded and disappeared altogether.

23

Johnny and Mia stood at the counter of the hospital coffee shop, waiting for their coffees to be made up.

'I'd say you'd like some time with Sarah alone,' Johnny said. 'I'll sit in the waiting room, and when you're finished, I'll pop in and say hi to her.'

'Say hi – it seems mad. We all treat her as if she's alive, even though she isn't,' Mia said quietly.

Mia hated the hospital, but she liked being in the room alone with her sister. It was the only place she felt at peace. Just she and Sarah, sitting quietly side by side. Sometimes she was silent, sometimes she talked to her sister, and sometimes she read her diary. It was the place Mia most wanted to be all the time.

Outside Sarah's room, the hustle and bustle of the hospital went on: machines beeping, doctors and nurses rushing about, laughing, chatting, gossiping, occasionally crying, and raised voices . . . Life went on. But in Sarah's room, when they'd finished checking her and prodding her and poking her and moving her and cleaning her, there was peace. Izzy's family portrait was stuck on the wall beside Sarah's bed, bringing some much-needed colour to the magnolia walls. Mummy, Daddy, Izzy and baby – she had labelled each of her stick characters. Sarah had long yellow hair and a big red smile.

Mia knew intellectually that her sister was dead, but in that room, when they were alone, Sarah didn't feel dead. She still seemed alive, and Mia felt close to her. Being in there was like a drug, an addiction, because it took away the pain of the truth. Mia wanted to run far away from the truth whenever she could.

Their last tiny sliver of hope had been dashed that morning when the Canadian neurologist had called Rob to concur with the prognosis. It had been the final punch to the gut.

'You look worn out, love.' Johnny took the steaming coffees from the counter and handed Mia hers. 'Please try to get home for some rest this afternoon. I'm worried about the toll this is taking on you.'

What was the point in trying to rest? Mia couldn't sleep. She'd nod off for about thirty minutes, then jerk awake and remember. Her mind would not stop whirring. Rest was not an option right now.

Johnny was pouring sugar into his coffee when a voice behind them said, 'I heard about the pregnant woman in here in a coma. I believe they're keeping her alive as an incubator.'

Mia's blood ran cold. She flicked her eyes to a good-looking young man chatting to the cashier.

'I know, isn't it desperately sad?' the woman said, as she took his money.

'God, the poor family,' he said insincerely. 'I know them a little bit, actually. Our kids go to the same school. Is there any hope she'll come out of the coma?'

'No,' the cashier said. 'Apparently not.'

'God, what a nightmare. Can the baby survive?'

Mia stepped forward, but Johnny grabbed her arm. 'Don't,' he hissed.

'No one really knows,' the cashier said, handing him some change. 'The doctors and nurses looking after the woman are in bits. I see them coming in here for their coffees so upset. They've never dealt with anything like it before.'

'Terrible situation. Do you know any of the doctors'

names? Maybe I could talk to them. My brother's a consultant in New York. Maybe he could help.'

Now the cashier seemed suspicious. 'No, I don't, and it wouldn't be right anyway.'

'Sure, yes, of course – I was only thinking if I could help in any way . . .'

The cashier looked past him to the next customer. He took his coffee and left.

'Johnny!' Mia was shaking with rage and fear. 'Do you recognize him?'

'No, but he's definitely a journalist. Tabloid, I'd say. Don't move.'

Johnny handed Mia his coffee and ran after the young man while Mia tried to figure out how he'd heard about Sarah. Only the family and some of the school staff knew. Then again, Izzy's class parents knew that her mum had collapsed and was 'asleep'. Two of the nice ones had texted Mia to say how sorry they were and that they'd be happy to look after Izzy. It probably wouldn't take a genius to figure out that she was in a coma. And they all knew Sarah was pregnant because, according to Vanessa Dixon, Izzy had proudly told the class last week in Show and Tell. People talked. Damn it. This could not get out. It would be a complete disaster.

No one outside the immediate family and the ICU staff knew that Sarah was brain dead. They'd specifically requested that the hospital keep that information on complete lockdown. They knew that if the news leaked and people found out they'd have opinions on it. Even they, Sarah's own family, didn't know what to think about it. The last thing they needed was other people knowing the awful truth. They had to stop this story getting out. It would be a media circus.

Mia went to the hospital entrance. People streamed in and out, visitors holding flowers and bags, patients smoking in hospital gowns. Some patients chatted in groups with family and friends, others stood alone, looking forlornly into the distance.

Mia wanted to shout at them: *Be grateful for your life. My sister is dead. Stop smoking. Don't ever take your health for granted. Appreciate what you have, hold your loved ones close and tell them you love them, because you never know when they may be ripped from you.*

Johnny walked back towards her, flushed.

'Well?'

'I got to him. He's new and hungry. He heard about it from his girlfriend, who heard about it from her friend who has a kid in your school. I told him to let it go and have some consideration for the family, but he couldn't give a toss. He knows it's a good story.'

Mia grabbed Johnny's jumper sleeve. 'What are we going to do?'

'He writes for the *Irish Daily News* which is owned by the *Irish Express*. I know Jimmy Dolan, the editor-in-chief. I'll talk to him and ask him to quash the story. He's tough, Jimmy, but he's a decent man. Don't worry. I'll sort it out, no matter what.'

Mia buried her face in his chest. 'Thank you. I'd die if it got into the papers. It would push all of us over the edge. This is our private pain and we don't need people judging us.'

'We'll have to talk to the staff here and the doctors, put a stop to any information being leaked. All information about Sarah has to be contained. I'll find Dr Mayhew and talk to him while you're with Sarah. Then I'll arrange a meeting with Jimmy Dolan.'

Mia leaned into her husband and welcomed his taking control of the situation. She didn't have the energy for it. All she wanted to do was be with her sister. It was all too much. 'Can you not just ring him?' she said desperately, wanting it sorted right now.

'It'll be harder for him to say no to quashing the story when I'm standing in front of him.' Johnny's jaw was set. 'See you later.'

Mia knew she could trust him to sort it out. She made her way back upstairs to ICU. In the reception area she bumped into Angela. The whole family had fallen a little in love with her – she was a saint in a uniform. Her little kindnesses, timely pats on the back, words of encouragement and cups of tea had kept them all going during the seemingly never-ending days and nights.

'Good morning, Mia.'

'Hi, Angela.'

'How are you today?'

'A bit freaked out, actually.' Mia filled her in on the journalist.

Angela was furious. 'Bloody scumbag. How dare he try to get a story out of this? Don't worry, I'll talk to all the staff here and make damn sure that no one says a word.' She squeezed Mia's arm. 'Now you go in there and be with your sister and I'll sort out some sugary tea for you after that shock.'

Mia wanted to weep with gratitude. 'Thanks.'

'The occupational therapist has just left, and Adam has gone off for a meeting with the consultant neurologist, so it's a good time to go in.'

'How is Sarah today?'

'I wanted to mention it before you saw her. She's a little swollen, but it's just fluid, so don't be alarmed.'

'Is it affecting the baby?'

'The baby seems fine, but the doctors will be keeping a close eye on it.'

Mia put on the protective gear and went into the room. She was glad Angela had forewarned her: Sarah's whole body had swollen. Mia gasped at the sight of her. Sarah would hate to look puffy. She was always so careful not to put on weight. Unlike Mia, who was always thin and never put on weight no matter what she ate, Sarah had always had to be careful with her diet. Mia reckoned their different metabolisms were down to her being a worrier and Sarah being laidback. Mia worried her weight off, while Sarah's positive attitude made her less nervy and thus more prone to gaining pounds.

But Sarah had incredible willpower so she ate very healthily, exercised every day and only allowed herself a few treats now and then. She baked brownies, cakes and scones that everyone else ate. Mia didn't know how she did it. She herself had tried to give up alcohol once and lasted three days. Life's too short: I want a beer or a glass of wine after work and I'm not going to feel guilty about it, she'd told herself on day three, as she'd popped the top off a bottle of beer.

Mia took a deep breath and sat down. 'Don't worry, Sarah. You're only a little bloated, still gorgeous,' she whispered. She took her sister's hand in hers. 'I wish you were here to go through this with me. Everything is such a mess. I need you.'

Sarah remained stock still, the machines breathing for her. Mia sighed and took out the diary. She still hadn't told any of the others about it, but she felt that Sarah wouldn't mind her keeping this one thing for herself. She turned to the back of the book and read Sarah's last entry. What were her sister's last thoughts?

April 2018

'*I'm having a son!!!!!!!!!!!!!!!!!!!!!!!!!!!!!*

'*I had the scan today, and it's a boy! Oh, thank you, God, for this beautiful baby. I know it's going to bring such joy to our family.*

'*Adam didn't make it to the scan and I was furious, but he was so emotional when I told him he was going to have a son. I'm so happy to*

188

be able to give him this. Our family will be complete. A beautiful little
girl and now a boy too. I can't wait to hold him in my arms. I hope he
looks like Adam, dark hair and gorgeous hazel eyes.

'Izzy is so like me, blonde and blue eyes, and I'd like Adam to have
his own mini-me. He is already talking about teaching our baby foot-
ball and taking him to rugby matches and watching Star Wars *with*
him. It's so lovely to see him so excited.

'I can't wait to go shopping for baby clothes. I know you shouldn't
tempt Fate, but I have a really good feeling about this baby. I just know
everything is going to be OK.'

Mia covered her mouth with her hand. To read her sister's
words and feel her joy leap off the page was agony. She
reached over and touched Sarah's cheek. 'I'm so sorry – this
should never have happened. You should still be here, enjoying this pregnancy and this baby. It's just not fair.'

Mia looked out of the window. Rain was coming down in
sheets. Black clouds covered the sky. It was weather for ducks
and shattered dreams. She shuffled around in the chair and tried
to get comfortable, but a body racked with grief is never still.

'I wanted to go shopping this morning, but I got a rotten headache. I'm
too scared to take any painkillers for it but it's pretty bad. I actually
had to pull over after dropping Izzy to school because my eyesight got
blurry.

'I'm in bed now resting and it's getting a little better. I'm probably low
on iron. I'll pop into the chemist on my way to collect Izzy and get some.

'I've had a few bad headaches with this pregnancy. I didn't have any
with Izzy, but I felt much more nauseous on her pregnancy. I was
constantly retching into the sink when I was pregnant with her. But it
passed after fifteen weeks. I'm sure these headaches will pass too.

'Anyway, who cares about a few headaches or nausea or any of it? I
have a beautiful daughter and I'm going to have a gorgeous son. It's so

worth it. I hate hearing women moaning about being pregnant – how hard it is and how they hate being "fat". It makes me so cross. First of all, you're so lucky to be pregnant, it's a blessing and not everyone is lucky enough to have children, and second of all, you're not fat, you have a baby inside you.

'Mind you, shifting Izzy's baby weight after she was born was a struggle. I used the excuse to eat for two when I was pregnant, and it took me a year to shift that extra stone. I'm going to try to be healthier in this pregnancy.

'I loved my bump with Izzy. This one isn't showing yet, but I can't wait until it is. I'll walk around sticking it out proudly. Dad is so thrilled. His eyes were all watery and he kept saying, "A grandson, imagine that."

'I think he would have liked a son. I know he adores Mia and me, but sometimes there were just too many women in the house for him. I'm so happy he's happy. He said he couldn't wait to tell Olivia. He really likes her. More than we realized. I'm glad he's happy, but she can be a little annoying. She doesn't bother me that much and she's nice to Dad, which is all that really matters, but Mia can't stand her and, being Mia, she doesn't exactly hide it. She can be quite rude at times. I know it bothers Dad. I said it to Mia, but she got all grumpy and said I was being fake-nice and she didn't do fake.

'She's so stubborn at times. I told her it was better to be fake-nice and not hurt Olivia's or Dad's feelings than always to say exactly what she thought. I reminded her that she has to be diplomatic in her job at school and she should try using those skills with Olivia too.

'I know why Mia hates Olivia so much – she's not Mum. Mia can't stand the thought of Mum being replaced. But Olivia isn't replacing her, and she never will. Mum was Mum. Olivia is just someone who is nice to Dad and keeps him busy.

'But Mia doesn't want Dad to move on: she wants the house to remain exactly the same. But Dad deserves to be happy. We all do. Mia needs to get over herself.'

Mia bristled. 'Get over myself! Huh. Thanks, Sarah. I'd like to see how you'd have reacted if the situation was reversed. I'd like to see how blasé you'd have been if Dad had died first and Mum had rocked up with some silver fox, who was all over her. I don't think you'd have liked it one bit, and you'd have found it a lot harder to be "fake-nice" to him.'

'I'm worried about Izzy feeling left out. She's mentioned one or two things about the baby taking up all of my time and wondered whether I'll love her the same when he's born. I've really tried to reassure her. I want her to know how loved and cherished she is. I want her to love her brother and not resent him. It's so important that they bond well. I don't know what I'd do without Mia. Even if she drives me nuts at times, and I know I bug her too, she's my person. No one in the world has my back like Mia and I'm the same with her. I'm allowed to give out about her from time to time, but when Adam does, it makes me furious.

'He finds Mia too strident – they clash all the time. I've tried to suggest to Mia that she doesn't pull him up on everything he says that she disagrees with, and I've said the exact same thing to Adam, but they can't help themselves. They disagree on so many things. If Mia says black, Adam says white.

'Adam told Mia last week that she was way too strict with Riley and that all her controlling was going to achieve was to push Riley away. He told her to chill out and let Riley live a little or she'd ruin her relationship with her daughter. He meant it in a nice way, because he loves Riley, but it came out a bit strong and preachy. Besides, no one wants to be told how to raise their kids, especially not Mia.'

Mia remembered it well – it was only a few weeks ago. She'd been furious with Adam for telling her how to raise her child. She remembered exactly what she'd said: 'You have no idea what it's like to have a teenager. Just you wait until

191

Izzy is fifteen. Then you'll see how bloody hard it is. It is my job to keep Riley safe from all the pitfalls out there and I don't appreciate your criticism. Keep your opinions to yourself.'

Adam was an authority on everything. He knew best. Well, he sure as hell didn't know what it was like to deal with an emotional, cranky, self-centred teen. Mia had watched her lovely smiley child turn into a sulky stranger who lashed out at her all the time. Mia had been to the talks and listened to the experts and read books about how to raise happy teens, but the reality of the day-to-day grind of dealing with Riley's moods, trying to keep her safe but giving her some independence, was the most challenging thing she'd ever faced.

Well, she'd thought it was the most challenging thing until now. Sarah had brought a whole new meaning to 'challenging'. It was amazing that in one moment your life changed. In just one tiny second, it can shatter until it's unrecognizable. One minute you're worried about your teenager getting drunk at a party, and the next your sister collapses and dies. Just like that. It all seemed so ridiculous.

'I felt bad for Mia. Adam and I don't know what it's like to have a teenager and I can see that Riley is challenging, but she's still the sweet girl underneath all that angst. Mia is tough on her. I know she worries she'll go off the rails with drink and even drugs, but Riley's got her head screwed on. Mia raised her to be strong-minded and not someone who will follow the herd. She's tough like Mia on the outside but all soft and kind and loving like Mia on the inside.

'Hopefully it's just a phase and they'll find each other again soon. They were such pals when Riley was younger – they need to find their way back. I know they will. Mia loves Riley more than anything and Riley adores her mum. They'll figure it out. I'm going to tell Mia to be more patient. It will definitely help things if she stops reacting so strongly

to Riley's moods. I know Mia is stressed and under pressure now, with Johnny losing his job, but I also know that Mia will be happier if she can reconnect with Riley.'

Mia laid the book on the bed and propped her elbows on her knees, cradling her face with her hands. 'You're so right, Sarah. It would really help if I could get back on track with Riley. I miss my daughter so much, the funny, lively girl I used to know. I'll try to be more patient, I promise.'

Mia was just closing the diary when a piercing alarm went off, splitting the silence. Within seconds, the door burst open and nurses and doctors swarmed into the room. Mia was briskly ushered out and the door was closed tight.

She stood outside in the corridor, clutching her sister's words to her chest, tears streaming down her face.

24

Riley sat looking at the back of Zach's neck. He was so close she could almost touch him. Drama was the only class they were in together. Riley was in the top stream for all the other subjects. Zach was in the second or third, and Zoë was in the bottom for all except French because she'd lived in France for the first nine years of her life, and her parents had a holiday house there. She added French words into conversation, like she was so bilingual she couldn't help herself. It was incredibly annoying and pretentious. Riley had actually heard her say, 'I love *pommes*, don't you? OMG, I obvs meant apples. What am I like?' Riley had almost puked.

Riley loved and hated seeing Zach now. Mostly she hated it but, like a scab you pick until it bleeds, she also liked seeing him, even though it hurt.

She inhaled deeply and could just make out his deodorant. Lynx Dark Temptation was the one he wore. She'd bought it and used to – OK, still did – spray it on her pillow.

Thankfully, Zoë didn't take drama so at least she was spared her nauseating perfume. Zoë drowned herself every five minutes in Victoria's Secret Bombshell. It made Riley want to gag. Every time Zoë walked by, she left a trail of sickly stink behind her.

Riley wore Comme des Garçons Floriental. It was a unisex perfume and smelt amazing. Sarah had given it to her last Christmas – she always gave her the coolest presents. It had even more meaning to her now. Riley held her wrist to her nose and inhaled. She fought a wave of emotion as she pictured

Sarah's face when her aunt was giving it to her. She pushed it down. Not now, not in school.

Zach used to say he loved her perfume. He said he hated really flowery scents. He'd obviously got over it or had had a permanent blocked nose since he'd started seeing Zoë.

Riley wanted to lean over and kiss his neck. She wanted to sit in his lap and tell him all about Sarah and the baby and how horrible everything was. She wanted to tell him how she was waking up every night crying because she didn't really understand how her aunt could be dead but not completely dead, and that she kept having the same nightmare – that the baby was a blackened, shrivelled corpse inside Sarah's body.

She missed him so much. She needed him. She needed his love. Why did he have to go off on her now, at the worst time in her life?

Riley forced her eyes away from his neck and focused on peeling off her navy nail varnish.

'Right, class. I've divided you up into pairs,' Mr Warren announced. 'I want you to work on a little project that I'm calling The Reasons Why. Each of you will have a book or play that you are to defend or disparage. I want a comprehensive paper delivered to me in three weeks' time with both sides of the argument clearly laid out. The best arguments for and against will win a prize. The prize will be . . . drumroll, please . . . two tickets to see Michael Fassbender starring in *Death of a Salesman* here in Dublin, in June.'

Oh, my God. Riley adored Michael Fassbender. He was awesome. She wanted those tickets badly. Mr Warren read out the pairs. 'Sam and Fiona, Harry and Juliette, Riley and Zach . . .'

Wait! What? Riley froze. Did he say Riley and Zach? She heard Harry snigger and mutter, 'Awkward.' She could feel her face turning a deep shade of scarlet. She ducked her head and let her hair fall around her, like a protective curtain. Damn it – Zach? Really?

'Dude, shocker getting paired with your psycho ex,' Harry hissed across at Zach. 'Be careful not to piss her off – she might stab you.'

Riley's blood boiled. 'The only person I'd bother stabbing is you, you ginger moron,' she hissed back.

'I might be ginger, but at least I'm not a freak show who burns her ex's stuff outside his house. Who does that?'

Riley looked up from behind her hair. 'I do, and I'll torch your precious mountain bike if you don't fuck off.'

'You wouldn't dare.'

'Wouldn't I?' Riley glared right at him. 'Do you really want to find out?'

'You're officially insane.'

'Dude, leave her alone,' Zach said.

'What's going on down there?' Mr Warren asked, from the front of the room. 'I don't want any comments about pairing. You are to work with the partner assigned to you and that's that.'

At the end of class, as everyone else made a dash for the door, Zach turned around slowly in his chair. 'How do you want to do this?' he asked. Those were the first words he'd spoken to her since the night she'd burned the stuff on the lawn. 'Once we decide on a book or play, we could each do our own part separately, then just submit it?'

So, he couldn't bear to be alone with her even for a minute. Riley hoped her face didn't betray how hurt she was. 'Sure, yeah, whatever.'

'What do you want to write about? I'll let you choose. I'm sure you have strong feelings about some play or book. But can you not choose something, like, totally intense?'

Riley's eyes narrowed. 'Sure, Zach. Why don't we do, let's

see, how about *Diary of a Wimpy Kid*? Is that good for you? Not too intense? Not too much to deal with? Not going to bore you? Funny enough for you? I don't want to ruin your life with my extreme choices or opinions, I mean, God forbid we'd actually do something that matters.'

Zach sighed. 'Come on, Riley, give me a break.'

'Like you gave me but didn't tell me? The break we were having but you forgot to mention?'

'Well, the next time you decide to crap all over someone's ambitions, I'd advise you to keep your opinion to yourself.'

'I've apologized for that, Zach. Come on, get over it already.'

'Your opinion mattered to me.'

Riley felt her chin wobbling. 'I'm sorry, Zach . . . Look, can you give me a break here? I'm going through a really shit time. My aunt is . . . she's . . .' A sob escaped Riley's lips. She didn't want to fall apart in front of Zach so she fled the room, ran to the toilets and locked herself into a cubicle. She put a hand over her mouth to muffle her sobs.

After five minutes, she began to calm down. She sat on the toilet lid and fished her concealer out of her bag. She'd have to try to hide her red, puffy eyes. She was about to unlock the cubicle door when she heard voices.

'OMG, Zoë, what a shocker for you,' someone said. It sounded like Danni Gard, but Riley wasn't sure.

'What are you talking about?' Zoë's voice said.

'Haven't you heard? Zach got paired with Riley, or should I say Debbie Downer, in drama. They'll be working together for weeks on some big project. Just the two of them.'

Riley held her breath.

'So what?' Zoë snapped. 'Zach is so over her. He can't stand her. He said she's all obsessed with people who, like, want to change the world and stuff and she totally doesn't get athletics. Look at her! She's a freak who wants to stay inside and read boring books about boring people no one gives a crap about. Zach will be furious he's stuck with her boring arse as a partner. I feel sorry for him. I'd better find him and cheer him up.'

Riley pulled out more toilet paper to wipe her tears. Zach was gone. She had to forget about him. He didn't even want to spend a minute alone with her doing a project. It was obvious he hated her.

The bell rang for break. Riley picked up her bag and headed out to the junior school playground to check on Izzy. At least she could do something right and help her little cousin. To hell with Zach, her aunt was dead and her cousin needed her.

25

Mia, Adam, Rob and Charlie paced up and down the ICU waiting room. What was going on? Mia had texted them immediately, thinking the alarm might have signalled the end. They had arrived in the last half-hour, all terrified. So far, no one had told them anything.

In the corner of the waiting room sat a woman of about seventy, her eyes closed, holding a set of rosary beads. She was praying quietly, completely immersed. It looked soothing, Mia thought. The woman's husband had been rushed in with kidney failure, but Mia had heard one of the doctors telling her that he was going to be all right.

Angela came out and told the woman she could see her husband. She stood up, calmly placed her beads in a little leather pouch and went out into the corridor.

'They'll talk to you shortly,' Angela said. 'Don't worry.'

The old woman's poise and composure were in stark contrast to Adam's mutterings and the rage Mia felt against the world. She had tried praying, but it had given her no peace. Seeing the woman and the comfort her rosary had given her, Mia wished she had stronger faith. To find consolation in some higher being would be a relief, but for her, no God could explain this or answer the questions she had. There was no God. How could a compassionate and loving God destroy Sarah's life? Mia envied the woman her faith, but she knew she'd never find solace there. There was no 'meaning' to this situation: it was just awful, terrible, random bad luck. People were always saying there was a reason for everything.

Bullshit. Sarah's death had no meaning: it was just the world being cruel and heartless.

After what seemed like hours, Dr Mayhew finally came in to talk to them. He looked exhausted.

'Is my baby OK?' Adam demanded.

'We had to perform an emergency ventriculostomy to treat the raised intracranial pressure by draining CSF and blood to relieve increased pressure inside Sarah's skull from the brain swelling. This basically means that Sarah now has a drain in her skull. It's vital that this does not become infected, so we will have to be extremely vigilant about visitors wearing protective clothing and gloves, too, now at all times.'

'And Ben?' Adam croaked.

'The foetus remains stable as of now,' Dr Mayhew said.

'Thank God!' Adam cried.

Charlie stepped forward. 'This drain, will it stay in permanently?'

'For the time being, yes.'

'What happens if it does get infected?'

Dr Mayhew paused. 'We must hope that it doesn't, and we'll do everything to ensure that it doesn't.'

'But what happens if it does?' Charlie persisted.

'An infection in Sarah's bloodstream would travel to the foetus and result in the rupture of the membranes, causing a pre-term delivery.'

Charlie's face was white. 'Jesus Christ, it's not right. None of this is right.'

'Ben's alive, Charlie. That's all that matters now,' Adam said.

'Charlie's just in shock,' Rob said gently. 'It's a very difficult situation, Adam.'

'No, it's not. It's perfectly straightforward,' Adam said, his voice rising. 'Ben is alive and that's our only focus.'

Dr Mayhew muttered that he had to check on Sarah and exited the room, leaving them to argue.

Charlie stood facing Adam. 'Sarah should die in peace. She's not an incubator, she's my daughter and she's dead. We need to let her go and bury her with dignity. This is not natural, Adam.'

'You don't understand, Charlie. This is Sarah's doing. She's fighting to keep the baby alive, and we have to help her.'

'No, she isn't, Adam. She's dead, son. The machines are keeping her body alive, not Sarah. She's full of tubes and drips and now she has a drain in her skull. Please, Adam, we need to let her go. No baby can survive in a dead mother's body for months.'

Adam stepped forward aggressively and shoved a finger into Charlie's face. 'While my son has a heartbeat, we will be keeping Sarah alive.'

Rob came and stood between them, making sure Adam didn't get any closer to Charlie.

'But she's not alive! I keep telling you – she's dead!' Charlie shouted. 'I was there at that scan you missed. I saw that little boy. I'd do anything to save him, Adam, but he can't survive in a dead mother's body. Cop yourself on and see the reality here.'

Adam looked as if he'd been slapped. 'He might, Charlie . . . he might survive. You aren't God. You can't tell me for certain that he won't. Ben is the priority here, and nothing and no one else matters. *I* will decide what happens. Me. That's my wife in there and my son, and I'll do anything to save him.'

The two men stared at each other, breathing heavily.

'Hey now,' Rob said quietly. 'Let's just take a step back.' He put his arm around Adam and physically moved him away. 'How about we go get a coffee?' he said, then steered his brother out of the room, casting a worried glance at Charlie.

The door closed, and Charlie turned to Mia, who was sitting quietly in the corner.

'Have you nothing to say? You normally have plenty to say about everything. You think it's OK, do you, your sister being used to keep alive a foetus that isn't going to make it? Her body is going to start deteriorating. It's inhuman. It's wrong, Mia. It's wrong.'

Mia felt nauseous at the thought of her sister's body breaking down. She couldn't bear it. 'I understand where you're coming from, Dad, but I can see Adam's point, too. While there is a chance of saving the baby, however tiny, he has to try. He'd have to live with the guilt afterwards if he didn't. Sarah wanted this baby more than anything. She was so happy to be pregnant. I really think she'd want us to try.'

'But the child won't survive. It'll be for nothing.'

Mia looked at her father, and knew he was at the end of his tether. This was killing him. 'Medicine has come a long way. Who knows what'll happen? Look, Dad, the whole situation is horrific. None of us can get our heads around it. I don't know what to say to people. My principal rang me and asked how Sarah was and I didn't have the words. So, I just said she's still non-responsive, but I'm not sure how long I can keep that up. When people find out, they'll have an opinion and I don't want to hear it. No one knows what it's like or what they'd do until they're in the situation. If you'd asked me a month ago if I'd think it was right to keep my dead sister alive as an incubator, I would have said no. But here we are, and the baby still has a heartbeat, so . . .'

Charlie sat down and rubbed his eyes. 'What a mess. What a total and utter mess. I can't mourn her, and I can't not mourn her. I think limbo might be worse than Hell.'

Mia reached over and squeezed his hand. 'I know what you mean.'

'How's Izzy?'

'She's holding up well, but I think Adam being in the hospital all the time is upsetting her too. She's so close to Sarah, and misses her so much, that she needs her dad now. But in fairness to Adam, he needs to be here for Sarah and the baby. I'm finding it impossible to explain it to Izzy. There is no explanation that a seven-year-old could possibly understand.'

'The poor little mite. I never even knew a situation like this could exist. I feel like I'm in a madhouse.'

Mia sighed. 'I'm hanging on by my fingernails. I just don't want this to break the family apart. That would really upset Sarah, if she was the cause of a falling-out. That's why I feel we have to back up Adam, even though it's incredibly difficult.'

Charlie didn't look convinced. Who was right? Charlie or Adam? What was the right thing to do? After reading Sarah's diary, Mia felt that Sarah would have wanted the baby to have the best chance possible. For now, while her heart went out to Charlie, she agreed with Adam.

26

Riley was in her room with Shocko, riffling through her bookshelf. Shocko was looking in her full-length mirror, admiring his new eyebrow piercing. 'It looks so good.'

'Are you allowed to wear it in school?'

'No. I'll have to take it out tomorrow morning and put it back in when I get home.'

'What did your parents say?'

'Dad told me I looked like a gobshite and Mum said she hoped it got infected because that would serve me right.'

Riley grinned. 'Well, if it makes you feel any better, I think it looks kind of cool.'

'Thanks. Me too.'

Riley threw another book onto the floor. The pile was getting higher. 'Damn it, I just can't decide which one to choose for the drama project.'

'Why don't you do that one you were telling me about? The one with the woman who wanted to be president of Brazil, then got kidnapped and tied up in the jungle for, like, a decade.'

'Ingrid Betancourt, it was Colombia and, no, Zach will just moan about how *intense* it is. I need something else.'

'I thought that book sounded good. If I was in your school and we got paired up, I'd be happy with it.'

'It is an incredible story, but I want to choose something Zach can't complain about.'

'The dude seems to complain about everything you do.' Shocko walked over to Riley's desk chair and picked up her guitar. He strummed it tunelessly. Riley wished he'd learn to play properly. She had offered to teach him but he wanted to learn organically, he said. In Shocko's case, that meant never at all.

Riley threw an armful of books onto the bed. 'I need help, Shocko. Which one would you choose?'

Shocko picked up the books and read out the titles. '*The Grapes of Wrath, Lean In, I Know Why the Caged Bird Sings, Man's Search for Meaning, I am Malala, Anne Frank's Diary, To Kill a Mockingbird, The Color Purple*, a biography of Gandhi, *A Long Walk to Freedom, We Wish to Inform You that Tomorrow We Will Be Killed with Our Families*.' He waved the last one in the air. 'Zach may have a point. These are all serious downers. I know you like to read about important stuff and real people who inspire and all, but *We Wish to Inform You that Tomorrow We Will Be Killed with Our Families*? That's a whole other level of depressing.'

Riley lay down beside him on the bed and groaned. 'When you put them all side by side they are a bit heavy jelly, but individually they're brilliant. None of them will work, though. I need something middle-ground. Something that's a good story but not too much.'

Shocko plucked the guitar strings while Riley tried to think.

'I was watching this show about these, like, midget people,' he said, as he strummed – badly.

'They don't like being called midgets.'

'Why?'

'They think it's offensive and derogatory.'

'But they are midgets.'

'No. They're Little People or people of small stature.'

'Seriously? They want to be called Little People? I would have thought *that* would be offensive.'

'No, that's fine.'

'How do you know this?'

'I watched a documentary about it.'

'Of course you did. Anyway, I was watching this show about a little woman and she –'

'That's it!' Riley sat up. '*Little Women.*'

'What?'

'We can do our project on *Little Women* and we can discuss why everyone thinks Laurie and Jo should have ended up together and not Amy and Laurie. Jo and Laurie are opposites. She's kind of like me and he's a bit like Zach, and they love each other and we can discuss it. Maybe I can make him see that opposites do attract and can work. If he's too lazy to read the book, he can watch the movie. It's perfect.'

'Hang on a second. Isn't Zach the guy you hate? Didn't you just burn all that stuff outside his house because he humiliated you and you think he's a dick?'

Riley nodded. 'Yes, but I hurt him badly too and if we can just get past all of that and get rid of Zoë, I think we could make it work. Maybe.'

'So you're into him again?'

'Kind of.'

'The burning and shouting was just a . . . ?'

'A reaction to him being with Zoë.'

'Women, you're all nuts.' Shocko sighed. 'Maybe I could write a song about it – "Nutty Women, Wacky Women, Crazy Chicks or Gaga Girls".'

Riley grinned and started putting the books back on her shelf.

Mia came through the door, kicked off her shoes and fell onto the couch. Johnny snapped his laptop shut. He'd been googling to see if there was anything online about Sarah. He was worried the story would get out if someone from the hospital talked.

'Well?'

Mia lay down and put her arm over her eyes. 'Nightmare. She's got a swelling on her brain and they've had to put a tube in. Dad and Adam had a row and I honestly don't know what to do any more.'

Johnny's heart sank. This was not good news. Sarah's body was beginning to crumble. He rubbed Mia's feet. 'Poor Sarah.'

'I actually found myself wishing she'd die so it would all be over. No more pain for her, peace at last, but she *is* dead. That's the head-wrecking part. Sarah is dead, but none of us can grieve her. Adam wants to keep his son alive and I get that, but is it right? Is it ethical? I just don't know what to think.'

'It's an impossible situation. There is no right or wrong,' Johnny said.

Mia sat up. 'But what should we do, Johnny? Should we turn off the life support?'

Johnny had thought about it a lot. Every time he went in to see Sarah, he felt more horrified. He'd barely slept the last few nights. Between Mia walking around the house, like a ghost, at night and his own head swirling with thoughts of Sarah, sleep was not forthcoming. What would he do?

'I think, if it was me and you were pregnant and there was any chance of saving the baby, I'd have to try. Imagine if it was Riley in there.'

'But the doctors all think the baby will die anyway.'

'I know.'

'I keep wondering what Sarah would want. That's the most important thing and, honestly, I think she'd want to try, even if it was a one-in-a-billion chance of the baby making it. She was a lioness when it came to Izzy, a protector and a fighter.'

Johnny patted her leg. 'Well, I guess there's your answer.'

Mia nodded. She pulled her legs under her and hugged a cushion. 'Angela told me that bastard of a reporter had been back asking questions, but they all stonewalled him. Security kicked him out and barred him. I thought you said you'd sort it with that guy Jimmy Dolan.'

Damn it, the reporter knew he was on to a good story. It was going to be very difficult to stop this coming out.

'Jimmy's been away the past two days, but I have a meeting with him tomorrow morning and I'll get it sorted then.'

'You have to, Johnny, because, honestly, Adam and Charlie are on their last nerves and it wouldn't take much to make them really lose it. I thought they were going to come to blows earlier. Thank God Rob was there to handle Adam.'

'I'm so sorry I wasn't,' Johnny said, feeling bad. 'Maybe I can talk to Adam, ask him to cool it with Charlie.'

Mia shrugged. 'Maybe. He's so wound up, though, I'm not sure he'd listen to anyone. The only one who can get through to him is Rob.'

'And what do you think Rob's take on it is?' Johnny asked.

Mia stared at the broken curtain rail. She reckoned it would never get fixed now. 'I'm not sure. He's just supporting Adam, but sometimes I wonder if he's thinking something different from Adam. When he looks at Sarah, he seems distressed. I might try to get him on his own, see what he feels about Adam's decision to keep her on the life support.'

'Yeah. If it comes to it and it's necessary to let Sarah go, Rob might be very important in getting Adam to accept that.'

'Definitely,' Mia said, nodding. 'I feel there's a distance creeping between us and Adam at the moment. He keeps shooting glances at Charlie like he doesn't trust him. It's really upsetting. We should be united, but Charlie really wants to let Sarah have a dignified death. He can't see Adam's point of view at all.'

'What about Olivia?' Johnny said.

'What about her?' Mia said brusquely.

'Could you ask her to talk to Charlie and maybe put Adam's view to him?'

'I don't think so,' Mia said. 'She feels the same way as Dad, that it's pointless and unnecessary.' Mia laid her head back against the couch.

Johnny stroked her face. 'And in the middle of all this madness, you've lost your sister and best friend,' he said gently. 'I'm so sorry, Mia. There are really no words.'

Tears were falling down her cheeks. 'I just keep talking to her, Johnny, because then it feels like she's going to wake up. But it's sort of disorienting and I have to remind myself she's gone. I feel like I'm in some strange in-between world. Nothing is solid. But when I allow myself to feel even a tiny bit of what I've lost, it's like I'm going to lose my mind as well.'

'Oh, Mia,' he said, resting his head against hers. 'It's impossible to imagine this family without Sarah in it.'

'I don't want to,' Mia said. She let her head fall onto her husband's chest and cried softly. There was only so much a person could take, could feel, and she was reaching the outer limits of her stamina. How long would it go on?

27

Izzy rolled over and kicked Adam in the balls. Ouch. Christ, sleeping with a wriggly seven-year-old was no fun. She'd thrashed about all night and he'd barely slept a wink.

Adam felt as if he was in a long, dark tunnel with no light. He was trying to process all the medical information, trying not to lose his mind about Sarah and trying to make the best decisions for their baby. His brain hurt with all the thinking. All he could do was cling to his gut instinct that Sarah wouldn't let her baby go without putting up a hell of a fight.

He wanted to pull the covers over his head, sleep for a long time and wake up with everything back to normal. How had his life become a living nightmare?

He wanted to wake up beside his beautiful wife. He wanted to hold her, smell her hair, feel the warmth of her body next to his. But he never would.

Adam buried his face in the pillow and tried to stifle his sobs.

'Daddy?' Izzy tapped him on the shoulder. 'Are you sad?'

'No, Sweet-pea, I'm just really tired.' Adam wiped his tears with the edge of the pillowcase and opened his arms to hug Izzy.

She snuggled up to him. 'Do you think I could see Mummy today?'

'I don't think so, love.'

'Oh.' Her little face fell.

Adam's heart sank. How could life be so cruel? How could it rip a loving mother from the life of a sweet, innocent child? 'Come on now, we're being lazy. Time to get up for school.'

'I don't want to go. I'm tired.' Izzy was sulky.

'Up you get.' Adam tickled her to get her up. She wriggled and writhed but eventually got out of the bed. 'You go and get dressed,' he told her, 'and I'll have a quick shower.'

Adam stood under the heavy fall of water and tried to wake up his exhausted body. What would today bring? He felt almost afraid to think of it. Would his son make it through another day? It was the only hope Adam had left. Without the prospect of his son surviving this horror, there was just a black hole.

Adam would not give up. He couldn't. He knew that if he gave up hope he'd fall apart, and he owed it to Sarah to keep trying. She had wanted this baby so much, had been so happy when she'd told him she was pregnant. It hurt to think of that glorious day. They'd felt so lucky.

Luck. What a joke. Two weeks ago Adam had felt like the luckiest man in the world, now his life was about as unlucky as it could possibly be.

He blamed himself. He'd known Sarah was getting head-aches and had told her to go and see the obstetrician, but she hadn't. He should have paid more attention – should have taken her there himself. She must have been worried, in pain, serious pain. Why hadn't she told him how bad the head-aches were?

He was angry with himself but also with her. Damn you, Sarah, why didn't you speak up? Why did you have to be so bloody stoic? They might have been able to operate and save your life – save ours too. Me and Izzy and the baby are lost without you. Adam thumped the shower wall, instantly regretting it as a sharp pain shot up his arm.

'FUCK!' he roared.

'Daddy,' a little voice behind him said.

Adam exhaled deeply. 'Yes, Izzy?'

'Breakfast is ready. I poured your cornflakes for you.'

'You are wonderful. I'll be down in two minutes.'

Izzy was eating her cereal quietly when Adam walked in. He felt marginally better after his shower and shout.

'Eat your breakfast, Daddy, or I'll be late for school.'

He kissed Izzy's head. 'Thanks for getting everything ready.'

'We need to hurry, Daddy. We have to make my lunch. I can't be late for school.' Izzy took off her glasses, picked up a tea-towel and began to clean them.

'I'll sort it out. Just let me have some coffee first. It'll help me wake up.'

While Adam drank a cup of strong coffee, Izzy finished her cereal and put her bowl in the dishwasher. She pulled out the pitta bread and the cheese and placed them on the counter.

Adam picked up a bread knife and tried to hack open the pitta. Lumps of bread sprayed all over the countertop. 'What the hell?'

'Stop, Daddy!' Izzy shouted. 'You have to toast it first. It goes all puffy in the toaster and then you can cut it and the cheese goes all melty when you put it in.'

'Fine.' Adam grabbed another pitta and placed it in the toaster. When it popped he reached in to take it out. 'Jesus!' he cried, dropping it on the floor. 'Bloody hell, that's hot.'

'Mummy made it pop out without touching it,' Izzy grumbled.

Adam picked it up and grasped the bread knife.

'I'm not eating that! It fell on the floor! It's all dirty and gross,' Izzy cried.

Adam gave it a rub with a tea-towel. 'It's fine. The floor is clean.'

'No, it isn't. Mummy cleaned the floor every day but you don't and it isn't clean now and I'm not eating disgusting dirty pitta.'

'I'll do another.'

They waited in silence as the pitta toasted. When it popped, Adam flipped it out of the toaster without using his burned fingertips. He carefully cut it open and laid the two sides face up, letting them cool down.

'No, Daddy, you can't let it go cold or the cheese won't melt. You're not supposed to cut it open fully. Only a bit so you can put the cheese inside, then close it and it melts. Now it won't melt.' She stamped her foot. 'I don't want it. Put on another one.'

'That was the last one.'

'You're the worst sandwich-maker ever. I have no lunch now. I'm going to starve in school.'

'Hold on, you can have a – a . . .' Adam frantically looked around for something. This was Sarah's territory, not his. He found some crackers in the cupboard. 'Here, cheese and crackers will be nice too.'

'I hate crackers. I have never, ever liked crackers. I like pitta with melty cheese. It's the only sandwich I really like.'

'Come on, Izzy, give me a break here. Just eat crackers today or else eat the pitta with cheese not fully melted. It really isn't that big a deal. I'll get you a chocolate bar in the garage beside school as a treat. OK?'

'No. We're not allowed chocolate in school. We're not allowed any sweet things. I don't want my teeth to go brown and fall out. I want a melty cheese pitta sandwich. I'm going to be hungry all day now. I hate you. You're the worst daddy *ever.*' Izzy collapsed on the floor, sobbing.

Adam put the knife and the crackers down and sat on the floor beside his little girl. He pulled her up onto his lap. 'I'm sorry about the sandwich. I know I'm a rubbish sandwich-maker. Mummy was the best at that. I'll try to do better tomorrow. You can help me. We'll do it really slowly and get it perfect. Just for today could we buy you a roll in the garage?'

'OK. Just for today.'

'That's my girl. I'm sorry, sweetie.'

'I miss her, Daddy.'

'I know you do, Izzy. I miss her too.' Adam buried his face in Izzy's hair and they both cried for the lost centre of their universe.

Adam was helping Izzy into her school coat when Rob came down the stairs, pushing his freshly showered hair out of his eyes. 'Morning.'

'Can you make pitta sandwiches?' Izzy asked.

'I sure can.'

'Good. You can teach Daddy while I'm in school,' Izzy said.

'I'd be happy to,' Rob said.

'I'm just going to drop Izzy to school. I'll be back in twenty minutes and we can catch up then.'

'Hey, let me do it. You look like you could use a coffee. I'd like to.'

'Yeah, I want Uncle Rob to bring me to school.'

'Great,' Adam said. 'Thank you.'

Adam watched Rob hold Izzy's hand as they headed out to the car. He wanted to weep with gratitude that his brother was there, on his side, on his team, helping to hold him up when all around him was crumbling.

28

Mia greeted the children as they arrived. After so many days at the hospital, she had decided that doing something 'normal' might be good for her. It was getting harder and harder to sit in that little waiting room in the ICU, slowly losing her mind. Instead, she had come into school and would pop in to see Sarah in the evening. This state of limbo could go on for months if the medical team could keep the baby alive, and it certainly wouldn't be good to live in that limbo the whole time. She had to be strong and try to live some sort of life as well.

Some parents dropped the children and hurried off, avoiding having to talk to Mia. Others were childminders who spoke little English, but a handful of parents said they'd heard her sister was unwell and hoped she'd recover soon. Mia smiled sadly, nodded and thanked them. She didn't want to get into a conversation with any parent about it. She had no answers and the reality of the situation was too complex to explain, and too painful to talk about.

Fiona Kelly, the headmistress, had told all of the other staff members and any parents who enquired that Isobel Brown's mother and Mia Wilson's sister was in a coma and was non-responsive. It was the line Mia had fed her and it kind of summed it up. If anyone had guessed otherwise, they didn't say so to her.

The last child ran in and Mia closed the door.

'Good morning, everyone,' she said.

'Good morning, Miss Mia,' the twenty-three children answered.

'What have you been up to while I've been away?'

Milly's hand shot up. 'Miss Hannah kept us up with our Communion work and we did our spellings and our maths.'

Sam's hand went up. 'Em . . . your sister is in a coma. I'm sorry, Miss Mia.'

'That's very kind of you, Sam, thanks.'

'What's a coma?' Kerry asked.

'It's when a person is lying down and sleeping but also kind of dead,' Sam explained.

'Don't say dead! My mum said not to say dead,' Conor stage-whispered.

Sam's eyes widened. 'Sorry, Miss Mia, I didn't mean dead.'

'Sam, it's fine. We should move on now, class. Take out your spelling books.'

'I saw Izzy crying at lunchtime yesterday,' Niamh said.

'Yeah, me too,' Kelly said.

'Did you go over to see if she was all right?' Mia asked.

'Yep, I did,' Niamh said. 'She said she was sad because her mummy won't wake up, but I said, "Izzy, she'll wake up just like Sleeping Beauty. Maybe your dad just needs to give her true love's kiss."'

'Eww, gross.' Conor made a vomiting face.

'You're so thick, Conor. If a husband kisses his wife, it's fine. If he kisses someone else's wife, that's bad.'

'My dad kissed someone else at a party and my mum was *suuuuuuuper*-cross,' Alexandra said.

Yikes, thought Mia. Alexandra's parents wouldn't want that broadcast around the school.

'My dad went off with his girlfriend and now they have a baby together and my mum hates the baby and says it's ugly and stupid. It's not nice to say a baby is stupid, though, is it?' Brona said.

'I think all babies are ugly. My twin sisters are rotten-looking,' Milo said.

'That's a terrible thing to say. God's listening and we're making our Communion really soon and it's a sin to be mean about your family.' Alexandra wagged her finger at him.

'No, actually, lying is a sin,' Milo retorted, 'so if I said they were cute, I'd be a liar. Jesus said we should tell the truth, so there. My granddad says he hopes they get better-looking or they'll be living at home for ever. Mum said that was a shocking thing to say, but Granddad thought it was hilarious.'

'All babies are beautiful because they are made in the image of God,' Alexandra said firmly.

'Ah-ha-ha!' Milo cracked up laughing. 'That means girls look like boys, which is why they're so ugly.'

'No, my mum said God isn't a man, he's a woman.'

'Well, how come in all the pictures he's a man?' Conor jumped in.

'Because people in the old days were thick and thought women weren't good enough to be God, but now we know women are brilliant. My mum says women are *waaaaaay* smarter than men. She has her own company, so there.' Grace was triumphant.

Mia was trying not to laugh, but she had to rein in this wide-ranging discussion.

'Right, class, let's get started. We have our Communion rehearsal after lunch, so we'd better get some good work done first.'

At lunchtime, Mia sat in her office while the children ran out to play. She saw Izzy on her own by the flowers. She seemed to be talking to herself, or maybe she was singing. The poor little dote looked so small and alone. Mia put down her sandwich and went to get her coat, but by the time she'd put it on Riley had appeared.

Mia watched as Riley picked up Izzy and swung her around. Izzy squealed happily. Mia opened the window, so she could hear them.

'How's my favourite person?'

'I'm a bit sad today, Riley.'

'About your mum?'

Izzy nodded. 'I just keep thinking about all those tubes and things all over her body. She was making this scary noise when she breathed, like a big clunky sound. Daddy said it was because of the ven– vent . . .'

'Ventilator.'

'Yes, that. It was horrible, and she didn't wake up even when I sang "Let It Go", even when I shaked her. She was still asleep.'

Riley crouched down and hugged her little cousin. 'Hey, I know it's scary for you and no one wants to see their mum sick like that. Don't feel you have to be all brave. If you want to cry about it, come to me. I'll be here every day at lunchtime and we can talk about it. You can cry or shout or even punch me if you feel angry. I won't mind. Deal?'

'I won't punch you.' Izzy giggled.

'I don't mind if you do. Sometimes when I'm really angry I want to punch things.'

'You seem angry a lot.'

Riley sighed. 'Being a teenager is difficult. I'm trying to be less angry and to be nicer to my mum. She's sad about Sarah too.'

'My daddy is super-sad. I heard him crying last night.'

'Oh, Izzy, it's just a really tough time. But things will get better. We have to look at the good things. You are loved by

218

so many people. You are gorgeous, smart, funny, cute and kind of adorable.'

'Gorgeous? Even with my stinky glasses?'

'Hey! Glasses rock. Do you want to look the same as everyone else? Hell, no. You want to stand out and be seen. You are a brilliant girl, Izzy. Don't ever forget that.'

'Jason called me Hedwig – like the owl in *Harry Potter*.'

Riley stood up. 'Which one is Jason?'

Izzy pointed to a boy with freckles.

Riley took her cousin's hand and went over to the group of boys Jason was with. 'Hey, Freckle Face, are you Jason?'

'Yes.' Jason looked up, eyes wide.

'Listen very carefully. If you ever make any comment to Izzy again about her glasses, in fact, if you even look at her sideways again, I will come down here and kick your arse. Do you understand me?' Riley poked him in the chest.

Jason nodded.

'And that goes for all of you. If anyone is mean or insensitive to Izzy, they will have to answer to me. Is that clear?'

All the boys nodded.

'Good.'

Izzy and Riley walked away.

'Wow, Riley, you were, like, really scary!'

'I wanted them to know I mean it.'

Izzy threw her arms around Riley's waist. 'I love you, Riley.'

'I love you too. You're going to be OK. I'm here for you. Now, you have my number in the special phone your dad gave you, don't you?'

'Yes, I have Daddy's number, Mia's, Johnny's, Granddad's and yours. Daddy said if I'm feeling bad or need to ask a question about Mummy, I can use it.'

'Well, call me anytime, day or night.'

'I will.'

'Gotta fly or I'll be late for class. See you tomorrow.'

'Bye.' Izzy waved as Riley jogged back to the senior school.

Mia smiled to herself. Her teenager still had a heart of gold buried beneath all the angst.

29

Johnny walked into the lobby of the *Irish Express* building. He filled in his visitor's badge, got into the lift and pressed the button for the fifth floor as instructed. He looked at his reflection in the mirror. He'd dressed up for this. His best navy suit and the light blue shirt Mia had bought him for his birthday. It was his interview suit, but this was no interview. This was crisis control.

He got out of the lift and looked around. He could see Jimmy in the distance, in a glass-fronted office. Johnny walked quickly past the rows of reporters and researchers bashing away on their laptops. He kept his head down. He recognized a few faces, but he did not want to get into a conversation with anyone as to why he was there. He strode quickly past a bank of printers churning out pages and a large water-cooler.

Johnny stood at the open door of Jimmy's office. The editor waved him in. The desk was covered with precarious towers of newspapers, paper, pens, books, photos and notebooks. There were bright green Post-its everywhere. The walls were lined with shelves crammed with books. A TV on the wall, muted, showed breaking news, and an orange couch was pushed up against the wall.

'Gotta go, I'll call you later.' Jimmy hung up the phone.

Johnny reached out to shake his hand, then sat down opposite him.

'How are you doing?' Jimmy asked. 'It's very hard when your outfit folds. I've been there.'

'Yep, it's hard,' Johnny said. There was no use lying to a

man as wily as Jimmy Dolan. 'I'm hunting for work, but there's slim pickings at the moment.'

Jimmy nodded. 'We're under siege, Johnny,' he said, walking behind him to close the door. 'The internet is hoovering up our readers. It's a bloodbath. Survival of the fittest.'

'I intend to survive,' Johnny said, exuding way more confidence than he was capable of feeling after five months of nothing.

'You're a good writer,' Jimmy said. 'You'll find something. If I hear of anything I'll give you a shout. So,' he said, sitting down in his chair, 'we have a matter that needs discussion.'

'Your reporter is sniffing around the hospital and you have to stop him.'

Jimmy stared at him. 'It's a good story, and you know it.'

'I'm asking you not to run it, Jimmy.'

'Why not? If this didn't involve your family, you'd be all over it. I've looked at your sister-in-law's Facebook page, and they're a very good-looking family. They tick all the boxes. It's heart-breaking, controversial and contentious, which makes it gold dust. Your reporter's instinct knows this. This is the real world, Johnny, and I've got a paper to keep going. And you know better than most how hard that is.'

Johnny looked down at his hands. He had to keep emotion out of this. 'Look, Jimmy, it is a good story, but my wife and her family are in shreds. If it was your family, you'd do everything to protect them. I'm asking you to sit on this for another while.'

Jimmy tugged at his already loose tie. 'When will it be over? This could go on for weeks as I understand it. Months, maybe.'

Johnny clasped his hands together. He needed to be vague and non-specific. He needed to buy time. 'Things are not going well, so I don't believe it will be much longer.'

Jimmy shook his head. 'I respect you and I feel for your wife's situation, but if I don't run this story, someone else will get it. At least if I run it, you know I'll be fair.'

Johnny stared at him. 'No, you won't,' he said. 'You'll be a good editor and wring everything out of it.'

Jimmy smiled. 'You know me well enough. Put yourself in my shoes, Johnny. There's no reason to sit on it. And we'll deal with it sensitively. I'll put my best guy on it. Denis Jacobs, you probably know him.'

Johnny did know Denis Jacobs and he was a decent journalist, but there was no way he was letting him break the story. 'What if it was worth your while to hold off?' Johnny said, his brain racing through the options. He had an idea. It was risky but, then, this was an unthinkable situation that needed a solution, and there was only one he could think of that might work.

'Go on,' Jimmy said, watching him closely.

'Sarah is my sister-in-law. I've known her for almost twenty years. I've been in the meetings with the medical team so I know the full story. How about you hold off in exchange for an exclusive?'

Jimmy's eyebrows arched upwards. 'Your instincts certainly haven't been blunted by bad luck,' he said.

'It's not like that,' Johnny said. 'I'm not doing it for me. I know it might be interpreted that way, but I'm doing it for my wife and her family. They are in hell. It would be cruel to run this story now.'

'So what will you give me?' Jimmy said. 'And when?'

'I'll give you an exclusive insight into the horrific dilemma the family is facing,' Johnny said, his palms sweating. There was no turning back now. 'I can describe the medical situation and the reasons why it's panning out as it is. As for when, give me two weeks.'

Jimmy picked up a pen and started clicking it. The noise set Johnny's teeth on edge, but he stayed quiet.

'OK,' Jimmy said. 'I'll want a good story, though, details. And I can give you a week, but that's all.'

'Jimmy, I'm begging you here. I promised my wife I'd keep it out of the press. She has no idea that the deal will involve me writing the exclusive. She'll probably divorce me when she finds out. I'm in deep shit here, Jimmy. Please don't make it worse. I promise you a brilliant piece, but in two weeks.'

Jimmy sat back and tapped the pen against his chin. 'The best I can do is a week, Johnny. If she's still alive in a week's time, I'm running it, with or without you. It's only a matter of time before someone else hears about it. If they do, before the week is up, we'll have to run it. I'll call to give you a heads-up if that happens.'

Johnny nodded. It was as fair as he was going to get. Most editors would have run the story and to hell with his family. 'All right. Thanks, Jimmy. I appreciate it.'

Jimmy stood up and held out his hand. 'I'm sorry for you, Johnny, honestly. I hope things work out for the best, whatever that is.'

Johnny walked quickly back through the open-plan office and into the lift. He couldn't look at himself in the mirror. He got out on the ground floor, went out of the glass front doors, turned left and made straight for Mulcahy's pub on the corner. There, he ordered a whiskey, carried it to the snug, sat down and took a big gulp. What had he done?

He tried to convince himself that he had done the only thing possible to save the situation, but his blood ran cold at the thought of how Mia would see it. Would she understand? He was risking everything if she didn't. But if he wrote the story, it would be compassionate and balanced. If it was any other journo, they'd go for the jugular on the sensationalism of their bizarre situation.

It felt like a crazy twist of Fate that he was now wishing for Sarah's little boy to die quickly so some hack wouldn't write a salacious story about his family. What a total mess. He could end up a pariah to the whole family. Adam would probably beat him up. God knew what Charlie would think. Johnny felt sick. He had no choice. If he could make them see that, everything would be OK. Surely they knew he wouldn't do anything that could harm or hurt Sarah. He adored her. He was doing this for her, so her death wasn't twisted into something macabre.

He swallowed the rest of the whiskey, feeling it burn all the way down his throat. For now, he had to pretend everything was fine, that the story was nixed and no longer a threat. It was his job to protect Mia from any more worry. He'd keep reassuring her, and he'd deal with the fallout later.

30

Mia's plan to inject some normality into her life by working each day had already fallen apart. She had been on her way to the hospital last night when Adam had called to say that the doctors didn't want Sarah to have any visitors until the following day. They had also called a meeting for the next morning, so Mia had rung Fiona Kelly to let her know that she probably wouldn't make it into the school that day.

In the waiting room, she sipped a cup of strong coffee and Charlie sat beside her, pretending to read the newspaper. He'd been staring at the same article for ten minutes. Mia's concentration had disappeared, too. She could barely understand what people said to her: it was as if she was in a fog. Everything was muffled and sounded far away. Riley had asked her for a red pen last night and Mia had made her repeat the question three times. Her brain didn't seem able to process anything except the medical information relating to her sister.

Maybe that was the problem: her brain was fried after all this medical jargon and she couldn't take in anything else.

Olivia bustled into the room. She was immaculately dressed, as always. Mia wondered briefly if she tattooed her lips red. Her lipstick never seemed to budge or fade. It didn't even come off on mugs or glasses. It was astonishing.

'Oh, my goodness, that car park is always full. I had to drive around four times before I got a space.'

'You should have let me park,' Charlie said.

'Not a bit of it. Sure you've enough to worry about without dealing with parking. Now, I brought us a flask of green tea.'

Olivia took out a flask and two cups. She poured Charlie some and handed it to him.

'Green tea?' Mia raised an eyebrow.

'I'm trying to get used to it,' Charlie said, grimacing as he sipped.

'It's very good for him, Mia. All this caffeine is making him jittery and he can't sleep. The poor man is worn out. He's up pacing the floors all night. I've to beg him to come to bed so I can massage him to sleep.'

Mia spluttered. Sweet Jesus, she really didn't want to picture that particular scenario. Damn it, now the image of Olivia in a frilly nightdress, with her boobs hanging out, massaging Charlie's naked body was in her head. Oh, Sarah, where are you when I need you? Mia groaned inwardly.

'Are the doctors in with her?' Olivia asked.

'Yes,' Charlie said. 'There seems to be a lot of activity around her, and Angela said we couldn't go in yet. The physiotherapist was in earlier and now the medical team are assessing her. They want to have a meeting with us at ten.'

Olivia handed Charlie a square cracker with seeds on it. He took it reluctantly. 'Would you like one, Mia? They're endurance crackers. I got them at this fabulous health shop that's just opened up beside the golf club. The man said they're extremely light and crispy while providing long-lasting energy. They're gluten-free, soy-free, nut-free, sugar-free and oil-free.'

'And taste-free, no doubt,' Mia said. 'No, thanks.'

Olivia tutted. 'You can't survive on coffee, Mia. You need to keep your strength up. You're bordering on skinny as it is. Breakfast is the most important meal of the day. Eat up, Charlie. The man said these fill you up and keep you going until lunchtime.'

Mia watched as her father chewed joylessly on the dry

crackers. Olivia's phone rang. She answered it and began to talk loudly, then got up and took her call outside into the corridor.

'Nice crackers, Dad?'

'I'd say cardboard tastes better.' Charlie tried to pick some seeds out of his teeth. 'Give me some of your coffee while she's distracted.' He grabbed Mia's cup and drank deeply. 'God, that's good. This auld green tea tastes like grass.'

'So tell her you hate it.'

'Ah, I wouldn't do that. She's only trying to help. She's a heart of gold.'

'Dad, you're in the horrors of Hell. If you want a coffee, drink a bloody coffee.'

'I do when she's not around, but she likes to fuss, and I don't want to hurt her feelings. Besides, it's nice to have someone caring for me, especially now.' Charlie looked down at his dry cracker.

Mia rubbed his back. 'I know, Dad. I'm glad you have Olivia.' He was right: it was lovely to have someone care for you. Johnny had got up early that morning and made Mia porridge with cinnamon, just the way she liked it.

'Well, try to be nicer to her,' Charlie said pointedly. 'Sarah always was. But sure she was nice to everyone.'

Yes, she was, Mia thought, but she didn't have the pressures I have. Why didn't her father ever acknowledge that Mia was doing a good job keeping things going, trying to save them from losing the house, juggling work and motherhood, trying to prevent Johnny from spiralling into depression and think of ways to get him a job? It was always 'Sarah's so nice.' Well, Mia was nice too, maybe not as nice as her sister but she had more shit to deal with. Charlie never, ever acknowledged that or praised her, and it hurt. Right now, it really bloody hurt. Sarah was dead, and only Mia and

Charlie were left. Mia needed her dad. She needed him to be kind to her and supportive, not critical and judgemental.

Mia felt tears pricking her eyes. She wanted to shake him. 'I'm all the family you've got left, Dad!' she wanted to shout. 'Let's be nice to each other.' Instead, she said nothing and pushed down the hurt she felt with the last gulp of her coffee.

'That was Robert.' Olivia came back in, beaming. 'He's just finished working on the Kerrigan tribunal. The newspapers were full of praise for him. But he's never had anything other than praise. He has such a brilliant mind. Honestly, people say he got it from me, but I don't know about that. He's such a wonderful son, always checking in with me. He was asking for you too, Charlie. He sends his best wishes.'

Mia tried not to stare, or laugh, at the big black seed stuck between Olivia's front teeth.

Adam came rushing through the door with Rob. 'Thank God! I thought I was late for the meeting with the medical team.'

'No, it's on at ten, another five minutes to go. Johnny's on his way too,' Mia said.

Adam fell into a chair. 'Izzy was acting up again this morning so we were late for school. Poor little thing, she's so upset.'

'She never stops asking about her mum – it'd break your heart,' Rob said.

Johnny walked in. 'Bloody bus was delayed,' he muttered, and sat down beside Mia.

'I don't know what to tell Izzy about Sarah. Should I tell her Sarah's never going to wake up?' Adam asked. 'Rob thinks I should start dropping hints.'

'In my humble opinion, honesty is always the best policy,' Olivia said.

'I agree with Rob,' Mia said. She had always liked Rob – he

was like a toned-down version of Adam. Less driven, softer. Mia had only got to know him a little at Sarah and Adam's wedding, then the odd time when he was home for Christmas or a week's holidays. Sarah had loved him. They'd hit it off from the minute they'd met.

Looking at Rob's fresh face, made Mia realize how much they'd all aged since Sarah's collapse. They were a haggard bunch, worn down by emotion and sleepless nights.

'Maybe start planting the idea gently, like mentioning she may not get better and things may get worse, just to try to prepare her,' Mia suggested.

'How can he tell Izzy that her mother's dead when she's in there being kept alive with a baby inside her?' Charlie pointed out. 'How can a little child get her head around that when I still can't?'

Olivia rushed over to him. 'Now, now, Charlie, calm yourself. You mustn't get upset. It's bad for your heart.'

His heart's broken, Mia wanted to say, but she held her tongue.

The door opened, and Angela came in. 'If you're ready, I'll take you upstairs.'

Charlie, Adam, Rob, Johnny and Mia followed her. Olivia stood up and kissed Charlie. 'I'll be here, waiting for you,' she said. 'Good luck.'

Angela brought them back to the same conference room on the fifth floor where they'd been told that Sarah would never recover. Mia hated it. She stood beside Rob, getting a coffee from the percolator in the corner of the room. The medical team filed in, led by Dr Mayhew. There were six of them, which immediately made Mia nervous. She hadn't met some of them before.

'What do you think this is about?' Rob whispered.

'I don't know, but I doubt it's good.'

Rob swore softly. 'I don't think Adam can take any more bad news. I'm worried he's going to have a breakdown.'

Mia put her hand on his arm. 'I think we all are, Rob. We just have to pull together.'

Dr Mayhew, Ms Johnston and Professor Irwin sat down. Mia and the others took the chairs opposite them.

'Good morning,' Dr Mayhew said. 'I'll start by introducing my colleagues whom you haven't been introduced to yet. They are helping us monitor Sarah's case and providing assistance to the key workers. This is Peter Long, consultant obstetrician, Karen Harrington, anaesthetist, and Kevin Strong, who heads up our neonatal paediatric team.'

'Is Ben OK?' Adam asked, the moment Dr Mayhew stopped speaking. It was a question he asked at least twenty times a day.

'Yes, for the moment,' Dr Mayhew said. Mia saw him take a deep breath. Uh-oh, this was definitely not going to be good news.

'I've asked you all here today as Sarah's closest relatives to discuss her treatment going forward. This is a tragic and most unusual case. We are all deeply sorry for you, her family, and we're mindful of the pain and confusion you're enduring. But we feel it's important to be honest with you and to keep you abreast of Sarah's condition. I'm sorry to say that it deteriorated late last night. She has unfortunately developed an infection in the drain site on her skull. There is fluid in her lungs and the additional complication of a urinary tract infection.'

'What?' Adam's face reddened. 'Well, you're not doing your job properly. You're not keeping her sterile or – or being careful enough with cleanliness. Give her antibiotics, clear it up.'

'Serious infection is almost inevitable in this case,' Professor Irwin said. 'You must understand, she has a huge amount of IV lines, central lines, catheters and drains, all of which are essential to monitor her condition and treat her ongoing problems, but they also mean that infection is essentially impossible to prevent, despite our best efforts.'

'But can't you cure the infection with antibiotics? Or will they harm the baby?' Mia asked.

'It's more serious than antibiotics,' Dr Mayhew answered. 'There is also evidence of cardiovascular instability now, which will require high doses of medication. There is evidence of hypertension relating to fluid overload. Sarah's body has now swollen further due to a build-up of fluid.'

'Sweet Jesus, my poor girl.' Charlie sobbed. Mia reached over to squeeze his hand. She tried to take in and understand all the medical information.

'Her pregnant abdomen is extremely swollen, and I have grave concerns that there may be an infection underneath,' Ms Johnston explained gently. 'We have not been able to identify all the sources of infection. Sarah's temperature rose to thirty-nine early this morning, which would mean the temperature in the uterus could be up to forty degrees. The foetus is not designed to be incubated in anything other than the normal temperature. The higher the foetus's temperature, the quicker the enzymes will work and the faster it will get through the available oxygen. The stretchmarks of the pregnancy are abnormally discoloured, indicating retained fluid. Sarah's blood pressure rose sky high and we have had to treat this with high doses of drugs. Some of the drugs and antibiotics we have had to administer, and will have to administer, to keep the body alive are not licensed for use in pregnancy.'

Leaning forward she added, 'This is a really pressing issue now. There is a very real threat of sepsis. If that occurs,

Sarah's blood pressure will plummet. If that happens, she will require inotropic support, which is not recommended for a foetus in utero.'

'Jesus,' Johnny muttered. 'Poor Sarah.'

'We have studied all the available data in great detail and discussed it at length. I am very sorry to say that we do not believe it is realistic, or indeed safe, to continue with somatic support until the foetus reaches viability,' Dr Mayhew concluded.

Mia didn't know what she felt – devastation? Relief? Grief? It was a blur. But a thought was growing at the edge of her mind and spreading out: It's finally over.

She looked at Charlie and Rob, and saw the same conflicting thoughts written on their faces. Then she looked at Adam, and she knew it wasn't over.

Adam's face was red and he was shaking with emotion. He pointed his finger across the table at the medical team. 'You're all trying to blind me with medical jargon. So, Sarah's gone downhill a bit and has fluid. Drain the fluid, get her infection under control and her blood pressure, and let's see what happens. Loads of pregnant women get high blood pressure and infections. It's not the end of the world. No one is pulling the plug on Ben. No one.'

Adam's bloodshot eyes were wild. 'Don't forget that report, the one Johnny found. The Heidelberg report said that babies of brain-dead mothers can survive. The problem here is you lot. Sarah should never have got an infection. That's on you. So fix it. Fix my wife. Do your bloody jobs.'

There was an uncomfortable silence following this outburst. Rob leaned on the arm of his chair, closer to his brother.

'If I may,' Peter Long spoke up. 'I'm afraid your reading of the Heidelberg report seems to have given you false hope.

I just want to talk you through the findings. Of the nineteen cases reported, there was one foetus that was fourteen weeks old when the mother was declared brain-dead. The baby died in the womb. There were two other cases involving foetuses that were thirteen weeks old – one was here in Ireland in 2004. The baby died in utero eight days after its mother suffered a blood clot in the brain. The other, whose mother was injured in an accident in Germany in 1993, survived for thirty-eight days before dying as a result of miscarriage.' Dr Peter Long paused. 'We estimate the foetus in this case to be about fifteen weeks now. We do not believe it is possible to continue life support for seven or eight more weeks. The chances of the foetus thriving and the baby being born alive are minuscule. I'm truly sorry to tell you this, but the foetus will not survive the storm going on around it. I'm very sorry to be blunt, but your wife's brain is now pouring toxins into the bloodstream. Her condition will continue to deteriorate and affect the baby detrimentally.'

Adam threw his hands into the air in frustration. 'I'll take minuscule. My wife is dead. My seven-year-old daughter is distraught. I have nothing but this tiny speck of hope that my son will survive and I'm taking it. We wanted this baby so much . . .' His voice broke, but he took a deep breath and carried on. 'Sarah was so happy. I know she would want me to fight until the end. I will not give up all hope. You will go in there and you will keep my son alive, do you hear me? *Alive.*'

'Hey,' Rob put his hand on Adam's shoulder, 'take it easy. No one is giving up.'

'It's not giving up,' Dr Mayhew said quietly. 'At this point, it's accepting the sad reality of the situation. We are trained to preserve life, that is our number-one priority, but we are also trained to recognize where life cannot be preserved.

Please, Adam, listen to the facts. We've done our level best, but we cannot save the foetus.'

'His name is Ben,' Adam roared at them. 'For Christ's sake, stop calling him "the foetus"!'

'Stop it,' Charlie croaked. 'Please, for the love of God, stop this, Adam. She's gone, and the baby has no chance of surviving. My girl is dead in there. It's not right. It has to stop.'

Mia put her arm round her sobbing father. She felt so many things at once, she couldn't think straight. But seeing Charlie so distraught was unbearable.

'Maybe it's time to think about letting go, Adam,' Johnny said.

'NO!' Adam shouted. '*No way!* No one is giving up on Ben. No one.' He stood up. '*Do your jobs!*' he shouted at the team, then stormed out of the room.

Dr Mayhew watched him go, then turned to them. He looked very shaken. 'We're truly sorry. We've never had a case like this and we're devastated for you all. It's the hardest thing I've faced, and I've been doing this job a long time.'

Mia looked at the doctors' faces. They were all in shock and distress too.

'It's a heartbreaking case,' Ms Johnston murmured. 'Just awful.'

'I'm very sorry for my brother's behaviour,' Rob said. 'He's not sleeping, and he's consumed by grief, so he isn't thinking as he normally would. I'm sure you can understand that.'

Dr Mayhew nodded. 'We can, of course. And we're sorry to have bombarded you all with the bleak details, but it's essential there is a clear understanding of the current situation. Perhaps you could talk to Adam,' he said to Rob. 'As next-of-kin, the decision rests with him. If Adam could see that the foetus has absolutely no hope of surviving, it would help him to make an informed decision.'

Rob rubbed his face. 'I do hear what you're saying, but Adam is in Hell right now and it is his decision and we have to respect that. Let's just give him some time.'

Johnny helped Charlie up and he and Rob led him slowly back to the waiting room. Olivia jumped out of the seat and rushed over. 'Oh dear. Bad news?'

Mia nodded. She was grateful that Olivia was there – she needed someone else to comfort Charlie. She couldn't do it right now. Olivia held Charlie in her arms and clucked over him lovingly.

'I'll go find Adam,' Rob said.

'Thank you,' Mia said. 'I know this is really hard on you, but you're being an incredible brother to him.'

'Thanks. He's my only family. We always have each other's back.'

Johnny hugged Mia. 'Hey, I'm so sorry but I have to get to the school.'

'Now?' Mia said, confused.

'Teacher-training. Half-day,' he said.

'Oh, God, I'd forgotten. Of course.'

'Will you be OK?' Johnny asked.

'I'll be fine. Thank God you remembered about the half-day. Go and get her. She's the priority. Thanks, Johnny.'

He left and Mia didn't want to sit in the room with Olivia and Charlie. Her mind was racing and she needed to think. There was only one place she could do that – with Sarah.

She went to the nurses' station and grabbed gloves, apron and mask and started to put them on. Angela came out of Sarah's room and froze when she saw her.

'Mia, I have to warn you, Sarah's had a bad turn.'

'I know, they told us.'

'She doesn't look good. You might get a bit of a fright. The swelling is very bad now.'

'I need to see my sister, Angela,' Mia said, tears rolling down her face.

'Of course you do. Would you like me to stay?'

Mia shook her head.

'Well, I'll wait outside in case you need me. I'll be just here.'

Mia opened the door and walked over to the bed. She looked down at her sister. Her hand flew up to her mouth and she screamed. The body lying in the bed wasn't Sarah. This body looked like a monster. She was completely bloated and puffy. Her eyes were so swollen that the lids would no longer close. Pus seeped out from the drain in her head. Oh, my God, Sarah? What have they done to you? What have *we* done to you?

Mia's vision was blurring and her head felt light. She heard running feet and her body was falling in space until hands grabbed her. Then blackness.

31

Mia came to in the ICU waiting room.

'Are you all right?' Charlie asked.

'Just give her a minute to catch her breath,' Angela told him.

Mia looked up. Adam, Rob, Charlie and Olivia were all staring at her.

Angela handed her a glass of orange juice. 'Drink that.'

Mia took a sip, then closed her eyes, but the image of her bloated sister flooded back and she opened them quickly.

'What happened?' Rob asked.

'Sarah,' Mia croaked. 'She looks . . . she looks like a corpse. I can't . . . Oh, God, she's really dead . . .'

'Jesus Christ,' Charlie said. 'This has to stop.'

'We have to stop it,' Mia said. 'It's not right. It's not Sarah in there, it's a . . . a rotting corpse. No baby could survive. I can't believe this is happening.' She sobbed. 'It's bad enough losing Sarah, but like this? Oh, my God, it's so cruel.'

'Is she that bad?' Charlie asked, looking at Mia in shock.

'Worse than you could imagine, Dad. I don't think you should go in.'

'No, Charlie, your heart can't take it,' Olivia said.

'She's not so bad, it's just bloating and infection,' Adam said. 'It'll clear up.'

'She's a monster,' Mia said, her shoulders shaking.

'Ben is alive! She's fighting for him,' Adam said.

'No, no, no. It's wrong. I see that now, Adam. She's gone. They're gone.' Mia's sobs filled the silent room.

Rob cleared his throat. 'Is there any way of halting the

deterioration or of clearing up the infections and bringing down the bloating?' he asked Angela.

She shook her head. 'I'm sorry, but it's probably going to get worse. Her body is breaking down.'

'Ah, God, my poor little girl.' Charlie buried his face in his big white hankie.

Olivia rubbed his back. 'Adam, please listen to them. Sarah is gone, the baby cannot survive. The experts have said so. You have to let her go now, for everyone's sake. Poor Charlie can't take much more. It's killing him.'

Adam stepped back from them. 'No. No, no, no, no. We keep going. We keep fighting, we do not give up. Ever. Do you all hear me? EVER.' He turned and strode out of the room.

Mia wiped her eyes. 'Rob, you're the only one he'll listen to. You have to talk to him. What we're doing to Sarah is not right.'

Rob nodded. 'I know. I get it. But he's just clinging on to the last thread of hope. You can't blame him for that. Let him calm down. I'll try talking to him. But don't push him on this. He's too angry and upset right now.'

Mia knew that Rob was right, but if they didn't make Adam stop this horror show, Sarah would suffer more and it would get worse and the outcome would be the same. Sarah and the baby were not going to survive. It was over. It had to be over. It was inhumane to let her decompose like that. They had to make Adam see.

Mia lay on the bed fully clothed while Johnny rummaged around in the chest-of-drawers.

'I know Adam's being difficult but the poor fellow's an emotional wreck and hasn't slept in days. Rob's really worried about his mental health.'

'We're all a mess,' Mia said. 'Poor Dad is in a terrible state. But we can still see that this has to stop.'

Johnny rustled around until he found the blue jumper he was looking for. 'Well, Adam's called this meeting for a reason. Maybe he's come around after seeing the state Sarah was in this morning.' Johnny's voice was muffled by the jumper as he pulled it over his head.

Mia hoped he was right. She couldn't take much more and her poor dad . . . She was really worried about Charlie. He looked broken.

Johnny picked up her handbag from the floor and held out his hand to her. Every bone in Mia's body ached. She felt like an old woman. She yearned to lie down on the bed and close her eyes for weeks and weeks. She wanted to sleep until it was all over.

'Come on, up you get.' Johnny pulled his wife to her feet. 'Adam said he wanted us to meet at his house at eight thirty sharp. Riley's been babysitting Izzy all afternoon, I'd say she's tired. Hopefully the meeting won't go on too long.'

As Johnny drove, Mia looked out of the window at people going about their daily lives. They have no idea, she thought, no idea that my sister is decomposing and the child inside her is dying too. They have no idea that their lives could be ripped apart in a second. One day your life is full of normal worries, like how to deal with bolshie teens and dwindling finances, and then, suddenly, BOOM. From nowhere life rips the rug from under your feet and turns your world upside-down and inside-out.

Mia felt scared all the time now. Anxious. She had always been a worrier, but now she felt permanently panicky. What if Riley was run over by a car? What if she had a tumour in her brain or got cancer? What if Mia got motor neurone or Johnny had Parkinson's? What if . . . what if . . . Mia knew now that nothing in life was certain or safe.

'What are you thinking?' Johnny asked, as they sat waiting for the traffic lights to turn green.

'That the guy there walking along with his take-out coffee could drop dead of a heart attack.'

'OK.' Johnny exhaled slowly.

Mia turned to face him. 'No, seriously, none of us knows what's going to happen. Everyone says, "Enjoy the now because we don't know what tomorrow will bring," or "Who knows what will happen?" but you never, ever, in your wildest dreams imagine that your pregnant younger sister will drop dead in front of you. You could never contemplate that her dead, rotting body would be incubating a child. You could not imagine sitting in meetings with teams of specialists discussing how her brain is now pouring toxins into the bloodstream that will probably kill her own child.'

Johnny reached over and took her hand in his. 'If I had brandy or whiskey or anything strong, I'd give it to you right now. But in lieu of that, breathe in and out slowly. You've had a terrible shock. Maybe you should ask the doctor for some Xanax or a mild sedative.'

'I'm not taking Xanax.'

'Mia,' Johnny said, letting go of her hand to switch gears, 'you've had a traumatic shock. You should consider taking something to help you.'

'I'm not chomping down Xanax. I'll probably become addicted to them and then die of an overdose.'

'That's why you need them, because you'll stop catastrophizing.'

Mia smiled sadly. 'Johnny, I'm not catastrophizing. I'm living in the middle of a real-life catastrophe.'

Johnny remained silent. What could he say? Mia was right. All of the years she'd spent worrying about bad things happening, well, now she was living right in the middle of one.

32

Riley answered the door to them. 'Be quiet, I've just got Izzy to sleep.'

Mia reached out to hug her. Riley patted her on the back awkwardly, then pulled away.

'Rob and Adam are only just back from the hospital. Granddad and Olivia are here.'

They walked into the kitchen where Charlie and Olivia were sitting at the kitchen table. Rob was busying himself, making tea and coffee for everyone. It felt so strange not to see Sarah by the kettle, bustling about in her kitchen. Mia felt a surge of pain. She sat down to catch her breath.

'I miss her brownies,' Riley said quietly, sitting beside Mia.

'Me too.' Mia smiled through tears.

'It's so weird here without her. It feels . . . I dunno, cold and lonely.' Riley sniffed.

She was right, it did. Even full of people, the kitchen felt bereft of Sarah.

Adam wandered in and went to help Rob organize the tea pot, coffee pot and mugs.

Mia turned to Riley. 'I'm not sure you should be here for this, love. It might get a bit intense,' she whispered.

'I loved Sarah as much as anyone and I want to know what's going on.' Riley's jaw was set.

'Let her stay,' Johnny said. 'If it gets out of hand, I'll take her home.'

'Forget the tea.' Charlie sounded weary. 'I couldn't drink anything anyway. It's been a really long and horrible day, so let's get to the point. What would you like to talk about, Adam?'

Her poor father looked old and utterly worn out, Mia thought. She tried to imagine what it was like to be a parent and see your child in that state. She couldn't even begin to imagine the pain of seeing Riley decomposing in a hospital bed. As a parent, you felt you had to protect your children, no matter what age they were. But this nightmare situation was beyond all the normal bounds, and there was nothing Charlie could do.

'I would like a glass of sparkling water, if that's all right,' Olivia piped up. 'My throat is very dry. I think it's the heat in the hospital – it's very dehydrating. Charlie could do with one too.'

'Could she be any more annoying?' Mia hissed under her breath.

Johnny put his hand on her leg. 'Take it easy.'

'If you had a slice of lemon handy, that would be super. It's very soothing on the throat.'

Mia couldn't take any more. 'Adam and Rob are not going to start looking for bloody lemons,' she snapped. 'Dad doesn't need a glass of sodding water with a slice of lemon, he needs a bottle of whiskey to deal with the shock of seeing his younger daughter in some horror show.'

'Go, Mum,' Riley muttered.

Olivia looked affronted. 'There's no need to be so aggressive, Mia. I was only trying to help your father.'

'You're not helping anyone,' Mia growled.

'Let's all calm down and take a moment,' Johnny said calmly, squeezing Mia's leg a bit tighter. 'Everyone had a terrible shock this morning.'

'I know, Johnny, but a degree of civility from Mia wouldn't go amiss.'

Mia was tempted to reach across the table, punch Olivia's annoying face and shout, 'Howdya like that for civility?'

It wasn't really Olivia's fault, but Mia wanted to hit someone. She wanted to scream at someone. She wanted to blame someone. But who? There was no one to blame. It was just a hideous twist of Fate. Brain damage. Such little words for such a life-altering, life-shattering thing. Mia thought of all the vile people who lived in the world – wife-beaters, rapists, bigots – and yet it was her lovely sister, who'd never hurt a fly, who was ripped from it.

Adam and Rob sat down at the table. While Rob poured glasses of water and mugs of tea, Adam talked. 'I asked you here to discuss the plan going forward.'

'The only plan is to bury my daughter with the scrap of dignity she has left,' Charlie said, his voice shaking with anger and grief.

Mia wanted to reach over and take his hands in hers, but Olivia got there first.

'A nice, dignified funeral where you can all say goodbye,' Olivia added.

'You all deserve the chance to bury her in peace,' Johnny agreed.

'It's time to let her go,' Mia said, looking at Adam.

Adam slammed his fists down on the table. The mugs jumped. When he spoke, he sounded like he was barely controlling a white-hot rage.

'The reason I asked you to come here is because I know that's what you're thinking. But I'm telling you that this is just a bump in the road. My child is still alive. I know Sarah looks . . . looks not like herself but our baby is alive. He hasn't been affected.'

'We don't know that,' Mia said. 'The doctors said they think the baby *is* being adversely affected by the infection, the excess fluid and all the drugs they're pumping into Sarah to keep her body alive. And there'll only be more and more drugs as this goes on. That's what I understood from this morning.'

Adam glared at her. 'They don't know for sure. They have no concrete knowledge, and while there is still a heartbeat and even the tiniest chance, I am not letting go.'

Charlie sat forward and looked straight at his son-in-law. 'Please, Adam, I know what losing your wife is like. I know admitting it's over is the worst pain, but there is no way you can let this go on. It's inhumane. That is no longer my daughter in that bed. We've let this go on for far too long. It's unbearable to see her deteriorate like this. It's wrong. My poor little girl. She needs to be at peace. She needs this to be over. Let her go.'

Adam shook his head. 'No, Charlie, I won't. Our baby is still alive.'

Charlie's face contorted with anger. 'What child can survive in a dead body?' he shouted. 'There is no hope. Stop this madness, Adam.'

Rob spoke up. His voice was quiet and measured. 'There is a lot of emotion here, and the situation is beyond awful, but Adam is Sarah's next-of-kin and that is his baby. And his baby has a heartbeat. Regardless of what we think, if he feels he wants to continue to give the baby a chance, we have to support him.'

Adam clenched his jaw. 'Exactly.'

Mia could see Adam was angry and defensive. She needed to approach this very gently. She took a deep breath. 'Look, Adam, I understand why you want to cling to hope. I know how much you and Sarah wanted this baby. I know how happy you were at the idea of having a son. Adam, I'm absolutely heartbroken, lost without her, but I'm having to accept the future as it's now going to be, and I really feel you have to do the same. The baby is absolutely tiny, so it really can't survive another seven or eight weeks. Even if it did by some miracle, it would probably die within days of being delivered, because very few babies born at twenty-four weeks survive. Look how much Sarah has deteriorated already. It's going to get worse day by day. The baby has no real chance. By dragging it out, you're only prolonging the agony. If I thought there was a screed of a chance the baby would survive, I'd back you, Adam. But I can't. Her deterioration has been so dramatic. It's horrific.' Mia paused to wipe away her tears. 'I know how hard this is for you, I really do, but you must face the facts, Adam. They're gone. Sarah and the baby are gone.'

Adam's eyes flashed. 'I will not quit on my baby or Sarah. Ever. Do you understand? None of you knows how much this baby meant to us, and especially to Sarah. After the second miscarriage, I wanted to give up trying but she insisted we keep going, and she was proven right. Don't you see? This baby was meant to be. We tried so hard to bring him into the world. I will not give up on him. None of you knows how much I loved her. I will fight on for her and for the baby.'

Charlie pulled out his handkerchief and wiped the tears running down his face. 'Of course we know how much you loved her, and we know how hard she tried to get pregnant. She was my daughter, and I loved her too. We're all broken here, son. But this is turning into a horror show, like Mia said. Do you think Sarah would want to end her life as a bloated corpse, infecting her own child?' Emotion overtook him and he whimpered and stared at the ceiling. His pain was evident on his face. 'She's gone. We've lost her, and the baby can't survive in there. We all have to be brave and compassionate and let Sarah go with the scrap of dignity she has left.'

Mia's heart ached for her father. 'Dad's right, Adam. We can't let Sarah deteriorate any further. We have to help her. We have to be her voice.'

Adam glared at Mia with such hatred, she gasped. He didn't even look like the Adam she knew any more. Grief and stress had transformed him.

'What happened to *I'm here for you, Adam. We're behind you, Adam*? Where's your loyalty now? I'm the only one who has the balls to make the hard decisions. It's my responsibility and I'm stepping up to it. So, just to be clear, no one is to mention letting Sarah go or switching off the machines or giving up. I don't want to hear those words. I am choosing hope.'

'I am here for you,' Mia said, desperately trying to get through to him. 'We all are. We've been doing everything we can to support you and Izzy. But you can't fight death. It's like fighting the tide, Adam. It's inevitable,' she pleaded with him.

'I will not be dictated to by you, Mia. I will decide. Me and only me.' He tapped his chest.

'For the love of God, make it stop,' Charlie shouted.

'NO!' Adam roared. 'I am her next-of-kin, not you, and I say she stays alive for as long as possible to save the baby. Do you understand? Is that clear?'

'Adam, the baby isn't going to make it,' Johnny said.

'What the fuck would you know?' Adam yelled. 'You can't even hold down a job.'

'How dare you –' Mia pulled Riley to her and shushed her.

Johnny blanched, but kept his voice calm and strong. 'I've done a lot of research into it, read everything I can get my hands on. I did that because I wanted to find an answer that would let the baby be born, Adam, but every single article and expert opinion says that the foetus is simply too young to survive. If Sarah was twenty-four weeks pregnant, we'd be having a very different conversation. But none of us can change the fact that she's only fifteen weeks.'

Adam turned on Johnny. 'What are you now, some kind of investigative journalist? A big medical expert? You googled a few things and you think you can tell me whether my child is viable or not? Do not come into my house and tell me what to do about my wife and my child.' Adam was spitting with fury.

Mia felt anger rise inside her. Johnny had been such a rock throughout all this. 'May I remind you, Adam, that Johnny has been looking after your daughter non-stop – cooking her meals, baking with her, picking her up from school, keeping her entertained and engaged and happy? Don't sit there all high and mighty and dictate to us. Sarah is my sister, she is Dad's daughter, she is the centre of our world. We should have a say in how she is treated.'

Adam stood up. 'Out. All of you. Get out of my house.' He punched his chest. 'I decide what happens to *my* wife and *my* child. I will not have you second-guessing me and ordering me about. I am her husband. I am the father of that baby and I will make the decisions. I don't want you interfering. Stay away from the hospital. Stay away from Sarah.'

Mia was stunned. Was he actually ordering them to stay away from their own flesh and blood? 'What? You can't make a rule like that. We'll bloody well see Sarah when we want to. You can't stop Dad seeing his daughter.'

Adam stood at the kitchen door, holding it open. 'Charlie doesn't want to see Sarah. He said himself he can't take it. So stay the hell away. I don't want you coming in and trying to guilt me into changing my mind. I don't want any of you telling me that I'm doing the wrong thing, that it's cruel and inhumane . . . I'm sick of it. I have too much to deal with, without you all wrecking my head with your opinions. I need peace. I need space. I need to be with my wife and baby. I will decide what happens and I don't want any of you near me or Sarah.'

Mia went over and stood in front of him. 'You're being ridiculous and you need to calm down. None of us are dictating to you. None of us are forcing you to do anything, but we are all Sarah's family and we care about her and we are allowed to have an opinion. You can't shut Dad off from seeing his daughter.'

Adam poked Mia in the chest with his finger. 'You're a control freak. A total dictator. You want to turn off the ventilator, and I know that as soon as my back is turned, you'll tell the doctors to do it. You always have to control everything. Sarah hated that, by the way. She said you suffocated her. You suffocate everyone – Johnny, Riley, everyone. Why don't you sort out your own life and leave me to sort out mine?'

Mia felt winded. She gasped for air.

Johnny strode over and put an arm around his wife, more to hold her up than to comfort her. 'That's enough, Adam. I'm going to give you some leeway because you're sleep-deprived and grieving, but I will not stay here and have you insult Mia, who was the best sister Sarah could have wished for and is a brilliant aunt to Izzy.'

Johnny marched Mia towards the front door. Riley jumped up and followed them.

'Get a grip on yourself,' Charlie said, to his son-in-law. 'Open your eyes and look at your wife. Look at what you're doing to her.'

'Let's not fall out over this,' Rob pleaded. 'Let's all get a night's rest and in the morning –'

Ignoring his brother's efforts to broker some calm, Adam shouted, 'I want you all out. Now. I don't need you. I'll deal with this myself, in my own way. Just leave us alone.'

'Fuck you, Adam! Everyone's been breaking their backs for you and Izzy, and you treat us like dirt. Fuck you!' Riley shouted.

For once Mia didn't mind her daughter's cursing.

'Adam, why don't you go and sit down? I'll walk these guys out.' Rob gently pushed his brother back into the kitchen and closed the door.

'I don't care how upset he is, he's a prick,' Johnny said angrily.

'Please don't,' Rob said. 'He's not a prick, he's a broken man.'

'Are you all right, Dad?' Mia asked her father, who was standing still, staring into space.

'I'm very far from it,' Charlie said. 'I don't want to see Sarah in that awful state, but I don't want to leave her alone either. I'd feel as if I was abandoning her if I didn't go to see her while that machine is keeping her alive.'

Mia tried to give him a reassuring smile. 'Of course. Don't mind Adam. He's not thinking straight tonight. He can't stop you seeing your own daughter. We'll go and see her together and you can just hold her hand, look out of the window and talk to her that way.'

'Yes, I suppose I could. Good girl, Mia, that's what we'll do.'

'Good. Now why don't you go home and have a nice hot whiskey and get some sleep?'

'Great idea,' Rob said. 'Why don't we all get some rest and perhaps we can smooth things over when everyone's calmed down?'

'We are calm,' Mia said pointedly. 'You've got to talk some sense into him, Rob. I don't mean force him to change his mind, but just make him see this affects all of us hugely, so we will have an opinion. But that doesn't mean it has to tear us apart.'

'I'll try,' Rob said. 'He's just so cut up about it, Mia. You're asking him to throw away his whole future, you know.'

Mia began to cry again — was there no end to the tears? 'I do know that, Rob. We're all shattered. But I have a child, as does Adam, and we have a responsibility to them too.'

Rob nodded tiredly. 'Jesus, no matter what he decides to do, it's painful.'

'I'll see you tomorrow,' Mia said. 'Let's see how things look then. Night, Rob.'

She followed the others outside. Johnny had offered Charlie his arm and was helping him to the car. Her heart filled with love for her husband. He was a gem.

'Well now,' Olivia was saying, as she walked along beside them, 'a hot whiskey won't really do any good. I think a nice cup of nettle tea would settle him just as well.'

'For the love of Jesus, Olivia,' Mia said, 'just give the man a strong drink for shock and also to help him sleep. He'll collapse if he doesn't get some rest. I'm really worried about him.'

'So am I, which is why I'm encouraging healthy options,' Olivia said. 'I lost one husband. I don't need to lose another.'

He's not your husband yet, Mia wanted to say. 'Just please make sure he gets rest.'

'Of course I will. I take great care of Charlie.' Olivia bristled. 'You should do the same with your husband. Men need to be minded.'

Mia closed her eyes and tried to block out Olivia's voice before she threw her a right hook.

Johnny steered Mia towards their car. Her hands were shaking so much, she couldn't click her seatbelt into place. Riley reached over and gently did it for her.

Johnny placed his hand on her shoulder. 'You can let go now.'

Mia bent over and howled. She cried for her beautiful sister, for the baby that would never live, for Izzy, for her father and for herself. She cried the tears of the broken-hearted.

33

Riley checked her face for the millionth time in her phone mirror. She'd spent her whole lunch break locked in this toilet cubicle, applying make-up and trying to make herself look as good as possible. She'd nicked her mum's push-up bra with the gel implants and opened her shirt button to show off her cleavage. Cleavage, for Riley, was a novelty. As Shocko had said, she had two fried eggs, but that was OK because she had good legs. It was rare to have both, her friend had told her.

Riley knew Zach was a leg man: he'd told her he loved her legs. But Zoë had really long, toned legs from jumping over the stupid hurdles all day long, and she had good boobs too. Not too big, not too small. More apples than fried eggs, but not melons.

Riley sprayed perfume on her neck and rubbed her hair in it. She wanted to be irresistible. She pulled at her eyes. No amount of concealer could hide her tiredness. She hadn't been able to sleep.

When they'd got home from that horrendous meeting last night, her mum had gone straight to bed. Riley had never seen anyone cry that much. She'd been really frightened by Mia's breakdown in the car.

She had wanted to check on her so she'd crept into the dark bedroom. Her mum was lying on her back, looking at the ceiling. Riley had gone to the side of the bed. Mia was lying in darkness, with just a sliver of daylight streaming through the curtains.

'Hi, Mum. I just wanted to see if you needed anything. I'm

sorry the meeting was so awful. I guess there is no hope for the baby, even though Adam thinks so?'

Mia shook her head. 'No, pet. The baby isn't going to make it.'

'Shit.'

'Yep, it is. Completely and utterly shit.'

'I'm sorry, Mum.'

'Me, too.'

'Can I get you anything? Tea, wine, vodka, Xanax?'

Mia gave her a weak smile. 'I'd like the last three, please. But, no, I'm just going to stay here and be sad for a while.'

'Like, for a day or a week or how long?'

'I don't know, Riley.'

'I'm just wondering because I kind of need a lift to school tomorrow and Dad has an interview.'

'Does he?'

'Oh, shit! I wasn't supposed to tell you – he doesn't want you getting your hopes up.' Dad would kill her. She'd over-heard him on the phone, so he'd told her about it, but he'd specifically said, 'Don't tell your mother. It might come to nothing.' Why had she opened her big mouth?

'Please, Mum, don't say anything to Dad about it.'

'I'll say nothing. Pray he gets it, Riley. We need some good news.'

'Does Izzy know about Sarah and the baby?'

'No, it's up to Adam to tell her.'

'Poor Izzy.'

'Yeah, poor little thing. Losing your mother is the worst.' Mia began to cry again.

'Well, losing your dad would suck too.'

'Losing your mother is worse.'

'I think losing either would be the same.'

Riley loved both of her parents equally. If she was being

honest, in the last year she'd probably loved Johnny more because he didn't nag her all the time.

'Sarah and Izzy were so close,' Mia said. 'They adored each other. It was such a beautiful relationship. Izzy is going to be crushed. Her life is ruined.'

'I know it's terrible, but she still has her dad.' Riley tried to reassure her mother.

'Adam's hardly dad of the year. He doesn't even know how to boil water.'

'True, but he'll probably meet someone.'

'What?'

Riley, not realizing what she was saying, had ploughed on: 'Well, he's decent-looking, has a few quid and isn't ancient, so he'll probably meet someone, and then Izzy will have a stepmum.'

'How could you say that? Sarah isn't even cold yet.'

'What? I didn't mean it like that – I didn't mean it like "Let's all forget about Sarah." I meant . . . Well, I meant Izzy will probably be looked after eventually by a woman who will be nice to her and stuff.'

'I just . . . How can you even say that? She's only . . .' Mia turned her head away and cried into her pillow.

Riley had stood, rooted to the spot. Crap. Now she'd upset her mother even more. Why did she always say the wrong thing? She'd meant to say that Izzy would hopefully end up with a loving stepmother who would mind her and love her. But now Mia thought she was a heartless bitch who was lining women up to marry her uncle.

'How about that Xanax?' Riley had tried.

Mia had closed her eyes. Riley had tiptoed out of the room, cursing herself.

Now, she applied one last layer of lip gloss, pushed away the thoughts of her messed-up family and unlocked the cubicle door. She strode into drama with as much confidence as she could muster. Her stomach was doing little flips.

Mr Warren had set up the desks, so each pair was facing each other. Riley went over and sat opposite Zach. He looked down and fiddled with his pen.

'Right,' Mr Warren said. 'I want you to discuss your chosen book or play and start working out some of the themes you're going to debate.'

'What are we doing then?' Zach finally looked up at Riley. God, his eyes. So blue, so sexy. 'The life and times of the Dalai Lama, I suppose.' Zach sighed.

Riley pretended the dig hadn't stung. *I'm raw*, she wanted to shout. *My aunt is dead, kind of, almost, and her baby is going to die and my mum's having a nervous breakdown and my uncle's being a prick and my dad has no job and my life is hell.*

Mia had barely spoken that morning when she was driving Riley to school. She looked so old and sad. Riley had tried to talk to her, but Mia just kept crying silently, like someone with serious mental-health issues. Riley was scared, really scared. Her mum was the rock of the family. Mia held them all together. She sorted out problems, paid bills, ordered everyone about. That was how they worked. That was their family rhythm. But now she was quiet and heartbroken, and Riley had felt sick all morning thinking about her mum being broken. She wanted Mia to shout at her or nag her or criticize her – something. But she was just like this empty shell of a person. Riley had leaned over to hug her, and Mia had stayed still, hands on the steering wheel, not moving, not noticing. It was as if Riley wasn't there. Mia had gone somewhere else in her mind and Riley was frightened.

'I chose *Little Women* actually.'

'Never heard of it. Is it about pygmies being mistreated in the Amazon or something?' Zach rolled his eyes.

Riley willed herself to stay calm. 'No, it's a novel about four sisters.'

'Not the one with Mr Darcy that my mum loves?' Zach groaned.

'No, it's about the March family. There are four teenage sisters. The dad has lost all his money and gone off to join the American Civil War as a pastor. Meg and Jo March, the two older girls, have to work to support the family. Beth, who is shy and delicate, stays at home and helps with house-work, and the youngest, Amy, is still at school. Meg is beautiful, Jo is a tomboy, Beth is a pianist, Amy is an art-ist. Their neighbour, Mr Laurence, who is really rich, has a grandson, Laurie, who Jo becomes best friends with, but then her sister Amy, who is spoilt, ends up running off with him, which is totally unfair because Laurie loves Jo. Like, he really loves her, but he just gets his head turned by Amy cos she's pretty and flirty, but she's thick and stupid and selfish, and Jo's brilliant and smart and strong. But Laurie marries Amy in the end, which is just wrong.'

'Well, maybe this Laurie guy is happy with the pretty, flirty sister.'

'Why would he be? Jo's so much better. He loves Jo.'

'Well, he obviously loves Amy more.'

'No, he doesn't. He just gets dazzled by her and she's a manipulative cow who lures him in when Jo isn't around.'

'Well, then, Laurie's a dork.'

'He isn't. He's a really nice guy, too nice.'

'A nice guy still isn't going to marry someone he doesn't love. He might shag Amy, but he wouldn't marry her.'

'They didn't go around shagging each other in the old days. No one had sex before marriage – they barely even kissed. And if Laurie had slept with Amy, I don't think Jo would ever have forgiven him or married him.'

'So why didn't she propose to him if she loved him? Why did she wait around for him to fall for her sister?'

'The thing is, Laurie proposed to Jo and she said no. But I don't think she really meant it. She did love him.'

Zach snorted. 'Come on! The dude asks her to marry him and she says no. No means no. Isn't that what we keep hearing women say? So if she says no, then what's he supposed to think? That she really meant "Not now, maybe later"? Whichever way you look at it, it's a kick in the face for him.'

'But he knew her. He understood her. He knew she was complicated. He should have just waited a bit and tried to persuade her more.'

Zach shook his head. 'Why? Why should he run around begging or waiting for years for Jo to finally decide to marry him? He asked, she said no, so why is it wrong of him to go for the sexy younger sister?'

'I never said she was sexy.'

'Pretty, cute, whatever.'

'She was selfish and vain, and thought she was better than everyone, and she just wanted Laurie because he was rich. Amy was not a good person like Jo was.'

'Maybe Laurie didn't care about that. Maybe he just wanted a hot wife.'

Riley glared at him. 'Are men really that shallow?'

'Why is it shallow to want a good-looking wife?'

'Don't men want someone they can talk to, not just look at? And, FYI, looks fade, minds grow.'

'Maybe some men want to marry someone who will look good and not want to discuss the American Civil War or whatever over breakfast every morning.'

'Maybe some men are pathetic and shallow, and when they look across the breakfast table one morning and see a woman with wrinkles and saggy boobs talking about getting a new bonnet, they'll want to shoot themselves.'

'What's a bonnet?'

'Hat.'

'I suppose that would be kind of boring.'

Riley beamed inside. Outwardly she just shrugged.

'Actually, I was thinking about you the other night.'

Riley's heart pounded. 'Yeah?' She tried to sound nonchalant.

'Yeah. My dad was watching this documentary about the Vietnam war and I sat down for just a minute but then I got really into it. Did you know that the Vietnam war lasted nearly twenty years and is the longest war in the history of the US? And, like, more than three million people were killed during the conflict? But only fifty-eight thousand of them were Americans.'

Riley grinned. She was about to say, 'Yes, I did know that because I read this really amazing book called *Born on the Fourth of July*', but instead she said, 'No, wow, that's really interesting.'

Zach beamed at her. 'I know, right?'

Riley basked in the glow of his smile. If she had to play down her knowledge a tiny bit, so what? He was worth it.

'So, what happens to the other two sisters in the story?' Zach asked, looking at the book Riley was holding and breaking that lovely spell.

'Meg marries Laurie's tutor and then Beth gets really sick. And Jo is the one who looks after her and tries to make her better. She loves Beth so much she just can't bear to see her so sick.'

'Does Beth get better?'

Riley shook her head. 'No, she doesn't, she gets worse, and Jo is so upset. And then Beth, well . . . she dies.' Riley ducked her head because she suddenly felt a tsunami of emotions rising inside her. Beth dies, just like Sarah and now the baby too. Riley could see her beautiful aunt in the hospital bed with all those tubes sticking out of her. She tried to shake away the memory and think of Sarah alive and smiling, but she couldn't.

'Uhm, are you OK?'

Riley croaked, 'Sorry, it's just my aunt.'

'The one in the coma?'

'She's dead,' Riley whispered.

Zach reached out and took her hand. 'Oh, God, I'm sorry. I know you were close to her. I remember you talking about her. Sarah, right?'

Riley nodded. He remembered.

'Look, do you want to go home? We can do this another time. You've got way too much going on.'

Riley shook her head. 'No, I want to stay here and do this. It's a good distraction.'

What she really wanted was for Zach to scoop her up. She wanted to sit on his knee and lay her head on his chest and feel his strong arms around her and hear him whisper in her ear, 'You rock.'

She wanted to tell him how much she hurt. She wanted to tell him she was doing everything wrong. She was saying the wrong things to her mother and father and everyone. She wanted to tell him that she loved him and that she needed him right now. She needed to know he was there for her. She wanted to talk, to FaceTime him for hours every night, and have him tell her she was great and that it was going to be OK. That her mum would be OK, that her little cousin would be OK, that her dad would get a job and they wouldn't be kicked out of the house, like she her heard her mum tell her dad they might. She wanted Zach to tell her she was gorgeous and special and not a stupid loser, who wasn't helping anyone and kept putting her foot in it. She wanted to tell him that she loved her mother and wanted Mia to know that, but she couldn't find the words. She wanted to tell him that her life at home was hell. She wanted to tell him that she had never felt so alone or sad.

'Are you sure?' Zach asked.

'Yeah, I'll be fine. You know me, I'm strong,' Riley said.

'Look, Riley, I'm sorry about –'

Harry's fat arse landed in the middle of their table. 'So, what are you guys doing? I bet Riley's making you do some worthy book like Nelson Mandela's autobiography that's, like, four thousand pages long.'

'No, we're doing *Little Women*.'

'What's that about? Midgets being discriminated against?'

'No, it's about these four sisters who –'

'Let me guess, lesbians looking for equality?' Harry cut across Zach.

'No, you fuckwit, it isn't,' Riley snapped.

'Oooooh, Riley's riled up. What are you going to do? Throw a drink over me while simultaneously concussing yourself?' Harry cracked up laughing. 'God, I wish someone had filmed that moment. Priceless.' Harry slapped Zach on the back. 'Zach really does have women falling at his feet.'

'Shut up,' Zach said.

'Relax. You can't help being a stud. I'd like a piece of Zoë action – now, *she*'s hot. You certainly traded up there,' Harry said. 'No offence, Riley.'

'Fuck off, Harry, you're being a dick,' Zach snapped.

'No offence taken, you vile ginger mutant,' Riley said, forcing tears back behind her eyeballs. No way was this bastard going to make her cry.

'Ginger is in. Look at Prince Harry, same name, same hair colour and he's with a ride.'

'I wonder would that have any little thing to do with the fact that he's a prince and you're a . . . a . . . What's the word? Oh, yeah – a lobotomized arsehole.'

Harry glared at her. 'What's lobotomized?'

Zach grinned. 'I think it means you're not just an arsehole, you're a stupid one too.' He winked at Riley. 'Right?'

'Exactly.'

Harry stomped off in a huff, muttering, 'I'll lobotomized you.'

Riley looked at Zach and they laughed.

'Sorry,' Zach said.

'Don't worry about it. I can handle Harry.'

'No,' Zach said, reaching out to squeeze her arm. 'I'm sorry for everything you're going through and for the whole Zoë thing. You're amazing, Riley.'

Riley's heart was pounding in her chest. Zach had realized his mistake. This was it.

Zach leaned towards her. 'You're so strong, no one can hurt you.' He patted her arm and stood up. 'Gotta go. I'm meeting Zoë to help her train for the Leinster finals this weekend.'

I hope she trips and smashes her stupid smug face into the ground, Riley thought.

'See you,' she said, as her heart shrivelled.

34

Rob read the last line of the book. He looked down at his sleepy niece and kissed her forehead. She was cleaning her glasses again. 'They're clean, sweetie. Let's put them down here.'

'No, I see a bit of dust.' Izzy rubbed harder.

'You can clean them again in the morning if you want to. But now you need some sleep.' Rob took them from her and placed them on her bedside locker. He pulled her pink princess duvet up to cover her shoulders. 'You're tired, Izzy. Will I leave the lamp on or switch it off?'

'On, please. I'm having bad dreams about Mummy and I hate waking up when it's all dark.'

Poor little kid. Rob remembered having lots of nightmares as a child. 'When I used to have nightmares, I'd wake Adam up and he'd talk to me until I fell back asleep. You should do that if you wake up. He's very good at making the nightmares go away.'

Izzy rolled onto her side and looked up at her uncle. 'I feel bad waking Daddy up. He's so tired, it feels mean to wake him.'

'Well, wake me up, then. I've lots of energy.'

Izzy wrinkled her nose. 'That would feel strange, but maybe. Are you and Ellen going to have kids?'

Rob smiled. 'I hope so. We've only been married two years, but we definitely want children. I'd be the happiest man alive if I had a gorgeous little girl like you.'

Izzy smiled. 'I hope you have babies soon. I want more cousins. I only have Riley. I was a bit worried at first about having a little brother, but now I'm excited. I think it'll be fun.'

Somehow Rob managed to keep his face blank. He busied himself placing the book on the locker beside Izzy's glasses. As he stood up to go Izzy called him. 'Uncle Rob?'

'Yes, sweetheart?'

'Do you remember your mummy?'

Rob shook his head. 'No, she died when Adam was three and I was only a few months old.'

'That's so sad. Was your daddy able to look after you and make your school lunches?'

If only you knew, he thought. 'Well, to be honest, Adam and I did a lot for ourselves growing up. Dad was working. Adam was the best big brother ever. He always looked after me. You know he'll always look after you, don't you?'

Izzy nodded. 'Yes, but I want Mummy back.'

Rob came back over and sat on the edge of the bed. 'Oh, love, I know you do. But just remember, you have a whole big family who love you and are here to look after you. Not just your dad, but Mia and Johnny and Riley and your grand-dad and me and Ellen too.'

Izzy's eyes narrowed. 'I know, but I want Mummy, and I know she'll come back to me. She always said she'd never leave me. She's going to wake up on my Communion Day, I just know it.'

Rob didn't want to get drawn into this minefield. He was terrified he'd say the wrong thing. He pointed to the clock on her bedside table. 'Look at the time! You need your beauty sleep, princess.' He kissed her.

'Uncle Rob?'

'Yes?'

'I'm glad you came over to help Daddy. He needs someone to mind him.'

'I'm very glad I can help in any way. I owe your dad a lot.'

'Uncle Rob?'

'Yes, pet?'

'Will you look up YouTube and teach Daddy how to do plaits?'

He smiled. 'I will. Now go to sleep, and remember, if you have bad dreams, come in and wake me up or, if you prefer, go in to your dad.'

'Night, night.'

Rob exited the room and prayed his poor little niece got a good night's sleep. He knew he wouldn't get a wink of sleep after the hospital that day. He'd spent about an hour in the room with Sarah and Adam, and it had taken every bit of will-power he possessed not to run screaming from the room. Even since he'd arrived in Ireland, Sarah's body had deteriorated hugely. Today Angela had warned them it was bad, but nothing could have prepared him. Sarah looked like something from a horror movie. It had shaken him to the core. He understood his brother wanted to try to keep Ben alive, but after today, Rob just couldn't see how any baby could survive in that situa-tion. It was unnatural and deeply unsettling. The thing was, he didn't think Adam could see it. God knew how that was pos-sible, but Adam kept kissing Sarah's face and whispering to her, and that was as unnerving as how Sarah looked.

Rob went into the living room carrying a tray of drinks and a plate of cheese and crackers. The room was painted and furnished in soft, soothing colours. Everything blended in. Beige, taupe and olive green sat side by side, complementing each other. Nothing jarred the senses.

'I love this room. I spent so many nights cuddled up on the couch with Sarah, watching movies and drinking wine.' Adam sounded so wistful.

Rob handed his brother a large gin and tonic, and Adam took a long sip. 'Bloody hell!' he spluttered. 'Is there any tonic in this?'

Rob sat down beside him on the couch. 'I thought you needed a strong one.' He knocked back half of his in one go.

'You clearly do,' Adam said.

'I've got to be honest with you, Adam, I was shocked when I saw Sarah today. Like, really shocked.'

Adam's jaw clenched. 'I know it's hard, but she's still fighting so I have to fight too. I will not give up on Ben.'

Rob remained silent and took another gulp of his drink.

Adam sipped his gin and tonic. 'I've been avoiding alcohol. I'm afraid if I start drinking, I may never stop.'

'Don't worry, I won't let you overdo it.'

'What if I have Dad's genes and end up an alcoholic?'

'Adam,' Rob said gently, 'you've always been able to have a few drinks without going overboard. You're never going to be like Dad.'

Adam pulled a cushion from behind his back. It was edged with little fabric bobbles. 'Sometimes, lately, in very dark moments, I kind of envy Dad. He just disappeared into a haze of booze. He felt no responsibility to anyone. He only thought about and loved himself. Maybe he had the right attitude – life would be easier if we didn't love or have to take care of others. There would be no pain or grief.'

Rob kicked off his shoes and placed his feet on the velvet footstool. 'He was a selfish, pathetic, shallow old bastard, who left this world without one person mourning him. Would you really want that? I know you're in Hell right now, but you loved and were loved. You have Izzy, who adores you and whom you adore. It's not what you wanted, it's not what you had, but it's still something good.'

Adam took another swig of his drink and let the numbing

effect of the alcohol wash over him. 'I'm not a good dad, Rob. I can't even make her bloody lunch. She needs Sarah – I need Sarah.' He began to cry.

Rob silently handed him a tissue.

'Sarah was our family. She was the centre. She was the most important person. I was so busy working all the time that I left raising Izzy to her. I should have been home more. She asked me – she made me promise that when our son was born I'd be home every night for dinner. I should have been here more, Rob. I wasn't a good husband or father.'

Rob put down his glass and sat forward. 'Hold on a minute here. You are a good husband and father. You provide for your family. You've given them a beautiful home, security, love and a good life. OK, so you weren't home every night, big bloody deal. I'm not home every night either. Ellen is always complaining that I work too hard. But they don't get it. We have to work hard! It's the only way we can feel safe. When you come from nothing, you never feel you have enough. You crave financial safety and security, but it's never enough.'

Adam nodded. 'You're the only one who really understands. No one else knows what it's like to live each day not knowing if there'd be food in the house, if Dad would be awake or unconscious. Oh, Rob, what am I going to do about the baby?' Adam asked, his voice breaking.

Rob chose his words very carefully. 'I can't tell you what to do. You have to look at the facts and make that decision yourself. Weigh up what the doctors are saying and make the decision that's best for your whole family – all four of you.'

Adam buried his face in his hands. 'I know what's happening to Sarah is awful, but my boy's heart is still beating. Sarah would have done anything for her kids. She once said she'd give up her life for Izzy.'

'You don't have to make a decision today or tomorrow. Take a breath.'

Rob was really worried that Adam was going to crack. He was teetering very close to the edge. His big brother had always been the strong one, the determined, driven, confident one. He had always been there for Rob, through thick and a lot of very thin. Adam was his hero, the person he looked up to and admired most. But now, looking at that broken man, Rob knew he had to be the supportive one. He had to be strong for Adam. If his brother wanted to keep Sarah alive, Rob would back him. Just like Adam had always backed Rob. No matter what curveballs life threw at them – and there had been many – they always had each other's back.

After seeing Sarah, Rob had called Ellen and sobbed down the phone. It was such a shock to see her in that terrible state. Ellen said she thought it was wrong and they should turn the machines off, but Rob said it was Adam's decision and he had to support him no matter what. They'd ended up arguing about it.

It was the ultimate impossible choice. Rob's heart broke for his brother. You'd think life would give Adam a break. Seriously, what kind of God lumps this on a man who has already had to claw his way through childhood? Rob drank deeply and enjoyed the burning sensation as the alcohol slid down his throat.

'I don't like fighting with Charlie and Mia, but it's my son.' Adam looked at Rob with eyes full of anguish. 'Dad gave up on us, and I won't give up on my Ben. If that means falling out with the others, then so be it. If I can't trust them, they can't be near Sarah. It's as simple as that.'

Rob knew it was very far from simple. 'Why don't I try to talk to Charlie and Mia, smooth things over? I'm with you, all the way.'

Adam wiped the tears from his face. 'Thanks, Rob. I feel like I'm going mad. My only sanity is you.'

Rob picked up his drink and knocked it back. He wanted to sleep, to pass out, to wipe out the gruesome image of Sarah's distended and distorted body. But he knew he had to get up tomorrow and face it again.

35

Johnny walked into the bedroom and placed a cup of tea on the bedside locker. 'Come on, up you come and drink your tea.' He placed his hands under Mia's arms and lifted his wife into a seated position. 'You've had an evening and a morning in bed crying. Time to get up now.'

Johnny gathered up the mound of tissues on the floor beside Mia and threw them into the wastepaper basket. He opened the curtains.

Mia winced as sunlight flooded the room. 'Stop, Johnny, it's too bright.'

He opened the window. Fresh air flowed into the room. 'Sunlight and fresh air are good for you. Drink your tea.' He handed her the mug. It had 'Number 1 Mum' on it. Riley had given it to her for Mother's Day when she was nine, still sweet and compliant.

Mia sipped the tea. 'Sugar?'

'I put some in to give you energy.'

'Nice.' Mia sipped again. Her head ached.

'I know you want to pull the covers over your head and stay there, but it's only going to make you feel worse. You need to get up and go to see Sarah. Talk to her. I know she looks awful, but hold her hand, talk to her, make your peace with her going and say what you want to say to her.'

'I'm not allowed near her, remember?' Mia said bitterly. 'Adam was very clear on that last night.'

'To hell with Adam. He can't stop you seeing your own sister. Besides, I checked. Angela's on duty this afternoon and Adam will be picking Izzy up from school, so you can slip in then. It'll make you feel better to see her. It'll help you get your head straight.'

Mia put down the mug of sweet tea. She reached up and pulled her husband close. 'I love you, Johnny. You're the best man there is.'

'Even unemployed?'

'Even unemployed.' She kissed him on the lips. They held each other for a minute, each enjoying the closeness and comfort of the other's arms.

Johnny pulled back first. 'Much as I love you and enjoy your hugs, you need a long shower. I'll make you something to eat and then drive you to the hospital.'

Mia smiled. 'Thank you. Thank you for marrying me even though I can be short-tempered, bossy and a pain in the arse.'

Johnny grinned. 'I like being bossed around and you aren't a pain in the arse, you're just very . . . uhm . . . decisive.'

Mia laughed. 'How tactfully put.'

Angela came straight over to Mia when she spotted her putting on an apron and mask.

'How are you doing, Mia? Yesterday was a very tough day. All the doctors were upset about the meeting and having to give such awful news.'

Mia sighed. 'It was very grim. Adam didn't take it well. He's banned me and Dad from seeing Sarah.'

Angela glanced around and whispered, 'He's told us all to keep you away.'

Mia rubbed the disinfectant soap into her hands and looked into Angela's eyes. 'I need to see Sarah, even if it's the last time.'

'Of course you do. You slip in there now and I'll keep an

eye out. If I hear him coming, I'll warn you. We don't want a scene in ICU, but I know how much you love your sister, and sure how could I deny you or poor Charlie seeing her?'

'Thanks, Angela, I really appreciate that.'

'Go on in now and I'll keep watch.'

Mia paused. 'Does she . . . is she . . . worse?'

Angela nodded. 'I'm so sorry, but yes. It's happening faster all the time. We can't prevent it, even with all the medication. You'll find it hard to look at her.'

Mia pulled her mask up over her mouth and took a deep breath. She braced herself as she walked in.

Sarah looked truly horrific. Mia closed her eyes to block out the awful sight. Part of her wanted to run away, but then she remembered what Johnny had said: 'Hold her hand and talk to her.'

Mia walked over to the bed. It was like another world in here. A separate universe where all the anger, angst and arguing were left behind. Here, she could talk to her sister in peace. Except for the whirring of the ventilator and the beep of the machines every now and then, it was like an oasis of calm away from the storm raging outside, with all of the people who loved Sarah fighting about her.

Mia sat down and took her sister's hand. Avoiding looking at her bulging eyes and bloated face, she concentrated on Sarah's hand. She took the lavender hand cream she'd brought with her out of her bag. She squirted a drop onto Sarah's right hand and began to massage it into her sister's dried-out fingers. The scent of lavender filled the room.

'I miss you so much, Sarah. We all do. Things are a bit tricky, I'm afraid. Everyone's so upset and emotions are running high. I know you'd hate to think we were fighting and arguing about you. We're all heartbroken. We love you so much and each of us wants the best for you and the baby, but we don't agree on what that is.' Mia didn't want to tell Sarah that her husband had gone crazy and was behaving like a total tyrant, treating her and Charlie like dirt.

'You'll be glad to know that Rob came over from Toronto to be with Adam. He hasn't left his side. I'm so sorry things have turned out like this. I know how much you wanted a baby. We're all just devastated. To be honest, Sarah, my head aches from trying to know what the right thing to do is. So, I'm going to give us both a break and just sit here and read you your diary.'

Mia flicked through the diary. 'Let's choose a happy memory. Oh, here, look! It's your wedding day.'

'I cannot believe I'm marrying the man of my dreams! I'm going to be Mrs Adam Brown. Mia thinks it's silly to take your husband's name. She still calls herself Mia Wilson, but I want to take Adam's name. I want to be Mrs Brown. I can't wait to be part of a married couple. I want to make Adam the happiest man ever and have lots of mini-Adams and mini-mes to look after. I think four kids would be perfect. Two boys and two girls. I want my daughter to have a sister. Sisters are the best. Mia always has my back. She's always been there for me, looking out for me and helping me and, yes, bossing me around too. I don't mind Mia's bossing, though, because she does it out of love and concern.

'I'm so happy I met Adam. He's perfect. I know that he will protect me and keep me safe and love me for ever. He's so good to me and he always makes me feel like the most gorgeous, precious thing in his life. I've never had a boyfriend who makes me feel this good about myself or so safe and loved and cherished. I feel like I could literally fly with Adam by my side.

'I'm so happy I could burst. I almost feel weepy about how happy I am. I have the best parents, the best sister and, in a few hours, I'll have the best husband in the world. I am one lucky girl.

'Oh, and the best flower girl. Riley looks adorable in her little dress. She is such a cutie although I can see Mum and Mia's personality in her. Riley knows what she likes and doesn't like and she's only seven! I reckon Mia will have her hands full when she's a teenager.'

Mia snorted. 'How right you were, Sarah. Riley is one big handful.'

'Mum always says that Mia was far more challenging than me as a teenager. But she always smiled when she said it. Mum adores Mia and loves that she challenges her and argues with her and debates all kinds of subjects with her. I think I'm too boring and placid for Mum. Don't get me wrong, Mum adores me, but she enjoys being with Mia more. I don't really get het up about things like Mum and Mia do. I just want a quiet, easy life. I know that may sound selfish and you should really go out and march for causes and all that, but to be honest, and I can only admit this here, I just want to be at home with Adam, snuggled up on the couch.

'I think Riley will be feisty like her mother and grandmother. Mum's going to get such a kick out of Riley when she gets older and more opinionated. It'll be fun to watch.'

Mia gulped back tears. 'I wish Mum had known Riley for longer. They got on so well. "Peas in a pod," Dad used to say. I wish Mum was here now to help me connect better with Riley. I need her, but even more, I need you, Sarah. You always told me to be more patient, to give Riley a break, and you were so good at getting me to take a step back and not react so quickly. I miss your advice. I miss you and your positivity and calmness and loveliness and . . . all of you.'

'I wonder what my children will be like. Will they be go-getters like Adam? Will they be sporty or smart or arty or all three? It doesn't

matter to me, as long as they're healthy and happy. When I look back now, I feel so grateful to have had such a happy childhood. I didn't appreciate it at the time but now, when I see what can happen to kids, I know how lucky I was to have Mum and Dad and Mia. I just hope I don't only have one child. I can't say that to Mia. I know how much she wanted another child and how upset she was when they found out they couldn't. My heart broke for both of them. Johnny was so crushed and he kept looking at Mia when they told us and you could see he was so devastated that he couldn't give her this important gift – another child. He loves her so much and, you know, she loves him just as much. She was amazing: she never made him feel like it was a problem. She said Riley was enough and she never looked back. Except sometimes, when she was alone with me and had had a few glasses of wine, her bravery would slip and she'd cry about it. I felt so bad for her. What can you say to someone who wants something they just can't have? It makes your heart sore.

'I loved having an older sister. I think having a sibling is so wonderful, I want that for my kids. I want them to have the bond that a sibling gives you and to know, whatever happens, that that person will always be there for you.'

Mia had to put the diary down and wipe her eyes. 'Oh, Sarah. I wanted Izzy to have a brother, and we tried to save him, but they said there's no hope. I'm so sorry. I prayed so hard – we all did. I promise you I'll keep an eye on Izzy, and Riley will be like an older sister to her. Actually, Sarah, you'd be so happy if you saw how sweet Riley is being with Izzy. It's made me so proud of her. She's taking Izzy under her wing. I guess it's a bit like I did with you. Five years between us and seven between them. They can be each other's sibling.'

'I'm looking at my wedding dress hanging up on the door of the wardrobe. It's so beautiful. Mia's sleeping soundly in the bed beside me. She

is such a deep sleeper. I want to wake her up and chat, but I'll let her sleep for another twenty minutes. She's exhausted from working and then Riley got an ear infection and didn't sleep for four nights. Poor Mia is worn out. OK, I'll let her sleep for a bit longer, but then I will wake her because I'm too excited to sit here alone. I think half past eight is a reasonable time to wake her up. I'll order a big breakfast in bed. I can't eat a thing, I'm too nervous, but Mia will enjoy it and we can chat while she's eating and maybe a cup of herbal tea will calm my nerves. Although they aren't really nerves, just excitement. Excitement about this being the best day of my life when I get to marry my true love and start on a new adventure with him by my side. I am truly the happiest girl alive!!!!!!!!!!!!!!!!!'

Mia closed the diary. She held her sister's hand between hers. 'Adam's upsetting me so much,' she said quietly, 'but you've reminded me how important he is to you. You really adored that man, and I know you're the most important thing in the world to him. Things aren't great at the moment, but I promise I'll talk to Adam and sort things out. I'll do it for you and Izzy.'

36

Mia put her apron and mask in the bin. She felt so old and weary. Her whole body ached with exhaustion and sadness. She had to try to patch things up with Adam. She must remember how upset he was, bite her tongue and give him the benefit of the doubt. He was well-intentioned, and she had to keep that firmly in mind.

Angela came over to her. 'Did you have a nice chat?'

Mia nodded. 'Yes, thanks. It was just what I needed.'

'You've all had a terrible shock and we're so sorry about the baby, too. It's been a nightmare for you.'

'Thanks, Angela. Everyone here has been so lovely to us.' Mia sighed. 'It's just amazing how one day your normal is going to school and teaching and the next your sister is brain dead and her baby is dying too. How is that? How can you process it?'

Angela patted her shoulder. 'ICU is full of people whose lives have changed in an instant. We see it all the time and it's so hard on the families and loved ones. You need to mind yourself, your dad too.'

Mia nodded, unable to speak. Kindness set her off. She blew her nose with a tissue. 'I need to go back to work.'

'Well, don't rush anything,' Angela said.

'I think it'll help to be there every day. The school have been so accommodating, but with the Communion coming up they need me to be around. Besides, the kids are so sweet and innocent, they lift my spirits.'

'If you think it'll help you, do it,' Angela said.

'Mum?'

Mia spun around. Riley was standing in her school uniform beside Johnny.

Johnny held up his hands in warning. 'There was a half-day in school for some teacher-training thing. Riley wanted to see Sarah, so I said she could because we don't know how long she has left.'

'I don't think it's a good idea.' Mia glanced towards the door to Sarah's room. Riley had no idea what lay behind it.

'I knew you'd say that,' Riley said, 'but I really want to see her, Mum. Dad told me she's all puffed up and stuff. I can handle it. I just want to say . . . goodbye.'

'I'm not sure you can handle it, Riley. I think you should remember Sarah as she was.'

'I want to see my aunt. I love her too, you know.' Riley's chin wobbled.

'Maybe it's no harm for Riley to see her and say a few words. You did say you found it comforting,' Angela suggested gently. 'I'll pop a pair of sunglasses over her eyes and make sure the sheet is covering her. Give me one second.'

'Thank you,' Mia said. At least if Sarah's bulging eyes and body were covered, Riley might get slightly less of a shock.

Angela handed protective gear to Riley, then disappeared into the room for a few minutes. She came back out and beckoned them over to the door.

'Now, you only have to go as far into the room as you wish,' Angela said. 'And the moment you want to leave, you do that. Don't feel it's disrespectful to leave quickly. It's a shock, and we don't want you to feel any pressure to stay with Sarah.'

Riley nodded.

Mia grabbed her hand. 'Riley, you need to prepare yourself. She looks awful . . . really, really awful.'

'It's OK, Mum,' Riley said, looking nervous. 'I understand. I'm ready.'

Mia helped her daughter with the apron and mask, then to disinfect her hands and put on gloves, and Johnny did the same. The three of them walked into the room.

Beside her, Mia heard Johnny gasp, 'Oh, Jesus.'

Riley walked straight over to the bed. 'Hi, Sarah, it's Riley and . . . Oh, my God!' she shrieked.

'I told you this was a bad idea,' Mia hissed to Johnny.

Riley covered her eyes. 'Oh, no . . . Sarah . . .'

Mia went over to comfort her, wrapping her in a tight hug. 'We'll leave, love. Let's go.'

Riley shrugged her arms away and took a deep breath. 'No, I'm OK. Sorry, Sarah.' She exhaled, walked over to the chair and sat down. She stared at Sarah, as Johnny and Mia stared at her.

'Poor Sarah,' Johnny whispered.

Riley picked up a brush from the bedside locker and began to brush Sarah's hair out across the pillow. She was gentle and tender and it hurt Mia's heart to see it.

'I always loved your hair, Sarah. It's movie-star hair. So silky and golden and wavy. Black is a bit crap, really. Maybe I'll dye mine blonde later.' Riley looked over at her parents. 'Honestly, it's OK now. You can go. I'll just stay for a few minutes.'

Mia and Johnny left the room, but Mia stood outside the door, leaving it slightly ajar so she could rush in if Riley panicked.

'I thought you'd like to know that Izzy is doing fine. I see her in the yard every day. She misses you big-time, but she's stronger than she looks. She's got your sweetness with a bit of Adam's toughness, which is good. Everyone keeps asking about you. It's hard to know what to say. I say you're in a

278

coma. I'm really sorry about the baby, Sarah. I know you wanted a sibling for Izzy. I used to hate being an only child, but I've kind of got used to it now. It's a bit intense because there is only you for your parents to focus on and you know what Mum is like – she's all over me like a rash, on my case twenty-four/seven. But then again, you get all your parents' love and attention, which is kind of cool too.

'I know you won't be there for Izzy, to see her grow up, and that totally sucks, but Mum will look out for her, and Dad and me and Granddad and Rob will, too. So she won't feel alone or not loved enough. We'll fill the gap, I promise.

'You were always so great to me. I loved calling into your house. There was always amazing home-cooked food and you were always so interested in me. You made Mum chill out and give me a break too. The only time I saw you annoyed was when I told Mum to shut up and you snapped at me and said, "Don't speak to your mother like that."

'When Mum went to the loo, you told me I should treasure her because she did so much for me. She worked so hard to provide me with everything and she was a brilliant mother. I was never to disrespect her and I should appreciate her. That made me think, and I realized you were right. I was mortified that you'd seen me being rude, and ashamed as well. Mum is great and I know how much she does for me. I guess some-times we just clash. Dad says it's because we're so similar, stubborn mules. I've tried to help and be kind since you've been in your coma, but I always seem to say the wrong thing. I dunno, it's like my brain wants to say one thing but it comes out of my mouth all wrong. I'm worried about Mum. She's so sad. I've never seen her like this. She spent half the day in bed yesterday. Yeah, I know! Mum in bed. I think she's depressed. I was scared she'd turn into one of those people who sits in a chair and rocks all day with dribble on their chin.

'I know her heart is broken in pieces. She cries a lot, and you know Mum never cries. It's hard seeing her so upset. But she loves you so much, she can't bear to say goodbye.

'I'm boring you now, amn't I? I guess I just wanted you to know that I'm trying to be a good daughter and I love you and I miss you and I still can't believe this has happened. God, Sarah, I really, really miss you. You were so brilliant to me.'

Mia could hear the sound of quiet crying. She bent her head and tried to fight back her own tears. Johnny came over and put his arms around her and she rested her head against him. From inside the room, they could hear Riley sniffing and taking deep breaths.

'I'm going to say goodbye, Sarah, even though I don't want to. But I'm not going to come in again because it really hurts to see you like this. I can't believe they're letting this happen to you. I'd pull that plug in a heartbeat if it were my choice . . . Oh, God, this is hard. I don't want to get up and go because then it's really over. I wish you were still here, Sarah. I'll remember you always. Love you.'

Through the crack in the door, Mia saw Riley stand up. Then she sat down again quickly, covering her face with her hands. Mia pointed silently and Johnny nodded. They pushed open the door and went inside. Mia went over and put her arm around Riley.

'Wherever she is, she heard you, and she adores you too,' she said. 'Come on, time to go now.'

She helped Riley to her feet and she and Johnny walked their daughter out of the room. Once outside, Johnny wrapped his arms around the two of them as they cried.

'What are you doing here?' a voice demanded.

Mia and Riley looked up, and Johnny took a step forward.

'Adam,' Johnny said, 'Riley wanted –'

'I thought I made it perfectly clear yesterday that you are not allowed near Sarah,' Adam snapped, as he walked towards them. 'You didn't do anything, did you?' he said, staring at them wildly. He ran past them into the room, glanced around, then came back out to them again.

'Adam, we wouldn't dream of touching any of the machines,' Johnny said calmly. 'I think you know that.'

'I know you're not with me on this,' Adam said. 'How the hell do I know what you would or wouldn't do? You can't be in there.'

'That is Mum's sister,' Riley said, her voice cracking. 'What if Rob was lying in a hospital bed and we said you couldn't visit him?'

Adam flinched, but then his face hardened again. 'You're just a kid, Riley. You don't understand this situation.'

'I understand enough,' Riley said. 'She's not Sarah any more. It's hard to be in there to see what's happening to her. I couldn't do that to someone I love.'

'You don't understand!' Adam shouted, and Johnny quickly stepped forward to protect Riley.

The two men squared up, anger flashing in their eyes.

'Stop that this minute,' Angela said, in a voice Mia had never heard her use before. She marched straight up and put a hand on each man's shoulder. 'Back away this instant or I'm getting security to put you both out.'

Johnny took a step away but remained warily on guard.

'They were just leaving,' Adam said.

'If they want to,' Angela said evenly. 'Mia is immediate family, so I'm not going to order her out.'

'I'm next-of-kin,' Adam said. 'My rights supersede hers and I don't want her in there.'

Mia took a deep breath. 'Adam, I'd really like to sort this out,' she said. 'It makes everything worse if we're fighting.'

Rob walked up to join them. 'What's going on?' he asked, sounding worried.

'I'm just explaining that they aren't to visit Sarah,' Adam said, staring hard at Mia.

'I was suggesting we talk it through and try to resolve this,' Mia said, forcing herself to stay calm and keep her voice low, non-threatening.

'That's a really good idea,' Rob said, clearly relieved. 'We really should talk as a family and work it out.'

Adam said nothing. He walked over to the nurses' station and went behind the counter. They all watched him, puzzled. Even Angela didn't say anything, just watched him in confusion. He rooted on the desk, then took up a pen and a blank sheet of paper. He wrote something on it in big letters, then pulled a piece of Sellotape off the dispenser and walked back towards them. He went straight into Sarah's room. They all crowded at the door, looking to see what he was doing.

He stuck the page on the ventilator machine and stood back. In big heavy letters he'd written: DO NOT TURN OFF!!!

'There,' he said. 'Now no one is going to do anything behind my back.'

'He's lost it,' Riley muttered.

Mia couldn't disagree. This was not the behaviour of a rational man. What was going on in his head?

'There's no need for that, Adam,' Angela said. 'Everyone knows the decision belongs to you, and that the doctors are the only ones with authority to handle the ventilator.'

'What people know and what people do are often different things,' Adam retorted. He pointed at Mia. '*She* is a control freak. She'd do it, I know she would.'

Mia gasped in shock.

'That is crazy,' Johnny said coldly. 'You've no idea what you're saying.'

'I wouldn't, Adam,' Mia said helplessly.

'You would,' Adam hissed.

'Outside,' Angela ordered. 'You're not arguing in here. Out.'

They all stood about in the corridor. Mia looked at Rob, and motioned with her head towards Adam, meaning 'Talk to him. Help us out here.'

Rob nodded, but he seemed half scared. 'Adam,' he said, moving towards his brother, 'Sarah would really hate this. Mia is willing to sit and talk it over, so why don't we go into the waiting room and do that?'

'I want to be with my wife now,' Adam said. 'Maybe we can talk another time.' With that, he grabbed some protective clothing and walked straight back into the room, closing the door behind him.

'Would you like me to ask Dr Mayhew to come down and talk to him?' Angela asked.

'Is he a shrink?' Riley asked. 'Because that's what he needs. He's lost it completely.'

'I'm so sorry,' Rob said, and Mia could see he was holding back tears. 'This isn't Adam. He's not sleeping or eating. He's crazy with grief.'

'He needs help,' Johnny said. 'Maybe the doctor can do something.'

Rob shook his head. 'When he's like this, there's no point. I don't think Mayhew could get through to him, especially when he's saying it's over.'

'I'll ring one of the social workers,' Angela said. 'I'll explain the situation and ask them to come and talk to him, not about the decision, just about what he's feeling. Would that be OK?'

'I guess,' Rob said.

Mia went over and hugged him. 'Rob, this isn't your fault. You're doing your best.'

'I feel like I'm losing my brother,' Rob said, then roughly rubbed away the tear that slid down his cheek.

'I'm not going to stay away from my sister,' Mia said, 'but we'll leave now. It might help him to calm down if we're gone. But if you need any time out, our door is always open.'

'Thanks,' Rob said. 'I'll get him a coffee and bring it in.'

'You do that,' Angela said. 'I'll make that phone call and we'll try to help him get things in perspective. The doctors are due down to check on Sarah in half an hour, so that will be a chance to talk it over as well.'

Mia, Johnny and Riley said goodbye to Rob and walked slowly through the corridors.

'Thank God Charlie wasn't here for that,' Mia said.

'When will the baby die?' Riley asked. 'I'm not being a bitch, I just want it to be over. Especially for you, Mum.'

Mia touched her daughter's cheek. 'I've absolutely no idea what will happen, Riley,' she said softly. 'It's just day by day.'

Day by day Sarah was crumbling into death. Day by day Adam was becoming more unhinged. Day by day Mia's heart was breaking more than she'd ever thought possible. Day by day they kept sinking further and further into this nightmare. Would it ever end?

37

Riley tried to concentrate on her arguments in favour of *Little Women* while Shocko howled along to an off-key guitar riff behind her. He had a large red bump on his eyebrow where his mother's wish had come true: an infection had developed. He'd had to take out the eyebrow ring and now he looked as if he had a huge zit above his eye.

'Seriously!' Riley swung around in her desk chair and glared at him.

'What? I'm trying to work on a new song. And it's not easy to play when you're sitting on a beanbag.'

'Maybe you should switch to the piano.'

'I don't own one.'

'Fine. Harmonica, then.'

'Like Bob Dylan?'

'Yes.'

Shocko grinned. 'Cool. Maybe I should. And he didn't have a great voice. I mean, I know he had good lyrics and all, but his voice wasn't so great. Maybe the harmonica would suit me better. I know my limitations. I can write amazing songs, but I don't have the best voice.'

'Neither did Leonard Cohen.'

'True. And neither does Kanye, really.'

'Well, there you go.'

'How much do you reckon a harmonica costs? I've only twenty quid left from my birthday money.'

'More than twenty quid.'

'How much more?'

Riley threw down her pen. 'I don't know – about fifty, I guess, for a decent starter one.'

'Do you think I should get one that you stick onto your guitar with the long steel bar? I bet they're more expensive.'

'I wasn't suggesting you do both. I think you should choose the harmonica *instead* of the guitar.'

Shocko leaned back on the beanbag, his floppy brown hair falling over his eyes. 'Yeah, but if I did both, that would be impressive. Especially if I did both at the same time. Harmonica and guitar – seriously cool.'

Riley peeled dark blue varnish off her thumbnail. 'I dunno, Shocko. I really don't think it would be that cool. A harmonica stuck onto a guitar looks kind of nerdy.'

'Really?'

'Yeah, like your mother made you play ten instruments because she thought you were *gifted* and you spent all of your childhood inside playing scales.'

Shocko pushed back his hair. 'Are you looking at it?'

'Hard to miss.' Riley smirked.

'That's why I gelled my hair down. It's supposed to cover it. Anyway, you're no one to talk – you've got a big zit on your chin.'

Riley's hand flew up to it. 'I thought I'd hidden it with concealer.'

Shocko laughed. 'You can see it from space.'

'Shit.' Riley pulled out a hand mirror from her desk drawer. 'Oh, God, it's way worse than it was this morning. It must be all the stress about Sarah.'

Damn. She had drama the next day with Zach. Riley wondered if she should pop it.

'And what's happening with your aunt?'

Riley sighed. 'There's no change. She's being kept alive because the baby shows a heartbeat. But it's so horrific.' She covered her face with her hands, as if blocking out the images in her head. 'I went to say goodbye and I nearly puked when I saw her. I hate to see her like that. No one should end up that way.'

'Will Adam pull the plug?' Shocko asked.

'No,' Riley said. 'He's gone psycho. No one can even talk to him about ending it. We visited the other day, so I could say goodbye, and he freaked at us for being there. He thinks Mum's going to switch off the machines or something. It's mental. And guess what arrived yesterday evening by courier?'

'What?' Shocko said, hanging on her every word.

'A solicitor's letter, telling Mum and Granddad they're banned from the hospital.'

'Jesus, can he do that?'

Riley shrugged. 'I don't know.'

'Banning them . . . That's harsh.'

'He's a prick. You should see my poor granddad. He's in bits. He looks about a hundred, and his annoying girlfriend keeps kissing him and massaging his shoulders. It's gross.'

'Do you think they're having sex? Do old people still do it?'

Riley made a face. 'I really don't know. I doubt it. I hope not.'

'What's the age you stop having sex? Fifty? Actually, no, it must be older. The one from *Sex and the City* who has loads of sex is fifty.'

'Yeah, but you do realize she's acting having sex, not *actually* having it.'

Shocko threw a stray sock at her. 'Duh, I know that, but I reckon she's up for it in real life too. Maybe it's sixty.'

'Well, Granddad is sixty-nine, so I guess he could still be at it.'

'Does your dick go all wrinkly like women's boobs?'

287

'Jesus, I don't know!'

'At least women can have boob jobs. Men can't have dick jobs.'

'Yeah, but men have Viagra. We don't have that.'

Shocko heaved himself off the beanbag and stretched his arms over his head. 'My dad says they need to invent female Viagra ASAP. He says it'll make marriages last way longer.'

Riley peeled off the last piece of varnish and flicked it into the wastepaper basket. 'I wonder if Adam will marry again. I bet he does. He's such a selfish bastard. I bet he marries some stupid young cow who wants sex all the time.'

Shocko rolled his shoulders to release the stiffness. 'I thought you liked your uncle – before all this, I mean.'

'I did like him. Sarah and he were crazy about each other. They had a brilliant relationship. They never seemed to fight . . . but, then, Sarah never fought with anyone.'

'God, it's World War Three in my house most days.'

'Yeah, my parents fight too,' Riley said. 'But I never saw Adam and Sarah arguing.'

Riley was worried about her family. The letter from the solicitor had pushed them over the edge. Her mum was really hurt now as well as being upset, and so was Granddad. He was coming over with annoying Olivia to discuss what to do.

Shocko picked up his guitar and waved a hand at Riley. 'Later. Call me if you can't sleep again – I'll leave my phone on.'

'Thanks, I will, and thanks for last night.'

'Hey, that's what best mates are for.'

He was leaving the room when Riley went up and hugged him from behind. 'You're the best, Shocko,' she said.

The night before she'd woken up, soaked in sweat and shaking, from a nightmare about Sarah's bloated face and the green gunk coming out of the tube in her head. She'd called

Shocko, who had talked to her for an hour until she'd felt calm enough to try to sleep again.

Shocko cleared his throat. 'Yeah, like, anytime.'

Riley heard voices downstairs, it was her granddad and Olivia arriving. She followed Shocko down, then ran to Charlie.

'Hi, Granddad.' She flung her arms around him.

Charlie clung to her. 'Hello, pet. It's good to see you.'

'Hello, Mr Wilson. I'm sorry for your . . . your, uhm, situation.' Shocko shook Charlie's hand.

'Oooh, is this your boyfriend, Riley?' Olivia looked Shocko up and down. 'He seems like a nice boy. Lovely manners anyway.'

Shocko's face turned a deep shade of red.

'No,' Riley said. 'Shocko's my best mate.'

Olivia smiled. 'Well, we all know that friends can turn to lovers. Charlie and I were friends first, weren't we?'

'I'm going to be sick,' Mia muttered.

'TMI!' Riley cried out.

'What's that?' Olivia asked.

'Too much information,' Johnny explained.

Olivia giggled. 'Falling in love is the most natural thing in the world. I think you two would make a lovely couple. And don't they always say men and women can't be best friends because one of them is always in love with the other?'

'Seriously?' Riley glared at Olivia. 'In this century guys and girls can be mates. Maybe back in the dark ages you couldn't, but we actually can.'

Olivia wagged a finger. 'Mark my words, one of you wants to be more than just a pal.'

Riley turned to her mother. 'Help, please.'

'Olivia, Shocko is our neighbour and a friend of the family. Leave them alone now. We've more important things to discuss.'

'What's more important than love?'

'My corpse of a sister and her dying baby,' Mia snapped.

'Well, I know that, but I was only trying to lighten the mood.' Olivia rearranged the scarf tied around her neck.

Riley would have liked to yank it tight to shut her up.

'So, I'm just gonna head out now,' Shocko said, as he sprinted through the front door.

Riley wanted to go after him, to apologize for her grand-dad's girlfriend being a total moron, but her dad put a hand on her shoulder. 'Make us a pot of tea, will you, love?'

While Riley boiled the kettle, the grown-ups sat around the kitchen table and discussed what to do about Adam turning into a total psycho.

'All of the doctors have said the baby will not make it past the next week or two,' Charlie said. 'But I can't stand to see her disintegrate any more. We need to give her some dignity, let poor Sarah go and have a funeral.'

'I know, Dad, but Adam is just clinging to hope.'

'There is no hope.'

'We've all accepted it, but I guess it'll take him a bit longer. Hopefully he'll come around in the next few days or . . . or the baby might die. Sarah's getting worse by the day.'

'It's wrong, Mia, wrong for us, her family, to let this happen. To allow her to be humiliated and demeaned. You can see the doctors think it's wrong too. I found Dr Harrington crying in the room with Sarah yesterday. She said it's the saddest case she's seen in thirty years. It's just so wrong.' Charlie began to cry.

'I know, Dad. I agree with you.'

'As if it's not bad enough, I get this letter from Adam's solicitor banning me from seeing my own child. My own little girl! As if he has the right to play God with her.' Charlie thumped the table. 'I won't have it.'

'Hush now, Charlie.' Olivia massaged his neck. 'Take a deep breath in.' Turning to Mia and Johnny she said, 'My Robert is a barrister, as you know. I rang him last night because Charlie was in such a state. He says you can send a letter back, telling Adam to basically sod off and that he has no right to stop you seeing your own flesh and blood.'

Mia ran a hand through her hair. 'Look, I'd like nothing better than to send Adam a letter telling him to go to Hell, but what would that achieve? A huge family feud, in all likelihood. He could keep Izzy from us, remember. We have to think of her. We must tread carefully here, for Sarah's sake. She'd want us to keep on good terms with Adam and, most of all, Izzy. That little girl needs us now.'

'I tried calling her last night, but her phone was switched off,' Charlie said.

'That's weird cos I called her this morning and she didn't answer either,' Riley said.

'Maybe Adam's taken the phone away,' Johnny said.

'I'll see her in school on Monday. I'll talk to her and find out.' Riley put the tea pot on the table. She reached over and handed Charlie a KitKat. 'I got this for you, Granddad. I think you need one today.'

Charlie smiled. 'I think I do. Thank you, Riley.'

'Well, it's a disgrace the way Adam's treating his father-in-law,' Olivia said. 'My Robert said you need to push back with bullies. Push back hard, he said. Show him you're not afraid of him and you will not be told what to do. He needs to know you're not doormats.'

'Amazingly, I agree with Olivia,' Mia said.

Johnny poured them all tea. 'But Mia's right, too. We need to tread carefully. If we end up in a legal fight with Adam, it could turn very nasty.'

'He's the one who's turned nasty,' Charlie said.

'I never in my wildest dreams thought I'd say this, but I'm now praying the baby will die soon.' Mia wiped her eyes with a tissue. 'I feel so bad for even thinking that.'

Riley handed her mum a KitKat too. Maybe it would help. Mia unwrapped it, broke off a piece and rolled it between her fingers. Riley could see the chocolate melting.

'I want it all to be over. It's too much pain and sadness,' Mia said.

'It is, pet, it really is.' Charlie reached over and took Mia's chocolaty hand in his.

'Do you think Rob can talk him round?' Johnny said. 'I've a feeling he's really torn about this.'

'Rob is just hanging in there, being the one ally Adam has,' Mia said. 'I suppose, as his brother, that's all he can do, regardless of what he thinks.'

'So what should we do, then?' Johnny said. 'Are we going to use Olivia's son and get legal?'

Mia and Charlie exchanged a look. 'I'd really rather not,' Mia said. 'It would be a dangerous move.'

'I'm sorely tempted,' Charlie said, 'but Adam is so much in shock, he's not capable of rational thought. A letter isn't going to change that.'

'Are you all going to stay away from the hospital?' Olivia asked.

'I don't really want to see Sarah again,' Charlie said quietly, 'but I'd still like to be able to go there, talk to the doctors and be near her.'

'Me too,' Mia said. 'The only time I'm at peace is when I'm next to her. I need that.'

Riley felt a stab of pain through her heart. She had lost her aunt, but she had no idea what it was like to lose a sister. She couldn't imagine what her mother was going through.

'Then we continue to visit and try not to antagonize Adam?' Johnny said.

'I suppose,' Mia said. 'Although he'll get riled up no matter how nice we are to him.' She sighed. 'There's no good option. It's one rotten choice after another.'

'Adam will come round,' Johnny said. 'I know it feels unending, but there's no way he can ignore what's happening to Sarah. He's resisting the truth, but it's there and he can't change it. It's hard to like him at the moment, but we have to treat him with kindness.'

'That's a tall order, Johnny,' Charlie said, shaking his head.

'We'll try,' Mia said, putting her other hand over Charlie's.

Riley wondered if she should get them some kitchen roll to wipe the chocolate off their hands, but she was afraid to move. Everyone was silent and still. Her heart ached, for her mum, for her granddad, for Sarah, but most of all for Izzy.

38

'Mummy always washes my hair,' Izzy screamed. 'Not you! Mummy! You don't know how. She dries it all fluffy and wavy and makes me look beautiful.'

'I'm sure I can do that, if you show me how,' Adam pleaded. 'Uncle Rob will help and we'll do it, I promise, Izzy.'

'Sure,' Rob said. He was leaning against the frame of the bathroom door, watching his brother be mentally defeated by a seven-year-old. 'I'm pretty good at doing hair, Izzy. You know that.'

Izzy crossed her arms. 'No hair washing. I told you, I want to go and see Mummy. If she knows my hair is dirty and knotty, she'll wake up. She hates dirty hair and knots. She always brushed my hair before I went to bed, like a real princess.'

'Izzy, I explained that you can't see Mummy right now.'

'Why?' she demanded, her bottom lip quivering.

Adam struggled to explain. 'Because she's very sick and only the doctors can see her at the moment.'

'Why can't they give her medicine to wake her up?' Izzy asked, tears welling in her eyes.

Adam reached out and held her hand. 'They're trying, Sweet-pea, but she can't wake up.'

'But why, Daddy?'

'Because she had this lump in her head and it made her very sick and now she's asleep and, to be honest, Izzy, she . . .' Adam tried to choose his words carefully. 'Mummy might not wake up.'

Izzy shook her head. 'Maybe not for the moment, but I

know for sure she'll wake up for my Communion. I know it for one hundred per cent sure. Mummy will not be asleep for my special day. No way.'

Adam didn't have the courage to tell her otherwise. How do you speak the words that will break a child's heart? He looked at Rob, who shrugged helplessly.

Izzy took off her glasses and began to clean them with the edge of her skirt. 'So, if Mummy can't do my hair, then Mia or Riley can. I can go over after school tomorrow and wash it there.'

'No, Izzy. I've told you I want you to stay away from Mia and Riley for the moment.'

'But I don't understand. You said you had a fight, so just say sorry and make up.'

'It's a bit more complicated than that.'

'But I want to see Riley and Mia and Johnny.'

'I know, but just for the moment we're going to let things cool off. It'll all be fine, but for now I need you to stay away.'

'But I don't want to. I love them. They're my family. Riley's my only cousin. I want Riley to do my hair.'

'Not at the moment, Izzy. I'll do it. You can show me how, and it'll be fun.'

'It's not fair!' Izzy shouted. 'You have Uncle Rob and I have no one. I want to see Riley.'

'You have me and Uncle Rob,' Adam said. 'We're here for you, Izzy.'

'I want to see Riley,' she moaned.

'Maybe we could . . .' Rob began, but Adam shot him a warning look.

'It'll be OK, Izzy, I promise. Me, you and Rob make a great team.'

'I hate you and I hate Mummy for not waking up and I hate everyone and everything and the whole stinky world and . . . and . . .' Izzy began to wail, her whole body shaking.

Adam held her close and rocked her. He couldn't look up at Rob. He didn't want to see the expression on his face. Izzy was distraught. He rocked her and rocked her until she fell asleep in his arms from sheer exhaustion, and he prayed that he was doing the right thing for his family.

Adam sat in the ICU waiting room, drinking a tepid coffee and trying to work himself up to go and sit with Sarah. Angela had just told him that Sarah's infection had got worse and he was dreading seeing her. A man of about his age was sitting on the couch opposite, talking quietly into his phone. Adam could hear snippets of his conversation.

'He's not good . . . You need to get a flight. He'll want to see you . . . Yeah, eighty-two is a good age . . . Still, he's our dad . . . OK . . . Call me with your flight time.'

Eighty-two *was* a good age. Eighty-two was the right age to die. Not thirty-four. Thirty-four was stupidly young – you had decades ahead of you. Sarah would never see Izzy grow up, graduate, get married, have babies. She was going to miss her daughter's whole life. Adam hunched over, trying to block out everything else and focus on the one positive: his son. Sarah's parting gift.

The man opposite got up to leave the room. He and Rob almost collided as Rob pushed open the door to come in.

'I brought fresh coffee,' Rob said, holding up two cups. 'Here.' He handed one to Adam. 'You'll probably never drink another coffee as long as you live after all this.'

They sat in silence for a few minutes. Then Rob said, 'Adam, I got a text from Mia to say she'd had a letter asking her to stay away. Is that true?'

'I had to do something,' Adam said. His heart was pounding with all the caffeine and he felt jittery and nauseous.

'You sent them a legal letter?' Rob said, and it was clear he was shocked. 'Jesus, no wonder Mia was so upset. Adam, this is your family. It's Sarah's family. Do you think that was fair?'

'Look, I have to keep Mia and Charlie away from her. I can't handle them telling me I'm wrong, telling me to switch off the ventilator, to let her go. It's like a drill in my head. I can't focus when they're around. I'm worried, Rob. I'm scared they'll talk to the doctors behind my back. This is my wife, my baby, my decision.'

Rob shook his head. 'I understand that it's your decision, and I'm with you on this, but locking them out from their own sister and daughter, that's kind of something else. I'm not sure you're thinking straight, man.'

'I didn't want to send the solicitor's letter,' Adam said defensively, 'but I'm afraid of them. I'm afraid they'll do something when I'm not here. I need them to go away and let me make my own decisions without their constant opinions in my ear, morning, noon and night. I just cannot take another lecture on why it's wrong to keep Sarah alive. It's like they don't realize how hard this is for me. Yes, it would be easier to say stop, but I have to give my boy every possible chance. Don't I, Rob? Don't I?'

Rob looked at him and bit his lip. 'Yes, you do. If there's a chance, I understand you want to take it. *If* there's a chance.'

'Don't you turn on me too,' Adam growled.

'I'm not,' Rob said quickly. 'I'm just saying that it's important we assess things realistically. Your son is very tiny and very vulnerable. We have to take everything into account.'

'That's what I'm doing,' Adam said, jumping up. His body felt restless and trapped. He ached in every joint and muscle from the stiff chairs and the lack of sleep. He was like an alien to himself.

'Calm down. We're just talking,' Rob said, raising his hands. 'That's all.'

Before Adam could answer, the waiting-room door pushed

open and he whirled round to make sure it wasn't Mia or Charlie. It was Dr Mayhew.

'Adam, I was wondering if I could have a word?'

'Sure, go ahead,' Adam said. 'You know my brother Rob. You can say anything in front of him.'

'Let's take a seat,' the doctor said. He sat across from Adam and threaded his fingers together. 'Adam, I know you've endured a singularly terrible trauma in what has happened to your wife, and while this is awful for you to hear, I feel it's important that you are made fully aware of the facts of Sarah's deterioration. Charlie and Mia have spoken to me and they are deeply concerned about Sarah's condition. I know you're the next-of-kin and that Sarah is your wife and this is your baby. I know you have issues with Mia and Charlie, but my staff and I can't enter into those disagreements. I hope you understand our impartiality.'

'Talk to them all you want,' Adam said, 'but I don't want them here and I've made that clear. Whatever they say to you doesn't hold weight with me. I'm just doing my best for Ben. That's all I care about.'

'It's good we understand each other. Now, I have to prepare you for today and the coming days, Adam, as the deterioration progresses. There are currently seven different syringe pumps needed to give Sarah the range of antibiotics necessary to combat the infections in her brain and body. These medications will affect the foetus. The wound in Sarah's head needs constant dressing. She has neurosurgical meningitis. She also has pneumonia, a urinary tract infection, a high temperature, a high white cell count, an increased heart rate, and liver dysfunction. I don't mean to be brutal or harsh, Adam, I'm sorry to be so blunt, but I need you to understand how dire the situation has become. There is evidence of a fungus growing on Sarah's brain.'

Shock jolted Adam and bile rose in his throat. He rushed across the room and threw up in a bin in the corner, his body heaving.

'Jesus, Doctor, go easy on him,' Rob said angrily. 'That's too much.'

'I'm sorry,' Dr Mayhew said, his voice full of emotion. 'I just need you to see the truth. This is the most difficult case I have ever worked on. I know this decision is unbearable, but your wife's body is literally falling apart and we can't stop it.'

Adam wiped his mouth with his hand. His brain was racing so fast he couldn't catch hold of the thoughts. He was capable of focusing on only one thing at a time. 'But the baby still has a heartbeat, right?'

Dr Mayhew sighed. 'We can detect a foetal heartbeat, yes, but the chances of survival are, at this point, non-existent. That is the considered opinion of every member of the medical team, from every discipline. It's unanimous.'

'Exactly. It's your opinion. You're not sitting here with anything other than an opinion. My opinion says heartbeat equals life. I choose life.'

'Adam,' Dr Mayhew said, sitting forward, 'please listen to me. The foetus is –'

'I need air,' Adam said. He couldn't take another second of this. The stale air of the waiting room was clawing at his throat. He pulled open the door and walked quickly down the hall, away from Dr Mayhew and his Doomsday scenarios.

Adam went towards the hospital exit. He heard running footsteps behind him and knew without turning that it would be Rob.

'I can't breathe,' he said, as Rob drew up alongside him.

'We're nearly there. Keep going. Fresh air will do you good,' Rob said, steering his brother by his elbow towards the door.

Adam stepped outside and drew in a huge lungful of fresh air. When he opened his eyes, he saw Mia. She was the last person he'd expected to be there.

'What are you doing here?'

'I've come to see my sister.'

'You're banned. I banned you.'

'Look, Adam, I don't want to argue with you. She's my sister. I want to see her, to talk to her.'

Adam felt his nerves jangling. Did Dr Mayhew arrange this? He'd said he'd been talking to her. Was this some sort of conspiracy designed to rob Sarah of her life? 'You've been talking to the doctors behind my back. Dr Mayhew just told me. I don't trust you. Stay away from her.'

'For God's sake, Adam, I'm not going to switch the bloody ventilator off. I just want to see her.'

'I don't want any of you near her. She is *my* wife and that's *my* baby.'

'Yes, we get it. You've only said it a million times,' Mia snapped, 'but she is also my sister and Dad's daughter. Can you imagine Izzy's husband blocking you from seeing her? Can you imagine what that feels like? You are hurting Dad terribly.'

Adam felt a fury rage through him. 'Don't you dare bring Izzy into this. This is typical of you, trying to control me and my decisions. Well, back the fuck away, Mia. I'm warning you.'

'Calm down, Adam,' Rob said, putting his hand on Adam's arm.

'Don't threaten me,' Mia shouted. 'I've had enough of you trying to bully Dad and me. We'll visit Sarah if we want to. I'm not going to follow suit and send you legal letters, but I did get advice and the legal situation is that you can't ban us.'

Adam curled his hands into fists. He wanted to smash something. Bloody Mia and her bloody self-righteousness.

'Sarah wouldn't want this, Adam. You're hurting her and the baby. What's happening to them is obscene.'

'You will not order me around,' Adam shouted. 'Get the hell out of my business.'

'Someone's going to call security,' Rob said, putting his face right up against Adam's. 'You have *got* to calm down. We can talk about this without the shouting.'

'She's my sister. You can't treat us like this, Adam. Do you honestly think Sarah would be happy with the way you're treating her family?'

People were staring at them, but Adam couldn't have cared less. 'Do you think she'd want me to give up on her baby?'

'Giving up and letting go are two totally different things,' Mia said.

A security guard walked over to them. 'Is everything all right here?' he asked.

'Just emotions running high,' Rob said. 'There's no problem.'

'This lady was leaving.' Adam glared at Mia.

Mia pulled her bag up on her shoulder, wiped her eyes and turned to walk away.

Instead of feeling triumphant, Adam felt sick. Sick, tired, worn out and drained. He no longer recognized his life. He was disoriented all the time.

'Let's go back inside,' Rob said wearily. 'We can work through what the doctor said.'

Adam let himself be led away, but he knew his own mind already. Sarah had always believed in miracles. She wished on rainbows, saluted magpies, bought unicorns for Izzy and adored stories of triumph against all the odds.

Sarah would send him a miracle. She would send him Ben.

39

Mia pulled up outside her childhood home. The grass needed cutting. She'd ask Johnny to do it. Olivia's car was in the driveway. Mia really didn't want to deal with her right now. She wanted a chat with her dad, alone.

She'd take him out for coffee if she had to: she was damned if Olivia was going to stick her nose in. Mia didn't think it was too much to ask for one private conversation with her father after all of the upheaval in their lives. She'd wanted to tell him about her run-in with Adam but had decided not to. Charlie was upset enough about Adam – she didn't need to make things worse.

She rang the doorbell. It felt strange not just putting her key in the lock and walking in, like she used to, but she had to respect Olivia's privacy, however grudgingly.

Olivia answered the door, dressed to the nines and fully made up with her red lipstick.

'Hi,' Mia said curtly and moved to walk past her. But her father's fiancée blocked the door. 'Hold on a minute there. I want a word with you. I'm on my way out to see my grandson performing in the school orchestra. He's a trombone player, such a talent. Of course, music was always in our family – I play the piano myself.'

'Is that it?' Mia asked. 'Is that what you wanted to tell me? That your grandson is a trombone prodigy?'

'No, that's not it. I want to make sure you're not going to upset your father. I'm very concerned about him. He has barely eaten or slept in over a week.'

Neither have I, Mia wanted to shout.

'He needs to be kept calm and not upset.'

Mia sighed. 'Right. Well, Olivia, to be fair, there isn't much I can do to make the situation of his daughter being brain dead any better.'

Olivia pursed her lips. 'No need to be snippy, Mia. I'm only looking after your father's welfare. As my Robert said to me, "That man is lucky to have you in his life to take good care of him."'

Mia was too tired, emotionally drained and sleep-deprived for Olivia's nonsense. 'What do you want, Olivia? A medal for being nice to Dad? Do you want me to get down on my knees and thank you for making him drink green tea?'

Olivia bristled. 'A simple acknowledgement of my support and care would be nice.'

Was this woman for real? Did she honestly think Mia owed her something? What did she want? A box of chocolates for being nice to Charlie, whom she was trying to railroad into marrying her? This was ridiculous. 'I'm sorry I haven't been praising you and showering you with gifts of thanks, but I've been kind of busy trying to deal with my sister and her baby.'

'I know it's been hard on you, but Charlie is considerably older and less able to cope with this trauma. He's desperately upset, and he even snapped at me this morning, which is most unlike him.'

'Why did he snap at you?'

'I was trying to get him to eat some quinoa porridge. I'd even added raspberries to it because I know he likes those. Quinoa is supposed to give you lots of energy and fill you up without bloating you and . . . Well, that's what the nice young man in the health shop told me. But Charlie pushed the dish aside and said it was something you'd feed pigs in a trough.'

Mia grinned.

'All very well for you to laugh. You're still young – you can survive on coffee and chocolate, but your father can't.'

Mia held up her hand to try to stop Olivia droning on. 'I know you're trying to help, but what Dad needs now is to drink ten cups of bloody coffee a day if he wants to, and if he wants to survive on doughnuts or chocolate, then let him. Stop trying to force him to eat healthily. Do that later. For now, just let him eat and drink whatever he wants to get through the day.'

Olivia picked up her handbag from the hall table. 'I most certainly will not let him survive on sugar and caffeine. If I did, I'd be neglecting my duties as a fiancée.' She pulled on her trench coat, then wagged a finger in Mia's face. 'I'll be back in an hour or so and I do not want to find Charlie high on caffeine and sugar. It's bad for his heart.'

'Off you go. You don't want to miss a beat of that wonderful trombone playing.'

Olivia glanced at her watch. 'Yes, I'd best be off.'

Mia resisted the urge to push her out of the door and opted to slam it instead.

'Mia? Is that you?' Charlie called from the kitchen.

'Yes, just coming Dad.'

Mia went in and found her father standing in front of the door that led into the back garden.

'Is she gone?'

'Yes.'

'Thank God. Did you bring them?'

Mia smiled. 'Yes, I did.' She pulled a packet of cigarettes from her bag and handed them to her father. 'I'm only letting you smoke one or two.'

'That'll do.'

'And Riley sent you two KitKats.'

'The little dote.'

'And I brought brandy. I'll make us some brandy coffees.'

'Thank you, pet. You're a good girl.'

Mia clung to the little compliment and allowed it to warm her heart.

They sat outside, Charlie insisting they were at the very end of the garden, so no smoke smell could waft into the house. 'If Olivia even thinks I was smoking, she'll never leave me alone again.'

Mia handed her father his coffee laced with brandy and lit his cigarette. 'Two things. First of all, this is your house and you can do whatever you want in or outside it. Second of all, you are sixty-nine years old and it's ridiculous that you're letting her boss you about.'

Charlie inhaled deeply on his cigarette and moaned with pleasure. 'Twenty-five years since I had my last, and it tastes wonderful.'

Mia only smoked the odd cigarette at very late-night parties, which she hardly ever went to now, but she joined her father in his illicit activity.

They puffed and drank in companionable silence.

'I'm used to bossy women,' Charlie admitted. 'Your mother was bossy, too.'

'Hang on a minute,' Mia said, annoyed. 'Mum was nothing like Olivia. Olivia is a whole other world of controlling. Don't let her take over your life, Dad.'

Charlie stubbed his cigarette out, then picked up the butt and threw it deep into the bushes. 'I barely know what day it is at the moment. Olivia is doing her best to keep me sane.'

'I'm here for you too, Dad. Don't forget that. I can't sleep, so you can call me anytime, day or night.'

'I wouldn't do that. Sure I'd wake up Johnny.'

'Honestly, Dad, I spend most nights pacing the house. Call me anytime.'

Charlie put his mug on the ground and lit his second ciga-rette. 'How did we end up here, Mia? I must have done something terrible in a past life. No man should see his beloved daughter in that state.' He rubbed his eyes. 'I can't get that image of her bloated face and bulging eyes out of my mind. It haunts me.'

'I brought some photos for us to look at, to try to remem-ber her as she was.'

Mia took one last long drag from her cigarette. They were sitting on two foldout chairs in the shade, under the 'climbing tree', as she and Sarah had called it when they were kids. The leaves rustled in the light breeze and all that could be heard were birds twittering and the very faint sound of cars on the road. Mia looked down the long, narrow garden to the back of the house. Home. This was our home, she thought.

A sharp memory flooded her mind. She remembered jumping in and out of the sprinklers with Sarah that really hot summer when she was about thirteen and Sarah was eight. She could picture her little sister in her red polka-dot swimsuit that she was so proud of. Mia bent over and pre-tended to put her cup down. She didn't want Charlie to know she was fighting to breathe because the pain of the memory was so great.

She felt a hand on her back. 'The memories come so sud-denly they can really knock you sideways,' Charlie said.

Mia sat up slowly. 'I could see her running around in her red polka-dot togs, jumping in and out of the sprinkler.'

Charlie nodded. 'I remember those. Your mother bought them for her in France. Sarah was like a peacock in them. Her "French togs".'

They both laughed. Mia pulled an envelope out of her bag. 'It's funny how we don't have photos, these days. They're all on our phones or in the i-cloud or whatever it's called. I miss physical photos. They really are snapshots of our lives.'

Mia handed him her favourite photo. It was of Charlie and Sarah standing in the archway of the church, about to walk down the aisle on her wedding day. They were looking at each other, beaming from ear to ear. Joy and love radiated from the photo.

'Oh,' Charlie whispered. He held it up to his face. 'She was magnificent.'

Mia nodded. She was gazing at the other photo she had brought. It was one of Mia, Sarah and their mum. They were all giggling. It was Sarah's tenth birthday and Penny had made an ice-cream cake, which was melting. Mia was trying to hold up the left side, and Penny tried to do the same with the other, while Sarah blew out the candles.

'You think when your daughters meet nice men, marry and have families of their own that your job is done. You can finally breathe easy. You can put your feet up and stop worrying. You can enjoy your grandchildren without any of the stress of parenting. And then . . .'

'It was so sudden.'

'She's gone but she's not gone. That's almost the hardest part. I want it to end now, Mia.' Charlie's voice was hoarse with exhaustion. 'I want to lay my little girl to rest.' He took a third cigarette out of the packet and lit it with shaking hands. 'I've actually started praying the baby will die. Imagine, a man praying that his own grandchild will die. But it's the only way Adam will stop this.'

Mia felt tears running down her cheeks. 'Me too. I want Sarah and the baby to be buried and at peace, together.'

'What a mess.' Charlie exhaled a long puff of smoke.

'I'll try talking to Adam again. Maybe he'll see sense.'

Charlie shook his head. 'He won't stop until it's over. And

I can understand it, in a way. I remember having to let your mother go. I didn't want to – I wanted to cling to her, wanted her to keep fighting, but she was so weak, it wasn't right. I had to let her go. It's a decision that Adam will live with for the rest of his life. I saw that little boy on the scan – good strong heartbeat. He looked so safe and alive. My heart breaks for Sarah. I'm glad she died before the baby – it would have killed her to lose him. As hard as it is for us, it's tougher on Adam. I suppose we need to remember that.'

'Yes, but he can't block us from seeing her. It's not right or fair.'

'I agree,' Charlie said. 'I just don't have any fight left in me.'

'I'll fight for you, Dad. I'll make sure you get in to see her and say goodbye.'

'Yes. I've decided I *would* like to see her one more time, after all, just to whisper a few words in her ear. The last time I saw her was so awful . . . I was so shocked.'

'We all were. I'll get you in, Dad. I'll talk to Angela and make sure we avoid Adam.'

'You're a good girl, Mia, a great girl. The brandy and cigarettes were a tonic.'

Mia smiled at her father and felt a kind of calm wash over her. This was a moment she'd remember, always.

'CHARLIE WILSON!' Olivia screeched. 'Put that filthy cancer stick down immediately.'

Charlie jumped and dropped the cigarette.

Olivia marched down the garden towards them, her face bright red. 'I leave you in charge for one hour and you have him smoking. Are you trying to kill him, is that it? Do you want him to die too?'

'Jeez, calm down Olivia, it was a couple of cigarettes.'

'My Gerald died of lung cancer due to smoking. I will not

let that happen to Charlie. You have just ruined twenty-five years of nicotine-free life for Charlie.'

'He's not going to die of lung cancer after three cigarettes or start smoking twenty a day again,' Mia said.

'You're a bad influence.'

Mia looked at Charlie. 'He said he enjoyed them.'

'Well, now, that's not exactly true. Mia thought they'd help me relax. I didn't even really like it. Rotten taste in my mouth. Don't get yourself worked up about it, Olivia, my darling. I won't smoke again.'

'That's what all addicts say,' Olivia retorted.

'I won't. Mia, take them with you and don't bring them to the house again, please.' Charlie handed her the packet.

Olivia turned to walk away.

'Judas,' Mia muttered.

'It's called self-preservation,' Charlie whispered. 'Hand me that packet.'

'No way! I'm not having her accusing me of trying to murder you.'

Charlie grabbed the packet from Mia's hand. 'I'll make sure she never finds them.'

Mia let go of the packet and watched her sixty-nine-year-old father stuff them down the front of his trousers, like a naughty schoolboy.

40

Riley stood in assembly with her hands clenched. Her nails made little half-moon indents in her palms.

The headmistress, Mrs Moloney, was beaming. 'And now a very special announcement. Zoë Karsdale came fourth in the All-Ireland hurdle final yesterday. We are very proud of Zoë and this incredible achievement.'

Everyone cheered and whooped. Riley wanted to throw up. Zoë pretended to be embarrassed, but still managed to wave and strut up to the stage to be congratulated by Mrs Moloney.

'As Zoë just missed out on a medal, we are presenting her with our very own medal here today.'

Zoë's hand flew up to her mouth in a fake 'What? No way!' move. Riley glanced at Zach – he was clapping and whooping with the rest.

Mrs Moloney put the fake medal around Zoë's neck and everyone cheered.

'*Merci* – I mean, thank you so much, Mrs Moloney,' Zoë gushed. 'I'm so touched by this gesture. I have to thank Mr Green, our sports teacher, for encouraging me and also I have to especially thank Zach for all the extra hours he put in, helping me to push harder and aim higher. Zach, you're amazing.'

All the boys around Zach began to whistle. He smiled and blushed bright red.

In a second Riley went from angry to devastated. He really liked her. He was into Zoë. It was over. She might as well accept it. Zach loved Zoë and Riley was never going to get him back.

Mr Warren raised his voice to get their attention. 'Class, I need everyone to really focus. This assignment needs to be in next week so I want to see some serious progress today. I'll be coming around to each pair to see how far you've progressed.'

Zach tapped his pen against his teeth. 'We need to get moving on this.'

Riley sat back in her chair and shrugged. She was done making an effort. She hadn't even put on lip gloss before class. What was the point? He wasn't into her. Zach wasn't going to scoop her into his arms and console her about Sarah. He wasn't going to tell her she was great and her dad would get a job and her mum would stop looking so heartbroken and that everything would go back to normal.

'Do you want to talk about our different points of view, then write some stuff down?' Zach suggested.

'Sure, whatever.' Riley bit her thumbnail.

'Psst, Zach,' Harry hissed, from the desk beside them. 'Does Frank Green know your extra training with Zoë includes a lot of horizontal jogging?' He sniggered.

'Shut up, Harry.' Zach frowned and turned back to Riley.

Riley concentrated really hard on her notes and not crying.

'I haven't had sex with Zoë,' Zach said quietly.

'What you do with Zoë is your own business.'

'Yeah, but I just wanted you to . . . Well, we haven't.'

Riley looked up. 'OK.'

Zach fiddled with his pen. 'So, I read the book.'

'Did you? Or did you watch the movie?'

'No, Riley, I read the book. I liked it.'

'Really?'

'Yeah, really. It's a bit slow to start and the mother is a bit too much of a saint to be real, but I liked the girls and Laurie and the granddad.'

'Which of the sisters did you like best?' Riley asked.

'Which do you think?'

'Amy.'

'Why?'

'Because she's pretty and fun and uncomplicated.'

'Selfish and conceited, too.'

Riley looked at him. 'Did you just say conceited?'

He grinned. 'Yeah, I had to look it up. But she is, she's really into herself.'

Riley nodded. 'But so are lots of girls. Half the girls in this school are obsessed with make-up and hair extensions.'

'You can be into how you look without being selfish. You wear make-up.'

'Yes, but I don't spend ninety per cent of my time focusing on how I look. I actually have a life outside staring in the mirror.'

'So do lots of other girls.'

'Like Zoë?'

'She spends a lot of her free time training, so she doesn't get all that much time to stare in the mirror.'

Riley didn't want to talk about Zoë. 'So you didn't like Amy?'

'No. I liked Meg, Beth, and I kind of liked Jo.'

Riley glared at him. 'How can you "kind of like" Jo? Jo is the heroine of the book. If it wasn't for Jo, the family would have starved. She is brave and ballsy and never pretends to be someone she isn't. She doesn't try to fit in with all those stupid, spoiled party girls. She is who she is and she's brilliant.'

'I agree. The reason I said I kind of liked her is because

she turns Laurie down. That drove me nuts. It's so stupid. Why does she do that? He's a great guy.'

'Well, she doesn't think they'd make a good couple because his life is all posh parties and small-talk and Jo hates all that stupid meaningless stuff. She doesn't want to talk about pointless crap, she wants to talk about real things and she wants to dress the way she likes and not have to look the same as everyone else. So, she knows she'll make Laurie's life difficult because his friends won't like her or approve of her.'

'He doesn't care about all that. He tells her he loves her and he wants to be with her. She turns him down. Laurie tries to persuade her.'

'Yeah, well, he should have tried harder. If you really love someone, you should never stop trying. I hate Laurie because he gave up too easily.'

'He's a great guy, generous, kind and fun too.'

'He's weak and he didn't fight for Jo.'

'If a girl turns you down, how are you supposed to know that if you just tried harder she'd change her mind?'

'Because, Zach, if you really love someone, you don't let them go, or if you do, you make sure you get them back.'

'I think Jo sometimes makes Laurie feel like he's not smart or serious enough.'

'Well, she's right, he isn't. He's so stupid and weak that he ends up marrying the wrong sister.'

'Why can't she look at his good traits?'

'She does, she loves him, but she knows he's too weak to be able to stand her never fitting into his crowd. Jo is so brave and generous that she lets him go.'

'Bullshit, she's the stupid one. She gives up the chance of a life of love, fun and luxury because she looks down on his friends.'

'It's called sacrifice. She sacrifices her happiness so he can

313

marry a stupid girl who'll slot into his life and won't make waves or embarrass him.'

Zach threw down his pen. 'It's called being stubborn and narrow-minded. Opposites do attract and marry and have great lives. She could have made it work. Instead she made him feel bad about his friends and his life and for having fun and being carefree.'

'That's not fair. She supported him and loved him and was a great friend to him. She just wanted him to be better, to be more, to reach his potential.'

'You should accept people the way they are and not try to change them.'

'I agree,' Riley said.

'Then what are we arguing about?'

'I don't know.' Riley chewed her lower lip.

'I never tried to change you,' Zach whispered.

'I'm sorry if you think I tried to change you.'

'You're my Jo.'

Riley smiled. 'I guess that makes you my Laurie.'

'Should we try to change the end of the story?'

'What about "Amy" and her hurdle training and her medals and her "fun" side?'

Zach grinned. '"Amy" is lovely, but I've had enough "fun". I miss Jo. I want Jo back.'

'But Laurie really seemed to like Amy.'

'He did, but Amy is a bit boring and all about herself. Laurie now realizes that Jo is the one he wants to be with.'

'Jo is having a really shit time and can't take any more knocks. Laurie needs to be absolutely positive about this. He can't change his mind and run back to Amy – because Jo can't take it.'

'He is positive. He will never hurt Jo and he wants to be there for her, to help her and comfort her.'

'He has to accept Jo – her love of books and serious issues.'

'He does. He misses her lectures.' Zach grinned. 'But Jo has to respect that Laurie's high jump is very important to him.'

'Jo will never, ever make fun of it and totally respects it. She will cheer him on.'

'Laurie has missed being challenged.'

'Jo has missed . . . well, she's missed everything.'

Zach reached out and took Riley's hand. 'The end.'

Week Three

41

Mia walked her class to the church, which was just around the corner from the school. Beside her was Vanessa Dixon, the other second form teacher.

'Good to see you back. How are you?' Vanessa asked.

'I'm getting there,' Mia lied.

'I believe your sister is still very unwell. I'm so sorry.'

'Thanks, Vanessa.'

Vanessa looked uncomfortable. Oh, no – had Adam said something to her? Mia's stomach lurched.

'Actually, Mia, I'm worried about Izzy. She's very withdrawn and she's developed this habit of cleaning her glasses all the time. She does it at least ten times a day in class. She gets very upset if they're not perfectly clean.'

'I think it's just her way of trying to control things while her mum is gone. It's a really difficult time. If you can just continue to support her and keep a close eye on her, I'd really appreciate it. She's confused and upset.'

Vanessa placed a hand on Mia's arm. 'Of course. I'm very fond of Izzy. She's a gorgeous girl. I'll help her in any way I can. Don't worry.'

'Thanks, that really does mean a lot.'

Mia turned away from Vanessa and busied herself ushering her class into the church, making sure the children who were reading prayers sat at the end of the pews.

Vanessa called them up one by one and they all read beautifully. Clearly, they'd been practising at home with proud parents.

As Mia and Vanessa ran through the Communion mass timetable, the children giggled, shuffled and wriggled in their seats. All except Izzy. Izzy sat still, looking small and sad.

When the practice was over and the children all rushed out of the church into the sunshine, Mia went to Izzy. 'Hello, sweetie, are you OK?'

Izzy shook her head. 'Daddy said I'm not supposed to talk to you and Riley and Granddad because you had a big fight. Why can't you just say sorry and make up, Mia?'

Mia wanted to kill Adam. 'I will – we all will. It happened because we're all tired and worried about your mum. It's nothing for you to worry about.'

'That's what Daddy said too, but for now I can't stay over with you. I really want a sleepover with Riley. I miss her.'

'I'll talk to your dad and see if we can sort it out. How are you feeling about your Communion?'

Izzy's chin jutted out. 'I'm excited because Mummy will wake up that day and I can't wait to see her. Although I hope she wakes up the day before, so she can do my hair. If she doesn't, can you or Riley do it for me? Daddy and Rob are no good.'

Mia tried to keep her face from crumpling. This poor, confused little girl really believed Sarah was going to wake up. How could they explain it to her? As much as Mia hated Adam right now, she didn't envy him that. No matter what he said or how he said it, his words would break Izzy's little heart, and part of it would remain broken for ever.

'Of course we will, pet.' If your psycho father lets us near you. 'You can look at pictures with Riley and decide how you want it.'

Izzy took off her glasses and began to clean them furiously, using the hem of her skirt. 'I know already. Me and Mummy looked at loads of photos of girls on their Communion Day and we decided on the nicest hairstyle. Mummy has a photo of it on her phone.'

'OK. Whatever happens, you will have beautiful hair and your stunning dress.'

'I love my dress. Do you remember when Mummy made me try it on for you and I kept twirling until I got dizzy and fell down?'

Mia smiled. 'Yes, I do.'

Izzy put her glasses back on. Her eyes shone. 'It's going to be an amazing day. Mummy will wake up and I'm having a bouncy castle and a chocolate fountain, and you and Daddy will be friends again and everything will be nice and no one will be sad. All the badness will be over.'

Mia bent down and hugged her.

'Ouch, Mia, too tight.'

'Sorry, pet. I just love you so much and your mum was always so proud of you.'

'I'm proud of her too. I know she's strong and she'll fight the lump in her head and wake up.'

Mia smiled and turned away before the tears came.

Johnny's head snapped up from the newspaper he was reading. He gripped Mia's arm. 'Do you hear that?'

Mia cocked her head. 'No, it couldn't be.'

'It must be the radio.'

They listened.

'I think it is,' Johnny said.

'She's singing.'

'She never sings.'

'Ever. Quick, I hear footsteps.'

Mia pulled Johnny away from the door and they pretended to be busy boiling the kettle together when Riley walked into the kitchen, still singing.

'Act normal,' Johnny whispered.

'Morning,' Riley said. 'How are you today, Mum? Did you sleep? Why don't you sit down and I'll get the coffee?'

'Go with it,' Johnny hissed.

'Fitfully, and I'd love you to make me coffee.' Mia winked at Johnny.

Riley hummed as she waited for the kettle to boil. Mia and Johnny eyed her suspiciously.

'She seems, dare I say it, happy,' Mia whispered. 'This is amazing. The teenage angst must be over. Everyone says it breaks at about sixteen and she's nearly sixteen. Hurrah.'

Johnny shook his head. 'I dunno, Mia. I've seen guys this happy and it's always after getting laid.'

'What?' Mia gasped.

Johnny shushed her. 'I'm not saying that's what it is, but I think a boy might be involved in this new-found joy.'

'We have to find out. You ask.' Mia poked him.

He poked her back. 'No way, you ask.'

'She'll bite my head off. You do it.'

Riley came over, bringing coffee and hot buttered toast. 'What are you two whispering about? Not more bad news, I hope. Oh, my God, Mum, is Sarah . . . ?'

'No, love, everything's the same,' Mia assured her.

Johnny sipped his coffee. 'So . . . you seem in good form today.'

Riley smiled. 'Yeah, I guess I am.'

'Any particular reason?' Johnny asked.

Riley blushed. 'Yes, but I'm not going to tell you.'

'Did you have sex?' Mia blurted out.

Riley spluttered. She wiped coffee off her chin. 'No, I did not, not that it's any of your business.'

'Thank God for that.'

'But there is a boy involved in all your . . . ah . . . shall we say, good form?' Johnny said.

'Stop digging, Dad. I'm not telling.'

'Riley, pet, you haven't sung or hummed or cracked much of a smile since 2015. Let us enjoy this moment.' Johnny grinned at her.

'Bit harsh,' Riley said.

'Is it?' Johnny replied.

'Yes. I smiled at Christmas when you got me the new iPhone.' Riley smirked.

'And there's another one. Jesus, Riley, stop or I'll have to put on sunglasses from the glare of your happiness.' Johnny laughed.

'Sod off, Dad, you're such a freak.'

'And now we're back to normal.' Johnny grinned.

'No, cos I'm still smiling.' Riley got up from the table and hummed as she left the kitchen.

Mia and Johnny turned to each other. 'She's happy and she didn't have sex, thank God,' Mia said.

'Yet,' Johnny said. 'A sixteen-year-old boy's involved in the bliss, and sex will be on the agenda. You need to talk to her.'

'Why me?'

'Because you're a woman.'

'Yes, but you're a man so you understand male urges. You can explain to her that she should not have sex until she's twenty-five, but that if she decides to, she needs to make this boy use a condom and that boys like girls who aren't easy.'

'Are you winding me up?'

'No, I'm deadly serious. It'll be much stronger coming from you. I'll talk to her about the pill, but you need to do the condom chat, and mention STDs too.'

'Ah, Jesus, Mia.'

Mia kissed his cheek. 'It's called parenting and protection, Johnny. Make sure you really drive home how much boys respect girls who don't have sex until they've been going out with each other for ages, like, a year or so.'

'Why can't you say it all in the car on the way to school?'

'I've just explained. You can do it later, while I visit Sarah, and then it'll be sorted.'

Johnny looked far from convinced. 'Are you heading to the hospital after school?'

Mia nodded. 'I need to see her. I don't know if I'll get in, but I have to try.'

'Keep calm if you bump into Adam.'

'I will.'

'Mia?'

'I'll try.'

As Mia was getting her car keys, Johnny's phone rang. He looked at the number and coloured. He moved into the lounge and closed the door. Mia went to the hall to put her coat on. She leaned towards the door. She could hear Johnny saying, 'Just give me a few more days to sort things out and I'll have the article for you.'

Riley joined her, bag slung over her shoulder. They headed out to the car.

'I just heard your dad saying something on the phone about an article,' Mia said. 'Wonder what that's about.'

'Yeah,' Riley said, 'there's definitely something happening. I heard him talking to someone yesterday and it sounded like he was working with them. He was talking about the article needing more time to fine-tune or something. I thought he was going to announce a new job.'

'Really?' Mia said, turning to look at her. 'You genuinely heard that?'

'Yeah,' Riley said. 'I could be wrong, like, but he was cagey about it when I asked, so I reckoned he wasn't ready to tell us yet. Maybe the article is, like, a test and then he'll get the job.'

Mia smiled. 'Finally some good news,' she said. 'These last months have been so bloody long and unending. If Johnny's found work, I'll be able to breathe a bit more again. Oh, please let him get the job.'

'It'd be great for you and him. Fingers crossed.'

They drove to school, Riley humming and Mia smiling. Johnny was being offered work. A weight lifted from her shoulders. It was a tiny sliver of bright hope in the horrible darkness Mia was living in right now. Riley was happy and Johnny was working. The world seemed a little less bleak.

42

Rob finished filling the dishwasher, popped in a tablet and pressed the button to start the programme. He looked around and nodded, satisfied. The kitchen was clean and tidy again, just as Sarah would like it. Adam had been too distracted to notice the mess. Rob felt it was important that the place looked like home to Izzy. He was so worried about her and was doing anything that would help to keep her life at least partly normal.

He went to check on Adam, who was packing a bag of fresh pyjamas for Sarah.

'Hey, are you heading to the hospital soon?' Rob asked.

'They just rang,' Adam said, as he folded Sarah's things carefully. 'There are some new complications that need attention, so they asked for no visitors until about one. I'll go in then.'

Rob spotted an opportunity for some time out, which he badly needed. 'Would you mind if I went for a walk?' he said. 'I'll be back by then.'

'Of course,' Adam replied. 'You don't need to check in with me, bro. Take a walk any time you need it.'

'Great,' Rob said, trying to keep the relief off his face. 'I'll change my shoes and head out for a while, then.'

He put on his trainers and a fresh T-shirt, called goodbye to Adam, then stepped outside. Alone. It was a warm May day, and it smelt beautiful. Rob felt like he'd never scrub the hospital smell off his skin as long as he lived: it was ingrained in his pores. The thought of a long walk in the fresh air made him giddy with excitement. He'd do anything for Adam, he *was* doing everything possible for Adam, but, man, it was hard. The days were just running together in their horrible routine: Sarah got a little worse every day, the doctors got more stressed and Adam more entrenched in his lonely position. It was taking every bit of Rob's strength just to get through the hours and stay patient and supportive.

He began to walk, not caring what direction. After ten minutes or so, he realized he was heading towards Izzy's school, although it would take another forty minutes' walking to get there. That sounded perfect. He could stretch his legs, maybe catch a private chat with Mia and also check in on Izzy. He strode along, enjoying using his muscles again.

When he reached the school gates, he suddenly realized that a random man turning up and standing outside was not a good idea. He could hear the kids in the yard, screaming like seagulls. He consulted his watch. Must be what Izzy calls 'little break'. He took out his phone and scrolled through to find Mia's number.

She answered breathlessly. 'Rob? Did something happen?'

'No, not at all. I just . . . Well, I know it's a bit mad but I came out for some fresh air and I actually walked to the school. I wondered if you'd have five minutes to chat.'

'You're outside our gate?' Mia said, sounding surprised.

'Yeah. I'm down the road a little because I don't want to be arrested.'

She laughed. 'I'd better come and save you, then. Be with you in two minutes.'

He walked slowly back towards the gate and Mia appeared, smiling at him. She unlocked it and let him in. They made their way through the kids barrelling around the yard like they'd just been let off leashes. It was mayhem.

'How do they not kill each other?' Rob said. 'There must be a hundred collisions a day.'

'You'd be amazed,' Mia said, opening the door to the school. 'It's like they have some inbuilt self-preservation navigation system. You see hair's breadth near-misses, but we have very few actual crashes.'

'Is Izzy out there?' he said.

'I let her go over to Riley's yard, the senior yard. It's quieter there and she can chat to Riley.' She looked at him guiltily. 'I'm not doing that to annoy Adam,' she said urgently. 'Please don't tell him I said that. I just thought Izzy needed . . .'

Rob put his hand on her arm. 'It's fine, Mia. I'm not here to spy on you. Whatever Izzy needs, I'm very happy to give her. She's missing you guys like crazy.'

Mia's face fell. 'We miss her. It's wrong for her to be caught in the crossfire.'

She led Rob into her office and closed the door behind him. A blissful silence descended when the screaming mob was blocked out.

'Sit down,' she said. 'Can I get you a coffee?'

Rob smiled. 'I've got caffeine running through my veins instead of blood. I am most definitely OK for coffee.'

'I hear you,' Mia said. 'I'm running on coffee and sorrow at the moment.'

'It's horrendous,' Rob said.

'You look exhausted,' Mia said. 'You get sidelined a lot, but I know this is really hard for you. You're in the middle, and you're trying to do your best by Adam.'

Rob sighed deeply. 'Yeah, it's been hard. I miss Ellen as well, but when I ring her, we argue because she's so appalled at what's happening to Sarah.'

'So it's not just me and Dad,' Mia said.

'No, it's really not. I can't bear to see Sarah as she is, and it gets harder every day.'

'But you can't get through to Adam?' Mia asked.

'No, I can't. I've really tried. I'm being his ally, because he needs one, but at the same time I'm questioning him and trying to get him to discuss the options.'

'Thank you,' Mia said.

'Don't thank me because I'm failing miserably to reach him,' Rob said. 'He's an island. Me, the doctors, you guys, Izzy, we're all circling but we can't get to him. To be fair to him, I reckon he feels under siege. He can't think straight.'

'I can't lie, I want to kill him at the moment,' Mia said, 'but at the same time I know he's hurting so much. It's a life sentence for him, and I suppose we can't be surprised that he's finding it impossible to accept.'

'Yeah, that's how I feel,' Rob said. 'That's why I'm going easy on him. The updates that Dr Mayhew gives him are unbelievably grim, but he's blocking it all out. He just can't let go.'

Mia nodded. 'I know, but time is going to force his hand anyway. I just hope there's a change sooner rather than later.'

'I'll keep trying,' Rob said, feeling weary at the thought. 'I did achieve one small victory last night, though.'

'What was that?'

'I talked to him a lot about you and Charlie, and he's agreed you can visit for one hour per day, under my supervision.'

'Really? Jesus, I'm amazed,' Mia said. 'The UN should hire you. That's some negotiating skill you've got.'

Rob laughed. It felt good, like a release. He felt like he hadn't laughed since landing in Ireland. 'It took a while, but behind the fear and the anger, Adam is still there, and Adam is a good guy, you know.'

'I do,' Mia said. 'We've never totally seen eye to eye, but I was so grateful that he adored Sarah and made her happy. When do my visiting rights start? I was planning to go in to see her after school today.'

'Shouldn't be a problem,' he said. 'Hang on.' He took out his phone and sent a text. A moment later, his phone lit up. He held up the screen for Mia to see. It said: *OK*.

'That's great,' Mia said. 'I was so worried about another confrontation today. I can't take much more.'

'Well, I'm glad I could help,' Rob said.

'And what about Izzy?' Mia said. 'Any chance of visitation rights there?'

'I'll work on it,' Rob said, 'but it's a touchy subject. I'm so worried about her, Mia. How do you think she's doing?'

Mia rubbed her forehead. Another headache was starting. 'Not good,' she said. 'Her teacher mentioned it to me as well. She's withdrawn, and she's started cleaning her glasses compulsively.'

Rob nodded. 'She does it, like, a thousand times at home every day.'

'It's a coping mechanism, I suppose,' Mia said, 'but it points to the stress she's under. The worst thing, though, is that she truly believes Sarah will wake up on her Communion Day. I honestly don't know how Adam could or should handle it, but she's pinned all her hopes on it. I'm terrified of what will happen that day.'

'Yeah, she keeps saying it to me too,' Rob said, sighing again. 'I can't tell her otherwise without Adam's say-so. He has gently tried to suggest Sarah won't wake up, but Izzy just tunes it out. Like father, like daughter!'

The bell rang, signalling the end of break.

'I'd better get out of your way,' Rob said.

'You're so good to have come all this way to tell me in person,' Mia said, smiling at him. 'We just have to keep believing we'll all get through this and come out the other side together.'

'It's hard to keep the faith right now, especially when

everyone is so worn down, but it can't stay like this for ever, that much is for sure.'

'I'll let Dad know that he can go in,' Mia said. 'He just wants one more visit, to say goodbye.'

'No problem,' Rob said. 'I'll be there to help him as well.'

'Are you going back there now?' Mia asked. 'Do you want a lift?'

'No, it's fine. They asked us to stay away this morning because they're treating some fresh complications.'

'Oh, God, no – what?' Mia asked worriedly.

'Adam didn't say, but we're going in for about one o'clock. So I'll walk back and then drive in with him. I just really needed the fresh air and exercise.'

'I know I've said it before, but feel free to walk over to us any time.'

'Thanks,' he said, standing up. 'And thanks for looking out for Izzy.'

'We'll do our best,' Mia said. 'I'll walk you out.'

Rob followed her back through the corridors and across the yard to the main gate. It was quiet now. She unlocked the gate and locked it again behind him.

'I guess I'll see you later,' Rob said.

'Yeah, I'll be in about half four, if you want to warn Adam. And thanks so much again for sorting this.'

Rob walked away, glad that he had helped, but also burdened by all that he couldn't change. His brother was locked away behind his grief and pain, and he was powerless to set him free.

43

Mia went through her usual routine of hand-sanitizing, apron, gloves and mask. Angela popped out of Sarah's room. 'Hi.'

'Hi there. Are you finished?' Mia asked.

'Yes, you can go in now. How long do you have?'

'One hour, on the clock,' Mia said.

'I'm glad you were able to work something out,' Angela said.

'Rob is supposed to sit in with me, but he's very kindly offered to stay in the waiting room so I can have some time alone with her. But if Adam should ask you, say that Rob and I were in there the whole time.'

'I get you. No worries.'

'Rob mentioned some fresh complications?' Mia said, afraid to hear the answer.

Angela nodded. 'The infections are getting worse, I'm sorry to say. We can't control them. They're coming from so many different sources. Her poor body is giving up.'

'And is the baby still . . .'

Angela's eyes welled up. 'Yes, we can still get that heartbeat, but I don't think it'll be long before it . . .'

'I hope so,' Mia said softly. 'I'll go in now.'

She opened the door and took a deep breath. She hadn't thought it possible for Sarah to look worse, but she did. Her eyes looked as if they were going to pop out of her head. Her body was even more bloated, while the wound in her head was oozing pus and now had a fungal infection. The team were masking the odours with creams, but Mia could still detect a sour smell that made her stomach turn.

She reached for the lavender hand cream in her bag, rubbed it into her gloves and inhaled deeply, then walked over and sat in the chair by the bed. As usual, she picked up Sarah's hands and began to massage the cream into them.

'I saw Izzy yesterday, Sarah. She's so excited about her Communion. We did a rehearsal in the church and she was perfect, as always. She was talking about her hair. I hope Riley and I can do a good job. She said you'd picked out a particular style and that the photo is on your phone. I'll have to contact Adam about it. He has your mobile. Things are still a bit strained between us, but we'll work it out. The only thing that matters is Izzy, and I'll swallow all my pride and anger for her, I promise.

'This might be my last time in to see you, sis. Angela and the doctors don't seem to hold out much hope for the baby lasting much longer, although they can't say for sure. We all just want you to be able to rest in peace now. You and Ben. At least you'll have him with you. It's a strange comfort.'

Mia looked at her unrecognizable sister, at all the monitors and machines that were slowly engulfing her. Sarah was disappearing inside the tangle of wires, drips and tubes. You wouldn't wish this on your worst enemy, Mia thought. Such a terrible death. If she could be granted one wish, it would be to die at home, in her warm bed, with no interventions, no doctors, no machines. Their noise filled the room, making Sarah's still silence seem even louder.

Mia pulled out the diary and flicked through the pages. She fell on Christmas 2017.

'I've just finished wrapping Izzy's gifts. We went overboard this year. I think the fact that she is still an only child made both me and Adam go a bit bonkers. It's as if we're filling the void and disappointment with gifts.

'I so want to give Adam a baby, but I have to accept that it may not happen and Izzy is enough. She is enough for anyone. She gets more beautiful and funny and wonderful by the minute. She's like my best friend. I know that sounds soppy and sad, but she really is. There is no one I'd rather spend time with than my seven-year-old daughter.'

Oh, Sarah, if only you'd known you'd be pregnant with Ben in the new year. Then again, if you'd known how that pregnancy would end your heart would have broken.

'They say that dads find it hard when their daughters get married and go off and live with someone else. I'll find it really hard. I want Izzy to live with me for ever. No man will ever be good enough for her. She's perfect in every way, and, yes, I'm obviously ridiculously biased, but she is.

'I'm dreading tomorrow a bit because it's our first time to meet Dad's new "friend" Olivia. He's bringing her to lunch here with all of us. He met her in the golf club about six weeks ago and seems very keen.

'Mia hates her already, even though she hasn't met her. Adam keeps winding Mia up saying, "Charlie seems really happy and full of beans. It must be all the sex." I told him to stop. I don't particularly want to think about Dad having sex with Olivia either. Although, to be fair, if he is, good on him.

'Johnny's lost his job. The newspaper closed down. So Mia's in bad form. I hope she doesn't drink too much wine. She's a bit spiky at the moment.'

So would you be if Adam had no job and few prospects. It's not easy, Sarah, I'm doing my best.

'I'm really looking forward to us all being together for Christmas lunch. I hope Mia doesn't argue with Riley. They're killing each other at the moment. Riley can be a bit grumpy, although you can see it's all just teenage awkwardness and angst. Mia reacts so quickly to her – they

spark off each other so much. But you can see the love there, the affec-
tion and the devotion. They are cut from the same cloth and I know
they'll find each other again when the teenage stuff is over. I hope it's
soon, though, because I can see how much Mia misses Riley and the
closeness they had.

'To be fair, Mia does have a lot on her plate. She's great the way she
works and looks after Riley and tries to make sure Johnny is getting
out and about, meeting people and networking, not letting the job loss
bring him down.

'I'd be useless if Adam lost his business. We'd be homeless. No one
would hire me – I'm not good at anything, really, except being a mum.
I do think I'm good at that, but no one is going to hire me for it.

'I hope tomorrow is nice. I love Christmas and I want us all to have
a good time. Dad seems happy with Olivia, so even if we don't like her,
I think we need to focus on the fact that he is happier than he has been
in years.

'Please God this year will bring a baby for us, a job for Johnny, love
for Dad, hormonal balance for Riley and joy and happiness for my
Izzy.'

Mia covered her face with her hands. Joy and happiness . . .
Izzy had heartbreak, grief and devastation to look forward
to. It was so cruelly unfair. She was such a little thing, so
young and innocent. But all of that innocence would be
crushed to pieces when she found out that her beloved
mummy was dead and never coming back. Mia wept into her
hands.

'Christmas Day, 10 p.m. Everyone has gone home and I'm lying on the
couch writing this while Adam snores beside me.

'I've just tucked a happy but exhausted little girl into bed. She
hugged me and said it was the "best Christmas ever", which made all
of the hard work and preparation worth it.

'Adam and Mia both drank too much and needled each other, but it didn't turn into an argument, thankfully. Johnny was quiet. I can see his confidence is low because of the prospect of being out of work. He is usually so much fun, but today he was definitely quieter. Riley spent most of the day on her new iPhone, but she did play with Izzy too.

'Olivia . . . Well, what can I say about Olivia? She pawed Dad all day and he seemed to love it. Mia and I did a lot of giggling into our wine glasses.

'All in all, it was a good day. But then Mia cried when she was leaving. Johnny and Riley had gone to the car and Mia was saying goodbye to me on the doorstep and thanking me for hosting Christmas and all that and then she burst into tears!

'It was so unlike her. She was quite drunk and her emotions just rose to the surface. She said she misses Mum and that Christmas morning was awful because Johnny and she had spent all of their money on Riley's phone and then they gave each other a book and that was it. She said Johnny had tried to make the house look Christmassy, but his heart wasn't in it and she was too tired to bother. She said she woke up and went downstairs on her own while Johnny and Riley slept in.

' "I miss Santa and the magic of Christmas and Riley being Izzy's age and – and feeling light and happy. I'm turning into a grumpy, stressed-out cow. I hate myself."

'I hugged her and tried to console her. I told her she's wonderful and brave and strong and loving and kind. I said, "This is just a phase. Johnny will get another job and Riley will come through her teenage years," and she'd be able to breathe easy again.

'She said they don't feel like a family any more, that Riley spends all of her time in her bedroom and Johnny is always on the computer and she's alone in the kitchen. They were all living separate lives and Mia said she feels really lonely.

'I felt so bad for her, but then Johnny honked the horn and she wiped her tears and left.

'I wanted to hug her and comfort her. I hate seeing her so upset.'

Mia sat back in her chair. She remembered crying. She'd hated every minute of Christmas Day. She'd woken up with an empty feeling in the pit of her stomach. She'd sat in the kitchen on her own, drinking coffee and looking at the small, cheap tree that Johnny had tried, in vain, to make cheerful. She'd felt deeply sad, lonely and low, very low. Was this her lot? Was she going to spend the next twenty years working to pay off the mortgage and worrying about Johnny and Riley? Where were the fun and the laughs she'd shared with the two most important people in her life? They felt like strangers to each other now.

Mia had felt so alone sitting in the kitchen that morning. But in a strange way, since Sarah had been in hospital, she had felt closer to Johnny and Riley. They were helping her – well, Johnny was, and Riley was trying. They were actually talking to each other. They weren't always rushing off to different rooms, burying their faces in phones, laptops and Netflix.

God, how she wished she could turn back time. She wouldn't have felt sorry for herself. She could slap that self-pitying woman in the face. She was lucky, so lucky. She'd had no idea how lucky she was that morning. If she'd known then what would happen five months later, she would not have been crying and moaning about stupid little problems. She would have been on her knees thanking God for life, health and her family.

'Oh, Sarah,' she whispered. 'I've been an idiot. I'll never complain again, and I'll make sure we spend more time together as a family. I'll drag Riley out of that bedroom and I'll make Johnny put his laptop away and I'll turn my phone off and we'll try harder.'

Mia read the last paragraph of the entry:

'*When I closed the door, I realized how lucky I am and how I must cherish Izzy and Adam even more. We are so lucky to have each other and to love each other so much. Our little unit, our little bubble of joy, is all I've ever wished for – and more.*'

Mia kissed the page and closed the diary. She held her sister's hand, watched the clouds sailing gently by the window and prayed for Sarah to be at peace.

44

Riley didn't hear them coming. If she had, she'd have run, but they would probably have caught her anyway, with all their fitness training. They slammed her against the wall of the science classroom.

'What the actual fuck?' Zoë screamed in her face. 'Zach just dumped me for you. *You* – Debbie Downer!'

'He's obviously having some kind of brain fart,' Cleo hissed.

Riley pushed against them and tried to wriggle out of their grasp, but they had arms of steel. They had her well and truly pinned to the wall.

'Zach and me are a couple. We're the sports couple. We train together and we cheer each other on. He is into me, not you. You're just a freak who thinks she's better than everyone because she reads boring books about boring people and dresses like a guy.'

'What did you say to Zach to make him break up with Zoë? Did you offer him sex every day? I bet you did, you slut,' Cleo sneered.

'Zach told me that I was beautiful and sexy and fun. He said he loved hanging out with me. He said you made him feel stupid and were always angry about the world. He hated being with you. He can't stand you, so what the hell did you do?' Zoë's face was contorted with rage.

Strangely, Riley felt sorry for Zoë. She knew how she felt. She'd felt like that when she'd seen Zach with her. She understood heartache and humiliation and the pain that comes with being dumped.

'Look, Zoë, you need to talk to Zach, not me.'

'I did talk to him,' she shrieked. 'We talked for three hours but he wouldn't change his mind. He kept saying he was sorry but he'd made a mistake breaking up with you and he had to see if he could make it work.'

Riley smiled. Had he really said that? That was so nice to hear.

'Do you think this is funny?' Cleo kicked Riley's leg. 'You won't be smiling next week when he dumps you and gets back with Zoë.'

'I don't think that's going to happen,' Riley said truthfully.

'Shut your mouth and listen to me.' Zoë put her face up to Riley's. Riley could smell her strawberry lip balm. 'I'm going to get Zach back. I'll use all of my sports talent and the fact that I'm *waaaay* hotter than you to get him to change his mind. You don't stand a chance.'

'You might as well give up because Zoë is, like, drop-dead gorgeous and you look like that lesbian in *Twilight* – whatshername?' Cleo tapped her head.

'Kristen Stewart,' Riley said.

'Yeah, her.'

'Well, I guess Zach likes that look,' Riley said.

'Shut up. Who gave you the right to speak?' Cleo snapped.

'You know what I think?' Zoë said. 'I think he's only going out with you because he feels sorry for you. Zach has such a big heart, he knows your aunt is in, like, a coma or whatever and he wants to be nice. He'll dump you when she wakes up or dies.'

Riley'd had enough. The mention of Sarah gave her the anger and strength she needed. She kicked out and hit Cleo in the shin. Cleo let go of Riley's arms and bent over to hold her leg. Then Riley shoved Zoë with all her might. She stumbled and fell back.

At that exact moment Mrs Moloney came around the corner. 'What's going on?'

'She attacked us,' Zoë said. 'She pushed me over. Look, I've cut my hand, and she kicked Cleo's leg. I could have been badly injured and missed my hurdles competition this weekend.'

Cleo showed the headmistress the red mark on her shin. 'I could be scarred for life.'

Mrs Moloney turned to Riley. 'I'd like a word in private, please.'

Riley trailed after the headmistress while Zoë and Cleo grinned and mouthed, 'You're dead,' at her.

Mrs Moloney said nothing until they got to her office. She closed the door and told Riley to sit down. The headmistress then handed her a glass of water.

'Now, I understand that your family is having a terrible time. Your mother called me and asked me to keep an eye on you. I believe you're very close to your aunt and this trauma is hard to bear. However, I cannot allow you to push and kick the other girls. You'll have to find a different way to deal with your pain. If you need to talk to someone, my door is always open. If you're having a bad day, come and speak to me or any of the teachers. They're all aware of the situation and will lend you an ear if you need it. I'm not going to punish you this time, but I must ask you to hold your temper, Riley. I can't have you injuring the girls. Zoë is a sports star. Injury could be detrimental to her career and she has brought such glory to the school.'

Riley thought, briefly, about trying to explain the situation and defend herself, but there was no point. She nodded, said it would never happen again and left as quickly as she could. She was in such a hurry to get away from the office that she bumped straight into Zach.

'Hey, I was looking for you. I heard you'd been hauled into Mrs Moloney's office for attacking Zoë and Cleo.'

Riley looked into his blue, blue eyes and willed him not to say the wrong thing. Do not say, 'Why did you do it?' Do not say, 'You need to control your temper.' Do not say, 'That was out of order.'

'I bet Zoë was giving you a hard time,' he said. 'She went mental yesterday when I broke up with her. Like, totally fricking mad. I saw a whole other side to her. I'm sorry if she was a bitch.'

Riley reached over and kissed Zach, in the corridor, outside the principal's office. She didn't care who saw. She loved him and she wanted to show it.

'Well, I guess you're OK.' Zach grinned.

'I'm better than that. I feel happy for the first time in ages.'

Zach took her hand. 'Your place or mine?'

'Let's go to mine.'

As they were leaving school, Riley saw Izzy walking out with Adam. She let go of Zach's hand and ran over to them. 'Izzy,' she called.

Izzy turned and ran towards her, but Adam grabbed her and pulled her back. Riley marched forward.

'Hey, gorgeous girl, are you excited about Sunday? Only two days to go.' Riley ignored Adam.

Izzy wrenched her hand free and threw her arms around Riley. 'Yes! I'm very excited and I want you to do my hair if Mummy hasn't woken up.'

'Of course I will. You can tell me exactly how you want it done.'

'Izzy!' Adam barked. 'Come on.'

'Hi, Adam.' Riley glared at him.

'Hi.' Adam barely looked at Riley. 'Izzy, we need to go.'

'So what time will I call over on Sunday? Nine? I'll need about an hour to do Izzy's hair and get her ready.'

'Me and Rob will do Izzy's hair,' Adam said.

Riley snorted. 'Yeah, right. She'll look a state.'

'We're fine, Riley. We don't need anyone's help.'

'But, Daddy, I want Riley to do my hair,' Izzy said.

'Uhm, Izzy, can you go and talk to my friend Zach? He's just over there. I want to talk to your dad for a minute.'

Izzy shrugged and went to Zach, who bent down to talk to her.

Riley rounded on Adam. 'Why are you trying to keep Izzy away from us? Keeping her away from us is just punishing her. We love her, we're her family.'

'I don't want any of you near her or me right now. I just need some space. You're all trying to force me to give up on Sarah and my son, but I won't.'

'I don't care what you do – ultimately, it's your decision, even if I think it's wrong. All I care about right now is Izzy. She's lost her mum and now you're trying to take her whole family away. Are you mad? She needs us more than ever. We're not going to say anything to her about Sarah or the baby or any of it. All we want to do is make her happy.'

'I don't trust any of you. You're all against me.'

Adam looked like crap. His eyes were red and small and stressed, and his face was so pale, like a grey pale, and he had stubble on his chin and his clothes were crumpled. He didn't look like the Adam she'd always known. Mr Smart, always perfectly dressed and shaved and full of life. He was a wreck. Like one of those people you see on TV shows who are all paranoid and weird. Riley almost felt sorry for him. He looked like he was going to collapse.

'Look, Adam, you need to stop being paranoid. No one is against you. All I want to do is call over and help Izzy with her hair, OK?'

He stared up at the sky briefly, then sighed. 'OK, but Mia

is not to come. Only you. I can't handle Mia telling me what to do.'

'Fine, but for the record, you're being a prick to Mum and Granddad. But I'll park it for Izzy's sake. I'll see you at nine. I'll bring all the clips and bows. Does she have a bag, tights and shoes?'

Adam rubbed his chin. 'I don't know, I think so. Sarah was always so . . .' he stumbled over the words '. . . organized.'

Riley turned away quickly so she wouldn't have to see the pain in his face. He was suffering more than all of them. He was losing half his family.

She walked over to Izzy.

'An ice-cream van too!' Zach was gushing.

'Yes, and a big ginormous chocolate cake with a little girl that looks like me on the top.'

Zach shook his head in awe. 'You are one lucky girl.'

Riley wanted to kiss him again. She felt emotions rising in her chest. Not now, not in front of Izzy. 'Hey, Izzy, your dad's waiting, but I just wanted to check. Do you have tights, shoes and a bag?'

'Oh, yes, Riley. Mummy got everything for me. It's all hanging up in her wardrobe, all wrapped up so not even "one speck of dust can get on it", Mummy said.'

'Great.' Riley smiled as widely as she could. 'I'll see you in two days. I can't wait to help you get ready – we'll have so much fun. I'll bring sweets, but don't tell your dad.'

Izzy hugged her. 'I can't wait, and the best part is that Mummy will wake up when she sees me in my dress. I know it for sure.'

Izzy ran back to Adam, who took her hand and marched her off without a glance in Riley's direction.

'Sweet kid,' Zach said quietly.

Riley bent her head. The tears flowed freely now. 'Her

heart is going to be smashed into pieces when Sarah doesn't wake up. It's just not fair.'

Zach put his arm around Riley and she leaned into him, sobbing. 'You're great with her,' he said.

'I love her.' Riley wept. 'She can drive me nuts at times because she never, ever stops talking, but I really love her.'

'I'm here for you, Riley.'

'Promise?'

'Promise.'

'You won't change your mind again and go back to Zoë?'

He smiled. 'Never. You're my Jo March.'

Riley felt her heart warm and her tears dry. With Zach by her side, things seemed a little less awful.

45

Mia opened the door and was greeted with the smell of roast beef. The house was warm and cosy. She rushed into the kitchen and threw her arms around Johnny. 'I'm so glad to be home.'

'Bad day?'

She nodded into his neck. 'But I feel so much better now. Did you cook beef? My favourite.'

He smiled. 'Yes, and roast potatoes and parsnips.'

Mia kissed him. 'I might just love you, Johnny.'

She looked at the table. It was set with a candle in the middle and their good plates. It was like a celebration. Mia's heart leaped. He must have got the job. Yes! That was it. Oh, thank God, some good news.

Mia felt like she smelt of hospital so she ran up the stairs to have a quick shower and wash away the horrible day. She wanted to have a nice meal with Johnny, one in which she didn't cry over her sister. One in which she didn't feel as if she was going to choke on her food.

She leaned against the shower wall and closed her eyes. She could picture her father hunched over in the chair beside Sarah's bed, weeping. He'd come to say a final goodbye to her today. Sarah was worse. More infections were ravaging her body and they were finding it impossible to get them all under control. He'd said he didn't want to remember his beautiful daughter like this. It was too painful. He wouldn't come again.

Mia and Rob had had to go in and lift him out of the chair

and into the waiting room. He was broken. Utterly broken. It had been devastating to see her father like that. Thank God Angela was there to talk to him and help him to recover enough to walk to the car. Mia had driven him home, where Olivia was waiting.

Mia wanted to stop seeing Sarah too, but she felt as if she'd be abandoning her. Even though she was dead, it felt wrong. She needed to keep going in until the end. Please, God, may the end be soon, she prayed.

Mia dried herself and decided to put on a dress. Since Johnny had gone to so much trouble, she wanted to make a little effort too. She patted concealer over the black bags under her eyes and put on some lipstick.

When she walked in, the dinner was waiting. Johnny produced a bottle of wine and poured her a big glass.

'Wow, wine. Fancy.'

'You deserve a glass or ten after the last few weeks.'

'Cheers.' Mia clinked with her husband. He must have got the job. They hadn't bought wine in months.

'Where's Riley?'

'Out with her new boyfriend. They went to the cinema. She'll be back by eleven.'

'Is she still in a good mood?'

'She's like a different person. I hope to Jesus this guy sticks around.'

Mia grinned. 'Me, too. If he breaks up with her, we'll have to leave the country.'

Johnny laughed. 'One-way ticket to Timbuktu.'

Mia tucked into the delicious dinner. 'This is so good. It's the first time I've actually enjoyed food in ages.'

'Good, you need a decent meal. You're fading away.'

Mia looked down. She supposed she had lost weight. Her dress was hanging off her. The grief diet, she thought sadly.

347

'Dare I ask, how are you feeling about the Communion on Sunday?'

Mia put down her wine glass. 'It's Izzy. She's convinced Sarah is going to wake up and I'm really worried about the fallout.'

'I suppose she has to find out sometime.'

'I know, but on her Communion Day?'

Johnny sighed. 'It's rough, but is there any good day to realize your mum isn't coming back?'

'I suppose not, but they're all so excited about the day and the dresses and the parties, and I just want Izzy to have a good time. Instead she's going to have her heart broken.'

'Poor kid.'

'I even feel sorry for Adam.'

'Really?'

Mia nodded. 'Yes. It's going to be hard for him to pick up the pieces of Izzy's heart. Imagine if it was Riley.'

Johnny shook his head. 'I can't even go there. You're right, though, it will be awful for Adam.'

'She's all he has left.' Mia reached across the table to hold Johnny's hand. 'I'm so glad I have you and Riley. We're so lucky. I never realized how lucky we are. But I do now. It doesn't matter that we'll never have a big bank account. What matters is that we're alive, healthy and here.'

'And we love each other, no matter what, right?' Johnny squeezed her hand hard.

'Well, yes, of course.' Mia was taken aback by his intensity.

'Because I love you, Mia. I love you and Riley and Charlie and Izzy and even Adam. And I really loved Sarah. You know that.'

Johnny was getting emotional. Mia felt bad. She had been so consumed by her own grief that she sometimes forgot how hard this was on Johnny.

'I know you do, love. Sarah adored you too.'

'She was a brilliant person, and this has been such a difficult time. It's hard to keep everyone safe and protected.'

Mia frowned. 'But, Johnny, we're all safe. You're a great dad, husband, son-in-law and brother-in-law, and an amazing uncle to Izzy. I'm sorry I haven't said that more. You've been a rock to all of us.'

'I just want you to know that I love your family and I'd do anything for them.' Johnny was getting choked up.

'I know that. Honestly, Johnny, we all know that.'

His phone buzzed. He jumped up and left the kitchen to take the call. Mia cocked her ear to listen. She could hear '. . . more time . . . I'm almost finished . . . Just a few details . . . It'll be all that and more . . . Yes . . . I appreciate that time is tight . . . OK.'

When he came back in, Mia pretended to be busy eating. 'Who was that?'

Johnny looked flustered. 'It was just . . . uhm . . .'

'Was it about a job?' Mia blurted out, unable to contain her excitement.

Johnny bit his lip. 'Kind of. Look, I might have an article coming out soon, but it's not what –'

Mia jumped up and threw her arms around his neck. 'I knew it! I knew you had good news! I'm so happy for you, Johnny. You deserve this. You're the best. Thank God something is finally going right for this family.'

Mia was too excited to notice that her husband's arms hung loosely at his sides.

46

Adam looked down at his sleeping child. 'If there is a God,' he whispered, 'let my son survive so this angel can have a sibling and not lose her mother and baby brother. If there is a God, give me the strength to get through this day.'

Adam sat on the end of the bed, shoulders bent, the grief sitting on his back like a demon. Sarah had been looking forward to today for months. She had been so excited about it. She'd spent so much time organizing and planning every detail. Her face had lit up when she'd shown him Izzy's dress and told him how beautiful Izzy looked in it and what a special day it was for all of them.

'It's my first memory,' Sarah had said. 'My Communion Day, the dress and all the fuss. Being the centre of attention. It's the first strong childhood memory I have and it's a really special one. I want it to be a perfect day for Izzy, one that she will remember with joy for the rest of her life. We're creating memories, Adam, memories for life.'

For most of the day before, vans had been pulling up outside their house. The bouncy castle, chocolate fountain and the cake, that Mia had organized, had arrived. Izzy had squealed and jumped up and down with excitement. She had set the table with Adam for all the guests. Sarah had invited twenty-five people – seventeen adults and eight kids. Friends, family . . .

Everyone had been texting. Is it cancelled? Do you want us to host it? Would you rather just be with Sarah's immediate family?

No, no, and definitely not. He did not want to be near Mia

or Charlie. He wanted friends and their kids to run about, distracting him and Izzy. He wanted to salvage some sense of the occasion for Izzy from the ruins of their lives. He wanted her to have the perfect day her mother had planned.

When he saw Izzy's little icing figurine sitting on top of the cake, he'd almost lost it. He'd had to leave the room, pretending to take a work call.

Adam reached over and kissed Izzy's arm, careful not to wake her yet. Sleep, he knew all too well, was oblivion, these days. When you were asleep you didn't have to think. Sleep was a reprieve from the nightmare of real life.

Adam inhaled and exhaled slowly and deeply. He had to muster all of his energy to make this day as good as it could be for Izzy. Today was her day. Everything else had to be pushed to the side. Thank God for Rob. He was Adam's source of strength, always there to keep him going. With the two of them either side of Izzy, they could get through this.

Adam checked the clock, then gently stroked Izzy's cheek. Her eyes fluttered as she began to wake up. She rolled over and then her eyes flew open.

'It's my Communion Day!' She punched the air. 'Woohoo! Quick, Daddy, what time is it? I have to get ready.'

Adam kissed her warm cheek. 'Sweet-pea, it's only eight fifteen. We have lots of time for breakfast.'

Izzy stretched like a cat in the bed. 'Oh, Daddy, I'm so super-excited.'

'Come on, I'll make you pancakes.'

'Really?'

'Yes. I looked up the recipe last night. It's easy.'

'Cool.' Izzy swung her legs out of bed and went into the bathroom to brush her teeth.

Rob emerged from his room, already dressed. 'C Day,' he said, grinning tiredly at Adam.

'Oh, yeah,' Adam said. 'She's wired.'

'It's great for her to have something else to think about for a whole day. It'll be great. She'll enjoy it.'

'We'll do our best,' Adam said, feeling less sure than he sounded. Today would be all about acting, and he had to turn in a masterclass.

Rob followed Adam to the kitchen and got the coffee going while Adam dumped flour, milk and eggs into a bowl and began to stir it with a fork.

'No, Daddy,' Izzy shouted from the kitchen door. 'You need the whisky thing.'

'What whisky thing?'

'It's what Mummy uses for making pancakes. It's silver and has lots of lines on it and it mixes stuff.'

'Do you know where it is?'

'No, but it should be in one of these drawers, where Mummy keeps her cooking things.'

Adam opened and closed drawers but saw no 'whisky thing'.

'It must be here – we have to find it. Otherwise the pancakes will be all lumpy.' Izzy's voice was getting louder. 'Mummy says you can't do it with a fork because it doesn't get the lumps out.'

Rob and Adam both opened drawers and riffled through them but couldn't find it.

'It doesn't matter, princess,' Rob said. 'For today we'll do it with a fork. Your dad's very fast at mixing – look.' Adam whisked furiously with the fork. 'That'll definitely get the lumps out, just like Sarah does.'

Izzy looked into the bowl. 'It looks disgusting. It's all lumpy. It's not right.' Her lip began to wobble.

'Sometimes things don't look great, but they taste fine,' Adam said, tipping the bowl into the frying pan.

'You put too much in,' Izzy said impatiently.

He swirled the pan around as the mixture ran to the sides,

leaving the lumps of flour stuck in the middle. It was a disaster. The heat was too high and the mixture began to burn.

'Damn,' Adam muttered, and pulled the pan from the heat.

'Yuck.'

'Never mind, we'll try another. Let's give Rob a turn at being chef.' Adam tried to keep up a façade of cheerfulness. He lowered the heat, scraped the first pancake into the bin and handed the pan to Rob. Same result.

'They're disgusting, Daddy. You two are the worst pancake-makers ever.'

'You might be right. How about cereal?'

'No, it's a special day. I don't want stinky cereal.'

'Well, then, toast with butter and jam?'

'Boring.'

'Eggs,' Rob said. 'I'll do some scrambled eggs on toast, delicious.'

'I don't want stupid eggs.'

Adam looked at his brother in desperation. 'I think we might have some sausages. Would you eat a sausage sandwich?'

'Maybe.'

'Let me have a look.' Adam opened the fridge. Milk, cheese, beer, yoghurts, but no sausages. 'Right, well, it seems we're out of sausages. Sorry. I need to go shopping.'

'Mummy always went shopping on Mondays and Fridays.'

Adam sighed. 'How about yoghurt and . . . and . . .' Rob yanked open a cupboard and pulled out a packet. 'And crackers?' Adam said hopefully.

Izzy climbed down from the stool at the kitchen counter. Her face was bright red and her eyes were full of tears. 'You are the worst daddy ever,' she screamed. 'This is the worst breakfast of my life. It's supposed to be a super-special day, but it's not. You can't cook or shop or do hair or anything

353

that Mummy does. I want Mummy, not you.' She pushed him out of the way and ran out of the room.

Adam turned to catch her, but Izzy was too quick for him. She had slammed and locked her bedroom door by the time he caught up with her. Rob stood in the corridor, head bent.

'Izzy, sweetheart, I'm sorry.' Adam stood outside the door, listening to his daughter's sobs.

'I don't want you. I want Mummy. I want everything to be the same, not all horrible. I hate this,' she bawled.

'Izzy, come on, let me in. I'll –'

The doorbell rang. Rob looked out through the glass and mouthed, 'Riley,' to Adam.

Damn, Adam thought. Now she was going to come in and see what a rubbish job he was doing. She'd tell Mia and Charlie and they'd all think he was a total loser, incapable of even cooking a decent breakfast for his daughter.

'Izzy, pet, just open the door and talk to me.'

'NO!' she shouted.

The doorbell rang again.

'Will I let her in?' Rob asked.

'All right,' Adam said, cursing under his breath.

Rob pulled open the door and smiled. 'Morning, Riley.'

'No need to rush, like, whenever you're ready.' Riley rubbed her bare arms in the cool morning shade.

'Look, Izzy's a bit upset, about her mum and stuff. She's locked herself in her bedroom. I'm not sure she'll come out for a bit. Do you want a cup of tea?'

Riley marched straight past him, then straight past Adam and went up to Izzy's door. 'Hey, Izzy, it's me. Listen, I've got up early to come over here and make you into the most stunning, drop-dead gorgeous Communion girl ever seen. I may also have brought some treats. So open up and let me work my magic on you.'

To Adam's surprise, the door lock clicked. Riley turned to grin at him and Rob. 'That cup of tea would be great.'

Izzy locked the door again. Riley held out her arms and her little cousin ran into them, sobbing into her chest.

'Hey, now, we can't have a blotchy face on your special day. Get it all out in one big cry and then we'll have to start work on making you perfect.'

'Daddy made horrible pancakes and I shouted at him and I feel bad now, but I feel bad a lot cos of Mummy and I just wish so much that she was here.'

Riley ran her hands over her cousin's hair. 'I know. It sucks. Like, it really, really sucks, and you're right to be sad and angry. Don't worry about shouting at your dad. I feel like shouting at him, too. I know today isn't exactly how you'd hoped it would be, but I'm going to make it as good as I can. Are you finished crying?'

Izzy pulled back and nodded. Riley tried not to mind the snot on her new T-shirt. She fished in her bag and handed Izzy a tissue. 'Let's get started.' She pulled out the little chair beside Izzy's desk and got her to sit down.

'Wait, I have to finish cleaning my glasses.' Izzy picked them up from her bed and rubbed them furiously with a cloth.

Riley sat beside her on the bed. 'If you rub any harder, they'll break. Besides, didn't you say you weren't going to wear your glasses on your Communion Day?'

'Yes, but they have to be clean.'

Riley laid her hand over Izzy's. 'It's OK, Izzy. I'm here now. We're going to get you all done up so everyone in the church gasps and falls over when they see your stunning beauty. They'll ask, "Who is that super-model?" and the priest will drop to his knees in front of you.'

Izzy giggled. 'You're crazy, Riley.'

While Izzy was distracted, Riley gently lifted the glasses out of her hands and put them behind her on the bed. 'Slight exaggeration, but come on, we need to get started on beautifying your already beautifulness.'

Izzy stood up and threw her hands into the air. 'I'm ready.'

Riley got Izzy to kneel up on her desk chair. She tipped her own make-up bag on the desk. Lipsticks, foundation, concealer, eyeliner and mascara rolled out. Then she pulled out clips, bobbins and her curling wand. She plugged the wand in and waited for it to heat up.

'Now, madam, we shall apply some cream and a little concealer to soothe those eyes. Lucky for you, I happen to carry make-up with me at all times.'

'You're not going to put all black on my eyes like yours, though, are you? I don't think Mrs Kelly would like it. She said no make-up at all. Hannah in third class got a spray tan last year and Mrs Kelly was not happy. She said we're to look natural.'

'Promise me you'll never get a spray tan. Girls who go around looking orange are dumb.'

'Mummy wears fake tan. She puts it on in the summer to make her legs look better.'

'Yeah, a little bit is fine, but the girls who put on so much that they look like walking tangerines are ridiculous.'

'You wear make-up, though.'

'Yeah, but that's different. Make-up is brilliant when you get older because it can make your eyes look bigger and hide spots and stuff.'

Make-up was the best invention since the wheel, as far as Riley was concerned. The way it hid spots and stupid freckles and made your eyes pop was bloody brilliant. She hated fake tan, though. The stink of it and the way it got all streaky and clumpy on your hands and feet was gross. Riley was fine about being pale. She never wanted to walk around in shorts, so she didn't care if her legs were white. Besides, her fashion idol, and lots of people said doppelgänger, Kristen Stewart, rocked the pale look.

'Now, we'll leave your eyes to cool down and start on your hair. My mum said you'd already picked the style.'

'Mummy has it on her phone.'

'Hang on,' Riley said. She unlocked the door and went down to the kitchen. Adam was sipping a coffee and talking quietly to Rob.

'What? What is it?' he said, jumping up. 'Is she all right?'

'She's fine,' Riley said. 'Sarah had picked out the hairstyle and there's a photo of it on her phone. Can you get it for me?'

Adam reached into the pocket of his jacket, hanging on the back of the chair, and pulled out Sarah's pink-covered phone. Riley felt teary at the sight of it.

Adam scrolled through her photos. 'There's some hair ones,' he said. 'How will I know which one it is?'

'You won't,' Riley said, 'but Izzy will. Can I have it?'

Adam handed her the phone, and Riley took it back to the bedroom.

'OK, Izzy, show me which one.'

She scrolled until Izzy said, 'That's the one me and Mummy liked. Mummy said it was, uhm ... Oh, what's her name? She's in *Robin Hood*.'

'Maid Marian?'

'Yes!'

Riley smiled. 'I like it.'

She bent over the picture and tried to figure out how to copy it. She tested the wand: it was hot enough. She picked up a comb and began to divide Izzy's hair into segments. Izzy's tummy rumbled.

'Sorry, I had no breakfast.'

Riley winked at her. 'I have something for you.' She pulled a big chocolate bar out of her bag. 'This is for you.'

'Yum.' Izzy clapped her hands.

'But I also brought you a banana, which you have to eat first.'

'Really?'

'Yes.'

'OK.' Izzy pretend-groaned.

While she peeled and ate the banana, Riley waved her hair with the wand and began to pull back the sides and clip them into place. By the time Izzy was halfway through the chocolate, Riley had finished.

'That's enough chocolate for now. Save some for later. I think you're going to be happy with your hair. I've added in some of these little white butterfly clips I found and it looks very cool.'

Riley brought Izzy to the mirror hanging on the back of her bedroom door. 'Ta-dah.'

Izzy's face lit up. '*Ooooooooh.*' She turned her head to get a better look at the butterfly clips. 'Riley,' she gazed up at her cousin, 'it's so beautiful. I can't wait for Mummy to see it when she wakes up later. She'll love it.'

Riley turned to get some hair spray and to fight back tears. Izzy continued to coo behind her.

When she had regained her composure, Riley held up the can. 'Now we need to spray loads of this in, so your waves don't move or fall or droop. Close your eyes and your mouth.'

There was a knock on the door. 'Is everything all right?' Adam asked.

Riley looked at Izzy. She nodded.

'All fine, thanks.'

'Daddy, I don't want you to see me until I have my dress on.'

'OK, Sweet-pea. We have to leave in five minutes.'

'Relax, she'll be ready,' Riley said.

Riley drowned Izzy's head in hair spray. Izzy coughed and spluttered as the fumes went up her nose.

'Do you have to spray so much?' She coughed again.

Riley shrugged. 'If you want it to last all day, then yes.'

Izzy put on her tights, then Riley carefully helped her into her dress and zipped up the back. When Izzy turned, Riley felt a huge lump form in her throat. She looked so young and innocent and beautiful. She was so like Sarah.

She fell on her knees in front of her cousin, pretending to bow at her feet, giving herself a moment to get herself under control. Izzy giggled.

'If I say so myself, I did a brilliant job. However, I have to admit that it was easy. You are absolutely stunning, Izzy. Don't move. I have to take a photo.'

Riley stood up and pulled her phone out of the back pocket of her jeans.

Izzy beamed into the camera. 'Show me?'

'Hold it just one more second,' Riley said. She grabbed Sarah's phone and took a photo. She didn't know why, but it made her feel like Sarah was there in spirit.

'Show me now?' Izzy said.

Riley showed her the photo and Izzy squealed. 'I do look like a princess. I really do. Mummy said I would and I do.'

She tried to throw her arms around Riley, but Riley pushed her back gently. 'No hugs allowed until after everyone has seen your perfect hair and dress. After everyone has seen how utterly gorgeous you are, you can hug and jump and do whatever you want. But I want you to be flawless when you arrive at the church.'

Izzy did a little dance. 'I'm so happy, Riley, thank you.'

'You're very welcome. I'm pleased with my work. Maybe I should forget about being a human-rights lawyer and become a stylist.'

Izzy was too busy twirling in front of her mirror to answer.

'We need to go, Izzy,' Adam called.

Riley packed up her stuff. She handed Izzy her white bag and helped her buckle her shoes. 'Ready?'

'Yes.' Izzy beamed.

Riley let Izzy go first and watched Adam's face when he saw her. Rob put his hand to his mouth.

'Oh, Izzy,' Adam said, his voice hoarse. 'You look so like . . . so like your mum. So . . . beautiful.' Adam rubbed his hand over his face and tried to get a grip. 'Sorry, Sweet-pea, Daddy's just so proud of you and blown away by your dress and everything.'

'It's OK, Daddy.' Izzy patted his arm. 'When Mummy sees me later, I bet she cries too.'

Rob and Riley exchanged a look. Adam swallowed hard and tried to speak, but no words came out. Riley knew he needed help.

She clapped her hands together. 'Come on, everyone! The Communion girl is not allowed to be late. I want Izzy to make a big entrance and for everyone to be awed by her magnificence.'

'Yes,' Adam agreed. 'Let's go, princess.' Izzy walked out through the front door and Adam turned back to Riley. 'Thank you,' he said.

'You're welcome, Adam.'

'You're an absolute star,' Rob said. 'This is so hard, but you're doing better than us.'

'It's all about Izzy,' Riley said.

They walked out together. Adam carefully helped Izzy into the car.

Riley waved them off and hopped on her bike. She rode away just as the tears began to fall. She gazed up at the blue sky. 'Oh, Sarah, you would be so proud of her,' she whispered.

47

Mia stood outside the church, welcoming her class as they arrived and showing the children and their parents to their allocated seats. She'd been awake most of the night, crying for her sister. She knew how much Sarah had been looking forward to Izzy's Communion Day, and how much work she had put into planning it so it would be perfect.

She hoped she'd cried out her daily allowance of tears, so that she would be able to hold it together today and be professional. Mrs Kelly had offered to let her skip the day, but Mia knew how much her class were looking forward to it and she wanted to be there for them. Besides, it was a distraction she needed badly.

Mia watched proud mothers holding their daughters' hands, fixing their hair, straightening their dresses and beaming down at them, love emanating from every pore. She felt herself wobble and pinched her arm to keep control.

She was doing quite well until she saw Izzy. It was as if a light was shining over the little girl's head. She looked so like Sarah. Mia felt a surge of pain as a memory hit her. Sarah was about ten: she'd got a new white dress and she'd slept with her hair in plaits so it would be wavy. That morning she'd burst into Mia's room where she was studying, and pranced about, swishing her hair and singing, 'I Feel Pretty'. Mia gazed at Izzy: she was Sarah in miniature, like a reincarnation. Mia clung to the railing at the side of the church as she tried to suppress the memory and the pain.

Izzy saw her and ran over. 'Hi, Mia! I want to hug you, but

Riley said not to until everyone has seen my dress and my hair. Do you like my hair? I love it. Riley is so clever.'

Somehow Mia pulled herself together. 'Yes, I love your hair. You're a vision of loveliness. Am I allowed to kiss your cheek?'

Izzy grinned and nodded.

Mia kissed her. She wanted to put her arms around the little girl and never let her go. She was as close to Sarah as Mia could get now: her sister's living, breathing child. Mini-Sarah.

'I have something for you,' Mia said. She fished in her pocket and pulled out a silver bracelet, with one charm hanging from it: a little silver angel.

'Ooh!' Izzy held out her arm as Mia closed the chain around her wrist.

'Every year on your birthday I'm going to buy you a new charm. This first one is an angel because you're an angel and also because it's like a guardian angel to watch over you.' Mia coughed to clear the lump in her throat.

'It's beautiful,' Izzy said quietly. 'Thank you, Mia. I'll show it to Mummy later. She'll love it, too!'

'Izzy,' Adam called, 'I told you not to run ahead.'

Izzy spun around. 'Look, Daddy, Mia bought me an angel bracelet.' She wriggled her arm in front of Adam's face.

Adam nodded. 'Very nice. Come on, we should go in.'

'Are you coming, Mia?' Izzy said, holding out her hand.

'You go on, sweetie. I'll see you inside.'

Izzy went ahead of her father and Mia grabbed his arm. 'Please don't ruin her day by freezing us out. You're only hurting her.'

'I think you'll find that trying to bully me into switching off the ventilator and give up on her little brother will hurt her a lot more,' Adam hissed. He pulled away from Mia and marched into the church.

Rob shrugged. 'Izzy keeps talking about Sarah waking up. He's barely hanging in there, Mia. All we can do is be here and try to support him.'

'Miss Mia,' Katy squealed, as she bustled forward in a big puffy dress.

'Don't you look gorgeous!' Mia nodded at Rob, who moved towards the church door, then arranged her face into a smile for her student. 'Where are your mum and dad, Katy?'

'They're fighting,' Katy said rolling her eyes. 'Mummy said my dress was like Belle's from *Beauty and the Beast*, Daddy said it looked like a – a whatsitcalled? Oh, yeah, a gypsy dress. They got into a big fight and Daddy said, "I can't believe that yoke cost five hundred euros," and Mummy said, "It was eight, actually," and Daddy got all red in the face and shouted, "What kind of arseology is this?"'

'I see,' Mia said, trying to hide her shock. 'Well, never mind. Mummies and daddies get a bit excited on Communion Day, too. Look, here they are.'

Mia watched Katy's mum marching ahead while her father followed behind muttering, 'Eight hundred bloody quid.'

'Good morning,' Mia said loudly. 'Lovely to see you and your gorgeous daughter. You must be so proud of her.'

'Good morning. Yes, we are.' Katy's mum smiled widely.

Mia turned to Katy's dad.

'Yes, yes, of course. She's a great girl.' He took Katy's hand in his. 'A really great girl.'

'Excellent. Take your seats and have a wonderful day. These days are very precious.'

Katy's mum squeezed her arm as she walked by. 'You hang in there. We're all praying for your sister.'

Mia turned to wipe her eyes. A handkerchief was put under her nose. 'How do you never have a hanky?' Charlie said.

'Dad? I didn't know you were coming.'

'Well, I said to him, "Charlie, you are not going to let Adam stop you seeing your granddaughter on her big day,"' Olivia's voice boomed. Mia turned. Olivia was standing behind her in a very bright orange flowery dress. 'That little pet needs her family now.'

'Thank you,' Mia said to Olivia.

Olivia nodded, then said brightly, 'Well, we'd best get in or all the seats will be taken and I'm not standing in these shoes, I can tell you.'

Mia led them in and found them seats at the back of the church. Izzy saw them and jumped out of her seat to come over.

'Oh, God,' Charlie croaked, as Izzy walked towards them. 'It's Sarah.'

Olivia gripped his arm. 'Hold it together, Charlie.'

'You came!' Izzy clapped her hands. She gave them a twirl. 'Do you like my dress? Riley did my hair.'

'You look sensational,' Charlie said.

'Spectacular,' Olivia added.

'Izzy!' Adam's voice rang out.

'You'd better take your seat. The mass is going to start soon,' Mia said.

'OK.' Izzy hugged Charlie. 'I'm so glad you're here, Granddad.'

'I wouldn't miss seeing you today for the world.'

Izzy skipped back to her seat beside Adam.

Charlie sat down heavily on the pew. 'I'm not sure how much more I can take of this, Mia,' he said. 'It's splitting the family apart.'

'Dad, we'll work it out. Rob is trying to broker a peace deal in the background. Don't worry.'

'I told you, Charlie, worrying will only make you sick. Tongue out.'

Charlie put out his tongue and Olivia sprayed Rescue Remedy on it. 'Now, deep breaths.'

'Can I have some?' Mia asked.

Olivia smiled at her. 'Tongue out and don't cough. We can't be passing around germs.'

Mia did as she was told. Olivia sprayed her tongue.

The choir began to sing. Mia hurried over to take her place beside her class. She closed her eyes and let the music glide over her. She saw Sarah twirling in her white dress, but this time the memory didn't floor her. This time the memory was beautiful.

48

Adam dug his fingernails into his palms as a trickle of sweat rolled down his back. He thought the veins on his neck were going to pop out with the effort he was making not to throw himself on the floor and howl.

The little girls' voices rose as they paraded out of the church singing 'Circle of Friends'. Izzy walked by, her hands held up in prayer, looking so innocent and angelic. Adam's hand shook as he tried to steady his phone to take a photo to show Sarah. He knew it was stupid, she was dead, but he liked to talk to her and show her photos and tell her all about Izzy. She'd want to know every detail about today.

He clicked wildly on his phone, hoping some of the pictures wouldn't be blurred. He had never felt so alone, sitting in the church, an empty space on one side of him. Sarah's seat. Well-meaning parents gave him sympathetic half-smiles across the church, but he couldn't bear it. He avoided eye contact.

He should be there with Sarah, nudging each other, whispering that Izzy was by far the most beautiful child in the church, beaming and waving at her up on the altar. Sarah would have been the most beautiful woman, the most stylish, too. Adam would have sat there bursting with pride. His wife and his daughter, the best, brightest stars in the place. His family, his perfect family.

But, no. Life had robbed him of that. Sarah had been ripped from him, torn from their lives, and the hole she had left was so deep. Every minute of every day felt like a lifetime.

Adam felt as if he was swimming against the strongest current. If he stopped or lost focus for even one tiny second, he'd drown. A lot of the time he wanted to give in, to let the water sweep him away, but he couldn't. He had to be strong for Izzy and Sarah and his baby.

He wanted to go to bed, pull the duvet over his head and never get up, but instead he got up every day and tried to do the right thing. What was the right thing? Adam didn't know. But he had to keep fighting or they would all drown.

He saw Izzy wave at someone. He craned his neck. Charlie was waving at her and dabbing his eyes with his big handkerchief. God, he looked old. Two weeks ago his hair had been salt-and-pepper grey, but now it was snow white. Adam looked at the church exit where the girls were streaming out into the sunshine. Mia was standing at the door, ushering them out. She looked awful, grey, exhausted and very thin. Her dress was hanging off her frame.

Adam touched the side of his face where he'd cut himself shaving that morning. He hadn't shaved in a week, but he'd wanted to be presentable for Izzy. In the mirror, he'd barely recognized himself. He'd tried to fix his hair and had put drops in to soothe his bloodshot eyes, but it had made little difference.

As parents stood up and talked with each other, complimenting dresses, daughters, the weather, Adam hung back. He didn't have the energy for chit-chat. Sarah was good at it. Mia used to laugh and say Sarah was the queen of small-talk. Mia liked to cut straight to the important things and have proper conversations with people, which freaked Sarah out. She wanted to keep it light. She didn't want to share her thoughts or intimacies with other people. She didn't want people telling her that their marriages were in crisis or they were having an affair, were secret alcoholics or hated sex with their husbands. Sarah had never been good with over-sharing. She'd always told Adam that she liked to keep her conversations to kids, holidays, fashion and light current affairs. 'I don't want a big gang of friends. I have you to talk to.'

He felt exactly the same way. She was his best friend, too. Sure he had mates to go to rugby games with, but Sarah was his best friend. He hadn't just lost his wife, he'd lost his closest friend, confidante, lover and the person he adored.

Adam had always thought people who self-harmed were insane, total nutters. But lately the thought of cutting himself to feel physical pain was attractive. Frighteningly attractive. He'd held a knife to his arm last night at three a.m. He hadn't cut himself, but he'd been close. It had frightened him. He was too close to the edge. He had to try to come back. He'd forced himself to look at the photos of Izzy that covered the kitchen walls and had put the knife down.

It hadn't been easy, but he'd done it. He couldn't start self-harming: that would be a dangerous spiral. He needed to stay strong and keep it together for Izzy, but it was very tempting to disappear into real pain instead of emotional agony.

Work was a mess, too. His managers had been fantastic, but he needed to get back to the office and deal with the mounting paperwork. The economy was buoyant again and the business was flying. Better than ever, they told him. But he didn't care. The special holiday they were going to take was gone now. No more family holidays. No more cocktails at sundown. No more walks on the beach. No more kissing Sarah and tasting the salt of the sea on her lips. No more . . .

'Adam? Are you all right?' a mother asked him.

He couldn't remember her name. 'Yes, fine. Just a bit hot in here,' he said.

'What a lovely ceremony,' Rob said, distracting the woman.

'Oh, yes, it really was. The girls were just lovely. Izzy looks wonderful. I'm so sorry about . . .'

Adam's throat tightened and his breath shortened. He had to get away from the woman before he broke down. He couldn't handle sympathy. 'I'm sorry, but I must find Izzy.' He pushed past her brusquely and rushed out of the church. He loosened his tie and sucked in gulps of air.

Where was Izzy? He spotted her talking to Charlie and Mia.

He marched over and took Izzy's hand. 'Come on, Izzy. We need to go.'

Rob joined them. 'Hi, guys,' he said. 'Thanks for coming today.'

'We're going to see Mummy now,' Izzy said. 'I'm going to wake her up. Today is the day.'

'Ah, pet, I don't think the doctors will agree to that,' Mia said lightly. 'I think you should get started on your party. I mean, a chocolate fountain, Izzy! I bet you can't wait to get home to that.'

Izzy shook her head firmly. 'No, Mummy first. Daddy is taking me to the hospital.'

'I don't think he can,' Charlie said. 'The doctors said Daddy couldn't bring in any other visitors, just himself.'

Adam felt the old rage rise up again, hearing Mia and her father taking over and throwing their weight about. 'The doctors didn't say that,' he said.

'Hey, Izzy, would you mind if I bring you over to that blossom tree for some photos?' Rob said. 'You'll look so pretty under those pink blossoms. I want to get a special picture for Ellen.'

Izzy went off happily, hand in hand with Rob.

Once Izzy was out of earshot, Adam fronted up for the argument.

'You're not seriously taking her to the hospital?' Mia said. 'She'll be so upset when she sees Sarah.'

'She's been asking me every five minutes for a week. I can't keep fobbing her off. If I don't take her in, she'll freak out.'

'So lie to her, tell her Sarah is in surgery or something. Tell her anything. Please, Adam, that's not a sight for a child.'

Adam gritted his teeth. 'I've used that excuse a hundred times already. She never stops asking. I'll ask Angela to make Sarah look more . . . more presentable. She can put on the sunglasses, put make-up on her face. It'll be OK.'

'No amount of make-up can hide the reality of Sarah's body,' Mia said. 'Izzy will be traumatized.'

Adam had had enough. Didn't they get it? He'd tried to put Izzy off. He'd come up with every excuse in the book but she asked non-stop. She got more and more upset every time he said, 'Not today.' She was desperate to see her mother. She would not let up until she did. What choice did he have?

'Back off, Mia. Stop telling me what to do. Just back the hell away.'

'Don't speak to Mia like that,' Charlie snapped. 'We're only concerned for Izzy.'

'I'm sick of all of you interfering in my life. Stay away from me and Izzy.'

Riley stepped forward and stood in front of her uncle. 'Adam, this is all kinds of crazy. I know you're in bits, and I know you adore Izzy and want to help her, but this isn't the way. I nearly lost my mind when I saw Sarah. Izzy is only seven. She seriously cannot cope with seeing her mother like that.'

'Like mother, like daughter,' Adam said. He felt sick at Riley's words, but he hated them all for judging him. He was a good father, but they were acting like he was an unfeeling monster. Where did they get off playing all high and mighty?

'I'm thinking of Izzy,' Riley said, her face flushed.

Mia put her hand on her daughter's arm. 'Yes, you are, love, but Adam can't hear us. This is a pointless conversation.'

Rob walked back towards them, Izzy holding his hand and babbling excitedly about Sarah.

'. . . and when she wakes up, do you know what we'll do? We'll bring her to the party and she can see everyone. She'll be so happy! I can't wait!'

'If she needs us,' Mia said, 'we'll still be here, Adam. You might hate us right now, but we'll always be here for Izzy. If she's upset later, Riley can come over.'

'She'll be fine,' Adam said, wanting desperately to get away from them now. 'I think it would be best if you don't come over later.'

'Adam –' Rob started, but Adam silenced him with a look.

He took Izzy's hand and walked her towards the car park.

Izzy waved at them over her shoulder. 'See you later at the party,' she shouted.

49

The hospital was quiet. It was a warm and sunny May afternoon so anyone who could bring their visitors outside to the grassy areas had done so. The corridors were much emptier than usual. Adam's heart was heavy, but he knew this moment of goodbye would be important for Izzy. She'd always remember that she got to say goodbye, and that would help with her grief.

'Adam,' Rob said quietly, 'are you absolutely sure about this? It's just –'

'I'll take it from here, Rob,' Adam said. 'I'll bring Izzy up myself.'

Rob flinched. He took a deep breath. 'You're making a mistake,' he said. 'Please don't do this.'

Adam shook his head. 'Even you,' he said, disappointed in his brother. He needed Rob to be strong, not swayed by the emotional blackmail of the others.

'It's not like that,' Rob said. 'I don't think you understand . . .'

'I understand everything,' Adam hissed.

'What's wrong?' Izzy said, looking fearfully from one to the other.

'Nothing at all, Sweet-pea,' Adam said, forcing a smile onto his face. 'Uncle Rob is going to get himself a coffee and wait outside in the sun. We'll go up to see Mummy ourselves.'

'Oh, that's a good idea,' Izzy said, beaming at them. 'Then, when she comes down with us, she'll get an amazing surprise to see Uncle Rob waiting for her.' She giggled. 'It's perfect. I won't tell her you're here, Uncle Rob, I promise.'

Rob nodded, but said nothing. He stopped walking, and

Adam took Izzy's hand and they made their way to the stairs, just the two of them.

Izzy's chatter stopped as they entered the ICU wing. She gripped Adam's hand tighter. He stopped and crouched down. 'Sweet-pea, you don't have to visit Mummy now. You can change your mind, it's absolutely fine. I've told you that Mummy is very sick. She's puffy and not like she used to look. It's a bit scary, but it's just the medicine they're giving her. I don't want you to get a fright. We can do this on another day.'

Izzy shook her head from side to side. 'No, Daddy. It has to be today. I have to see her today to wake her up. Mummy would never not wake up to see me on my Communion Day.'

Adam bit his lip. 'OK, but remember I told you that the medicine also makes her sleep, so she probably won't wake up, Izzy.'

Izzy placed her hands on her father's shoulders. 'Daddy, stop worrying. Mummy will start getting better today. Everything is going to be fine now.'

Adam didn't know what to say. He knew that if he tried to stop her seeing Sarah today, she'd have a complete meltdown and never forgive him. In a way, it might be a good thing, easing her into the realization that Sarah wasn't going to get better. She needed to see her mother, and Adam hadn't the heart to stop her.

Angela came over to them, smiling widely. She held her hand up to her chest. 'Oh, my goodness, you're a vision. Give me a twirl.' She handed Izzy a ten-euro note.

'Oh, no, I couldn't take your money. Daddy says nurses get paid really badly and treated like servants and I should only ever be a doctor when I grow up.'

Adam wanted the floor to swallow him.

Angela laughed. 'Well, he's right, we do, but I saved this especially for you.'

'Are you sure?' Izzy asked.

'Positive.'

'Well, thank you very much. Let's see Mummy now,' Izzy said.

'Yes,' Adam said, 'but we have to put on the special clothes. I know you're wearing your beautiful dress, but I have to give you an apron, a little mask and gloves. We can't let our germs get onto Mummy because she's not strong enough to fight them.'

'Where's my apron?'

Adam got the gear and helped Izzy into hers. Izzy was washing her hands when Angela pulled Adam aside. 'Adam, are you sure about this? I've tried to make Sarah look somewhat presentable but I have to stress once again that I don't think it's a good idea.'

'She needs to see her,' Adam said. 'She won't stop until she does.'

Angela crouched down. 'Izzy, as I'm sure your daddy told you, your mummy doesn't look like before because of all the medicine. I had to put sunglasses on her eyes to protect them and –'

Izzy held up her hand. 'I know Mummy is sick and the medicine is strong and she's puffy and sleepy, but it doesn't matter because today all that is going to change. Come on, Daddy, let's go.'

As they approached the door, the occupational therapist came out. She stopped dead when she saw Izzy.

'Thank you for helping my mummy,' Izzy said to her. 'I'm Izzy, her daughter, and today is my Communion Day, I'm going to wake her up.'

'Oh, but –' She looked frantically at Angela and then at Adam. 'She can't . . . It's not . . .'

Adam looked at the horrified face of the therapist and

paused at the door. 'You know what, Izzy? Let me pop in first and see that Mummy's OK. I'll just be a second.'

'*Daddy!* Hurry up.' Izzy groaned.

The door shut behind him and Adam stood in the room he had become so familiar with. He walked over to the bed. The tubes, the machines, the infections, the fungus . . . Suddenly he saw it. He saw his wife through Izzy's eyes. The eyes of an innocent seven-year-old, who remembered her mother as a beautiful, living, smiling, laughing woman.

He saw her for what she had become. He saw her for the first time not as his wife, his beloved, but the bloated corpse she was.

How could he bring Izzy in here? How could he let her last memory of her mother be this horrific sight? Adam bent over and pain shot through his heart.

'Sarah. I'm sorry. I'm so sorry. How did I let this happen? My beautiful Sarah. I'm so sorry. Forgive me. Please forgive me. I wanted to keep you and Ben alive – I wanted to fight. I wanted never to let go.'

He slid to the floor. 'Sarah,' he wept, 'forgive me.'

There was a bang on the door. 'Daddy! I want to come in.'

Adam moved to the door to block it. 'No, Izzy. I'm sorry, but you can't see Mummy.'

'You promised!' Izzy shouted.

'I know, and I'm so sorry. It was stupid of me and wrong of me. You can't come in, Izzy.'

'I can and I will,' Izzy screamed. 'Let me see my mummy. I need to wake her up. Let me in, Daddy! She needs to see my dress.'

'I can't, Izzy. I'm so sorry.'

'Mummy? Mummy! It's Izzy! Wake up!' she cried. 'I'm here to see you.'

Adam heard Angela's voice. 'Hey, now, Izzy, will you be

the best girl and just sit outside for a minute and I'll go in and see what's happening? Your mummy might need some extra medicine.'

Angela knocked gently on the door. He opened it to let her in. With one look, Angela knew. 'You've made the right decision, Adam. She shouldn't see her mother like this.'

'I've been so blind and stupid,' Adam sobbed. 'How could I have even considered bringing Izzy in?'

'She's a very determined little lady who wanted to see her mother. You're just doing your best under the circumstances.'

'Look at her!' Adam cried. 'She's a stranger, a corpse. That is not my wife. That is not Izzy's mother. Ben could never survive in there – I see it now. Oh, God, I see it. I've lost them, Angela, I've lost them.'

Angela held him while his body convulsed and he wept.

'Now, Adam, you need to take a deep breath and go out there to talk to that confused little girl. It's going to be hard but at least she'll know, instead of living in this awful limbo.'

'It's going to break her little heart.' Adam gulped back tears.

Angela wiped away a tear from her cheek. 'Come on, now. You can do this, Adam. You're a good father and she needs you. Children are amazingly resilient. Just keep telling her that you're there for her.'

Adam dug deep into the depths of his body to find the willpower to walk down the corridor and tell Izzy the news that would shatter her.

'Daddy! I'm sick of waiting,' Izzy snapped, when she saw Adam.

'Izzy, I need you to sit down. I need to tell you something.'

Izzy's eyes grew wide and frightened. 'Is it bad?' she asked, her chin trembling.

Adam nodded. 'I'm so sorry, Sweet-pea, but Mummy isn't going to wake up, ever. Mummy has died and gone to Heaven.'

'But she can't have.' Izzy clutched her little white bag to her chest. 'She can't be dead. Today is the day she wakes up. Let me see her, Daddy. I can wake her up. I know I can.' Izzy jumped up. 'Let me talk to her. Mummy!' she shouted.

Adam grabbed her waist to stop her running. 'Izzy, Mummy is gone. Only the machines were keeping her alive, but even they can't save her now.'

Izzy saw Angela standing in the corner. 'Is it true?'

'Yes, pet, it is. Your mummy is gone.'

'For ever?'

Angela nodded, biting her lip to hold back the tears.

'But – but it's my special day.'

'I know, Izzy,' Adam choked back tears, 'and I'm here for you. I'll do everything I can to make it better.'

Izzy looked at him, a little crease in the middle of her forehead. 'You can't make it better. No one can make it better. Mummy is gone. My mummy is gone. I . . . Who's going to look after me?' Izzy's eyes were wild with fear. 'Who's going to wash my hair and make my lunch and bake with me and watch movies with me and hug me and sing me songs and read me bedtime stories and – and . . .' She sank to the floor, legs straight out, her dress spread around her, like a doll's.

Adam sat beside her and put his arms around her. 'I will. I will do all those things.'

'But you're always working.'

'I'm not going to work so much any more. I'm going to be home to look after you. I'll learn to cook and do your hair, and I'll do all the things that Mummy did. We can do this together. I'm here for you, Izzy. Daddy's here.'

'But I want Mummy,' Izzy sobbed.

'I know you do.'

'She's my special person.'

'She was mine too.'

'Everyone has a mummy.'

'Actually . . .' Rob walked down the corridor carrying two coffees. He set them down and knelt beside Izzy and Adam. '. . . your dad and I had no mummy. Our mummy died when we were very small. We were very sad in the beginning, but we were OK.'

Izzy sniffed. 'Did you have a good daddy?'

Rob put his hand on Adam's shoulder. 'Not even close to as good as your daddy is. Your daddy loves you enough for two people and more.'

'Mummy said she loved me more than the whole world.' Izzy bunched her fists against her eyes.

'She did,' Adam said, 'but she's still with you, Izzy. She's here.' He touched Izzy's heart. 'She will always be in your heart. She is you and you are her.'

'And you've got so many people who love you and want to help look after you, like Riley and Mia and Johnny and Granddad and me and Ellen,' Rob said.

'But they're not Mummy.'

'No one is as special as your mummy. But we'll all help you through this. You and your daddy,' Rob said, touching Izzy's cheek.

Izzy looked up wearily at Adam. 'I'm tired, Daddy. Can we go home?'

'Yes, we can. Maybe you'd like to look at photos and videos of Mummy in the car. Remember the fun times.'

Izzy nodded and took his phone.

On the way home, Rob drove in silence while Izzy and Adam sat in the back together, watching videos of Sarah – alive, vibrant, beautiful, loving and laughing. Adam felt Izzy's body relax. She even managed a little laugh at the video of Sarah trying to do cartwheels with her on the beach.

Maybe they would get through this, maybe . . .

50

Riley stood in the kitchen, hands on hips. 'So, let me get this straight. We were invited to the house after the Communion, then disinvited, then re-invited to call over at six o'clock when the party is essentially over? I had plans and you've called me back home for this?'

'Yes,' Mia said. Adam had sent her a text asking if she, her father and the others would please come to the house. *It would mean a lot to Izzy*, he'd written.

'We're doing it for Sarah, and most of all for Izzy,' Mia said.

'We're all going, even Granddad?'

'Yes, because it's Izzy's day.'

'Even though Adam is a prick?'

'Language, and yes.' Mia had wanted to tell him where to shove his last-minute invitation, but when she thought of Izzy in her dress, so hopeful and so sure her mum would wake up, she knew she had to go there.

'Dad?' Riley turned to Johnny. 'What do you think?'

Johnny swung his car keys around his finger. 'We need to focus on Izzy. It's up to us to be there for her out of respect for Sarah. If, God forbid, anything happened to Mia, I'd have wanted Sarah to show up for you.'

'Yeah, but you wouldn't have shouted at her and banned her from the hospital or the house, like Adam has.'

'Who knows how I'd behave if I was in his situation? Lookit, I agree he's treated Mia and Granddad terribly, but he's deranged with grief.'

'He's deranged all right,' Riley said. 'Mum, don't die because I'm not living with Dad if he turns into Adam.'

Mia finished wiping down the countertop. 'I'll do my best. By the way, you were great with Izzy this morning. She looked perfect. Well done.'

Riley shrugged. 'I was happy to. I remember my Communion Day as being a really great day and Izzy's is . . . well, it sucks.'

'Yeah, it doesn't get worse than having your mum being in a brain-dead coma on your Communion Day,' Shocko agreed. 'I thought mine was bad because my dad got really drunk and started doing Elvis impressions.'

'And he's so bad at them.' Riley grinned.

'The worst,' Shocko said. 'But after a few whiskeys he actually thinks he is Elvis.'

'Parents can be so embarrassing.'

'Yours are pretty cool,' Shocko said.

'Thanks, Shocko.' Johnny patted his shoulder. 'Although I'm not sure Riley agrees with you.'

Riley dipped a biscuit into her tea. 'You're not the worst.'

'Gee, thanks,' Mia said.

Riley grinned at her. Mia smiled back.

'We should go.' Johnny looked at his watch.

'Why don't you come too, Shocko?' Mia suggested.

'Oh, no. I don't want to crash the party.'

Johnny held up his car keys. 'The more the merrier, and Riley's always happier when you're around.'

'It's not me that makes Riley happy, it's Zach.'

'Zach?' Mia spun around.

'Dude!' Riley hissed.

'Sorry, I thought they knew.'

'So Zach's the guy?' Johnny asked. 'Is he your boyfriend now?'

'No . . . Well, kind of.'

'Are you a couple?' Mia asked.

'See?' Riley glared at Shocko. 'Now I'm going to get interrogated.'

Shocko held up his hands. 'I'm sorry.'

'It's still very early days and I don't want to talk about it,' Riley said.

'Is that who you were with this morning?'

'I was with Shocko too.'

'Threesome!' Johnny winked.

'Dad!'

'Joking, love.'

'I don't think I could do a threesome with another guy. Two girls, definitely,' Shocko said.

'Is he in school with you?' Mia was determined to get as much information as possible before Riley shut down.

'Yes.'

'Is he nice?'

'Yes, Mum.'

Mia looked at Shocko.

'Yeah, and he's sporty,' Shocko told her.

'Now we're talking.' Johnny rubbed his hands together. 'Rugby? Soccer?'

Silence.

'Tennis? Basketball?' Johnny continued listing sports.

Shocko grinned. 'What is it he's into again, Riley?'

'He's into high jump,' Riley muttered.

'High jump?' Johnny repeated. 'As in high jump?' He tried to suppress a chuckle.

'Yes, Dad.'

'Right. Not the most macho of sports, but good enough.'

'It's actually really skilled and he trains all the time and he's really fit and good at it.'

'Good for him. It shows he's focused and dedicated,' Mia said. 'Kids who are good at sports tend to stay on the straight and narrow.'

'Oh, Mum, you're making him sound like a nerd now.'

Silence.

'He's not a nerd. He's actually quite cool.' Riley crossed her arms defensively.

'Really?' Johnny sounded doubtful.

'Yes, really.'

'He sounds lovely, Riley.'

'Mum, don't say lovely. When parents say a boy is lovely it means he's a total loser.'

'True for girls, too. My parents told me their friend's daughter was "lovely". She was five feet tall and five feet wide, with a face like a slapped fish,' Shocko said.

'Fine. He sounds nice,' Mia said.

'That's worse.' Riley groaned.

'Oh, for goodness' sake, sporty, cool, whatever. Can we please go now?' Mia huffed. 'We've more important things to be doing. I want to see Izzy and make sure she's OK. She went to see Sarah this morning and I'm really worried about her.'

'Let's go,' Johnny said, putting his arm around Mia.

Riley linked Shocko's arm. 'You're coming, too, to protect me from Mum's inquisition about Zach.'

They walked out, Mia praying Adam would behave and not start another argument. She didn't have the energy for it.

51

They all stood at the doorstep.

'What do you think this is about?' Charlie asked. 'An olive branch?'

'I think Izzy went to see Sarah and is traumatized and he wants us to be there for her,' Mia whispered.

'I cannot believe he let her see her mother like that. I don't think I'll ever be able to forgive him.'

'I agree completely, Dad, but to be fair to him, Izzy was absolutely insistent.'

'Well, if he says one rude, insensitive thing, I'm out of here,' Charlie said.

'Quite right, Charlie, and I'll be behind you,' Olivia said. 'If he even looks at you sideways, I'll start the car.'

'What if he looks at him sideways by accident, like, not in a dodgy way, just in an oh-look-there's-Charlie way?' Shocko asked.

Olivia regarded him for a moment. 'Are you Riley's boyfriend yet?' she asked.

'Steady, Olivia,' Mia said. 'Shocko is her best friend, you know that. Her boyfriend is a boy called Zach. Apparently he's very good at the high jump.'

'Shut up, Mum,' Riley said, making a face.

'High jump?' Charlie didn't sound impressed.

'Yes, Granddad.'

'Pity it isn't football.'

'Too right,' Johnny said. 'Or rugby.'

'Oh, yes, that would be nice.'

'Can you all please stop picking on Zach?'

'Can you pick on someone if they're not actually, like, present?' Shocko asked.

'I don't think so,' Johnny said.

'Well, stop dissing him, then.'

'What's dissing?' Olivia asked.

'Dismissing,' Mia explained.

'Why don't you just say that?' Olivia asked Riley.

'Because dissing is more street,' Shocko said.

'What in God's name is he talking about?' Olivia asked Charlie.

'I think he means it's more modern,' Charlie said, smiling.

'Oh, you lot with your LOLs and your FOMOs, I can't keep up,' Olivia huffed. 'Why can't you just use proper English?'

'Correct English,' Riley said.

'What?' Olivia asked.

'It's actually "pardon", if you're so keen on manners.' Riley smirked.

'Are you going to let her speak to me like that?' Olivia glared at Mia and Johnny.

'I think you mean "allow her to",' Mia said, with a grin.

'Well, I never –' Olivia's huffing was interrupted by the front door opening.

Adam stood in front of them. His shirt was hanging out and he looked like hell. 'Thanks for coming,' was all he said, as he stood aside to let them in.

They trooped past him into the kitchen. The counter was laden with party food that lay untouched. The bouncy castle in the garden was deflated. The chocolate fountain was turned off.

'What happened?' Mia asked.

'I couldn't go through with it,' Adam said.

'Oh, thank God. So Izzy didn't see her?' Mia said.

'No.'

384

'You made the right decision,' Charlie said.

Adam nodded. Rob came in with Izzy. She was in a pink unicorn onesie. Her eyes were red and swollen from crying.

Mia's heart melted. She rushed over and hugged her. 'How's my little pet?'

Izzy shook her head. 'I had a real bad day.'

'Oh, Izzy.'

'Mummy is gone. She's – she's not coming back. The machine was just making her breathe, but Mummy is not there.'

Mia looked up at Adam. He nodded sadly.

'Well, when I look at you, all I see is Sarah. Your mummy is in you, Izzy,' Mia said gently.

'Daddy said she's in my heart.' Izzy began to sob.

Mia nodded. 'He's right, Izzy, she is. She's always in your heart, but also in your eyes and your hair and your smile and your gorgeous personality, too.'

Johnny handed Mia a tissue. She wiped Izzy's eyes and then her own.

'Sarah would be very proud of you,' Charlie croaked.

Izzy's eyes were bright with more tears. 'I'm proud of her too. But I wish . . . I wish she wasn't gone. I thought she was going to wake up for my special day. I really believed it.'

'It was the same with Granny Penny. Sometimes when you get super-sick you just can't fight it.' Mia held Izzy close. 'But your mummy loved you more than anything or anyone. You were her world and she'll always be watching over you, minding you, guiding you and protecting you.'

'And you can still talk to her,' Charlie said. 'I still talk to Penny all the time.'

Olivia stiffened. 'Do you?'

'Uh-oh,' Shocko whispered.

'Yes, and she gives me great advice,' Charlie said to Izzy.

'Does she?' Izzy said. 'Can you hear her voice?'

385

'In my head and my heart. If you listen, you'll hear Sarah.'

Izzy stayed still. 'I don't hear her.'

'It won't happen all the time, but at night when you're lying in bed, talk to her and see what happens,' Charlie told her.

'If he's talking to your gran in bed, he mustn't be shagging Olivia,' Shocko whispered. 'I mean, that would be way too weird.'

'Sssh,' Riley hissed.

'I'll do it tonight, Granddad.'

'That's my girl.' Charlie kissed Izzy's head.

'We're all here for you, pet,' Johnny said. 'If you feel sad or want to talk to Riley or Mia or Granddad or me or anyone, just pick up the phone. Anytime.'

'Thank you, Johnny.'

'We love you, Izzy. We love you so much. We'll always be here for you,' Mia said.

'But that's what Mummy said and now she's gone,' Izzy whispered.

Silence.

Riley wiped her eyes with her T-shirt and sniffed. 'Well, I'm not going anywhere. Come on, this is supposed to be a good day for you. Let's turn on that chocolate fountain and eat chocolate marshmallows until we puke. OK?'

Izzy half smiled. 'OK.'

Shocko took out his phone and put on some music.

While Riley and Shocko distracted Izzy, Adam asked the adults to come into the lounge. They sat on the two couches, facing each other, and waited for him to speak.

Adam stood in the middle of the room, Rob beside him. From outside the door they could hear Riley saying, 'No stopping until we puke,' and Izzy giving a little laugh.

Adam smiled. 'She's great with Izzy.'

'Yes, she is,' Mia agreed.

'First, I owe you all a big apology. I've behaved really badly and I'm sorry. I – I've been so terrified, angry, upset and freaked out since Sarah collapsed. I can't sleep or eat. I thought I was doing the right thing. I really thought keeping Sarah alive was the best thing to do. I was clinging to a screed of hope, like a drowning man. I felt so alone. I needed to believe I could salvage something from this horror. But when I went into that room this morning and I looked at Sarah through Izzy's eyes, I saw – I saw what she's become. I saw . . . I saw that she was gone, really gone. Not an ounce of that person is my wife. I finally saw the reality and . . . and I knew that no baby could survive in there. If he was older, if she'd died when he was twenty-four weeks or even more, then maybe he could have made it.' Adam began to choke up. 'But I see now that it's hopeless. I have to give up on my baby boy. I've lost them both. All I have is Izzy.' His face collapsed, and he sobbed the tears of a broken man. A man who had had his heart ripped out. Rob put an arm around him and cried with him.

Everyone was crying. Mia stood up and went over to her brother-in-law. 'You have us and Rob. We're your family. We're here for you,' she said, as she put her arms around him and patted his back.

'Why did God have to take them both?' Adam wept. 'One was bad enough, but both of them? It's just too much.' He cried into Mia's shoulder.

Mia heard the door open and close and open again. 'Here you go, mate, sit down and have a drink of this,' Johnny said.

He led Adam to the couch and helped him sit down, then handed him a glass of whiskey. 'Drink it. You need it.' Rob patted his shoulder.

Adam swallowed it in one. 'Thanks.'

Charlie stood up and went over to sit on the arm of the couch. 'Look, Adam, you've had a terrible time. We all have.

But if I've learned one thing from losing Penny, it's that you need your family. Don't push us away. We want to help you. We'll all help with Izzy. There will be days when you can't get out of bed for the grief. On those days, call us. We'll take Izzy to school or mind her for the day. There'll be days when the pain of loss will bend you double. Let it flood you, don't fight it. It will pass . . . and I know this is impossible to believe now, but it will slowly, very slowly, get a bit easier to bear.'

'Thank you, Charlie.' Adam squeezed his father-in-law's hand. 'I really need to cling to that hope because, right now, I can only see and feel pain. Every time I look at Izzy, I want to put my fist through the wall. I'm so angry for her. She deserves to have a mother. She deserves to have Sarah in her life. The person who adored her most in the world is now gone. It's just not fair. She'll never see her grow up. I'm so angry for her and for Sarah. She was the best mother.' Adam began to sob. 'Who is Izzy going to talk to when she's a teenager with girl problems?'

'Me.' Riley stood at the door, carrying a tray laden with some of the uneaten food, coffee and wine. 'I'll help her. I'll talk to her. I'll have her back. I promise.'

Adam dabbed his eyes with his soggy tissue. 'Thanks.'

Johnny helped Riley put the tray on the coffee-table and kissed the top of her head.

'I promise I'll be there for her,' Riley said. 'Even when she's a bolshie teenager – yes, Mum, I know, it takes one to know one – I'll be there. I'll make sure no boy ever treats her badly and no girl ever tries to bully her. I've got it covered, Adam. And Mum will be there for her too. She can keep an eye on her in school and be like a surrogate mother. Mum loves Izzy and Izzy loves Mum – and she's a pretty amazing mother.'

Mia's heart swelled. She wanted to run over and crush

Riley in the biggest hug, but she held herself back and just beamed at her daughter.

'We've got it covered. We all love Izzy and we all love . . .' Riley's voice caught '. . . loved Sarah. She was awesome.'

Mia went over and put her arm around Riley's shoulders. Her daughter didn't shove it off. Instead she leaned in.

Johnny's phone rang and he scurried out of the room. How could he take a call now? Mia was stunned. It must be about the new job.

Mia turned to her brother-in-law. 'Adam, no one will ever replace Sarah in Izzy's life, but we'll all try to fill the gap. We'll be with her every step of the way. Trust us. Let us in.'

Adam rubbed his eyes. 'Thank you. All of you. I'm sorry for pushing you away. I want you in Izzy's life. She needs all of you and your support means the world to her and to me.'

'And I'll visit more, and you guys can come and stay with us. We're all in this together. We're all here for you, Adam. You're not alone,' Rob said.

Rob handed everyone a glass of wine.

'Not for me, thank you. I'm driving,' Olivia said pointedly.

Riley grabbed a glass. Mia removed it from her hand and handed her a cup of tea.

'Seriously?'

'Yes.'

They all drank deeply to the sounds of Shocko singing 'Let It Go' with Izzy outside.

Adam cleared his throat. 'There is something else. I've made the decision to turn off the ventilator. I've spoken to Dr Mayhew. We're doing it tomorrow morning at ten. It's time to say goodbye. I'd like you all to be there, but I totally understand if you'd rather not.'

Shocko and Izzy's voices rose to a crescendo *'Let it go . . .'*

52

Mia slipped quietly into the ICU. It was late and, despite the clanking of machines, raspy breathing, murmurs of voices, the place felt calm.

Angela came over to her. 'I heard the news. We're all so relieved that Adam has come around to making the right decision. How are you?'

Mia thought. How was she? 'Sad. Just really, deeply sad.'

'Oh, love.' Angela hugged her. 'This has been the most heartbreaking case I've ever witnessed, and I've worked in ICU for twenty-five years. I don't know how you're all still standing.'

'Me neither. I guess we're all stronger than we think. Talking to Adam this evening was incredible. It was like he'd come back to us. In a strange and complicated way, we had a good day, despite everything.'

'I'm so glad to hear that. Families need to stick together in times of sorrow.'

Mia nodded. 'Yes, they do.'

'Do you want to go in and see her?'

'Yes. Adam says the machine will be switched off tomorrow. I want to say a final goodbye.'

'Of course you do. I'll make sure no one disturbs you.'

Mia sat in the hospital room and listened to the ventilator. The familiar noise soothed her. She took out a scented candle – Jo Malone Peony & Blush Suede, Sarah's favourite – and lit it.

As the scent filled the room, Mia pulled a sheet of paper out of her bag. Johnny had barely looked up when she'd left the house. He'd been locked away in the bedroom on his computer since they'd got back. He seemed very stressed about the article he was working on. Mia hoped to God it would get him the job.

Watching him, she'd thought she should write down what she wanted to say to Sarah. Get her thoughts straight before her final conversation. She'd scribbled down her thoughts.

'Hey, Sarah, it's me. This is goodbye, my darling. I'll never be the same again, not without you, but I'm so glad Adam is ready to let you go. It's awful, but it's the right thing to do. I wrote down some final thoughts and things I want to say to you. And I'm afraid you can't get away, so you'll have to hear me out.' She smiled sadly at her sister.

'I can't believe this day has come. I know you left us a while ago, but in the weirdest, most messed up of ways I still felt as if you were here. This has been the most awful, unimaginably difficult few weeks of all our lives. Our grief for you is so acute, it matches our love for you.

'And, Sarah, you are deeply loved. You are adored. We are heart-broken without you. For a while we were lost. But I think, now, maybe we can see our way back.

'I don't think I ever realized what a central point you were in our family. You were the core. You loved and were loved by all of us. Every-one else has little issues and grumbles with the others, but not you. Everyone loved you.

'I used to get frustrated with you for not doing more with your life. What a fool I was. What a complete idiot.

'Your simplicity was the best thing about you. You never looked for more, just appreciated deeply what you had. You were content. I think I'll spend my whole life looking for contentment, but you had it. You

knew how lucky you were. You knew how good your life was. You loved deeply and were loved deeply in return.

'People spend thousands of pounds and a lifetime seeking what you had – pure and simple happiness. Satisfaction with your lot.

'You were never grumpy or stressed or overwhelmed, because you didn't let yourself be. You were so much smarter than me, than all of us. You kept your life small and perfect. You had time for those you loved. You didn't waste time on people who were not important to you. You focused on your loved ones and never wanted what others had because you had all that you wanted.

'You didn't need a bigger circle. You didn't need more people in your life, more noise, more commitments, more stuff. You knew what was important and you nurtured that. Adam and Izzy were your world.

'I remember getting really cross with you when you said you wouldn't come to the theatre with me to see an all-star cast in Glengarry Glen Ross. *I'd bought you a ticket as a birthday gift and you said you were sorry, but you had planned a birthday dinner with Adam and Izzy that night. I told you to do your birthday dinner the night before or the night after, that this was a one-off performance, a chance to see incredible actors in a wonderful play.*

'"I'm sorry, Mia," you said, "but I've told Adam and Izzy we're having a celebration dinner that night and I won't change it."

'You were polite but firm. I knew you wouldn't budge, and I was cross. But you were right. You were right to prioritize your husband and daughter. You were right not to let them down and change your plans. They were the loves of your life.

'When I tried to suggest you get a part-time job because you "must be bored", you were firm then too. "I am in the lucky position that I don't need to work and I'm choosing not to. I want to be here for Izzy. If she's sick, I want to look after her. If she forgets her lunch or her tennis racquet, I want to bring it in to her. If she has one line in the school play, I want to be in the front row. I don't want to have anything that gets in the way of being her mother."

'I thought it was ridiculous, but you would not budge. Again, you were right. Your relationship with Izzy was incredible. The love you had for her, and her for you was extraordinary.'

Mia paused and took a minute to gather herself. This was hard. Every time she thought of the huge loss in Izzy's life she felt as if she was being stabbed in the heart.

'And Dad. You were so good to Dad when Mum died. Always there for him. Giving him so much time and help, constantly checking in on him so I didn't have to. You took on the lion's share of looking after Dad. You kept saying, "I'm not working, it's easy for me." But it wasn't easy for you. You were grieving Mum's death too. But you put Dad and me first. You gave me space to grieve and not feel guilty about looking after Dad, and you gave him all the support he needed.

'I don't know if I ever thanked you properly for that. And even with Olivia. I hated her on sight, but you kept pointing out, "It's good for Dad," and again, you were right. Even though she is the most annoying person on earth, she is good for Dad. I do see that now.

'And Riley, you were so good with her. You always pointed out her good qualities and reminded me of how wonderful she is underneath her prickly exterior. Reading your diary has reminded me of how lucky I am to have a wonderful daughter and how I need to ease up on Riley and stop being on her back all the time.

'You always sang Johnny's praises, gently suggesting I back off and stop hounding him about job interviews and networking. You told me to trust him and not suffocate him. You reminded me time and again of what a good man he is. How much he loves me and Riley. What a great dad he is.

'You've taught me that I need to change. I need to see life through your lens. I must stop and look at all the wonderful things I have, appreciate the people I love and stop seeking more. I have to stop pushing myself and them to achieve more and just enjoy my life. Reading

your diary has shown me that I need to stop and smell the roses. Thank you for that.

'You saw the world through the eyes of a happy person. You saw the good, the hope, the kindness in life. You saw the world simply and clearly.

'You knew what mattered most and ignored the rest. You focused on the positives. You loved with a full heart. Please know that you were loved profoundly in return. The depth of our loss and grief is testament to how much we love you. I'm so angry that you're going to miss out on Izzy's life, but I know you'd tell me not to waste time and energy on anger. "What's the point of being angry, Mia?" you said once. "Anger just eats away at your soul and makes you ill. You have to let it go."

'Sarah, as long as I have breath in my body I will look out for Izzy. I will love her, protect her, mind her, care for her and try my best to fill her life with joy. I owe you that and I will be honoured to do so.

'And wherever you are, be proud. Be proud of a life well lived, of having loved and been loved and of creating the most incredible little girl in the world (apart from Riley!).

'I love you, Sarah, and I will miss you every single day until the day I die.'

53

Mia decided to wear red. It was Sarah's favourite colour. It felt wrong to wear black. It wasn't a funeral. It was a farewell. She wanted to look nice for Sarah, even though she knew her sister could neither see nor hear her.

It was silly, really, but these little things helped. Riley was in her school uniform because she had an exam that afternoon, which Mia wasn't letting her miss.

'It's so unfair.'

Mia was firm. 'Life has to go on, Riley. We need to try to get things back to normal. Well, the new normal.'

Adam had dropped Izzy to school, not telling her what was happening. Her mother was dead: she didn't need to know the terrible details. No one did. That was something the family would keep to themselves. The trauma, pain and awfulness of what they had lived through had been contained, thanks to Johnny. Mia was so grateful to him for that.

Their choices and decisions, made under the most horrendous circumstances, were for no one else to judge. How could anyone judge anyway? Mia thought. No one could ever imagine this happening because it doesn't happen. Ever.

Johnny was in the kitchen on his laptop. 'We have to go,' Mia said, glancing at the clock on the wall.

'Just give me a minute.'

Mia stood for a minute. 'Johnny!' she said.

'I'm coming,' he grumbled.

In the car, Johnny seemed preoccupied and distant.

'What is this article you're working on anyway, Dad?'

Riley asked. 'It must be really long – you're always on your laptop.'

'It's just difficult,' he said, looking at Mia.

She patted his arm. 'It'll be worth the hard work to get the job in the bag.' She smiled at him.

Johnny flushed and concentrated on the road. He seemed very tense, but everyone was tense, these days, and a job was riding on this article. Mia looked out of the window and up at the clouds. I'm coming, Sarah, she thought. I'm coming to say goodbye and let you be at peace. It's nearly over, sis.

They stood in a semi-circle around the bed. Adam, Rob, Mia, Charlie, Johnny and Riley.

Angela and Dr Mayhew stood to the side, waiting. The window was open, letting sunshine and fresh air and the sound of birds flood the room. Sarah looked even worse, but it didn't hurt to see her now because it was all going to be over soon.

In the breeze, Izzy's picture fluttered. They looked up. Stick figures labelled Mummy, Daddy, Izzy and Baby, with wide crayon smiles and huge hands. Izzy's family, now about to be halved.

Adam cleared his throat. 'Thanks for being here. It means a lot. I've said what I had to say yesterday to the family. It just leaves me to thank you, Dr Mayhew, and all of your team, and you, Angela, for being such a rock of support and sense to all of us. It is some small comfort to know that Sarah has been cared for by such good people. I never in my wildest dreams imagined I would have to make such a heart-breaking decision, but Sarah and Ben are gone and it's time to let them be at peace.' Adam's voice broke. Rob put a hand on his shoulder.

Adam nodded to Dr Mayhew. One by one, the alarms and monitors were turned off and then, finally, the ventilator.

Silence. Complete silence. Nobody moved. Mia felt as if her feet were frozen to the spot. It was over. The nightmare was over. No more wondering, What if? No more arguing and agonizing over what to do next. Sarah was at peace and maybe now they could be, too. No more fighting, no more cruel and angry words.

Mia knew that she had to find a way to get on with Adam. She needed to support him and, more importantly, Izzy, and for that to happen, she had to be on better terms with him. She owed it to Sarah.

'Well, she's at peace now, thank God,' Charlie said. 'She's with Penny.'

'May she rest in peace,' Rob said.

'Amen,' Johnny added.

'Goodbye, Sarah, love you,' Riley whispered.

Mia put an arm around her daughter. 'Goodbye, Sarah. Mum will look after you and Ben now. Rest easy.'

Adam laid a single rose on Sarah's chest. He leaned over and kissed her cheek. 'Goodbye, my love. Thank you for loving me and allowing me to love you. You taught me what true love is and you made me a better man.'

They all wiped tears from their eyes and filed out of the room. There, lined up along the corridor, were the medical team and the ICU nurses. They shook their hands and the eyes of each one were full of tears.

Saying goodbye to Angela was the hardest. She cried openly. 'It's been an honour to care for Sarah and get to know you all,' she said, embracing them one by one. 'You are a wonderful family. Stay close and be kind to each other.' Her beeper sounded, and she turned to go back to the ICU, to help another patient and another family.

They walked through the waiting room, where they had spent so much time over the last three weeks, went down in the lift, then through hospital Reception and out into the warm summer's day.

'Coffee?' Adam suggested.

'Sure,' Mia said.

'I've got to head off.' Johnny took out his car keys.

'I thought you were taking Riley back to school,' Mia said.

'Yeah, no, I can't, sorry. I have to work on that – I have to go.'

Before Mia could say anything else, Johnny had scuttled off.

'I can drop Riley to school and you home,' Charlie said.

'Thanks, Dad,' Mia said, but she was annoyed with Johnny for rushing off like that, especially now, after what had just happened.

They walked to the coffee shop across the road from the hospital. Rob ordered coffee, cake and buns.

'We need sugar and comfort,' he said, placing a big plate laden with food on the table.

They all looked at it, but no one felt like eating.

Adam reached into his jacket pocket and pulled out two velvet pouches. Looking at Mia and Riley he said, 'Now that I'm thinking clearly again, I want you to know how much it means to me that you have been so brilliant to Izzy and to me over this godawful time. I wanted to give you these as a thank-you from me – well, from Sarah – to you.' He handed one to Riley and one to Mia.

'What are they?' Riley asked.

'Something of Sarah's that I know she'd like you to have and that I want you to have. Izzy helped me choose them.'

Riley opened hers, and gasped. It was a pair of diamond stud earrings. 'Oh, Adam, are you sure?'

'Positive. You've been a rock, Riley, and I'm sorry I was so awful to you.'

Riley grinned. 'These will help me forget a lot quicker.' She pulled out her little silver studs and put in the diamonds.

Mia's hands were shaking so she took a little longer to open her pouch. Inside was Sarah's Tiffany necklace, the one she wore every day. It had a thin silver chain and a diamond S. 'Oh, Adam.' She burst into tears.

He reached for her hand. 'It'll keep her close to you. No one deserves to wear it more than you.'

'Thank you. I'll never take it off.' Riley helped her with the clasp. Mia held the S to her neck and felt a rush of warmth.

Charlie patted Adam's shoulder. 'Well done. That's a lovely gesture.'

Adam took a box out of his pocket. 'This is for you, Charlie.'

'I don't need diamonds.' Charlie smiled.

'It's not.'

Charlie opened the box. Inside he found a lock of Sarah's hair. 'Oh . . . oh . . . it's . . .' He picked up the lock of hair and held it tenderly in the palm of his hand. 'My golden girl,' he whispered. 'Beautiful.'

'Well done, man,' Rob said.

'Thanks, Adam. Sorry for calling you a prick.' Riley smiled sheepishly at her uncle.

'I was behaving like one. I need people to call me out when I'm being an arse.'

'Happy to oblige.' Riley grinned.

Rob looked at his watch. 'I'm really sorry to break up this moment, but I've got to go to the airport.'

'And I need to get Riley to school,' Mia said. They all stood up.

'We'll miss you, Rob.' Mia hugged him. 'You've been an absolute rock. Thank you for everything.'

'I'm glad I could help in some small way.' Then Rob

whispered in her ear, 'Look out for Adam, won't you? He needs you guys. I know he can be difficult, but he's a good man.'

Mia patted him on the back. 'I promise you that we will.'

Adam picked up his car keys. 'Well, I'd better get you to your flight on time or Ellen will never forgive me. What am I going to do without you, bro? I've got used to having you around.'

'You'll be all right. You've got a big family right here who have your back.'

'Why don't you bring Izzy over for dinner tonight?' Mia suggested.

'Thanks, Mia, but I'll pass. I feel pretty shattered, to be honest, but tomorrow would be lovely,' Adam said.

'Great, we'll see you then.'

They waved goodbye to Rob and Adam.

'Well, now.' Charlie turned to Mia. 'The man has a heart after all.'

Mia smiled. 'Yes, he does, and we need to nurture it.'

'I'm kind of wrecked. Can I skip my exam?' Riley asked.

'No, love, not a chance.'

Riley groaned and climbed into the back of Charlie's car.

'Do you think we're going to be OK, Dad?' Mia asked.

Charlie looked up at the sky. 'We just keep putting one foot in front of the other, Mia. That's all we can do.'

Mia walked around and climbed into the passenger seat. He was right: there was no miracle cure, it was just life – getting on with it and waiting for the pain to subside.

54

Mia was dabbing night cream around her red, puffy eyes when Johnny came into the bathroom. He stood beside her, leaning against the white-tiled wall. 'I need to talk to you about something. I've tried to find the right time but there hasn't been any right time lately.'

Mia washed the cream off her hands. It would take a miracle to make her eyes look better. She'd aged so much in the last three weeks. They all had.

She smiled at Johnny in the mirror. 'You got the job, didn't you?'

Johnny put his hands in his trouser pockets. 'No. It's about the journalist in the hospital and Sarah's story.'

Mia's hand flew to her mouth. 'Oh, no! Tell me the story's not coming out.'

Johnny cleared his throat. 'Not exactly.'

'What do you mean?'

'Remember when I went to talk to Jimmy Dolan about quashing the story?'

'Yes, and he said he would.'

'Well, that's not exactly what happened.'

Mia's hand froze mid-air. 'What the hell is going on, Johnny?'

'When I spoke to Jimmy, he was very reluctant to pass on it because, let's face it, it's a great story from a news editor's point of view. I tried everything to get him to drop it, but there was only one way I could do it. I had to offer him a deal.'

Mia's eyes widened. 'What? What deal?'

Johnny sighed. 'It wasn't a good solution, Mia, but it was the only solution.'

'What did you do?' Mia said hoarsely.

'Jimmy was going to run the story one way or another. I couldn't get him to drop it. He already had a pile of research done – they had pulled photos from Sarah's Facebook account, they knew what was going on and it was being printed, no matter what. The only concession I could get . . .' He stopped and looked at her.

Mia felt like her world was about to explode all over again when the next words left his mouth.

'The only way I was able to stop the story coming out was to offer an exclusive written by me.'

Mia backed away from him into the bedroom. She sat down suddenly on the bed.

Johnny followed her and hunkered down in front of her. 'Please don't freak out, Mia. I know it sounds awful, but it's the best outcome for us. I got him to hold off until now, and with Adam putting an end to things today, that means the story comes out when it's over, not while Sarah is still lying in the hospital. That's really good. You have to see that. And I've written it from our point of view, stressing how difficult this has been for the family, how there was no good option available to us. This way, we get our point across before the tabloids row in, twist and sensationalize it. It gives us con- trol, Mia. That's why I did it.'

'Have you lost your mind?' Mia shouted. 'You told me it wasn't going to come out. That is my *sister*! Are you using my family tragedy to get in with Jimmy and his newspaper, Johnny? Is that what this is really about?'

Johnny rocked back on his heels. 'Jesus, Mia, of course not. I'm trying to protect you all from some tabloid exposé that would cast the family as monsters.'

'You told me it was sorted out. Now you're telling me that you're going to expose my family publicly. You lied to me. Are you getting a job out of this? Is using my sister's life the only way you can get a bloody job?'

Johnny's face set in a hard line. 'Listen to what I'm saying. I'm not using Sarah for anything. They were going to run the story no matter what, so I did sort it out. I did stop it, in the only way possible.'

Mia poked her husband in the chest. 'No, you bloody didn't. I don't want people reading about my sister and her baby. It's our private horror. The last thing we need is people weighing in and telling us how awful we are or how right or how wrong. I asked you to sort out one thing, just one thing, and you couldn't even do that!' Mia screamed. 'I'm having a nervous breakdown here, yet I'm still going to work and pay-ing the bloody mortgage and all the bills while you're sitting around on your arse fucking things up.'

She put her head into her hands, but Johnny pulled her hands away and forced her to look at him. 'I am not sitting on my arse. Who the hell do you think has been keeping everything together at home? Me. I've been looking after Izzy and Riley and you and everyone. I've hunted for a job every day since I was made redundant. I feel enough of a failure without you shoving it in my face. If it wasn't for me, Sarah's story would have been splashed all over every tabloid last week. I had to beg Jimmy to hold off.'

Mia stared at him. She hated him right now. 'Well, it'll be splashed all over the papers soon enough anyway, so I'd hardly say you saved the day, Johnny. You did nothing but postpone it. I can't believe this is your idea of sorting things out. You have lied to me and betrayed my family. Thanks a lot, Johnny. You're a real rock.'

'There's no need to be such a —'

Mia glared at him. 'What? Bitch? I'm not a bitch. I'm a woman with a shattered heart who has lost her sister and best friend and all the while, instead of falling apart and crying into my pillow, I'm working to keep a roof over our bloody heads.'

Mia grabbed her pillow and stormed down the stairs. She pulled the spare duvet out of the hall cupboard and flung herself onto the couch.

'What are you doing?' Johnny asked from the doorway.

'Go away.'

'You're not sleeping on the couch.'

'I am not sleeping with you.'

Johnny walked in. He pulled her up. 'Mia, I will sleep on the couch. You've had a hell of a day. Go upstairs to bed. You need sleep.'

'How can I sleep knowing you've betrayed me and my family?' Mia shouted.

'I did the only thing I could to keep it out of the papers, Mia.'

'Well, it's going into the papers anyway, so you did sweet fuck-all. How the hell am I supposed to explain this to Dad and to Adam? Jesus, Johnny, how could you do this to us? After all we've been through. I will never forgive you.'

Mia picked up her pillow, slammed the door shut and walked back upstairs. Riley was hovering on the landing.

'What's going on?'

'You'll find out tomorrow, so I might as well tell you. Your father wasn't working on an article for a new job, he was writing an exposé on our family and Sarah's horrific death. It's going to be splashed all over the paper tomorrow and everyone will know our private and painful business.'

Riley frowned. 'But Dad would never do anything to hurt you. He loves you. You know that.'

'I thought I did.' Mia's voice caught. 'But apparently he

has decided to betray me. I come home from witnessing the end of my sister's life and think my husband might hug me or tell me I'm going to be OK, or that he has a job and all the financial pressure will be off my shoulders but no — oh, no. Instead he tells me the whole country is about to know all the painful and intimate details of Sarah's death.'

Riley wasn't convinced. 'Dad must have had a reason, Mum. He'd never betray anyone, least of all you.'

'He swore to me that the story had been quashed. Now he says it was going to come out anyway — if it was, I'd prefer to have been betrayed by a stranger than by my own husband.' Mia slammed her bedroom door and locked it.

She had thought Johnny was going to hug her and tell her how brave she was and how sorry he was that she had just said goodbye to her beloved sister. But, no, he'd landed this on her instead. Mia stared up at the ceiling and wondered how she was going to explain Johnny's betrayal to her father and to Adam. It made her feel dead inside, like Sarah. She didn't think she would ever be able to forgive her husband.

55

Mia sat outside in a garden chair, wrapped in her dressing-gown. She watched the sun rise. It was spectacular. The sky slowly went from navy-blue to pink as the rays burst through, announcing the birth of another day.

Mia's first day without her sister. Her first day with nowhere to go, no one to visit. It was over. She felt empty, depleted. Was she really supposed to 'get back to normal' now? Was she supposed to get dressed and go to work as if her world had not been ripped apart? Would she have to talk about the weather and the news and which movie stars were sleeping together? Mia shuddered. All she wanted to do was talk about Sarah. She wanted to say her name over and over so that she would not be forgotten. She wanted people to know her, to understand how wonderful she was. To know how unbear-able it was to lose your sister and her baby.

Mia wanted to run down the road and scream at people, 'Do you know how lucky you are?' Maybe she was going mad from grief and lack of sleep, but how can you sleep when your heart is broken, when you have seen your sister's body decomposing in front of your eyes? Sleep had not come.

Johnny's bombshell had rocked her to the core. She had lain awake, thinking about Sarah, then feeling huge waves of anger as she thought of what Johnny had done. She didn't want to remember all she'd said to Sarah during that final goodbye, but it kept rearing up to confront her: she had talked of love and cherishing and going easy on herself and every-one. Was this the first test?

It had gone round her thoughts in a loop, exhausting her, and the only person she wanted to talk to about it was Sarah. What would Sarah have said? She'd always listened carefully to Mia, but then she was always so fair and generous to Riley and Johnny. Mia knew Sarah would tell her to give him the benefit of the doubt, but she kept pushing that voice away because she didn't want to hear it. What he had done was so huge. How was she supposed to get past it?

The door opened and Mia heard footsteps. She looked up. Johnny handed her a cup of tea.

'I don't want it.'

'Mia, I know you're upset about the article but –'

'I'm not upset, I'm furious. You let me down. You betrayed us, you –'

'Mia,' Johnny snapped. 'I had no choice. You have to believe me. I wouldn't lie to you about this. I've been torn apart ever since that meeting with Jimmy, but it was honestly the only way to resolve it. You're my world, Mia.' He stopped, trying to compose himself. 'Please, Mia. Read it before you judge me. I went to get the first edition. It's out today. Why don't you read it and then decide if you're going to forgive me or not?'

He handed her the newspaper and placed the cup of tea on the ground beside her. 'I'm going for a walk. I need to clear my head.'

Good riddance, Mia thought. She was so angry with him, she could barely look at him. She threw down the newspaper and looked back up at the sky. She stared at the colours until her eyes watered. It was going to be another lovely day.

As she watched, a thrush with a speckled breast landed on a branch of the ash tree. It was a beautiful bird, its eyes darting with curiosity. Mia stayed perfectly still. The bird hopped onto a lower branch, then a lower one. It was coming closer to her with each hop. She could see the yellow feathers mixed with the creamy-white and brown ones. She'd had no idea a thrush had so many colours. It flew from the low branch, landing neatly on the path, only about a metre from her chair. It walked delicately towards her, watching her intently all the time. It stopped just an arm's reach away and regarded her without any fear.

My God, Mia thought. She'd never been so close to a wild bird.

She stared at the bird and it stared back, and for some reason she thought of Sarah. She was sure she'd read somewhere of a belief that the souls of the dead revisited in the form of a bird. She couldn't help it, she reached out slowly with her hand towards the thrush. It hopped back a step, then took flight, out of reach, landing on the willow tree further down the garden. It began to sing, and the sound made Mia shiver with delight.

It was utterly daft, but she felt as if Sarah had come to say goodbye.

Mia sat up straight to watch the bird fly off, and felt warmth spread over her. The newspaper at her feet caught her eye. It was folded over, but she could see Sarah's mouth smiling at her from the main photo. She reached down and picked it up.

When she unfolded it, she gasped. It was a photo of Sarah and Adam, taken at Cousin Julie's wedding last year. Sarah was absolutely radiant, stunning in a yellow silk dress, her gorgeous hair loose and wavy about her shoulders. She was laughing, and Adam was gazing at her with nothing short of adoration.

Mia closed her eyes against the hot tears. She didn't want to, but she started to read.

An impossible choice
Johnny Hegarty

On 15 April, Sarah Brown collapsed at her home. She was thirty-four years old, healthy and pregnant with a yearned-for baby boy. Sarah never woke up again.

She was rushed to hospital, where the medical team worked hard to find out the cause of her collapse. After three days of tests and waiting, they advised Sarah's family that she had suffered a severe brain injury and would never survive off life support.

Sarah was my sister-in-law. I had known her for almost twenty years and she had been one of my best friends for all that time. She was an adored sister, daughter, wife and mother, and the family was utterly devastated by this news. The only tiny sliver of hope lay in Sarah's womb, where her then fourteen-week-old foetus still showed a heartbeat. Sarah had gone through years of anguish trying to conceive this baby, and we knew she would fight for it with every breath in her body. She couldn't fight any more, so we had to do it for her.

Sarah was put on a ventilator and somehow, against all the odds, the baby continued to survive.

The experts told us that the baby would most likely die too . . . but he still had a heartbeat. There was the slimmest chance that he might survive. What else could a loving family do but take that chance?

Yes, it meant Sarah became an incubator and we could not give her a dignified death and burial, but we weighed up the situation and decided to give her little boy, Ben, that chance.

But how could he survive? How could a baby survive in a dead woman's body? She was brain dead, but not physically dead. She was warm to the touch, no corpse-like pallor. She looked like Sarah.

But was it right? Was it ethical to keep a dead woman alive for this purpose?

We listened to the experts; we got second and third opinions. We researched, we read medical papers, we trawled the internet until our eyes bled. We talked, we argued. We agreed and then we disagreed. We wept, we prayed, we begged for a miracle.

Some may sit in judgement of us and our decision, but this was an unprecedented case. There was no 'how to' guide that we could consult. The doctors couldn't advise us based on past experience – no, we were very much on our own, trying to do the right thing in a gruelling situation where there was no right decision, and where there could be no good outcome. No matter what we did, Sarah would be lost to us forever.

We came together, we pulled apart, but we found our way back. In the end, it was the innocence of Sarah's seven-year-old daughter who pulled us back. She made us see sense. She showed us how much we need to stick together and not allow grief, anger, frustration and heartbreak to tear us apart.

In the end, there was only one decision. Sarah's body began to fall apart. The baby could not survive. I cannot begin to describe the horrors we witnessed.

And yet, turning off the ventilator was not a decision that came easily. When it comes to the death of a loved one, the hardest part is letting them go. The desire to hold on to them is so strong, it can obliterate all other thought. But we came to understand that the only kindness we could show Sarah was to let her go, to give her our blessing to leave us.

On 7 May, we stood around her bed as the doctor switched off the ventilator. Sarah's husband showed incredible courage in making that final call. It fell to him and, in the end, he shouldered that burden with compassion.

When the machine clicked off, we fell into a silence that drowned us. That clicking and whirring had been the soundtrack of our grief, and when it stopped, the silence was deafening. I don't think any of us will ever fully recover from that silence. We can't, because we loved Sarah so much.

I wouldn't wish this experience on anyone else. It was cruel and random and devastating. Sarah leaves behind a little girl

who adored her mother, who is bereft without her. It will be a
long road to recovery.

 As a family, we faced an unthinkable dilemma: accept Sarah's
death, and allow her unborn baby to die with her; or keep
Sarah alive, even as her body began to decompose, in order to
give her unborn baby its minuscule chance of survival. We may
be judged for our actions, but we did our best. We honoured
Sarah by respecting her deepest wish to give birth to Ben.
Finally, we honoured our beloved Sarah by letting her rest
in peace.

 Sarah Brown and Ben Brown, 7 May 2018, RIP.

Mia bowed her head and cried. Her shoulders shook as
the grief cut through her. She looked up at the garden. The
thrush was still in the willow tree, gazing at her. She suddenly jumped up from her chair and ran. She ran through
the kitchen, where a startled Riley called, 'What are you
doing?' She didn't answer her. She ran down the hall, yanked
open the front door, and ran outside in her dressing-gown
and slippers.

She had to find him.

She ran into the park and looked around frantically. There
he was, ahead of her, walking towards the pond.

She ran, feeling her legs shake as she pushed them on.
When she reached him, she tried to call his name, but only a
sob escaped.

He turned around. Mia fell into her husband's arms.

'It's beautiful,' Mia sobbed. 'It's exactly how it was.' She
gasped for breath. 'You didn't hang Adam out to dry,' she
said. 'It was just us, the family, and it was her. It was Sarah.
Oh, God, I'm sorry, Johnny.'

Johnny pressed her to him. 'Does this mean I'm forgiven?'

She nodded into his chest.

Mia pulled her head back. 'I'm sorry for doubting you. I know the story would have come out, given that that guy was snooping around the hospital. The staff will probably talk now that it's over. I just wasn't ready for the world to know. I wanted more time. But the words, Johnny. You wrote it so beautifully. You explained it so well. You really do have a gift. I'm sorry I was a bitch.'

'You're not a bitch. You were just devastated.'

'I forgot how hard this was for you, too. I've been so wrapped up in my own grief, I forgot about you and Riley. I know how much you loved Sarah. I'm sorry, Johnny.'

Johnny kissed her lightly on the lips. 'You have nothing to apologize for. You're the most amazing woman and wife, mother, sister and daughter. Never forget that, Mia. You were a brilliant sister.'

'I miss her so much.' Mia gulped back tears.

'I know you do. But I'm here and so is Riley. Don't push us away, pull us in. We want to support you and help you. It's our turn to look after you.'

Mia buried her face in her husband's chest and wept for all that she had, and all that she had lost.

Week Four

56

Riley hovered in the hall, biting her thumbnail.

'You'll have no thumb left if you keep that up,' Johnny said, as he came down the stairs.

Riley pulled her thumb out of her mouth and stuck it into her skirt pocket.

'You look lovely. Skirts suit you.'

She shrugged. 'I wanted to make an effort today. You know, for Sarah and Mum.'

'Well, I approve mightily.' Johnny smiled at her. 'What time is he due?'

'Around now,' Riley said. 'Promise you won't embarrass me, Dad?'

'How could I? I'm the coolest dad around.'

'Oh, God.' Riley rolled her eyes. 'This is going to be a disaster.'

'You invited him,' Johnny reminded her.

He was right. She had. It had been a moment of weakness. She'd been crying about Sarah and the scattering of her ashes, and Zach had said he'd like to come and support her, so she'd said he could.

But now he was going to meet everyone, all at once, and they'd be asking questions and it would be mortifying.

'How are you doing?' Johnny asked.

Riley looked up at him. 'I couldn't sleep last night. I keep thinking this is all a dream and Sarah will come through the door any minute. I guess this all makes it very final.'

Johnny sighed. 'Yes, it does. It's been a horrendous few weeks. You've been great with Izzy, I'm so proud of you.'

'Stop, Dad. Don't make me cry.' She held her fingers up to her eyes.

'Can I hug you?'

'No, that'll definitely set me off. But thanks.'

'You're welcome.'

The doorbell rang. Riley jumped. With a warning finger pointed at her father, she opened the door. Zach was standing there in a shirt and tie. He was holding a big bunch of flowers. 'Hey,' he said.

'Hey.'

'You look nice.'

'So do you, a bit dorky, but nice.'

Zach grinned. He handed her the flowers. 'These are for you and kind of for your mum, too.'

'Thanks, they're beautiful.'

Riley wanted to lean into his chest and inhale his scent, but her dad was behind her, watching.

'Hello, I'm Johnny, Riley's dad.' Johnny came forward. 'Come on in.'

Zach proffered his hand and shook Johnny's firmly. 'Very nice to meet you, Mr Hegarty.'

'You too, Zach. We've heard a lot about you. I believe you're a great man for the high jump.'

Riley glared at her father.

Zach smiled. 'Yes, I'm pretty keen, all right.'

'Good for you. I'd be very grateful if you could encourage this one to get into sports.' Johnny poked Riley in the back.

'Get off, Dad.'

Zach grinned. 'I've tried, but she's pretty stubborn.'

Johnny whooped. 'I'm delighted to hear that it's not just with us then.'

Zach laughed. 'I don't think Riley ever does anything she doesn't want to do.'

'Indeed she doesn't.'

'It's actually one of the things I like most about her,' Zach said.

Riley felt her stomach dance.

'Me too, son. Me too.' Johnny smiled at Zach.

They heard footsteps on the stairs. Mia came down. She was wearing a long navy dress with little sleeves. It was hanging off her. She's got so thin, Riley thought. Despite her make-up, she looked exhausted.

'You must be Zach.' She held out her hand.

'Lovely to meet you, Mrs Hegarty. I'm so sorry about your sister.'

Riley wanted to kiss him. He was perfect, saying all the right things.

'Thank you, Zach. I'm sorry we have to meet for the first time on such a sad day, but I'm glad you're here for Riley.'

'I'm happy to help in any small way.'

'I appreciate that,' Mia said.

'Right, coffee's on. We've got ten minutes. I'll pop some bagels in the toaster. I want you to eat something, Mia,' Johnny said.

'I couldn't, Johnny. Not this morning.'

Johnny touched her cheek with the back of his hand. 'OK, love. Coffee it is.'

They went into the kitchen and Johnny handed round the filled mugs.

'So where is this beach exactly?' Riley asked.

'It's kind of hidden. You have to climb down lots of steps to reach it. Sarah liked to walk there,' Mia said.

'That's a lovely place to do it,' Zach said. 'I'm sorry I never got to meet your sister. Riley speaks so highly of her.'

'She was kind of wonderful,' Mia said quietly.

For a while they were silent.

'Zach's keen on the high jump,' Johnny said.

'Oh, yes. That's nice.' Mia nodded absentmindedly.

'We should probably go now.' Riley stood up. The whole thing was way too awkward.

Johnny grabbed his keys and they all got into the car. They drove in silence to the beach. He parked on the edge of the road and they each took a small bunch of white balloons from the boot.

The steps down to the beach were steep. Below them, they could see everyone waiting. The day was calm and clear. The sky met the sea in an infinity of blue. Two people walked their dog along the shore.

When they reached the others on the sand, Mia and Riley handed white balloons to Adam, Izzy, Charlie and Olivia. Izzy was clinging to Adam's leg.

Riley went over to her. 'Hey, Izzy, here's your balloon. It has a little card attached to the bottom. You can write a message on it, if you like. Will I help you?'

Izzy nodded. Riley bent down and held up the pen.

'You write it,' Izzy said.

'What do you want to say?'

'"I wish you weren't dead. I miss you. I will always love you for ever and ever and ever."' Izzy began to cry.

Riley finished writing the note and cuddled her. 'I know it's hard, Izzy. I'm so sorry for you. But I'm here for you. I'll be your big sister and your best friend and your sleepover person and your hairdresser and your shopping buddy and whatever else you want me to be.'

Izzy put her little arms around Riley's neck and held her tightly.

Mia wrote her card. It was simple. 'We love you and we

miss you.' That was it really. Love and missing. Throw in heartbreak too and that pretty much summed it up.

Charlie came over to her. 'Tough day, but I'm glad we finally get to let her go.'

Mia nodded. 'Yes, Dad, me too.'

'She's at peace now with that little baby. The suffering is over. I can finally remember her as she was, my lovely Sarah.' He reached out and took Mia's hand. 'You're a good girl, Mia. You've been wonderful through this whole nightmare. You were a great sister. Sarah always looked up to you. She was mad about you. Olivia told me I don't praise you enough, so I want you to know that I'm very proud of you.'

Mia leaned into her father and laid her head on his shoulder. 'Thank you, Dad. That means the world to me.'

They stood in silence looking out over the bay. Mia made a mental note to be nicer to Olivia from now on.

Adam approached them. 'I've written my message. I think everyone has. We should probably let them go soon – Izzy's getting overwhelmed.'

'Sure.' Mia wiped her eyes and followed him to Izzy. 'Are you ready, pet?' she asked.

'Yes,' Izzy said.

'Let's get everyone to line up, then, and we'll count to three and let them go up into the sky to Sarah.'

'Will she get them, Mia? Will she read them?'

'I think so, Izzy, I really do.'

'Is she lonely up there?'

'Well, she has baby Ben with her and Granny Penny, and she has all of our love going up to her in the sky, so I think she's OK.'

Izzy turned to Charlie. 'Granddad, I talked to Mummy last night and she answered me.'

'Isn't that wonderful?' Charlie smiled down at her.

'She said, "I will always love you, Sweet-pea."'

'Did it make you feel a little bit better?' Charlie asked.

Izzy nodded. 'Yes. But I still miss her.'

They lined up. Mia watched Zach slip his hand into Riley's and her daughter leaned close to him. He was a good kid. Mia could tell the good from the bad after years of teaching. Zach was a good one.

Don't interfere, Mia could almost hear her sister saying. I won't, Sarah, I'll trust her.

Izzy was holding Adam's hand. 'Are you ready, sweetie?' he asked.

'Yes, Daddy.'

'Let's show Mummy how much we love her, then. One, two, three!' Adam shouted.

They all let go of their balloons. Eight white balloons sailed up into the sky. They bobbed among the clouds. Up and away. Floating towards the sky, Heaven and Sarah.

'We love you, Mummy,' Izzy shouted, as she chased the balloons down to the water's edge.

Adam mouthed up at the sky, 'I love you.'

Mia's heart ached for him. He had lost so much.

'You OK?' Johnny asked.

'Yes, thanks. I think the ashes will be harder,' Mia said.

Adam walked over to where the urn was sitting carefully in a box. He took it out, kissed it and walked down to the water's edge. He called Izzy over.

Slowly Adam removed the top of the urn and held it out. Everyone took a handful of ashes.

'This is my first time scattering ashes. What do we do?' Zach whispered to Riley.

'Mum said we throw them into the sea,' Riley told him.

Izzy took a handful of the ashes. 'Is this really Mummy?'

'No. Mummy is up in Heaven. This is like a kind of symbol of her,' Adam said – fudging it well, Mia thought.

'Thank you, Sarah. Thank you for being my best friend and for being my guiding light, even in death,' Mia whispered, as she let her sister go, out to sea, out into the other world.

Mia saw Johnny wiping away tears. She went over to him and put her arms around his waist. 'I love you, Johnny Hegarty,' she said. 'Thanks for being my rock these past few weeks. I know you loved her too.'

Johnny held her hand and squeezed. 'She was one of my favourite people in the world.'

'Me too,' Mia said.

'Me three,' Riley said, behind them. She put her arms around her mother and kissed her cheek. 'I'm here for you, Mum. I know that no one can ever replace Sarah, but I'm going to try to be a better daughter and a friend to you as well.'

Mia smiled at her and stroked her cheek. 'Thank you.'

They stood and held each other as Sarah's ashes sailed away on the ocean. Gone but not forgotten.

July

57

Mia watched out of the window as they pulled up in the car. She could see suitcases piled high in the back. She ran down to greet them.

Izzy bounded towards her. 'Daddy said you have a super-special present for me!' she said.

'Yes, I do. Come on in.'

Mia kissed Adam's cheek and the three of them went into the kitchen. She looked at Adam. He nodded. She bent down and handed Izzy a package.

'What is it?' Izzy asked.

'It's a very special gift that your mummy left for you. I wanted to wait until the right time to give them to you, when things were calmer and you had time to read them with your daddy. Your mummy wrote seven letters to you. One for each year of your life.'

'Wow. I didn't know that she'd done that,' Adam said.

'I found them in her diary, which I wanted to give to you.' She handed it to him.

'I was wondering where that was,' Adam said.

'I kept it because it made me feel close to her. I'm sorry, I should have given it to you before but I . . . Well, sorry.'

Adam hugged it to his chest. 'I wouldn't have been able to handle reading it before now anyway.'

Mia knodded and turned to Izzy. 'I thought you could read the letters on the plane with your dad. It'll help pass some of the time.'

425

'I can't wait.' Izzy's eyes shone.

'It'll be like a really special present from your mum.'

Adam held out his hand. 'Will I keep those safe for you, Izzy, so we can read them later – just the two of us?'

Izzy nodded. 'Yes, please, Daddy. Keep them super-safe.'

'Riley's upstairs if you want to say hi,' Mia told her.

Izzy darted out of the room and up to see her cousin.

'So,' Mia said.

'So.' Adam smiled.

'Are you looking forward to Canada?'

Adam nodded. 'We need a change. The house is so quiet without her. It feels like a stranger's home. I want to take Izzy away from all the sorrow and let her be a kid again. Being with Rob and Ellen will be good for both of us.'

'It will. It'll be nice for you to have Rob's support too.'

'Yes, he's been great. He's on the phone constantly.'

'You need a break. You've been through so much.'

'We all have,' Adam said.

'Yes, but you most of all. You must look after yourself. Izzy needs you.'

'I know. I've started sleeping a bit more and my appetite is slowly coming back. I feel slightly more human.'

Mia smiled. She knew how he felt. She'd begun to sleep and eat again. Not much, but things were slowly improving. 'We'll miss you.'

'You'll miss Izzy.' Adam smiled wryly.

'We'll miss both of you. You will come back, won't you?'

'Yes. My business is here, and Izzy's family is here too. But we'll try to spend a month or two in Canada every summer, if we can. I'd like Rob to see more of Izzy. I want him and Ellen to be involved in her life, too.'

'Of course, and I'm sure Izzy will love it. We'll be dying to hear all about it.'

'Izzy's made me promise to Skype you every Sunday and I'll send you photos and videos too.'

'Great, I'd love that. So would Riley.'

Adam pulled his hands out of the pockets of his trousers. 'Look, Mia, I'm sorry about –'

Mia held up a hand. 'You have nothing to apologize for. You were in Hell. You wanted to save your son. I get it. We all get it. I probably would have done the same in your position.'

'But I treated you and Charlie badly and I'm truly sorry for that.'

'It was an impossible situation. You're a great dad, Adam. Izzy is lucky to have you.'

'I mess up every day. But I'm trying. I can make good pancakes now, so that's a start.' He tried to smile, but his face crumpled. 'God, I miss her so much.'

Mia hugged him. 'I know you do. She adored you. You made her so happy.'

'I was so lucky to have her in my life.' He sobbed.

'We all were,' Mia said.

Adam pulled back slowly. 'Look at us. Sarah would be delighted to see us getting on so well. She always wanted us to be closer.' He smiled through his tears.

Mia laughed. 'She's controlling us even from the grave.'

'*Daaaaaaddyyyyy!*' Izzy raced into the room.

Adam quickly wiped his eyes. 'Yes?'

'Look what Riley got me.' Izzy held up a huge Beanie Boo owl.

'Wow.'

Riley came in after Izzy.

'Thank you, Riley. I'm not sure how we're going to fit it into the case, but thanks.'

'I knew she wanted it, so . . .'

Mia knew they cost a lot of money. While Adam and Izzy

427

admired the owl, Mia turned to Riley. 'That was really thoughtful, love, but how . . .'

'I sold my guitar.'

'Oh, Riley.'

'It's no big deal. I hardly ever played it. Izzy deserves it.' She held out an envelope. 'I got you this with the rest of the money. Open it later.'

Mia put the envelope into her pocket. 'Thank you.'

'Well, we'd better go. Tell Johnny goodbye from us.'

'You know he'd have been here if it wasn't his second day at his new job,' Mia said.

'I'm delighted he's working again – it's brilliant news.'

It wasn't a great job, but while he waited for a journalism job to come up Johnny had decided to teach English to foreign students. The pay was quite good and he was happy to be busy and contributing again.

'Did Dad call you?' Mia asked.

'Charlie FaceTimed last night. Their cruise had just reached Capri. He looked well.'

Mia smiled. 'He needed to get away. Olivia was right to drag him off.' She bent down and picked up Izzy. 'Well, my beautiful and most favourite niece, I'm going to miss you. But I want you to promise me you'll have the best time ever. Enjoy this exciting adventure in Canada.'

'I will,' Izzy said. 'But I wish you were coming too.'

'We'll Skype every week and the time will fly by.' Mia kissed her.

'I love you, Mia, you're the best aunty in the world.'

'I love you too.' She put her down and Izzy ran to Riley.

'Thanks for my owl. I love him.'

'No problem. And, hey, have fun! Come back soon. I'll miss our sleepovers and our chats. I'll have my bed ready for the night you come back – we can stay up all night and have a midnight feast and you can tell me all about Canada. OK?'

'OK. Promise you won't get a new best friend when I'm gone?'

'No one could ever be better than you.' Riley kissed her.

Adam took his daughter's hand. 'Come on, time to go.'

They walked out to the hall. Izzy hugged them one last time and began to cry.

'No tears now, go and have fun. We love you and we're here for you.' Mia nudged her gently towards the car.

As they drove off, Izzy waved out of the back window and Mia felt tears running down her face.

Riley ran into the house, sobbing. She raced up to her room and closed the door.

Mia shut the front door and went back to the kitchen, her hands in her pockets. She felt a rustle. It was the envelope Riley had given her.

She opened it. Inside was a memory stick. Mia opened her laptop and plugged it in.

Music started playing – Whitney Houston singing 'I Will Always Love You' – and then photos . . . lots and lots of photos . . . memories . . . beautiful memories. Sarah as a baby, Sarah as a toddler. Mia and Sarah, Penny and Sarah, Charlie and Sarah, all of them together. Holidays, Christmases, Halloweens, weddings, christenings and then the final photo, Mia and Sarah roaring laughing into the camera. Sisters. Best friends.

Mia put her head in her hands and wept.

She heard a noise behind her. 'I didn't mean to upset you.'

Mia stood up and threw her arms around her daughter. 'I love it – I love you. I love you more than I can ever say. Thank you. Thank you for this precious gift.'

'I love you, Mum, and I think you rock and I know I don't

say it enough, but I do. I probably won't say it again for ages because it's just really awkward.'

Mia smiled. 'This is enough, Riley. You are enough. I have everything I need, right here in this house. I am so lucky. It took Sarah dying to make me realize how lucky.'

'We'll be OK, Mum. I'm here for you and so is Dad. And now that Dad is earning money again, you don't need to worry so much, and I'm going to get a summer job and make my own money too. I don't want you to worry about anything.'

'Thanks, Riley, you're just great.'

'I'm going to meet Zach now. Are you going to be all right? Do you want me to stay?'

'No, pet, go and have fun.'

'Are you sure?'

Mia nodded. 'Yes.'

She watched her daughter leave. Mia blew kisses behind her back as she walked out.

She sat down and pressed Play. She wanted to be with Sarah again. Back to the beginning, where it all started. Two sisters, beginning life full of hope and dreams. Two sisters, united for ever by family and love.

My darling Izzy

We read your mother's seven beautiful letters of love. Now, I'm going to try to write the eighth.

Mummy told you about your first step, smile, tooth and word. She wrote about your first day at school and your first Christmas play, where you were the most beautiful angel.

I missed a lot of those precious moments because I was too busy working. I'm sorry, Izzy. I'm sorry for not being there more. I promise you that I will be a better father.

The last few months have been heartbreaking. But through it all you, my very own angel, have kept me going. When I look at you my heart bursts with pride. I sometimes think it's going to explode out of my chest.

You are the light and love of my life. You are so like Sarah. Sometimes when I look at you, my heart skips a beat. It's like looking at Sarah. You have her beauty, her big heart, her kindness and her strength.

I know you miss her. I know your little heart is broken. I hate that life has shown you how cruel it can be at such a young age.

I hate that you're not going to have Sarah sitting in the front row at every school event. But I'll be there. I promise you, Izzy, I will be there, clapping and cheering as loudly as I can.

I'll keep trying to get better at cooking and hair-plaiting and shopping.

We can do this. You and me. And we're lucky because we have so many people who will help us and who love you and want to be part of your life. I promise that I will make sure that you see your mum's family all the time.

I promise that I will do everything in my power to make your life happy. I will keep you safe and I will try to love you enough for two people.

It's you and me, Izzy, you and me against the world, and there is no one I'd rather go through life with than you.

I love you,
Daddy

Acknowledgements

This book was originally inspired by a devastating court case I read about a few years ago. The story of that woman stayed with me. I wondered, at the time, what would you do if . . .

As always I have many people to thank.

Biggest thank-you goes to Rachel Pierce, my editor, who was a huge help in getting this across the finishing line; Patricia Deevy, for her great insight, ideas and cheerleading; Michael McLoughlin, Cliona Lewis, Carrie Anderson, Aimee Johnston, Brian Walker and all the team at Penguin Ireland for their continued support and help; to all in the Penguin UK office, especially Tom Weldon, Joanna Prior and the fantastic sales, marketing and creative teams. To my agent Marianne Gunn O'Connor for being a great agent and always knowing the right thing to say, and for her unwavering support and loyalty. To Hazel Orme, for her wonderful copy-editing and for being such a positive force. To Colin Murphy, for helping me with the complex details of the medical procedures and processes that arise in this book. Any and all mistakes are my own.

To my fellow writers: thanks for your support, encouragement and for always knowing when a kind ear or a coffee and a bolstering chat are needed.

To my mum, sister, brother and extended family: thanks for always being there.

To all of my friends: thanks for your support and love, and for your wise words and counsel.

To Hugo, Geordy and Amy – the brightest stars in my sky.

To Troy, for being my other half.